ANCASTA

Diana Jackson is an English, business studies and personal tutor at a local college in Bedfordshire. Her passions are social history, gardening, cooking her own produce, travelling and following her husband's Rock and Roll band.

Ancasta is her second novel and takes her first novel Riduna to the next generation. This series of books, which will eventually be a trilogy, have been inspired by her family history, especially her great grandmother, born on the Channel Island of Alderney UK. Diana's novels are works of fiction, although Ancasta has a few real characters woven through the plot.

You can 'meet' Diana through her blog where she writes a great deal about her research and the background to her writing, on Twitter and on her Facebook Page, or face to face if you keep an eye open on her Diary Blog linked to her website.

www.dianamaryjackson.co.uk
www.dianamj.wordpress.com

Riduna on Twitter

Diana Jackson's Author Page on Facebook

Diana Jackson

ANCASTA

GUIDE ME SWIFTLY HOME

*Ancasta is the goddess of the River Itchen,
Hampshire, England, from which this novel flows.*

EVENTISPRESS

Eventispress

A CIP catalogue record for this title is
available from the British Library.

Cover designs and illustrations copyright Colin van Geffen 2012

978-0-9572520-2-8 Ancasta - Guide Me Swiftly Home (eBook-PDF)
978-0-9572520-0-4 Ancasta - Guide Me Swiftly Home (Paperback)

EVENTISPRESS
www.eventispress.co.uk

First Published in 2012
Eventispress,
Bedfordshire England

Printed & Bound by CPI Group Ltd

Dedication

Diana Jackson would like to dedicate this novel to her parents Mr & Mrs Jackson who were both brought up in Woolston, Southampton and also her grandpa and uncle who both worked at Supermarine.

Acknowledgements

THERE ARE SO many people who have walked along side me on this journey of discovery; Colin Van Geffen who I originally met at Solent Sky, but he is now the curator of Calshot Castle, the Southampton aircraft museum, has produced the art work for the cover, made suggestions and ensured any references to the history of flying boat development are accurate; Richard Greaves and John Benjamin who gave me a great deal of support whilst researching at The Shuttleworth Collection Archives and also read my manuscript to check for historical accuracy of early flight and The Great War; Rachel Holmes and Lt Colonel Colin Bulleid from The Hampshire Regimental Museum in Winchester who gave me valuable feedback; Martyn Basford from The Bitterne Society, who rooted out relevant books to read, answering my many questions about the Woolston area and its people and David Moore from the Palmerstone Fort Society.

I need to give a special thanks to many good folks on Alderney including Francis Jeens, the curator of Alderney Museum who spent hours finding relevant items from their archives and also Trevor Davenport who checked relevant chapters referring to Alderney; to Mark Harding for the enjoyable few hours on Alderney being tutored in the arts of fishing, precariously balanced on rocks near Crabby Bay, an occupation I knew absolutely nothing about before this research. With fishing in mind, Victor Petit too, has given me fantastic suggestions and a valuable insight into life on the island at the time of his father and grandfather and shared with me many memorable fishing related stories.

Here in Bedfordshire closer to home, Brenda and Marcus have tirelessly proof read my manuscript finding many of the errors I had missed, but have also accompanied us on a camping trip to Hamble in order to carry out research. Finally I cannot forget Lorna Joy, my writing partner who lifted my spirits in times of doubt and my husband Roger for his patience and encouragement. I could add now my writer's group, twitter followers, facebook friends and readers, all of whom kept me motivated and kept me company during my lonely days of writing.

Finally, and more recently all those who have helped to bring 'Ancasta' into print.

Foreword

IN THE DAWNING light of the new century the world was changing rapidly. A new age was emerging from Victorian formality to the socially more relaxed lifestyle of the Edwardian era. The amazing advances of the previous decades had seen the birth of new technologies and industries including the steam turbine engine, put to use in all forms of working life from mining, light, medium and heavy engineering and electricity-generation, to powering the modern giant ocean-going liners; and later the internal combustion engine, powering all forms of transport from the 'horse-less carriage' to the newest invention of the new century, the aeroplane. At the time no-one could foretell the significant role these new forms of power and manufacturing would play in the forthcoming conflict of the 'Great War' which would change the principles of combat, the way of life and the face of the world forever.

Against this background of the new 20th century we are re-introduced to the progress of life for the next generations of the growing Newton family, now living at Woolston, near Southampton on the south coast of England. This area was once occupied by the Romans who, it is believed, worshipped the goddess *Ancasta* 'to ensure a swift and safe journey on the River Itchen', which cleaved its way from the chalk downs above Winchester, to the larger body of Southampton Water and in so doing cut a path between the port of Southampton and neighbouring boat-building town of Woolston.

Through this period of social upheaval, turmoil and tragedy we are lead through the stark realities of those emotional times whilst not being spared the realities of more tragedy and loss in the lives of these families. We are carried through the localities with a close attention to detail of life as it was lived in those far-gone days and in our journey we are reminded of the growth of ships and shipping and the quest for speed at sea with the tragedy of the Titanic disaster and in the air the contrast of the excitement of the Schneider Trophy contests of the time, seeking to achieve ever-greater speed in the air, and the birth of the soon-to-become world famous Supermarine Aviation Works.

Continuing with her successful technique of writing in the present and reverting to the past in the lives of these characters and with ever more unexpected twists and turns, Diana Jackson succeeds in jolting the reader's emotions to give a clear understanding of how things were for so many 'ordinary' people in those dark days of wartime, followed so soon after by the Spanish flu epidemic which swept the world with terrifying devastation claiming more lives, of all generations, in the next two years than had that terrible War. No families were spared the loss or sacrifice of a loved one, but life had to go on.

It was my pleasure to accept Diana's invitation to offer 'technical' support concerning the local history of this region (particularly with regard to the aviation developments which are close to my heart) and then to be invited to illustrate the cover, which has been my privilege. To then be asked to write this *foreword* might seem to be greedy to some, but for me it is the icing on my cake to be a part of this gripping and moving look at the continuing lives of the families we first met in *Riduna,* with their friends.

Colin van Geffen
Artist, Public Speaker and Local Historian

The Prologue

In a state of half-sleep Harriet's mind was flitting between memories. At first she was standing with her late husband Joe at Sarah's wedding, his face alight with pleasure as he led their daughter down the aisle towards Anthony, who waited proudly in his army uniform.

Harriet absentmindedly reached out but, finding Joe's side of the bed empty and cold, in a state of loneliness she drew his pillow tight to herself, stilling her racing heart until she breathed softly once more.

A thick fog swirled around her mind but as a gentle breeze brushed against her cheek, an occasional break in the white revealed the slopes she knew instinctively to be Les Butes, almost as if each blade of grass was familiar to her. Her feet were standing on Riduna, the island of her birth. A foghorn sounded, echoing a stark warning of the invisible, treacherous waters which she knew surrounded her.

Occasionally Harriet felt the subdued glow of the sun attempting to penetrate the gloom, until finally she had her first glimpse of the harbour and breakwater below her, on which was standing a solitary figure patiently staring out to sea. She recognised herself at only sixteen years of age, the vision stirring emotions of waiting, longing and hoping which still churned deep within her.

The scene soon faded, consumed by the dense fog. After a few moments of blankness a further scene broke free to the right of the harbour, which was now no longer visible. Harriet looked down on Braye Common, where two young people stood. She held her breath as she observed the young man, Edward, her childhood sweetheart, holding something out to her. Memories flooded back of the day

Edward had given her a beautiful silver locket as they had stood above Braye Beach on the day before he left for a life at sea, but as he held Harriet close to him the scene was hidden once more.

This time, in sheer agitation, she remembered searching for the locket and the feelings of devastation when she finally admitted defeat. Her loss, swamped by her recent bereavement, left her shivering as her dream world mixed with the reality of her present life. She pulled her covers up, though in her mind it was her cloak which she wrapped tightly around her, keeping out the damp, cold day. Upon hearing footsteps she turned to see the familiar figure of her father, who paused and smiled before striding purposefully on towards St Anne. Next, through the mist she saw the face of her friend and rival, Charlotte, who joined her brother Michael before disappearing in the ghostly air, and finally there was Jane, her best friend and confidante, who stood waving to her from the edge of the town. As each face faded Harriet was overwhelmed by the warmth of belonging. Here was her home, the island of her birth, the place her mind returned to in times of distress to soothe and comfort her and give her peace.

Chapter 1

August 1910

EDWARD SAT IN the Captain's cabin on the London South Western Railway's *Princess Ena*, a time when he usually enjoyed a moment's peace before finding his way to the bridge, to guide his ship on its path to France. It was a tall funnelled vessel which, although quite new, looked a little old-fashioned, much like her captain. Edward's bearded rugged face, worn by the travelling adventures of his youth, sea air and sunshine, still had a twinkle of boyishness beneath the frown he wore today. At 47 years of age, he had long since chosen to avoid the long distance routes across the Atlantic or round the notorious Cape towards India, content now in the knowledge that a home cooked meal and a warm bed awaited him on his return to Hythe. Nonetheless it wasn't an easy task negotiating a route across the busy English Channel to Caen from Southampton and he certainly felt the weighty responsibility for his four hundred passengers, although this was tiny in comparison to the *Edinburgh Castle*, the ocean liner they had followed into Southampton docks the previous morning.

Edward sipped a cup of strong coffee. He really

preferred the hard stuff given the choice, but the caffeine helped to keep tiredness at bay and fill him with that extra sense of alertness, to be one step ahead of trouble at sea, or on land for that matter. Even after years of sometimes dangerous but stimulating voyages for cargos of tea, to satisfy the English's unquenchable thirst for the brown liquid, he still didn't understand its appeal.

Edward closed his eyes momentarily, but seeing two faces staring at him from behind his eyelids he changed his mind, preferring to escape his dilemma by daydreaming with his eyes wide open.

He sat in his sparsely equipped cabin and looked around him. This room bore no resemblance to his earlier Atlantic voyages where, as captain, he had enjoyed the privilege of a polished mahogany desk with studded leather inlay and matching armchair. Settled in this luxury he had pored over the charts strewn in front of him.

As he tried to relax today, in a dream-like state of mind, a face filled his mind's vision and wouldn't retreat. This was not surprising since Harriet, his childhood sweetheart back on the island of Riduna all those years ago, had been like the thumb on his right hand from the moment he could grasp her tiny fingers. Edward couldn't shed the last glimpse of her quiet dignified figure as she had watched the *Itchen Ferry* or *Floating Bridge* as the locals called it, depart from Woolston shore a couple of hours before. They had walked the long way back from Weston Shore and, not wanting to say goodbye at her home, she had continued with him along Victoria Street towards Lipton's the grocers. Edward had wanted to embrace her then. Her face so familiar, the lines of pain from the bereavement for the sudden death of her husband Joe, did little to mask her beauty, to his way of thinking. Instead of the embrace he longed to give her, she had held out her hand and as he had taken it to his lips, always the gentleman in her opinion; their eyes had met momentarily.

'I'll call as often as I can,' he'd promised recklessly.

'I hope so,' Harriet had replied: words which conveyed more doubt than confidence in him.

Had he always let her down, he wondered, his mind wracked with guilt.

'My cousin Joe was a very lucky man.'

His voice had cracked as he had turned his back on her to catch the waiting ferry, which would take him over the River Itchen to Southampton and his waiting vessel.

His mind reran the conversation in so many different ways. Had he made a promise that he was unable to keep?

His thoughts then turned to his early life on Riduna and his gnawing longing to leave the island of his birth. He had never questioned this decision, or dwelt too long on how it had changed his destiny. When he was a young lad he had frequently watched ships pass by their tiny island, with the desire to escape out into the wider world seeping deep inside him. In that moment the truth dawned on him that his single-minded quest had lost him Harriet, maybe forever.

He consoled himself that he'd achieved so much since his first position on the *Stella,* travelling from Southampton to St. Peter Port. It had been such tragic news when the *Stella* went down. He remembered with affection so many of the crew who had lost their lives that day. Fortunately for his family he'd chosen more adventurous routes by then, and his cousin Joe had also admitted to having no sea legs and had returned to find work on land. He felt a twinge of jealousy as his thoughts turned to his visits to Joe and Harriet in Woolston over the years. He loved showering their children with gifts and exotic stories, but also felt a little guilty that he'd not made the effort to attend Joe's funeral, having no personal wish to return to either Sarnia or Riduna himself.

Next, Edward's thoughts relived saying goodbye to Marie that very morning.

'Why are you really leaving so early?' she'd demanded, hands on hips.

'I've just got things to do,' he'd replied rather lamely, aware that she'd gleaned the hint of dishonesty in his eyes.

Women; they can read you like a chart, second guessing which direction your mind will journey next and always there if you lose your way, so to speak.

Marie, his wife in his eyes and all but for that bit of paper, knew only too well that his crew were so well trained and loyal, that they would have everything under control when their captain returned. Edward and Marie shared a small but comfortable cottage in Hythe, just over the cobbled street from the pier, as far from water as he ever wanted to be. It was a bed sock and night capped life, cosy and voluptuous, like Marie herself. He rarely thought of the life of ill repute he'd rescued her from all those years ago, preferring to dwell on the contentment they shared in an arrangement that was harmonious and mutually beneficial.

Edward was also a creature of habit, despite his early desires for new adventures, and he always left home after a hearty lunch.

'My last home cooking for a few days,' he often remarked, grinning cheekily. They would share a warm embrace, almost as if he were setting off for a voyage which would take a few months. Then he would enjoy the stroll along the wooden pier, to arrive just in time to catch the *Hotspur* which would take him over Southampton Water to the jetty beside the newly built pavilion.

Later, as the *Ena* sailed effortlessly along Southampton

Water, Edward Johnson stood on the bridge, ever mindful of the course they were taking and the many smaller vessels scrambling to get out of their way.

Uncharacteristically, Edward experienced a lapse in concentration. Across the waters, jutting out from Weston Shore, a sand bank appeared before his eyes. The solitary figure of Harriet stood there, holding a single rose bud, silently gazing into the space before her. She seemed to look straight through his ship, as she held her hand high to cast the rose far into the waters. His rational mind knew that it was not low tide. She was in grave danger of being swept away by the currents. Edward yelled out an agonised warning.

'Captain!' was all his Second Officer had to bark to bring Edward to his senses, in time to alter his course in line with the marker buoys, outlining the narrow permissible shipping lane to the right of the channel.

As Edward regained his control and concentration he glanced back over his shoulder. Harriet had vanished. The sandbank he had seen so clearly a moment earlier had also disappeared below the lapping shoreline. Edward quickly dismissed the vision from his mind, as is the habit of many men with experiences they cannot comprehend, and he focussed once more on the task in hand.

The instant he did so Edward was not surprised to see another lady standing on the nearside quay at Hythe, waving in his direction. The petite but ample figure of Marie stood only a couple of hundred yards from their little cottage. Edward could just make out her mischievous smile and he returned her wave, sighing inadvertently.

From then on he gave the vital matter of navigation his undivided attention. They sailed past the imposing Royal Victoria Hospital, a quarter of a mile of chateaux-like turrets and towers majestically overshadowing the shoreline. The ship entered The Solent and, with Cowes and then Ryde on their right and Portsmouth Harbour on their left, they made their way to the open sea of the English Channel.

Chapter 2

NOT FAR AWAY from where the *Princess Ena* sailed across the English Channel towards Caen, a family had gathered together on the island of Sarnia. Sarah, Harriet's daughter, was feeling quite alone amongst the strangers in her aunt's drawing room. No longer a young girl and yet barely an adult, she sat absentmindedly flicking an escaped curl from her mop of auburn hair, which she had tried to tame with numerous pins hidden beneath her simple black bonnet. Her face was etched with a mixture of sorrow and frustration.

She looked across the sea of unfamiliar faces. Her gaze paused momentarily on each of her sombrely clad brothers. The twins, Tom and Jack, were deep in conversation with cousins she remembered being introduced to for the first time earlier that day, and her eldest brother Ernest looked so grown up as he talked at length to his Uncle Walter. Although she was unable to lip read all of their conversation, she gleaned from the occasional word that it was about air machines, Bleriot's exciting cross channel flight the previous year and the unimaginable rumours of a transatlantic airship attempt in the near future. Sarah was just wondering what Uncle Walter's reply was going to be to Ernest's question about whether flight would be important to Sarnia when a lady stepped up behind her.

'It is Sarah, Joe's daughter isn't it?'

The voice penetrated her distracted thoughts. Sarah turned to see a friendly woman who appeared to be much the same age as her mother. She was dressed in black crepe out of respect, her bodice trimmed with lace and the straight skirt with fine embroidered stitching. Long, tailored sleeves led the eyes to delicate fingers adorned with gold rings, making it obvious to Sarah that the lady's class was superior to most of the assembled group.

'Yes it is...' she replied tentatively.

'I believe I am your namesake, Miss Sarah Mortimer,' she said, reaching out and gently grasping Sarah's hands between her own.

It reminded Miss Mortimer of another first meeting about twenty years ago when she had met Sarah's mother Harriet for the first time in similar circumstances. To Miss Mortimer, Sarah was instantly recognisable, having a striking resemblance to her mother, with her tall slender figure and attractive face. Unlike the Harriet she remembered though, who had frequently worn the expression of a lost soul, Miss Mortimer noticed a steely determination behind these sad grey, green eyes.

'I knew your father many years ago. I was so sorry to hear the news. Joe, your father, was a much respected young man here on Sarnia.'

'Thank you Miss Mortimer; that's very kind of you,' Sarah replied. 'I think I have heard your name mentioned in the past,' Sarah attempted to return the lady's warm smile and she paused, struggling to control her emotions.

'Please call me Rose,' Miss Mortimer said, trying to put Sarah at her ease. 'All my friends do.' Sensing Sarah's continued discomfort, and concerned about her companion's pale complexion, she suggested in a quiet voice, 'Would you like some fresh air and to go for a stroll with me down to the harbour?'

'I, er, Rose, I'm not sure,' Sarah stumbled with her reply, 'Aunt Pamela might need my help.'

'I am sure that your aunt could spare you for half an hour,' Rose replied as she gestured towards the two young maids who were waiting almost invisibly by the door.

They had walked amongst the guests, replenishing empty glasses and offering plates of food, and were now alert for Aunt Pamela's signal to begin clearing away.

'We shall ask!' Rose said, as she scanned the guests for their hostess, the proprietor of this small guest house near the centre of St Peter Port and sister of Joe, Sarah's father, whom they had buried at eleven o'clock that morning.

Sarah observed their whispering and occasional glances in her direction and, before she could protest, she found herself being ushered to the door. Although it was a warm day in early summer, Sarah collected a light shawl to fend off any sea breezes at the harbour's edge.

They strolled in companionable silence down the short cobbled slope of Well Road, between the rows of harbourmen's cottages. The road narrowed and turned, the way ahead being covered with shadows, before suddenly emerging into the sunlight, with the harbour in front of them. Small boats mingled, chattering messages as they fidgeted against the glittering water. They dodged a Hansom Cab racing towards the jetty and joined the wave of people walking towards the waiting steamer to England. A few were carrying their own bags or cases but most were following on the heels of one of the many barrow boys, who frequently turned their capped heads to smile or make some light-hearted and humorous comment to check that the owners of their burdens were not too far behind. Sarah heard glimpses of conversations: sad farewells, fond recollections of their stay on the island, exciting plans for future visits or the journey ahead as she tuned in and out between the channels of her own thoughts and the reality around her.

Rose led Sarah to an area above the waiting ship, where wooden slatted seats were occupied by folks enjoying a rest or admiring the view. They found a place to sit beside an elderly couple with lined, contented faces, walking sticks leaning at their sides and wrinkled hands clasped together in eternal love and friendship. The couple beamed as the ladies joined them and it struck Sarah just how similar their features had become as they had aged together.

Sarah sighed.

'It's difficult to explain. Suddenly I feel that I hardly knew my father at all. Here is a world, a place I have barely heard him speak of, the beautiful home of his birth where he grew up, family, friends and a life I have very little knowledge or understanding of. It's disconcerting, to say the least.'

Rose thought for a few moments, wishing to give the right words of comfort to this confused young woman. The day had been a long one. That morning Joe Newton had been buried according to his wishes in a grave alongside his parents, far away from his home in England.

'Your father was many people: father, husband, son, brother, cousin and friend. Each facet had its own character and its own life, just like a different scene in a play. In each scene he was a special man and lived to please the people around him whenever he could.'

'I understand what you are saying. During the long journey here yesterday I had time to think. I was wracked with guilt that my father had come over here on a visit and died alone, so far away from his family. His heart attack had been so sudden. He was tired when he left but I never imagined he was ill. I had visions of him being so far away from my mother and his children, just when he needed us most – but it wasn't like that at all, was it?'

'My poor girl! You must rest assured that he had his sister and many members of his family nearby. Also the nuns up at Les Cotils are very loving, caring people. He could not have been in better hands.'

There was another silence as they watched how basket after basket of tomatoes and luggage were hauled effortlessly on to the waiting ship and stowed securely by the stevedores, the line of laden carts queuing at the dock edge gradually dwindling.

'Would you mind telling me about my father as you knew him, Rose? You mentioned that he was much respected, but he must have been quite young when he left Sarnia.'

'Your father worked hard from the moment he was out of short trousers. In fact, well before that. First he would meet and greet travellers coming to lodge at his parents' guest house, carrying their trunks on his barrow. Even at ten years old he was known for his smile and his way with words as he touted for business. It was rare for the Marina to have vacancies in season, mainly thanks to Joe. He pushed his barrow up the steep slope with ease, talking merrily as he led his guests, slipping items of local gossip amongst informative descriptions of the island's attractions.'

'He became a special painter, didn't he?' Sarah asked.

'Yes, that's right. He met an old chap on Riduna on one of his visits; the time he fell in love with your mother over there, I think. He was so excited to tell me about it. He became an apprentice in decorative gold leaf painting at the various forts on Riduna. Once he had learnt his skill he returned to Sarnia to practice it. There was so much work at the time that he took on a couple of apprentices and he had quite a business going. And of course he had dealings with officers, officials and island dignitaries in this line of work. Anyone who thought they were somebody, in fact!'

'He told me once that he had to travel to France for his work,' Sarah remarked.

'Yes, that's right. He went to pick up the pigment for his craft,' Rose replied.

'I doubt if he enjoyed those trips very much,' added Sarah.

'No I'm sure he didn't, but did you know that your father once went to sea? He quickly discovered that he had no sea legs though, and was so relieved to return to dry land, unlike your Uncle Edward, who was born to be at sea.'

'You knew Uncle Edward?' Sarah asked in surprise.

'Yes, I met him several times when he was staying with your father. He attended many of the island's dances, I seem to recall, sometimes uninvited, which was a bit of a scandal in those days! Do you know if he ever settled down with anyone?' Rose asked casually.

'That's another funny thing. My father took me to see Uncle Edward and Marie several times when I was young. It was our little secret, even from my mother. It was an adventure, taking the floating bridge over to Southampton, walking around to the pier and catching the ferry over to Hythe. It is a quaint place with a long wooden jetty, where the *Hotspur* docks. I never questioned why we didn't tell my mother and only broke my promise the other day. Do you know why it had to be kept a secret?'

'I am not sure,' Rose replied in all honesty. 'I hear though that you have recently married and must offer my congratulations, but where is the fortunate young man?' she enquired feeling it diplomatic to change the subject.

She had heard rumours about Edward but dismissed it as jealous conjecture.

'My husband, Anthony, is in the army. He was unable to

accompany me because he is currently training in Woolwich. He caught the train to London two weeks after we were married, but when he returns we will be stationed at Fort Gilkicker at Alverstoke Bay in Hampshire.'

'And are you still living at home then, Sarah?'

'No, we went away to Ryde in the Isle of Wight for a weekend after the wedding and then we returned to move in with Anthony's parents in Hamble until married quarters are completed at the Fort. In the brief moments we had together when he was allowed home for a weekend on compassionate leave, we decided it might be best for me to return to my mother's for a few weeks.'

'Your aunt was saying that you have two free days before you return to England. It would be a pleasure for me to show you some of Sarnia's most beautiful sites, if you would care to join me. Your brothers would also be more than welcome,' Rose added, remembering the occasions she had accompanied Sarah's parents, Joe and Harriet, and Harriet's cousin Florence all those years ago.

Seeing this as a wonderful opportunity to find out more about the island of her father's birth, Sarah replied,

'If Aunt Pamela and my brothers approve of the outing then I would be most grateful to you.' Sarah hesitated for a moment. 'Do you mind me asking why everyone calls you Rose and not Sarah?'

Rose laughed,

'Not at all. My father was so fond of the roses in his garden that he used to say, "pretty as a rose!" whenever I ran out to him. Then he shortened it to "Ah Rose!" And the name sort of stuck.'

'It's a pretty name,' replied Sarah as they strolled away from the harbour, just as the last rope was thrown on to the waiting deck of the steamer before it started to inch away from the dockside.

Chapter 3

THE FOLLOWING DAY, two buggies left Well Road, laden with family and food for a picnic lunch. The horses trotted along the familiar Esplanade, slowing up for other carriages joining from the many steep side streets, and the pedestrians who chose that moment to rush across, right into their path. It was a beautiful day. They passed prettily clad ladies holding parasols to protect their pale features from the noon day sun. There was also a band of the local militia turning to march along Castle Pier to Castle Cornet in their red uniforms, buttons sparkling as brightly as the ripples of silver water in the harbour. Then the ponies pulled their loads up the steep winding slopes, the view of the islands of Sark and Herm disappearing behind dense woodland.

Rose, who today wore a deep blue tailored suit, befitting of a well dressed lady of independent means, quite in contrast to the sombre, plain, black attire of Sarah and her brothers, talked as they sped along.

'Down a very steep slope over there on our left is the nearest bay to St Peter Port, Fermain Bay, which is quite stony but very popular. The best way to reach it is by ferry from the town, but I would like us to go a bit further before we stop, along to one of the most beautiful secluded bays on the island. The climb down is very steep, but you are all young and fit and I assure you that it is worth the effort!'

They turned to their left down a narrow lane which wound through farmland and among occasional cottages until a panoramic view of the smaller islands in the sea panned out to their left. The men carried the rugs and baskets between them, leaving Rose to lead them along a rugged cliff path, with ever-changing breathtaking views, the likes of which Sarah had never seen before. Rose suddenly disappeared to the left down a sharp drop and, tentatively following her, they reached a set of steps carved out of the rocks. She turned to them momentarily, doubt written on her face.

'I think it would be better to have our picnic over there on that grassy bank before climbing down the cliff steps; don't you think?'

Relieved to turn back with their burdens, the party settled in the sunshine and enjoyed a communal picnic, taking their minds off the reason for their visit to the island. For Ernest it was nothing new, having travelled with his father on a couple of occasions in the past. He realised how fortunate he had been and wished his father was still alive to accompany them all.

Sarah wondered at the beauty around her, so different to the world she knew. After many moments when they sat quietly digesting their repast, Sarah turned towards their hostess.

'Yesterday you were telling me about my father, Rose. Why did he leave Sarnia if his business was going so well?'

'He married your mother in St Saviour's Church near the market and then your brothers were soon on your way. Unfortunately, after a few years the islands went through a difficult time. The numbers of visiting military personnel had declined, the building work had long since been completed and work was short. Many men, at that time, were travelling abroad to earn a living.'

'It couldn't have been easy for my father to take his family with him.'

'No, that's right. In some ways I was desperately sorry for young Harriet, your mother, because she had suffered so much already. In another way though, she was one of the fortunate ones, since Joe was so determined to take Harriet with him. Many men left their wives here to struggle on their own and sent money over when they could, but I'm afraid to say that some even started new lives and never returned. As you say, it wasn't easy for them, but your father adored Harriet. He wouldn't have left her behind.'

On that positive note they left their empty baskets with one of Rose's servants and the group inched its way gingerly down the steep steps. The bay, Petit Bot, was almost deserted except for a couple of young people and their dog, who bounded back and forth, in and out of the water and across the white sand, leaving a criss cross of virgin paw prints. At shore level the sea breeze was quietened by the imposing rock face on either side and the peace was only disturbed by the energetic sea, rushing in between isolated rocks on the edge of the bay, making rivers which turned into rock pools as it retreated. The group ambled about and the young men even took off their shoes to paddle in the cool water's edge. The ladies settled on the rugs and sat in silence for a while, Sarah's head clearing for the first time in days as she felt the soothing peace of the sea.

Their climb back up, a couple of hours later, was filled with less enthusiasm and a lot of panting and groaning, but soon they emerged at the top, full of self-praise for their worthy achievement, as if they had scaled a high mountain peak. Rose hid her amusement.

On the following afternoon the buggies followed the steep slopes out of St Peter Port in a northerly direction. Leaving the town behind they weaved though farmland and the occasional hamlet to reach the northern end of the island. As they pulled up to a halt, the sea breeze caught Sarah's face, caressing it and inadvertently lifting wisps of her hair as she faced the wind and breathed in deeply. She climbed down from the buggy and walked across the grassy bank towards the sea, her eyes sweeping along the wide and open bay, a contrast to Petit Bot. If Sarah had been listening she would have heard Rose giving a description of the bay.

'We are at the most northerly bay on Sarnia which is easily accessible by buggy, called L'Ancresse, with the small forts of Pembroke to our right and Le Marchant to the left. It can be quite windy here, even in summer.'

Rose's enthusiastic voice dispersed in the sound of the breeze and rolling waves, as Sarah's whole self was uplifted by the sight of the bay and the rose tinted rocks in the distance. It was mid-afternoon and although the morning had been crystal clear, now the horizon was softened by a haze, so that there was a blur between sea and sky.

Sarah's mind wandered to her new marriage of a matter of weeks and, as she thought of her reunion with Anthony in a few weeks' time she blushed, remembering the tentative way they had explored each other's bodies in the newness of their union. She was aware that Rose's voice had momentarily ceased and she could hear the less familiar *chugga chugga* sound of one of those motor cars rolling into view, disquieting the horses as they waited patiently. As she turned her back towards them she could hear the animated conversation between her brothers and the driver of his new Model T Ford, recently shipped over from America. The proud driver was only too willing to discuss his most prized possession, since it was only one of twenty cars on the island. It had arrived at the port in the spring in packing cases, with the wings and wheels still to be attached. He explained that a local company, the Bougourd Brothers, had recently expanded into the motor car trade from a successful business selling bicycles. Ernest was particularly impressed by the gleaming black steel panelled body and detachable roof, excellent for all seasons, whereas Jack was firing questions about the up to the minute mechanical features. They all agreed that it was a beautiful car and the driver, a local land owner, puffed up with pride.

'So unnecessary on a small island like this!' tutted Rose to Sarah.

Sarah's attention was drawn, as if by some magnetic force, back to the horizon and she was sure that she could just about make out another island in the mist. It was as if Rose was reading her thoughts as she exclaimed,

'Oh! That's Riduna, the island of your mother's birth. You are so lucky to be able to see it!'

After a pause, as the information penetrated through to her consciousness, Sarah asked,

'And how long does it take to travel to Riduna?'

'The journey is less than two hours on a good day, but if a sea fog descends it has been known to take more than a day! As it happens I will be travelling there myself tomorrow, after your departure for England. My father used to be a patron of the school, as he was here on Sarnia, but since he passed away I have tried to continue his good works. He believed so much in a good education for all, even the girls. His attitude was well before his time, but many are grateful for his legacy.'

Knowing how her father had struggled sometimes with his reading, having never been taught formally at school, Sarah realised that this had not always been the case for everyone here.

An irrepressible excitement grew in Sarah's mind. She calculated that Anthony would not return to Woolston to collect her from her mother's for another three weeks. If she were to travel on to visit Riduna, what a lovely opportunity it would be to meet distant relatives and to see the island of which she had heard so many stories. But where could she stay? She could not afford lodgings. Her relatives may not take too kindly to her appearing on their doorstep and may not even welcome her. After all they had not made the effort to travel to attend her father's funeral.

As if reading Sarah's thoughts a second time Rose exclaimed,

'If you would care to join me, then I am sure my sister would be more than happy to accommodate you for a couple of days. She runs a boarding house on the island but I feel sure that she would welcome you as her personal guest.'

Sarah hesitated only for a moment before she accepted the offer with good grace.

After the motor car had driven away they took a stroll along the bay together. Later, when they returned to the buggy Sarah looked back over towards Riduna, but the hazy horizon blended with the sea as one and there was now no visible sign of the island.

'If we are to reach your aunt's before the light fades, then I think we should be heading back now,' Rose said.

'I agree Miss Mortimer,' replied Ernest, 'and thank you so much. I'm sure I speak on behalf of my sister Sarah and my brothers to say that you have made our unfortunate trip over to Sarnia much more pleasant to bear.'

As yet Ernest was unaware of Sarah's plans to extend her stay, so deep had he been in conversation with the car owner.

'My pleasure,' replied Rose as they climbed back into the buggy.

They rode back to Marine Lodge, where Aunt Pamela

had prepared a hearty meal of Coq au Vin and Pear Torte with lashings of rich island cream. The influence of nearby France on her aunt's menu fascinated Sarah and she relished the new experiences, hugging the thought of tomorrow's adventure close to her, as her brothers made ready for their departure to England the following morning. She could see that Aunt Pamela was more than surprised to hear of her plans but neither her aunt nor her brothers could think of reasons to dissuade her from this venture. They could see that Sarah's mind was set.

Chapter 4

SARAH STOOD NEXT to Rose on the quayside across the harbour from the steamer where her brothers were on deck waiting to depart for England. As she watched them Ernest held up his hand in a single wave. He was angry that he had failed to dissuade her and so she stood silently, like a child awaiting a new and forbidden adventure, with a mixture of anticipation and apprehension for the days ahead. Ernest took with him a letter to her husband Anthony, explaining the reasons for her spontaneous change of plan and reassuring him that by the time he had received this letter, she should already be on her return to England. This was a journey she was compelled to take, driven by a deep need to learn more about the island of her mother's birth.

The *Courier* was to depart for Riduna a short distance along the jetty from where they stood. The tall cream and black funnel was her only proud symbol of importance, compared to that of her larger cousin the *Alberta* which had just left her berth and was steaming towards the harbour's mouth.

The journey was uneventful. They stood on the deck of the *Courier* for a while as they left the harbour and passed Herm and Sark to their right. Soon they sought shelter from the sea breeze, trying to seek comfort on the slatted wooden benches below. There they remained for most of the journey until Sarah overheard a fellow traveller mention that Riduna was quite close now and so she persuaded Rose to return to the deck. Unfortunately, as Rose climbed up the steep wooden ladder-like steps, she tripped and one of her silver buttons was caught between the hand rails. A kindly gentleman helped her back to her feet and up the remaining steps. Sarah followed behind, but noticing an object glisten between the slats, she shivered with the strangest of sensations, as she grasped the silver button and placed it in her pocket. For some inexplicable reason she was reminded suddenly of the mysterious silver locket which she had found amongst her father's possessions as she had cleared out his trunk in the attic at home.

On reaching Rose, who was now deep in conversation with the gentlemen who had come to her aid, Sarah had time to absorb the view before her. At first the island was just a hazy outline, an unforgettable shape which would imprint upon her memory for some time to come. Gradually the outline was filled in with details: fields of cows, crops and craggy isolated rocks covered with a multitude of gannets. An almost familiar fort came into view next, not dissimilar to those she had seen on Sarnia, sitting out majestically in front of a crescent-shaped sandy bay. It was as if an artist had sketched a scene roughly at first but now he was filling in the details. They passed two more fortresses flanking picture postcard bays on either side: tiny sandy coves where occasional holidaymakers were enjoying a picnic or afternoon stroll along the water's edge. Sarah was stirred out of her daydream as she realised that the gentleman was directing his conversation towards her.

'That is Fort Albert to our left and Braye Beach sweeps around to the harbour. Fort Grosnez sits guarding us on our right, just behind the jetty and fishing harbour, which is hidden from view at present,' he explained, gesticulating as he spoke.

Sarah was in awe of the natural beauty of Braye Beach, a more complete view from the sea than she would have had if she were walking along the beach. It was as if she had known Riduna all her life, but had not realised it. It was so familiar and yet she had never set foot on the island: too many contradictions.

Rose's sister waved from her waiting buggy. Even if the *Courier* was late, which it was not on this occasion, the news of its arrival would soon filter through. All those who were expecting guests from Sarnia, provisions, or a delivery of some kind, would find their way down to the jetty, in plenty of time to have a gossip while they watched the approaching vessel out of the corner of their eyes. The post boy, who had come for the mail, was the only person impatient to pull his load quickly up the slope to St. Anne, to be sorted and collected at the Post Office.

Sarah stood back discreetly as Rose quietly spoke to her sister, who nodded encouragingly. It had been impossible to give her sister prior warning since this was the first visit of the *Courier* in two days and there was no other form of communication, unless you were lucky enough to find a sailor heading this way and willing to take a message. Even then there was no guarantee that it would have arrived before them. Sarah stepped forward towards Mrs Hammond, who smiled warmly, offering her hand.

'Welcome to Riduna, my dear. Let us get you home for some refreshments. There will be plenty of time to talk later over supper.'

She watched Sarah step up into the buggy, looking down over her dark apparel, which she realised was a sign of Sarah's recent loss. Young ladies on Riduna on the whole still wore smocks, simply gathered above their waist and along the neckline, whereas she noticed that the line of Sarah's formal dress was brought in tightly at the waist and flowed down in panels below a narrow sash. Mrs Hammond was always alert to any changes in fashion apparent when visitors came to Riduna, because it incensed her to think that visitors might think the islanders backward. She was always the first to have a quiet word with her favourite dressmaker, who did her best to keep a good customer happy. The majority of the islanders lacked both the means and the inclination for such frippery.

The sisters continued to talk about the trip, the weather and the frustration of isolation of the island: topics Sarah was sure had engaged them on frequent occasions in the past. As they headed away from the small harbour development and up Braye Road, they passed by the rather grand entrance to Scott's Hotel on their right hand side, where the gentleman they had met on the *Courier* was in deep conversation with quite a dashing young man. The two men turned and waved simultaneously, though Sarah had to turn away quickly as the younger man's piercing blue eyes met hers.

At the top of the hill they veered to the right, with the large imposing Methodist Chapel before them and then they turned immediately left into Victoria Street, which was obviously the main cobbled road of the small and only town of St Anne.

'Named after the late Queen's royal visit,' Mrs Hammond explained. 'I am told that it was a day to remember. I wasn't here myself. I married Mr Hammond in 1895 and came over here from Sarnia.'

They passed, among others, a couple of butchers' shops and grocers, a bakery, the Post Office, a drapers, a shoe maker, milliner and dress makers. Enough shops, Sarah noted, to satisfy the island's needs. She noticed that the hats in the milliner's were a little dated by Southampton standards, but nevertheless there was an element of choice from simple straw, ribboned ones to the decorative and quite elaborate bonnets on display. Sarah was quite impressed. There was a pleasant but relaxed bustle of activity, an unhurried air of people going about their daily business, intermingled with smiling holiday-makers, enjoying the change of scenery and a break from their busy lives at home. She overheard English mainly but also the local language, not dissimilar to French, but she was also surprised to hear unmistakeable American accents as they passed by. Seeing Sarah's puzzled expression,

Mrs Hammond explained,

'It's our famous cows they come for. We export Ridunas all the way to Canada and America now!'

At the top of the street they turned left again, passing rows of terraced stone cottages and a couple of public houses, until the road widened and they pulled up at a large gate on their left hand side. A gardener appeared and they continued along the short drive to the house, grand by the island's standards with eight large sash windows, and a ninth with a balcony overlooking a neat central flower bed in front of imposing carved oak doors.

Once inside, a maid was called and Sarah was shown into the drawing room, where tea was provided until her room could be made ready. Soon Sarah was shown to her room where she was able to rest and refresh herself following the long journey, before it was time for supper. A jug of water, soft towel and scented soap were left on a washstand beside the door. As she gazed out of the window she was pleased to see a glimmer of the sea through the trees at the end of the garden. Sarah sighed.

That evening after supper, when only pleasantries were being exchanged about the journey and life on Riduna, the ladies were again in the drawing room.

'It must be nearly twenty years since your mother left Riduna, wasn't it Sarah? I am sorry that you too have lost your father and wish your visit was in happier circumstances. What would you like to do during your short stay?'

'I would very much like to spend some time exploring the island, but there are people I might call upon if I am able to,' Harriet replied. 'My mother has talked of her friends Charlotte, John and Michael and her teacher, Jane, who I believed married the doctor. There was also Annie and Joseph, my mother's next door neighbours, but I am sure that they have passed away by now. I also have second cousins living somewhere on the island. I have written down their address as far as I can remember it.'

'I think that the Charlotte you speak of must be Mrs Dunn at the Rose and Crown who is married to John Dunn. Michael, Charlotte's brother, runs the bakery with his wife from Sarnia. Both couples took over the businesses from their parents some years ago. As to the Mary of whom you speak, I know several ladies of that name, but none are married to doctors, either past or present, as far as I am aware. Maybe Mrs Dunn, that's Charlotte, will know of whom you speak? I think Charlotte would also be able to tell you about the other couple. As to your second cousins, I will write a note and send a maid with it directly. I will keep it short and simple and we will await their reply. It would be better not to arrive unannounced, although Charlotte is such a good-natured, welcoming lady, and a dear friend of mine; I am sure she would be overjoyed to receive you. Please call me Cynthia, by the way.'

The sisters laughed as if they shared a joke.

'My sister's name is really Anne, but in the spring time our father loved hyacinths,' Rose explained.

'I would tolerate my father calling me Hyacinth but, as

you can imagine, I was happier when all the family shortened it to Cynthia.'

'That's more than kind of you, Cynthia,' Sarah replied, smiling.

'Well, I am sure that you are tired after your journey and would like to go to your room now.'

'Yes, I would truly appreciate that; thank you.'

Chapter 5

THE NEXT MORNING Sarah joined Rose and Cynthia for a light breakfast.

'Sarah, while my sister is occupied with her duties, I would see it as a personal pleasure to escort you to see places and people whom you wish to call upon...... No, don't thank me,' Cynthia continued, raising her hand slightly to discourage any protest.

Sarah usually preferred her independence, but she could see that her hostess would not easily be dissuaded.

'That would be lovely,' she replied, her eyes softening with uncharacteristic meekness.

'We shall go to visit Charlotte first, since she is a personal friend of mine. We have also received a hand-delivered note from your family, who would be happy for you to call this evening. First we will walk to The Rose and Crown, since the exercise will be good for us both and my sister can use the buggy.'

They set off towards the town, passing the top end of Victoria Street. They continued down the sloping street, passing the entrance to the school house on their right. A little further down the hill on the left hand side, hanging above the narrow footpath, was the sign of The Rose and Crown.

Cynthia pushed the door open. A cheery buxom blonde, whose few white strands of curls which escaped from the loose bun above her round face were the only signs of her forty six years, came forward to greet her.

Momentarily, Charlotte was lost for words as she spied Sarah behind Cynthia.

'My word,' she exclaimed. 'You must be Harriet's daughter. You're the spitting image of her!'

Thinking this a bit of an exaggeration, but pleased that she was recognised nevertheless, Sarah moved forward, her hand held out in greeting.

'Hello, Mrs ....,' she stumbled over the words as Charlotte moved forward too, and gave Sarah a tight embrace.

'Sit down and call me Charlotte, do. Now, tell me all about your mother. How is she and how many brothers and sisters do you have now?'

Sarah sat down where she was bidden and talked about her family, finishing with her recent loss and the reason for her sudden trip to Riduna.

'Oh you poor dear, and my word, poor dear Harriet. I'll make us a coffee, shall I?' she asked, already bustling through to the stove in the kitchen behind the bar, not expecting a reply.

'I am so sorry to hear about your father. Such a nice man. I could see from the moment he set his eyes on Harriet that he was smitten, but I thought at the time he didn't stand a chance.'

Realising she might have said too much she added,

'Well I did think the news of their wedding was rather sudden. We all wondered…'

There was a pause as the meaning of Charlotte's words sank in and she was yet again flustered.

'These things happen,' she finished lamely, her words trailing off.

'It was a lovely wedding. I remember it well,' exclaimed Cynthia trying to defuse the embarrassing moment as best she could, 'and just after a year later,' she added, with emphasis on certain words as she looked pointedly at Charlotte to warn her to be a little more diplomatic, 'everyone was thrilled when your eldest brother Ernest was born,' she ended with a flourish making her meaning perfectly clear.

'Oh well, all's well that ends well,' added Charlotte, not taking a blind bit of notice of the warning.

'Do you know what happened to Harriet's friend Mary and her doctor husband?' asked Cynthia, diplomatically changing the subject.

'When the old doctor passed away, he was such a good doctor, well liked by everyone on the island. Well, young Mary, she was so much younger than him anyway; she stayed on the island for a while. It was a bit lonely for her so she moved to Sarnia, I think. Her little daughter must have been around ten years old by then. I'm not sure if she's still there. Is your mother still in touch with Jane, then?' Charlotte mused.

'She last heard from Jane when she went to serve as a nurse in South Africa. Mother has written a couple of times but doesn't even know if she came back alive.'

'Oh, the poor dear. What a thing!' exclaimed a shocked Charlotte, whose one trip off the island to Sarnia had taken her weeks to recover from.

'And Annie and Joseph?' Sarah enquired.

'Buried in the grave right next to your grandparents. Seemed right somehow, them being neighbours all those years. I haven't seen Edward since the day of the funeral. You'd think he'd visit from time to time, the rascal.'

Sarah was surprised that Charlotte spoke of her Uncle Edward as if he were a child.

'Uncle Edward calls in at home from time to time. I used to love his visits as a child, with his tales of his sea travels and his unusual presents. I always call him uncle but he isn't really,' Sarah exclaimed.

Charlotte just stopped herself from showing her surprise about Edward's visits when she took heed of the glance from Cynthia, which brought the conversation to a natural close.

'Well, it *has* been lovely to meet you, Sarah. I am sorry you haven't met the family. My youngest is still at school and my eldest has joined the militia. The middle two are down at the harbour preparing our fishing boat and tackle for the night ahead and John, bless him, has gone to check on some supplies we need delivered from Rose Farm.'

She reached out to give Sarah a lighter embrace.

'Enjoy the rest of your stay. I am so sorry to hear about your father; such a kind man,' she repeated.

As they were about to leave, Cynthia suggested that Charlotte might find time to join them in a drive around the island; after all she grew up with Sarah's mother and would be more knowledgeable about Harriet's life when she was young. Sarah and Cynthia continued walking down the street until they reached Marais Square, where two horses were tied to a nearby water trough. Just as they were passing the door to the Marais Hall Hotel it swung open and out sauntered the young man whom they had seen the previous day. He gave them a wave of recognition and Sarah found it hard to conceal her blushing face from Cynthia. She gave a slight nod as they turned to walk away, leaving the smiling young man standing watching them with some amusement, his eyes burning through Sarah's back. Relieved to be out of his sight they turned towards the recently renamed Royal Connaught Square, passed the Island Hall and turned right up a quiet lane behind the churchyard of St Anne's. Sarah enjoyed time to absorb her surroundings.

'We'll continue our walk taking a different route home. You will soon get your bearings. It's such a small town.'

As they strolled along the cobbled streets Sarah soon recognised the Methodist Chapel and the island's dairy as they made their way back to Cynthia's house on Longy Road.

After a light lunch Sarah and Cynthia returned to The Rose and Crown where Charlotte was ready and waiting for them, having organised her staff to manage in her absence. Charlotte and Cynthia agreed the route and so they headed down Le Petit Val, the more scenic lane following the route of a stream on its way down to the village of Crabby. Charlotte took a detour here to the right, where they briefly paused to overlook the fishing harbour. Several men were still hard at work cleaning their nets and baskets; the pungent salty smell of fresh fish and crustaceans filling the air.

'Those are my boys,' gestured Charlotte proudly as the two young men worked hard to land their catch below them.

Instinctively they looked up and waved. Charlotte laughed as she returned their wave and then as they watched the men return to their work Charlotte suggested that Cynthia direct the buggy towards Crabby Bay.

Sarah was touched by the charmed and happy life her mother's childhood friend enjoyed. She was pondering on the merits and drawbacks of this existence when they pulled up outside a row of cottages in Crabby village. Charlotte did not have to explain because Sarah knew instinctively that this was where her mother was born. Her eyes slowly followed the row of cottages, trying to imagine her mother's early life with grandparents whom Sarah had never had the pleasure to meet.

'Which was the actual cottage?' she asked Charlotte, her hands trembling.

Charlotte pointed to the mid-terraced stone built cottage. 'That's where your mother grew up with your grandparents, Annie and Jack. Beth and Joseph lived next door on the right hand side with their only son, Edward. Handsome young man he was then, his head in the clouds though, if you see what I mean!'

Sarah gazed around her, deep in thought. She tried to picture what it might have been like, so different from the red brick terraced back street in Woolston where she had grown up, with only more houses on the other side of the street. She wondered how her mother could bear to leave the island and even more puzzled as to why she was adamant that she had no wish to return. It was stunning; not the same as the beauty of Braye Beach, with its long sandy shores sheltered by the harbour and breakwater, but in a wild and natural way, with the white tips of a restless sea exposing dark rocks or signalling their presence below the surface of swirling foam. On such a lovely day it was impossible for Sarah to imagine the bleak winters with no protection from the winds and storms.

After a while Sarah broke the spell of her thoughts and almost reluctantly her gaze was drawn towards the dangerous stretch of waters between the shore and the deserted island of Burhou.

Following her eyes, Cynthia filled the silence.

'The only inhabitants of Burhou are gannets and puffins. Occasionally there are boat trips around the island and it is so quaint to see them. The dangerous waters you are looking at, us islanders call The Swinge.'

They continued their tour, passing the imposing walls of Fort Tourgis, barracks to the dwindling numbers of troops on the island, and they took the right hand fork which followed below the steep rock face and grassy slopes, until Fort Clonque was a stone's throw away. This fortress was surrounded by water but Cynthia and Charlotte assured her that it was not the case at low tide, when a causeway would appear. Sarah was charmed by this picture, an ideal fairy story setting for a stranded princess awaiting rescue. Next, they walked beside the buggy as the horse pulled up the steep slopes of the path, known affectionately by the locals as the Zig-Zag. Then they continued on, passing Rose Farm as they headed back to

St Anne. Unfortunately there was no time to go to Saye Bay or Corblet's Bay, on the other side of the island, but Sarah assured her hostess that she had seen the pretty little coves when approaching Riduna on the *Courier*.

That evening Sarah was dropped off at the Braye Inn near the harbour in Newtown, which she guessed used to be her great grandparents' inn, but was now run by her second cousins, Albert and Evelyn. At first Sarah felt uncomfortable, having never been allowed to enter a public house at home, but everyone was so good-natured that she soon relaxed. The bar seemed to be filled with relations and people who had a story to tell about her mother.

'Did you know, young Harriet, your mother, started the tradition of a Sunday picnic? You can let her know we still go from time to time, just like we did in her day. Only it's now our children we watch playing in the sand,' said one friendly man, who was obviously a quarryman. 'Sad business though, about her parents.'

Before Sarah had a chance to form a reply, and realising that the man must be referring to the death of her grandparents, another man changed the subject.

'I remember your mother well. She was a wonderful dancer; looked like an angel and her feet barely touched the ground.'

'That's not what I remember. When our teacher gave us lessons, my feet were sore for days,' joined in the first man.

'I bet you didn't have young Harriet as a partner then. I tell you, she could spin on a sixpence, that lass.'

'It was Edward, wasn't it, her partner?'

The speaker was obviously another fisherman about the age of her Uncle Edward.

'No, you've got it wrong there. Edward danced with Charlotte,' and he winked knowingly at the other speaker.

'Oh yes, young Edward was a one with the ladies all right,' he laughed. 'First it was Charlotte and then...

'Stop your idle tongue, Thomas Howard. That's no talk for a young lady to hear, especially when her nearest and dearest's concerned. You should show some respect. Can you manage the bar on your own for a while, Albert?' Evelyn, normally a quiet woman, raised her voice to bring the speaker's tale to an abrupt close.

Albert nodded as he turned back to his customers.

'Come along with me, Sarah. We'll have a good natter in the kitchen at the back, out of the way of this rude bunch.'

Sarah followed Evelyn with some reluctance, since she was so inquisitive to hear about her mother's early life. Nevertheless, she was pleased to listen to her relation describing her extended family there on Riduna, whose names were too many to remember. Sarah in turn talked about her brothers and her recent marriage and the sad death of her father which had brought the family, all but her mother, to Sarnia.

'It's a shame your mother didn't come with you. There are many who would be pleased to see her again.'

Just at that moment, Mr Hammond appeared at the door, heralding the moment when Sarah should say her goodbyes and return to the safety of Longy Road, giving no chance to explain her mother's reluctance to revisit the island of her birth.

Chapter 6

BEFORE THEY SET sail the following afternoon, Charlotte had suggested that they meet at St Anne's churchyard for Sarah to pay her respects. Sarah followed Charlotte in and out of the gravestones, until she paused and nodded at a pair of stones positioned in close proximity. With sensitivity unusual to her nature, Charlotte made an excuse to walk to fetch some water, leaving Sarah to have a few moments' peace with her own thoughts. As she gazed down on the graves of her grandparents Annie and Jack Loveridge, Sarah read the inscription quietly:

'Though tragic their passing, may they be reunited in death.'

She had been given permission to pick some roses out of Cynthia's large garden and so the red roses were gently arranged at the foot of the grave. After a few moments of thoughtful silence she placed the yellow roses at the foot of the adjoining grave, whose inscription was of a more humorous nature, which Sarah rightly attributed to her Uncle Edward.

'May Elizabeth Johnson and Joseph Johnson now laugh together in heaven.'

After paying her respects, Sarah asked if she could call into a shop to purchase gifts for her mother and husband. She chose a small picture of shells for her mother, a reminder of the island of her birth, and a small box of marzipan sweets for Anthony, who she knew had a sweet tooth. She was just emerging from the shop when she yet again bumped headlong into the handsome stranger.

'We meet again,' he exclaimed, bowing his head and doffing his cap. 'Third time lucky, they do say,' he continued, totally ignoring her embarrassment.

'I will not apologize for colliding in such an opportune manner with a lovely lady,' he added brashly and was about to add something more daring as he reached for her hand when saw her ringed finger.

'Oh, I should have known from the very start that you would be spoken for. I do apologize for my ill mannered behaviour,' he added with such a boyish twinkle in his eyes that she knew he was not to be taken seriously.

'Apologies accepted,' Sarah replied before moving quickly out of the shop, her heart pounding as she caught her breath.

Charlotte and Cynthia diplomatically chose to ignore the altercation, while Sarah regained her composure.

'Are you ready for your journey home, my dear?' Cynthia asked, adding as a form of excuse for the incident as she dismissed the matter, 'I do apologize for that young man's behaviour. Young people today have no manners.'

Before they made their way back to Cynthia's boarding house to join Rose for an early lunch, Charlotte explained that Sarah could not leave the island without a walk to Les Butes and so the three ladies made their way slowly down Victoria Street. Not that they wanted to make haste, but it was impossible in Charlotte's company not to pause to talk to several islanders en route, especially those inquisitive to meet Harriet's daughter.

Once on Les Butes they stood looking out over the sweep of Braye Beach and the harbour. Sarah imagined her mother standing there all those years ago and it was as if history was repeating itself when the ladies noticed that the *Courier* had rounded the headland at Fort Albert and was steaming towards the jetty. It was Charlotte who was filled by the memories of the past and fleetingly thought of her rivalry for Edward's affections. She had fallen for his charms all those years ago when they had learnt to dance together and it had nearly destroyed her friendship with Sarah's mother, Harriet. She dismissed the intruding thought as she also noticed her sons returning in their fishing boat and she smiled indulgently as she pointed them out to Sarah.

'Do you think your mother might return to see us one day, Sarah?' Charlotte asked after a pause.

'She always says that she will never return, but I'm not so sure.'

'"Never say never" my mother always said,' added Charlotte knowingly.

In the quiet of the next moment Sarah was about to thank Charlotte for her company when her eyes were drawn to the small golden cross which she wore around her neck.

'I hope that you don't think me impertinent, but that is a pretty chain you are wearing. Do you happen to recall if my mother ever wore a silver locket when she was young?' Sarah asked.

'My word no, my dear,' Charlotte replied. 'We didn't have money for luxuries in those days, but I'm glad you like it. My John bought it for my birthday last year and it was such a surprise.'

'We must get back now, otherwise you will have no time for a light lunch before your departure,' encouraged Cynthia.

'And so must I, my dear. Please send my warmest wishes to your mother and tell her to come and visit us soon,' responded Charlotte.

'I will, I promise and thank you for spending some time with me.'

With that said, Charlotte gave Sarah one last embrace.

'That's nothing, ducks. I still can't get over how much you look like our Harriet. Everyone says so.'

As Charlotte walked away, Sarah took one last hypnotic gaze down towards the harbour below. Finally, with reluctance, she turned away and followed the other two ladies. She could not hear their words as they parted company but rushed to join Cynthia and they returned to her hostess' house, where Rose was already waiting for them. While lunch was being served, she went up to her guest room to finish packing her valise, which was collected by the maid and loaded into the waiting buggy. The atmosphere at lunch was as light and bright as the lunch itself but all too soon they were on their way down to the harbour.

Sarah felt a knot of sadness to be leaving Riduna but she had a feeling deep inside that one day she would return. She stood on the deck of the *Courier* long after Rose had sought refuge from the wind. She watched Riduna disappear into the misty horizon just as her mother had done. It was strange that on Sarnia she had been able to see the outline of Riduna so clearly. She tried to envisage her mother's emotions as she had left Riduna for the first time all those years ago, but it was beyond her imagination. Unlike her mother, Sarah had the security of her family at home in England and she would soon be reunited with her husband.

Below deck she was reminded yet again of the silver locket and so she decided to take the opportunity, during their voyage ahead, to broach the subject.

'Rose, do you mind me asking if you have any

recollection of a silver locket in my father's possession when he lived on Sarnia, by any chance?'

Her travelling companion was about to deny all knowledge of it but her eyes suddenly lit up with a hidden memory.

'I do remember, on one occasion, meeting your father and Edward outside one of the second hand jeweller's shops near the harbour in St Peter Port. I recall that he was trying to persuade Edward to buy something, but I'm not really sure what it was, or if in any event they made a purchase. Is it important?' she added inquisitively.

'No. It's not important. It is just that I found a silver locket amongst my father's possessions in his old trunk in the attic. It's a bit of a mystery,' she replied.

'Have you asked your mother about it?' Rose enquired.

'No, I haven't as yet. It doesn't seem right at this moment in time and I don't want to upset her.'

'I understand,' Rose replied knowingly.

Sarah's last evening on Sarnia was spent in the warm company of her Aunt Pamela and Uncle Walter, who made a special effort to leave their guest house for a little while to escort their niece to the Southampton steamer the next morning. Rose also joined the small group of now familiar relations and friends who waved at the quayside as she left Sarnia.

Sarah stood on deck of the *Alberta*, the mail steamer from Sarnia to England. She looked wistfully towards the disappearing islands of Sark and Herm and, even though there were now no other passengers on deck, she remained steadfast, pulling her coat tightly around her against the chilling breeze.

Five weeks ago her life was full of certainty; she had

walked down the aisle on her father's arm towards Anthony in the parish church of St Mark's. They had shared two carefree days in Ryde before returning to live with Anthony's parents in the large old house in Hamble. It had been the first time she had travelled more than a few miles from her home in Woolston and Sarah had been so full of happiness and excitement. She realised for the first time that she had never questioned or really appreciated her good fortune in enjoying a secure and comfortable childhood with parents who adored her.

Her perspective on life had shifted irreversibly as she realised how little she knew of her parents' early lives and the pain of the loss she felt was far greater now that she could no longer turn to her father and talk to him. All those questions she would have asked him and memories he could have shared seemed to hang in the mist and swell in the wake of the ship.

Gradually, as the unmistakable but faint shape of Riduna appeared, Sarah's thoughts turned to her mother. Her memories of her recent visit, an adventure she would never have imagined possible only a few weeks before, gave her the feeling that her life would never be quite the same again.

Chapter 7

BACK IN WOOLSTON, Harriet sat quietly staring into the cold fireplace. During the week following the news that her husband Joe had suffered a fatal heart attack whilst visiting his family on Sarnia, Harriet's world had been a blur. Her neighbour, Mrs Groom, a widow, called in to see her morning and night, bringing meals with which to tempt her, although they frequently remained untouched. In her absence while Mrs Groom was visiting her elderly mother in Bitterne up the hill, her twelve year old daughter Jennie popped in to make a cup of tea and talked about anything that came into her head. It was the summer holidays and she would usually go with her mother to see her gran, but she had always enjoyed a special relationship with Harriet since she was tiny; for her age, she was a very alert and perceptive young lady, who reminded Harriet of her good friend Jane when she was a young girl. In fact, Jennie had the same caring nature and was always tending to children who had tumbled in the street or animals and birds she'd found suffering. She'd once nurtured a baby blackbird back to life, rescuing it from the mouth of their old ginger Tom, despite her father remarking that the kindest thing would be to hit it on the head and end its sufferings. The little thing, now almost full grown, still chirped in the back yard for tit bits from time to time, even though it now kept at arm's length.

At first Jennie talked endlessly about anything that came to mind: the antics of her brothers, the new bright red sweets she had seen at Mrs Green's sweet shop and the motor car that made her jump out of the way as it tooted along Victoria Road the other day, not even pausing before it swept into Portsmouth Road to catch the *Floating Bridge*. Its wooden panels had been polished so brightly that she could almost see her face in the side, and oh those big round eyes on the front.

'Gave me such a fright, I can tell you.'

Soon Jennie realised that what Harriet needed was just a bit of quiet so she would potter around and sit on the rag rug by Harriet's side and rest her head on Harriet's lap, like she had done as a child when Harriet had told her a good story or two. After a couple of days, when she felt sure that Sarah, Ernest and the twins would soon be home, Jennie decided it was time to talk again. Harriet was sitting in her armchair, the other chair by its side filling the room with its emptiness, and an untouched meal lay on the table behind her.

'If me father had died and me mother stopped eating, it would worry me so,' she began thoughtfully. 'When Sarah and Ernest come back they don't want the worry of you too, Mrs Newton. You're sad. It's only natural. I was so sad when me kitten died. It was such a sweet little thing, but me father said that I was very lucky to have had me kitten as a friend. Even for a little while.'

Jennie paused, glancing at Harriet's downturned face, but determined not to be defeated she continued,

'And Mr Newton. He was such a good man. Whenever he brought sweets home for the others he would always share them with me if I was around, which I always was, if there were sweets around, that is. Please, Mrs Newton, try and eat your supper. It was that nice too, me favourite steak and kidney. I'll heat it up for you if you like?'

Harriet looked up, suddenly focussing on the child who had such a concerned loving look on her face. Harriet smiled a watery smile.

'Come here, Jennie,' and so Jennie went into Harriet's waiting arms and they shared a meaningful embrace.

'You're such a good girl and you are right to be cross with me. Sarah would be too, if she were here!' Harriet exclaimed as she tried to hold back a stream of tears.

A few drops fell. They say that tears heal the mind and cleanse the soul and so from that moment on, Harriet felt her burden lift, ever so slightly. The following day was Sunday and so she went to St Mark's Church to the morning service and as she knelt in prayer she thanked God for Joe, their life together and the children she was so blessed to have. She didn't ask why her husband had been taken away from her, but asked that her children be brought safely back home soon.

On the last evening before the expected return of her family, Harriet strolled down to the river side. It was a hot, airless summer's evening and so she rested against a mooring bollard as she watched *The Sarnia* steam into the harbour on the opposite bank of the River Itchen.

Harriet remembered the moment when her young family had arrived in England all those years before, leaving the familiarity of her island life in Sarnia far behind and the secluded life on Riduna just a distant memory. She and Joe had maintained a facade of strength and cheerfulness for the sake of their young family who clutched their hands nervously.

Following a couple of nights squeezed into a single room at The Cliff Hotel they had set up a temporary home in one bedroomed lodgings in Florence Road, before they found their feet. Soon Joe had found enough painting work to feed his family, but with another mouth to feed on the way they were both relieved when Joe was offered more secure work at White's, the boat builders in Itchen Ferry, the small hamlet on the northern side of the *'Floating Bridge'* hard: a settlement which existed long before the village of Wooston, when small fishing boats carried people across the river to Southampton on the west bank of the river.

A mate Joe had met down at The Victoria had put in a good word for him and the foreman, realising how useful his skills could be for them, offered Joe a job the next day. Initially he painted and varnished the hulls and internal woodwork of the boats, but occasionally his skill of gold leaf painting was put to good use when more elaborate work was required on the larger yachts and vessels for their more prestigious clients.

With a new baby imminent, the family felt secure enough to move to a more permanent place of their own in St John's Road in the next street. It was no distance to move their meagre belongings to the modest three up two down dwelling, snug in a row of red brick terraced houses. Harriet was relieved to have her own back yard and scullery, so that she no longer had to share a place to do the washing. Now they had made it comfortable with rose curtains at the windows, a solid oak table and chairs. Two time-worn armchairs stood beside the hearth with a clean newly made rag rug at their feet, which softened the look of the recently laid linoleum, which Joe had been so proud of.

Yes, in those days it had been very different. Harriet once had to sweep the bare wooden floorboards daily because there was so much dust, until, that is, Joe had managed to find the money and time to lime wash the walls. The candles downstairs had now been replaced by gas lamps which they

45

only used sparingly, but they still lit candles to find their way up to bed at night. It was here that Harriet had found the first true feelings of contentment since leaving Riduna, as she cherished her growing family.

While Harriet watched some of the passengers make their way towards the *Floating Bridge* she thought of her eldest son Ernest who had been about five years old when they first arrived: too old to hold her hand but not too old to grasp hold of his father Joe's coat as he waited for the strange flat boat to arrive on the shore, while Harriet struggled with a twin on each hand.

Ernest had now settled with his childhood sweetheart in his own little cottage in Itchen Ferry village. The pair had been inseparable since the family had moved into St John's Road all those years ago and reminded Harriet of Edward, her childhood friend and sweetheart back on Riduna. Harriet's eyes misted over once more as she pulled her thoughts back to Ernest and Ethel, who now had an adorable little girl of their own and she was sure, by the secret twinkle in their eyes on the night of Sarah's wedding, that there might be another one on the way. It was the most natural thing in the world for Ernest to follow his father into the boatyard. From a very young age he had found pieces of driftwood and roughly at first, had chiselled out the shape of an animal, boat and even a working toy, as his skills developed. It was no surprise when he was accepted as an apprentice boat builder, learning to carve and shape the beautiful wooden hulls, smoothing them to perfection.

Jack, one of the twins, was also married and settled. He had always been the lively one of the pair and could have chosen from a number of young girls who were smitten with him over the years. To everyone's astonishment he had chosen Hannah, a plain, quiet lass, so much in contrast to his own nature. They do say that opposites attract, she mused. He was the brains of the family and was always trying to find out how things worked. He had been so fascinated by the first motor car he had seen that he'd been too excited to sleep. Then there was the day recently, he'd come home reading in the newspaper about ER Moon landing the first aircraft in nearby Eastleigh. He was beside himself with enthusiasm so that Joe and Harriet were not surprised when he applied for an apprenticeship as a mechanic.

Tom, on the other hand, was the quietest of the three boys. Harriet had the occasional private thought that Hannah would have been a more suitable partner for Tom, but she kept this to herself. Tom also turned out to be mechanically minded like his twin brother. They looked so alike but there the similarities ended. Yes, when they were young they were inseparable, but as time passed Jack was out and about more and more, leaving his quieter twin at home reading or taking their dog Spike for a walk, with his little sister Sarah in tow. As soon as Joe had saved up to buy Tom a second hand bicycle, their son had found his niche in life. He was forever at old

Mr Palmer's bicycle shop on Bridge Road next to the greengrocers, and it was no surprise to everyone when Mr Palmer offered his young helper a job. He was teaching Tom all he knew about bicycle repair and people were in no doubt that he would take over the shop one day.

After Jack's marriage Tom became very restless at home and so, when old

Mr Palmer offered him his spare room over the shop, to keep an eye on things and offer some security at night, Tom was grateful of the chance. The abruptness of his departure hurt Harriet for a while until Joe gently pointed out to her that their son needed his independence and with his routine shattered he needed a new one. Harriet was surprised at how astute her husband had been on this occasion, when Tom soon settled into coming home for supper on Monday, Wednesday and Saturday nights and for afternoon tea on Sundays.

Harriet watched the *Floating Bridge* make its way towards the hard, not far away from where she sat remembering her feelings of insecurity as the family had boarded the ferry on that very first occasion. Unlike any boat she had seen or travelled on in the past, it was disconcerting that it was so flat and that they were so close to the water level. Joe had tried to reassure her by pointing out the strong chains which pulled the ferry to the opposite shore towards their new life. The little cottages of the village of Itchen Ferry, set amongst trees on the hillside, had reminded her of St Peter Port in some respects, though the ship builder's yards in the foreground were in stark contrast to her memory of St Peter Port harbour, with numerous sailing boats whose moorings were overshadowed by Castle Cornet.

As the *Floating Bridge* clanked to a halt not far from where she sat, a sombrely clad Harriet slowly made her way home, passing familiar faces who nodded in sad acknowledgement of her loss. Joe had been well liked in both villages.

Once inside, the door had closed behind her, Harriet felt the sorrow of her solitude overwhelming her. Joe had been her stability, her rock, the level–headed, ever optimistic side of their partnership, which had happily spanned over twenty years. The gnawing emptiness consumed her with a heaviness which left her devoid of strength. She sat in her chair, feeling much older than her forty four years, far too young to be left alone. She drifted off to sleep, dreaming of her life on Riduna and Sarnia and, even when Jennie crept in to place a cold supper by her side, she hardly stirred. She had a fitful sleep until the early hours of the morning, when she woke up with aching limbs.

Remembering the importance of the day, she repeated her prayer for the safe return of her family and, with a faint glimmer of motivation, was able to busy herself with jobs around the cottage for the first time in nearly a week.

Her prayers were partially answered because late that evening her three handsome sons burst into her quietness. As Ernest embraced his mother he looked at her sheepishly because he did not know how Harriet would react to Sarah's reckless and, in his opinion, thoughtless decision to travel on to the island of Riduna for a couple of days.

Harriet sat down in surprise, when she heard the news.

'Well!' she exclaimed. 'What made her think of doing such a thing?' she asked, staring at the empty fireplace as if to fathom an answer from its depths.

'I tried to reason with her, mother, but she is so stubborn at times,' Ernest replied.

Tom and Jack came over to Harriet's chair, Tom putting his hand on her arm in greeting and Jack, always the more loving one, kissed her gently on her head.

'I think that she felt that she had seen Sarnia, our father's birthplace, and she wanted to visit where you were born too,' Tom explained.

'I hope you're not telling me that she travelled over to Riduna on her own,' exclaimed Harriet frowning at Ernest, who, as the head of the family now, should have known better than to allow his sister to go.

'No, as it happens, Miss Mortimer, who I think you remember, was kind enough to take us to some interesting places on Sarnia while we were there. She is accompanying Sarah. They will both be staying at Miss Mortimer's sister's house for a couple of nights and then she will return to Sarnia before catching the next available steamer to England.'

Ernest searched his mother's face for reassurance that

she understood and was relieved when Harriet's shoulders finally relaxed and she struggled to her feet. Just at that moment, Mrs Groom and Jennie bustled in and placed a cold supper on the table for the returning travellers.

'We won't disturb you but thought you'd like something t' eat,' she muttered as they headed back out of the door, nodding to Harriet.

The young men thanked them profusely as Mrs Groom and Jennie pulled the door shut and then they tucked into the brawn, bread and chutney laid before them. They had not realised just how hungry they were.

After that, Ernest and Jack reluctantly took leave of their mother, since they had wives who would be waiting for their return. Ernest was still fuming that Sarah had not come home to keep his mother company and so he was relieved that Tom volunteered to stay for the next few days until Sarah's return.

Chapter 8

ANOTHER IMPORTANT PERSON in Harriet's life was also travelling towards Woolston at that time. Jane, Harriet's best friend and confidante when she was a young girl, had also left her home on Riduna twenty years before. Unlike Harriet, though, she had visited the island occasionally while her father had still been alive. Now she was on her way to Southampton to begin her new job.

Jane tried to concentrate on an article about the research into a cure for malaria by R S Christopher. Her mind wandered and she was lulled by the regular, rhythmic rumble of the wheels on the track below. She thought of the meeting she had recently had with Professor Blackney, where he virtually gave her orders to take up a position at the world renowned Royal Victoria Hospital in Netley in charge of training nurses for terms serving abroad. Her time had been busy at St Thomas' since her return from South Africa, after a period of much needed recuperation from the mental and physical demands of her role in Natal Province. The hustle and bustle of the busy London hospital, for Jane, was tame compared to the knife-edged world far away, which seemed bleak at times, but where she had strangely felt most at one with herself.

'At the Victoria you will be able to share a lifetime of

expertise and experience, passing on your wide knowledge of operating in a constant state of emergency, coping with unexpected crises and challenges where you were stretched to the absolute limit of endurance.'

The Professor's words still echoed in Jane's mind as a distraction from the printed words which swam before her eyes.

'I know of no other nurse with such proficient skills, knowledge and understanding of the real world which these young girls may now face. Do you remember how wide-eyed and innocent you were as you trained here in St Thomas' before your first posting? Too many girls hear about Florence Nightingale and her works and paint a fairytale image of what life for her was like. Their aspirations to follow in such honoured footsteps are admirable but nevertheless, I know of no other person who could add a touch of much needed realism to prepare these innocents. Do you?'

Jane had remained quiet as the intonation of his voice made it clear that the question was rhetorical. The professor had watched Jane quite closely. She knew in her heart that she was keen to travel again and since returning from South Africa she had thought of possibly offering her much sought after services on a mission to Kenya, or returning to Natal Province, where they were rebuilding order from the ashes as it were. The professor's offer (or was it a command, Jane was not entirely certain) had other compensations, though. A recent letter from her dearest friend Harriet was carefully folded in her pocket. Harriet had written directly to the hospital since Jane confessed to being reticent to write from abroad and had lost touch for a few years.

As Jane had discussed her thoughts with a close nursing friend later that night, she explained,

'Harriet was my dearest friend as we grew up on Riduna, but whereas I could write freely to my father and brother about the chaotic, almost nightmarish world in which I lived from day to day, I found it impossible to write to Harriet. Her world was so simple and domestic - children, home, family - all those things I knew now that I would never experience, but to share my foreign world with her, it would be far too shocking. On the other hand I could not bring myself to lie, or to make the truth sound rosier, and so we lost contact. Wrong of me I know, but there it is. I can't turn the clock back and always had the excuse that I was far too busy and exhausted, which to some extent was the truth.'

Harriet's loss of Joe hit Jane hard and left her with a guilty conscience which only a meeting face to face might heal. As she had rushed from the hansom cab, which had brought her the short journey from the hospital to the entrance of the grand Waterloo Station, she was halted in her tracks by the familiar sight of baskets and boxes of tomatoes being unloaded on to waiting carts, which she knew would be taken directly to Covent Garden. It was amazing what memories a basket of tomatoes could invoke as Jane thought of the last time she had said goodbye to Harriet on the harbour's edge in St Peter Port. Was it really over twenty years ago and would we recognise each other, she wondered.

A whistle sounded, bringing Jane back to the present. The train was now leaving Eastleigh Station and she knew that Southampton was to follow. The last time she had been here she had continued on the train to the very end of the line to Southampton Docks. On that occasion they had abandoned their meagre, carefully labelled luggage to be brought on in carts and Jane and her two nurse travelling companions had walked excitedly to the waiting ship, not knowing that their services would be needed so soon, as several members of the crew went down with a fever even before their ship had reached the coast of Spain.

Today, as the train came to a halt, a kindly looking young gentleman in uniform helped Jane with her large brown leather case while she alighted, carrying her smaller valise herself. He walked over to the opposite platform where she had intended to catch the train directly to Hamble. On impulse she decided she could wait no longer to see Harriet and made the decision to break her short journey at Woolston on the way. There was half an hour to wait, just enough time to sip a cup of welcoming tea, which this young man had kindly brought to her. He explained that he had travelled, not from London, but from Woolwich and that he was on his way back to the barracks at Gilkicker - a place of which Jane had never heard, but which she would be strangely familiar in the next few months.

At Woolston Station he yet again helped Jane with her case and waved a porter over to her aid. Little did he know that she had struggled with much more weighty and awkward loads in Natal as she had assisted in the hasty retreat of all their belongings and equipment to the edge of immediate danger during an intense period of fighting. The young man returned to his carriage just in time to give a cheery wave, and Jane thought wistfully that he could have been her son in a different life.

The porter kindly booked Jane's case into a left luggage area and gave her careful directions to St John's Road and so, gripping her small valise in one hand and her letter from Harriet in the other, she walked across the busy Portsmouth Road, along Victoria Street, passing the many shops on her way. Taking two left hand turns she was faced with rows of neat red brick terraced cottages, just as she had imagined, and was soon at the front door of number fourteen, which opened directly on to the narrow street.

Harriet's face was a picture as she opened the door to Jane and she need not have worried. It was as if the years between them evaporated as they first drank in the sight of each other's faces, showing a few lines of all their years and experience, but both still shining with that inner beauty of the young girls within. Jane reached out her arms and they held each other tightly for several moments. She didn't realise it, but it was at that point that Harriet's tears began to flow freely at last, as if Jane's healing skills worked their magic as the friends connected in mind, body and spirit. It was so good for Jane to see Harriet again and she knew instinctively that Harriet felt the same.

The friends sat and talked for hours and although Jane helped herself to some cold meat and bread from the table, ravenous after her journey, she noted with concern that hardly a crumb entered Harriet's lips. After Harriet had answered Jane's sensitive questions about Joe, they relaxed as they talked about the missing ten years of their lives when they'd lost touch.

'When were you last on Riduna, Jane?'

'After I last wrote to you, letting you know my plans to travel to Natal and to wish you good fortune for the new century, I visited Riduna. My father was happy and well at that time, enjoying life with Mary and his daughter, Edith. It was quite a shock, only a year later, to hear from Mary that he had died suddenly, suffering from a brain haemorrhage.'

'Oh, I'm so sorry. I didn't know.'

'I'm afraid I agreed with my brother at the time, who said that there was little point in me coming home, because I would certainly not arrive in time for the funeral, so I just concentrated all my energies on my all-consuming work. I gave myself little time to dwell on it.'

'What happened to Mary then? Are you still in touch?'

'Yes, I am, as a matter of fact. We exchange a letter most Christmases, but I have only seen her once since. She now lives on Sarnia with Edith. She returned to teaching there when Edith was old enough to go to school, but I saw them on one occasion recently when they were travelling on to family in Sussex. They visited me in London for the day, but I'm sure that Mary was quite shocked as to how unwell I looked at the time. She didn't stay long. Maybe she was worried about Edith catching something tropical. I'm surprised that you lost touch with her; after all, you were closer to her than me, I thought.'

'I'm afraid I wasn't very sociable when I left Riduna, or should I say when I was sent away. In fact, looking back, I know I was suffering greatly after losing both of my parents like that, but there must have been a hot-headed, stubborn side of my nature too. I just cut myself off from everyone on Riduna, trying to forget. Especially when I thought that Edward had been lost at sea.'

'Have you kept in contact with Edward at all, Harriet?'

'It's strange you should ask that but he actually turned up on the day of Joe's funeral and we went for a walk to Weston Shore as if it was the most natural thing in the world. Mind you, he has visited the family several times over the years and he adored Sarah!'

Jane watched her friend carefully for any telltale signs of hidden emotion but was too discreet to mention that Harriet's eyes shone just a little bit brighter when she talked about her childhood sweetheart, Edward.

'Joe felt that it would have been good for me to return to the islands to see everyone again. It used to frustrate him at times that I was so determined not to do so.'

'Maybe he's got a point there. Hanging on to anger or sadness all these years is not in your nature, but if you've buried them deep within, then you do need to heal sometime. I think your Joe was very wise indeed.'

'And if I had travelled with him, I would have been there for him when he needed me.....'

At that point Harriet burst into loud sobbing tears yet again and Jane went to her to give her comfort.

'You did what you felt was best at the time. You mustn't blame yourself Harriet. It sounds as if there was really nothing you could do and I'm sure that he was in good hands.'

'Oh, Jane! It is so good to see you again.'

And with that her tears began to flow, but more gently this time.

'I'm so glad to be here,' Jane replied and for the first time she really felt it in her heart, though a few unsettled doubts lingered deep within.

All too soon it was time for Jane to catch her train to continue her short journey to Hamble and Harriet threw on her shawl to walk Jane back to the station. Jane could tell that a glimmer of light had returned to Harriet's sad eyes as she realised that Jane would be living so close again. Her heart, too, was lighter and her struggle with a desire to travel to distant shores again diminished, as she realised that she was in the place that she was truly meant to be.

Nothing prepared Jane, though, for her first sight of The Royal Victoria Hospital. She had heard of its grandeur and knew that it was the largest hospital in the world but to set eyes on it for the first time close up filled her with awe. She did not take the train directly into the purpose-built station in the hospital grounds, because at her age she preferred a certain amount of independence and distance between her work and her home life. Instead she had alighted at Netley Station and had been taken by horse and trap to the small but adequate lodging house near the Royal Consort, a grand public house with gilded, rather pretentious pillars, right on the main street. She was to live around the corner from the establishment, a short but pleasant walk to the hospital.

Passing the hospital gatehouse, Jane stood in wonder as this imposing building spread before her, a quarter of a mile long. The hospitals in London were large, but this was all the more stunning because it was standing in isolation, other buildings carefully hidden behind, where a station and an almost entire village community was thriving. As Jane was to discover later on, the complex continued almost the same distance at the back, where the Red Cross Training buildings lay, with row upon row of green Nissen huts.

Jane walked up to the main entrance and if she had been in awe of the imposing structure from the outside, nothing prepared her for the display of a full size white elephant skeleton in the centre of the vestibule. Human skulls and all manner of exotic stuffed reptiles and animals filled the main lobby and continued along the corridors to left and right. This almost macabre sight before Jane gave her an insight into the eccentric nature of the man who had designed the hospital, and whereas many a person's instinct might have been to take flight at the sight of row upon row of skulls facing them as they entered the hospital, she found them quite fascinating.

A porter showed her to the office of the Ward Master, who asked his assistant to take Jane for some refreshments before showing her around the massive building. She was accustomed to nursing alongside the military and so walking amongst uniformed staff and blue pyjama suited patients was quite familiar to her. Everywhere they went orderlies were mopping the floors and scrubbing the multitude of wards. Although she was struck by the wonderful brightness of the shore-fronted corridors, with their high arched windows looking out on to Southampton Water, she was also reminded of her patron and personal heroine Florence Nightingale's word *'disaster'*, regarding the many wards leading away from this bright channel, plunging her into relative darkness. With little daylight and lack of fresh air in these side wards, she could see why it was difficult to keep morale up in such a contrasting environment.

Jane found it hard to believe that such a large building could function so efficiently, despite its drawbacks. It was quiet at that present time, the numbers of patients few, but the unrest in Europe between Italy and Turkey, which seemed so much closer to home than the Boer War and the more recent struggles in India, gave an atmosphere of quietly efficient preparation.

Although she was glad that the social reforms of the Liberals had made progress in making health and social welfare more accessible to the masses, she knew that this type of environment rarely benefitted local people. In fact, apart from affecting the economy of the local service providers at Woolston and the market gardeners at Sholing, she soon realised that the local people knew little about life at the hospital and the vast majority of the hospital community rarely ventured beyond the proximity of the hospital grounds.

Jane's role would be to train nurses for service both here and overseas and to bring present staff up to date with the modern practices at St Thomas'. With less research into tropical diseases taking place here in Netley, compared to in its heyday in the late nineteenth century, Jane could not help but wish she had been given the opportunity to work here earlier in her life. Nevertheless, she soon observed that there was much to do and it did not take long for her to settle in. It was actually to the huts that she was drawn most to seek company. There she found like-minded nurses, who had shared similar experiences of serving abroad in South Africa. She spent many a break or evening sitting outside one of the huts sharing tales and drinking coffee. Jane was unaware of it at the time, but eventually she would be posted to the huts in order to train the Voluntary Aided Defence nurses for service. For now she had a programme to set up and trainee nurse schedules to organise in the main hospital wards, which took all of her waking time.

The following weekend she joined the routine gathering of staff and patients alike, for a service in the vast chapel, where patients, still in their blue pyjama suits, were either wheeled in or walked independently under the careful eye of one of the many auxiliary nurses. During the somewhat moving service, she could not help but bring to mind those people she knew personally who had lost their lives and those whose lives had been irreparably damaged by the futility of war. She was aware of the stark contrast to surroundings at the military hospital camp in Natal, where here the congregation spilled out across lush green lawns, heading towards the wooden pier on the shoreline, in order to enjoy the late summer sea air.

As she stood looking out across Southampton Water, watching the ferries and small sailing vessels weave about their daily journeys, she couldn't help but wonder why the Professor had been so keen to send her to this sleepy idyllic backwater. Whether she had choice in the matter she had little doubt, but she felt wistfully trapped like a ship in a bottle, as she gazed towards the Solent and imagined the open seas beyond.

Chapter 9

THE NEXT SUNDAY afternoon Jane had free, she asked an acquaintance, who transported supplies to and from the hospital, if he would take her along the shore to Woolston to see Harriet. When she arrived, Jane was not at all surprised to see that Sarah, Harriet's daughter, had returned from Sarnia and she settled with a cup of tea to listen to Sarah's account of her trips to Sarnia and Riduna.

Sarah was just as she imagined a daughter of Harriet to be, her enthusiasm shining as she described her experiences, but also tinged with a dignified quietness, reflecting the family's recent bereavement. Harriet said little as she listened to Sarah's tales, but Jane saw the concern on her face.

Sarah was also keen to hear some of the less gruesome tales of Jane's travels to Natal, and was spellbound as Jane recalled the events of the sudden evacuation of the Red Cross Hospital camp with sounds of fighting in the air. Harriet was a little in awe of her friend as she tried to imagine caring for the injured in such conditions.

'I was torn with a desire to continue in that desperate work, when I was ordered to escort a troop ship of injured soldiers back to England. I knew that my nurse superior understood that I was mentally and physically exhausted, and that, had I stayed, I may have become seriously ill and thus of no use to anyone, but the mixture of relief and regret was a continual struggle. Despite being reassured that a person of my experience was needed to care for the brave men as we journeyed home, I still yearned to be back in Natal.'

'What did you do when you reached England?' Sarah asked.

'I was given indefinite leave and stayed with my brother's family for six months to convalesce. I am afraid I contacted no one and was like a hermit, not wanting to venture out of the house. My sister-in-law was really kind and it was my young nephew and niece who brought me back into the land of the living again. They first encouraged me to walk with them to Hyde Park, which was only a short distance from the square where they lived. We started going on a regular basis after school and eventually I had the courage to walk by myself at lunchtime and sit listening to the occasional band playing.'

'But you returned to nursing in the end?' Harriet prompted.

'Yes, I think my brother became impatient that I was wasting my life away. As a London surgeon, his daily life was full of the sufferings of others, but he had no comprehension of my experiences. He organised an interview for me at St Thomas' in the study of tropical medicine. He felt a research post might satisfy my enquiring mind, but protect me from the everyday strains of a nurse's life.'

'I imagine you would enjoy that type of work. You always had an inquisitive nature,' Harriet recalled.

'Yes I did for a while, but Dr Manson, though grateful for my contribution, realised that my gifts lay more in the caring for others and that I should be back in a nursing capacity again. It was he who recommended me for the post at The Royal Victoria, training and supervising nurses both at the hospital and to prepare them for service overseas.'

'It seems a position made for you, with all of your experience,' exclaimed Sarah.

'Yes, that's what Professor Blackney said when I was interviewed. In the end I am not sure if it was me being interviewed for the position or whether he had already decided my fate. A bit of both I expect, but what an amazing place. It took my breath away. I remember passing it by as the mail ship brought me back from St Peter Port all those years ago, but I never dreamed I would work here one day.'

'Yes, I remember my first journey along Southampton Water as if it were yesterday. Joe and I stood on deck gripping the children's hands. You weren't born then, of course,' Harriet smiled at Sarah. 'Joe pointed out The Royal Victoria and I could hardly believe such a building existed, let alone think of it as a hospital. I had no comprehension of the wars overseas. Occasionally the islanders joined up and volunteered for service, some not returning, but not among our closest friends.'

Time passed all too quickly. It was getting late and Jane had to be back before dark. Fortunately Sarah was returning to Hamble to collect her few belongings from Anthony's parents and so they were able to share transport. Jane was also pleased to hear that Sarah was intending to return to stay with her mother for two weeks, until her husband returned from training and they were able to move into the new married quarters at Gilkicker.

'Oh, that's a coincidence,' exclaimed Jane. 'There was this most charming and thoughtful young man, who helped me with my luggage at Southampton Station. He was returning to Gilkicker Fort too.'

Jack arrived at that moment to take his sister to Hamble. He was introduced to Jane and as he helped her step up into the buggy, which he had borrowed from the brewery near to his home, Jane could see a resemblance not of Joe, but of Edward. This was especially noticeable in his light-hearted banter and his irresistible ability to flirt with any lady, young or old. Since Joe and Edward had been cousins, she decided that the similarities were hardly surprising.

Harriet looked a little like a lost child as she stood to wave them on their way. As perceptive to his mother's loneliness as his father would have been, Jack gave her a hug and said that he would call back in on his way home.

'After all,' he winked at Jane as he leapt lithely into the front seat, picking up the reins all in one movement, 'I haven't had a piece of your lovely fruit cake, mother, and you know my wife can't cook cakes to save her life.'

'Oh be gone with you and don't be so cheeky about Hannah,' Harriet smiled nonetheless.

'Come again soon, Jane. It's wonderful to have you so close again,' Harriet called after them.

Maybe Jack's acquired his dad's kind nature after all, mused Jane as they trotted along Weston Shore.

After a little while it was Sarah who broke their silence.

'I am trying to persuade mother to offer her spare rooms as lodgings,' she explained. 'She did speak of it when father was alive, but I really think that she needs a purpose now we've all left home. As soon as I leave too, she's going to be so lonely.'

Sarah and Jane discussed the merits of this idea all the way to Hamble, when it was decided to take Jane to her own lodgings first, before returning to the cottage in the village where Anthony's parents lived.

Jane was exhausted as her head hit the pillow that night. Her morning would begin at 6am and so she had little time to contemplate her new circumstances or that of her friend Harriet, before she was fast asleep.

Sarah and Jack, on the other hand, were greeted warmly

by Mr and Mrs Parker and Jack went into the front room to share a brandy, while Sarah went up to pack her few belongings. She thought briefly of the short time between her wedding and Anthony's departure, when they had shared this delightful room as man and wife and she suddenly felt an overwhelming sense of shyness as she tried to imagine their reunion, but little prepared her for the reality of their meeting.

'Are you nearly ready?' called an impatient Jack, who was eager to get back to his mother and then home to his wife and child.

Sarah hugged her parents-in-law warmly and they in turn gave reassurances that she would always be welcome to stay at anytime, but they understood that she needed to be with her mother. It was dark when the buggy finally arrived back at St John's Road and soon Sarah and Harriet found the comfort of sleep.

After a restless night Sarah came down to the kitchen to find her mother already sitting by the range, surrounded by various items from around the house. She poured Sarah a cup of tea.

'You might find these handy when you set up home,' she explained, nodding at the pile as she passed the cup to her daughter.

Since there was also a small pile of her father's belongings sat in the corner of the room, including the trunk returned from Sarnia, Sarah offered to put it all in the attic.

Harriet carefully passed the trunk up to Sarah, who spent several minutes transferring items from a large cardboard box back into it. She found the small pouch that she had discovered a few weeks earlier before her father had travelled to Sarnia. Without thinking, she slipped it into her apron pocket and quickly completed her task, passing the large box back down to her mother who was waiting below.

They spent a companionable hour filling the box with all sorts of items which would not only be useful to Sarah but remind her of home.

Once their task was complete, Sarah tidied her other belongings into her old bedroom where she would be sleeping for a while. She gently closed the door before taking out the small pouch and emptying the beautiful silver locket into her other hand. She held it up, trying to decide whether she should open it and wondering what secrets it might hold. When Harriet called up, Sarah carefully hid the pouch amongst her belongings in her case, still none the wiser as to its origins, and returned downstairs.

Sarah decided to spend the days ahead, before Anthony was due back clearing the other spare room which the boys had shared, as well as her own, just in case her mother changed her mind about lodgers. In the afternoons they went out for a walk and Sarah helped Harriet to face the future. Although Harriet had some savings she would need to earn money to pay the rent and it was with a heavy heart that she decided she should take on sewing yet again, to make ends meet. There was always mending work to do from the large houses at Peartree and they called at Colonel Grimstone's[4] in order to seek some work.

This gave Harriet the much needed financial security she required, but since she was also proficient at embroidery they also called into Lancaster and Gate, the local department store. The assistant manageress of the haberdashery section promised to consider Harriet's work if she produced some samples in the next few days. This kept Harriet occupied while Sarah began systematically sorting through her brother's and her belongings and so time passed quickly until it was just a day before Anthony's expected return.

It was Sunday and Jane had called for afternoon tea, catching the train from Netley. Sarah was relieved that Jane hoped to call as often as she could, because she knew that once she and Anthony had moved to Gilkicker, it would be too far away to visit frequently and she was concerned about her mother. The afternoon passed quickly. This time, as Harriet said goodbye to Sarah, her heart was heavy as she thought fleetingly that the future without Sarah would be so much easier to face if Joe were still here by her side.

Sarah too was fighting back her tears. Jack was waiting impatiently in the buggy, a collection of cases and boxes of donated household items neatly packed behind them. As Harriet waved and turned back to step inside her quiet and empty cottage, Sarah, Jane and Jack headed towards Weston Shore.

It was while they rode along, that Sarah picked up the courage to ask Jane about the locket.

'Jane, I hope you don't mind me asking, but do you know whether my mother ever had a silver locket when she was young?'

Jane hoped to hide her immediate surprise, before she replied in a guarded manner,

'That's a strange question, Sarah. Do you mind me enquiring why you are asking?'

'It's just that while I was sorting through my father's possessions in our attic at home, I came across this pretty silver locket. I have never seen my mother wearing it, as far as I can remember, and it puzzled me.'

'You didn't think to ask your mother about it, then?' Jane asked, still trying to avoid a direct answer.

'It wasn't the right time, if you understand me. I didn't want to distress mother any further. It was such a shock when my father passed away.'

'Yes, I can understand that,' Jane agreed.

There was a short pause when Jane tried to decide how to respond.

'I can honestly say that I do not remember your mother ever *wearing* a silver locket on Riduna, but....' and here she paused again, 'I really think that you should ask her about it one day, when you think she feels more herself.'

Sarah was a little disappointed, because she was so sure that Jane was going to give her some clues to solve the mystery of the locket. While they sat in silence, Jane too was struggling with conflicting thoughts. She had been telling the truth when she said that she had never seen the locket, but it was not the case that she knew nothing about it. The last time she had heard it mentioned was in a distraught letter from Harriet, not long after they had travelled together to Sarnia all those years ago, about losing the locket, but how it had got amongst Joe's belongings she could not guess.

Soon they parted company and Jane wished Sarah well in her new life as she and Jack continued on to Hamble.

Chapter 10

SARAH WAS SPENDING a night at Anthony's parents, before meeting him off the early morning train. She was so nervous about seeing him again after so long and pondered with an uncharacteristic shyness as to how they would cope in their new life together at Gilkicker Fort, so far away from family, friends and anything familiar to them.

As it happened, there was little time for an emotional reunion. Early the following morning, Anthony jumped down on to the station platform, swinging his kit bag over his shoulder as he marched proudly over to Sarah, head held high befitting of his new stripes. Though little taller than Sarah in stature, Anthony's handsome balanced features could turn many a young girl's head, especially in uniform. He gave her a light peck on the cheek and then they walked briskly the short distance towards his home, with Sarah trotting by his side. Anthony was aware that their journey would be a long one and was keen to be on their way as soon as possible. They had time to say a hasty goodbye to his parents, whose manservant pulled a handheld cart with all their belongings, down the cobbled street to the quay, to wait for the small passenger ferry to Warsash. Anthony commented with irritation on the amount of luggage as he loaded it on to the ferry but gave little time for Sarah to reply. Within minutes they had reached the far side of this narrow waterway where Anthony's parents had hired the grocer from the little hamlet of Warsash to transport them on the journey to Gilkicker.

Soon Anthony began to relax and they exchanged pleasantries, much like strangers, a far cry from the excitement she had felt on her wedding day. Anthony appeared to have grown up in this short time and, having passed his training, seemed to Sarah to have gained in self-assurance, so that she was a little in awe of him. Anthony, on the other hand, no longer saw the young, light-hearted, carefree girl he had married but a young woman who, through tragedy and experience, had shown herself to be self-willed and independent and he, too, felt a little uneasy.

The journey was tiring, first winding their way inland towards the village of Titchfield where the horse was happy to enjoy a drink at the trough while the men gained refreshments at The Bugle Inn. Sarah chose to remain with the horse and trap, eating some bread and cheese which her mother-in-law had wrapped for her in a muslin cloth. Soon they were on their way again and the narrow lane wound its way through small hamlets and farming settlements until they reached the outskirts of Gosport where, with the forbidding Brockhurst Fort in front of them, they took a right hand turn, passing the Palmerstone Forts of Rowner and Grange. It was clear they had reached an area important to the military, since most of the travellers they passed were in uniform, whether in buggies like themselves, marching or on horseback and Anthony sat up straighter by Sarah's side.

They followed the route not far from the railway line, down towards the shore. Sarah was relieved to reach Stokes

Bay, where many were enjoying the late summer sunshine, sitting on the shingly beach or walking along the pier where they could also see passengers embarking on the Isle of Wight Ferry.

Sarah and Anthony were nearing their destination, as the bay swept before them towards Gilkicker Point. Soon they could see the fort which was strategically placed to defend the entrance to Portsmouth Harbour and the Solent. Sarah could just make out the shape of the red brick building with its row of tall chimney pots, the only sign of its more domestic purposes. Her heart sank as the horse was guided through the marshy land away from the gay day trippers towards the isolated building which was to be their home, a far cry from the cosy terrace in which she grew up.

Sarah pulled her shawl more tightly around her as gusts of wind blew across the long grass.

In front of them lay Fort Gilkicker, a sweeping semi circle of Cornish Granite overlooking the sea. Only the row of archways at the eastern end was visible to them, as they followed the track along a moat beside the bay. The gun emplacements had long since been removed and instead the NCOs manned the nearby Fort Monckton, an imposing building which would be Anthony's life in the months to come.

As they reached the entrance to the fort late in the afternoon, they veered to the left towards a prison like arch, on which the name 'Gilkicker' was emblazoned. They waited for the gates to be opened before they were ushered inside. Men came to help unload their belongings and Anthony thanked and tipped the driver generously.

Anthony and Sarah were shown to the newly built married quarters, the red brick section, clean but spartan, which comprised a bedroom, scullery and living room, the quite modern toilet facilities being at the back of the barracks. Sarah was left alone to begin to unpack and make the place more homely and it was not long before the three bare rooms began to look more welcoming. Main items of furniture were provided for by the military, including ample shelves and cupboards where Sarah placed their belongings. As she unpacked she was constantly reminded of home but she had to admit that these newly refurbished married quarters were better than she had imagined. She was used to gas and water on tap at home but as she made the acquaintance of her two immediate neighbours, Irene and Nell and heard of conditions they had lived in on previous postings, she realised how fortunate she was. Irene and Nell would play a huge role in making her life at the fort bearable in the months to come.

By the time Anthony came back that evening, tired and ready for rest and sustenance, Sarah was feeling a great deal more cheerful. As they ate, there was still a tense atmosphere. They had been on their own very little since his return from Woolwich and Anthony, although sensitive to Sarah's need to feel comfortable in her new life, reluctantly challenged her behaviour in his absence.

'I was really worried when I received your letter to say that you were travelling on to Riduna and not returning with your brothers from Sarnia. What possessed you to disappear on a trip of your own, when you knew that none of your brothers approved?'

Anthony wanted to add that Sarah had not been able to ask his permission either, but he felt that she might take offence. He had heard the headline news, time and time again, about the ridiculous fight for women's rights but it made him less sure of his ground nevertheless.

'It was such a wonderful opportunity to visit Riduna, Anthony. I have no regrets. I feel that I understand my parents far more now that I am aware of where they both came from. It's such a beautiful island; in fact Riduna and Sarnia are both charming in their own ways. I only wished I had visited Sarnia when my father was alive.'

Sarah's eyes looked up at her husband's with determination whilst her fingers fiddled nervously with her fork.

'But to travel on your own, Sarah! It was irresponsible when you knew that both your mother and I would worry. Your mother has been through enough recently without your behaviour adding to her concerns,' Anthony continued, feeling that he had every right to make his feelings plain to his wayward wife.

'As I explained in my letter, I was certainly not alone and I still don't regret my actions and so I can't apologize.'

Sarah rose to clear away their dishes, glad to be busy to still her shaking hands, but nevertheless defiant.

Anthony sighed and lit his pipe, knowing that to continue would be futile. Once he had relaxed he decided to retire, having no idea how to resolve the fragile atmosphere between them. Each made themselves ready to retire for the night, avoiding the other's gaze, partly through embarrassment but mainly due to the icy atmosphere between them. Each moved towards their chosen side of the narrow bed, Sarah curling up and Anthony remaining rigid and straight as they fell into a fitful sleep. Anthony could not help but think of the difference between this night and the first two nights of their married lives, when they had overcome their nervousness and enjoyed nights of passion. As he lay there, he thought of turning towards Sarah to try to awaken some of the warmth they had shared, but feeling her unyielding back against his, he sought the solace of sleep.

When Sarah woke up the next morning, Anthony had already left to take up his duties, leaving a subdued but nevertheless unyielding Sarah to continue to unpack, feeling both trapped and uncomfortable. After a couple of hours she asked to be allowed out of the fort and walked down to the shore. It was a cool and windy day and the few members of the public were far in the distance. She walked aimlessly for a while along this windswept shore, her eyes close to tears, feeling alone in her isolation. It was as if her unspoken prayer was answered, because she heard her name being called across the grassy ridge. She recognised her neighbour, Nell, and answered her wave. As the girls walked back along the beach towards the fort, Sarah found herself sharing her frustrations about her misunderstandings with her husband and her concerns about life at Gilkicker.

'Give it time,' suggested Nell wisely. 'I've been here two weeks now and everyone's so friendly. You've been married not much longer than that. It's been quite a shock for you. Me and Bert, well, we were married a year ago. It was easier for us 'cos we'd known each other most of our lives. Anyway, I'm only next door and I'm sure we'll soon have far too much to think about,' she added, patting her extended belly. 'Have you seen the wash house? Cor, it's a sight of pleasure compared to our last place. Come and look.'

Sarah had barely time to reply as she raced after Nell and they admired the laundry, with its copper tubs, mangles and drying chamber. Once inside they were joined by Irene and it was impossible to remain stony-faced for long, when hearing Irene's wicked sense of humour. It was their friendliness which brought Sarah to her senses and helped her to relax, so that when Anthony came home that lunchtime, to his great relief, she was more warm and welcoming.

Chapter 11

AFTER THAT SARAH, adjusted to her new life in a more positive way and Anthony settled into the routine life of a Bombardier, ensuring both his men from The Royal Artillery and the armaments were in top condition. Though his duties as a Bombardier were in the nearby Fort Monckton, he involved himself in Gilkicker by taking charge of the accounts. On the evenings when he was busy working on the figures at their table, Sarah sat in the armchair by the range doing sewing work for the higher ranking officers. Able to supplement his meagre income in this way, both lived quite comfortably and wanted for nothing of a material nature.

Nevertheless Sarah found the bleak winter months of the first year the most difficult and although her cheerful companions made her life bearable, she could not help but be homesick for her cosy home in Woolston. Sometimes she would escape from the fort and walk along the stony shore of Stokes Bay, the pier now empty and even the infrequent train bringing only a handful of military personnel back to the fort or carrying them away.

On one occasion, she stood alone, holding her bonnet in place with her gloved hand. She had swept her hair under her bonnet, secured with a multitude of hatpins, but even so, locks were escaping in wisps across her face. She looked out over the grey restless waters towards the open ocean, allowing the wind to blow away her restlessness. She stood with her back to the fort, her prison-like home just out of her line of vision. She focussed on the dark shape of a ship in the misty distance and imagined that it might be on its way to Sarnia. Her thoughts turned to Riduna. It was as if the island's magic had worked on her during her short visit and the pull of her ancestors were drawing her to return.

As the following summer approached once more and the holiday-makers and day trippers returned to their bathing huts, this feeling was forgotten as Sarah realised that she was with child. This was to begin a couple of years of greater contentment for her, as she and Anthony began life as a family. On the outside Anthony, too, was proud that he had achieved the status of a Bombardier at a very early age. Also, due to their expanding family, they had gained the privilege of being upgraded to B grade accommodation, where he and Sarah would now enjoy two bedrooms. He had a lot to be thankful for and yet he was becoming more restless within.

It all began on a day back in May 1911 when he and Sarah were taking a stroll along the Haslar sea wall, not far from Gilkicker and Fort Monckton. First they heard the unusual clattering noise in the distance and were amazed to see a large flying machine, a box-like contraption with bicycle wheels hanging below, swooping towards them. It was the closest either Sarah or Anthony had been to a sight such as this, and they gazed at it in wonder. Anthony later discovered that it was a Bristol Boxkite Biplane which had flown only a few yards above their heads. He had waved his cap at the pilot, who waved cheerfully back at them and it was the talk of both forts for weeks to come. From then onward, if Sarah was harbouring any secret thoughts of

Riduna when she fell asleep at night, Anthony was dreaming of a time when he could fly, and try as he might he couldn't get the thought out of his mind.

In her letter to her mother Sarah wrote the good news of the expected arrival and also gave a vivid description of the experience:

30th May 1911

My dear Mother,

I hope that you are well and are not too despondent with all the sewing we organised for you to do. If you are, then maybe you will have given serious thought to our idea of having paying guests in your spare rooms.

I have some exciting news. You will soon be a grandma once more, because Anthony and I are to have a baby and I believe that it will be due by the autumn. I hope that you are as thrilled as I am and I assure you that I am truly lucky to have such a wonderful role model as yourself!

I have made two lovely friends here at Gilkicker. Irene is always light-hearted and fun to be with, but Nell is so warm and kind. I feel that I've known her all my life. Nell and Irene have been so supportive and I really don't know how I would have coped without their care and friendship.

I have some other exciting news which Anthony insists I share with you so that you can tell my brothers. On Sunday afternoon Anthony and I were taking a stroll nearby in the sunshine when, and I quote Anthony here, we saw a Bristol Boxkite Biplane just above our heads. It was amazing, with two box wings and a box tail, which looked so fragile, and wheels like an oversized pram hanging down below. You'd never believe it. We were so close to the pilot that I could even see him smile. He was having such fun. Anthony has not stopped talking about it since, and the baby of course!

Although it is lovely here during the summer, when I can pretend to be a day tripper and sometimes eat ice cream and mingle with the crowds, it is very bleak and unwelcoming during the long winter months and I cannot help but feel homesick and long to see you again.

Thinking of you as always
   Sarah

A couple of weeks later Sarah received a reply which heartened her:

14th June 1911

My dear Sarah,

What lovely news! I am so happy and hope that I can save enough to travel by train to see you when the baby is due, if you think that might be possible.

I settled into a routine here for a while, but just as I was beginning to think that I could not face another sheet to mend or garment to darn, Jack came in one evening after work to ask if I wouldn't mind taking in some guests. The Cliff House Hotel was full with people from the Admiralty, who had come to discuss the next ship to be built, following the launch of the Miranda last year. He explained that there had been an unfortunate muddle of bookings, since there was also a party arrived early for a family wedding at Pear Tree Church, and so I had three fee paying guests over the weekend.

It is just as well that the couple were pleasant, although their eight year old thought my home was well beneath him. His father soon put him in his place when he complained and we didn't hear another peep out of him. A sullen ill-mannered little boy if ever there was one.

Following the success of the weekend, the manager of The Cliff House was so relieved that he promised to put more work my way when he could. That was two weeks ago and I have already entertained two travelling businessmen, much to the irritation and concern of my over observant, curtain twitching neighbours. If my hospitality continues to be this popular, I will be able to cancel the sewing batches for good.

I also see Jane when I can, which is usually every fortnight. You cannot imagine what a joy it is for us to meet again after all these years and I was so glad that you have made two good friends at the Fort. A lesson I have learnt is that if you can make one really good friend in your lifetime, then you are fortunate and you should treasure it with your heart.

I must go now to do some shopping and post this letter before returning to prepare the evening meal for my guests, but before I go I have to admit that you were right in your suggestion. This has given me a renewed purpose in life and I'm sure that the arrival of your child will complete your world too.

All my love,
    Mother

Sarah was gratified to hear that her mother had opened her home to paying guests and quietly praised the quick thinking of her brother, Jack.

Chapter 12

AFTER BABY TIMOTHY was born on 15th September 1911, Harriet made a space in her bookings and clutching her overnight bag, she headed for Woolston Station. She fumbled for change in her purse before waiting nervously for the train. As she watched Sholing speed past, her fear turned to excitement and with the helpful advice of a friendly porter she even coped with the change at the junction at Fort Rowner. He ensured that Harriet waited for the branch line to Gilkicker, rather than to Lee on the Solent, so that by the time the train pulled up at the pier at Stokes Bay, she was quite proud of her accomplishments. It was an emotional but happy reunion and she was given special permission to stay in Sarah and Anthony's spare room, which they were now preparing for Timothy. Harriet walked with Sarah along the shore, as proud as a princess to be pushing the pram holding her grandson and she smiled to all who passed them by.

'You are looking so well, Sarah,' Harriet commented, 'Motherhood suits you.'

'Oh Mother, it's made us both so happy. This little man takes up all my waking moments.'

Mother and daughter gazed down at the tiny rounded features of little Timothy, his wide eyes returning their gaze.

'That tuft of golden hair reminds me so much of you!' Harriet whispered as she gently lifted the bundle into her arms. 'Here is your grandma come to see you little one. That's nice isn't it?' Harriet cooed, unable to take her eyes off her grandson as he gurgled in reply. 'You're a miracle and everyone's happy now you're here.'

'But it *has* been hard Mother. You can't imagine what it's been like for me to move out here.'

Harriet looked up and replied sharply,

'Oh I certainly can, Sarah. Sometimes life throws us into unfamiliar places and situations. We can't spend all our time wishing and dwelling on what life might have been. When you chose to marry Anthony you married his way of life too, remember.'

'I know Mother, but I miss you all so much and don't be deceived by this perfectly sunny day. In the winter it's bleak and unwelcoming and I'm quite overwhelmed at times.'

'I'm glad that young Timothy here has brought you to your senses. Your father and I enjoyed every moment of our family life. Well, nearly every moment! You were always a bit of a wilful child.'

Harriet laughed and mother and daughter shared memories of some of the antics of Sarah's childhood.

'Do you remember the time I came home with that little kitten? Father was allergic to it and banned it from the house, but every time we opened a window or door it would creep back in.'

'And you would sneak it up to your bedroom and hide it in your bed. How cross your father was when he found you snuggled up together. You looked so sweet but I had rarely seen him so angry!'

They laughed together as they paused before returning along the beach.

'How about you, Mother? You are looking very well too.'

Harriet looked smart in her deep maroon suite dress, with its puffed shoulders, round neck and a bodice of tucks, flatteringly tapered to her waist before the skirt flared down to the floor. Her cheeks were flushed and the lines on her face few for a woman of her age.

'My new venture at home has been so successful that I don't have time to dwell on life. It was hard at first but your brothers have been very encouraging.'

'I'm so pleased for you, Mother!'

'That's lovely of you to say so, Sarah. I must admit to feeling quite proud of myself too. I never thought that I'd be a woman of independent means!'

On the Sunday a small christening service was held at Alverstoke village church and Sarah was pleased to see her brothers, their families and Jane gathered for the happy celebration.

The only event to mar the whole memory for Harriet was the shock that Edward arrived with his lady friend Marie at his side. It was not a surprise that Sarah had invited them both, after hearing about the secret visits Joe had made with Sarah over the years. It was just that Sarah was unaware of the mixed emotions her mother still experienced in his presence. At one point Harriet could hear Jack and Ernest's wives clucking behind their handkerchiefs that Edward had the audacity to bring this hussy into a house of God. Although at first Harriet experienced a strange sensation of dizziness on setting eyes on Edward, she did not have time to analyse her feelings. Out of the corner of her eyes Harriet watched Sarah introduce them to Anthony before they settled in the pew at the back of the church for the commencement of the service.

Later, when the group had gathered together in the village hall, Harriet yet again felt an agonising pain in her heart as she watched Edward cradle little Timothy in his arms. She was relieved when the couple announced quietly to Sarah that they had to leave not long after the service because Edward's ship would be departing that very evening, although she had to admit in confidence to Jane later that Marie sounded a friendly, pleasant lady nonetheless.

Just as Marie and Edward were leaving, Marie's eyes met Harriet's in a knowing way and she tucked her arm through Edward's as if to claim her possession, before the couple finally went out of the door.

Harriet shivered, but determined to enjoy what little time she had left with her daughter, she put the incident from her mind. When it was finally time for her catch her train later that afternoon Harriet was even more emotional.

'Take care of my little grandson, Sarah,' she said as she gave her daughter a hug, 'and look after that handsome husband of yours.'

'I'll make sure of it,' laughed Anthony, coming over to shake her hand and put an arm protectively around his wife's shoulders.

'Come back soon, Mother,' called Sarah, as the buggy set off to take Harriet and Jane to the station.

'I will,' called Harriet over her shoulder.

Fortunately for Harriet, Jane was able to share some of the journey with her. They travelled together until Netley Station, where Jane had to take the branch line to Netley Hospital, the local name for The Royal Victoria Hospital, to begin her evening shift.

On the journey there was no need for Jane to ask how Harriet was feeling, so great was their mutual understanding. Instead they discussed the new challenges which they were experiencing and gave each other some much needed encouragement and moral support. Jane, although capable, had never acted in a training role before and so was feeling rather nervous of showing an appropriate air of authority to the younger nurses in her charge. On the other hand, though Harriet was a natural hostess, she was concerned that the well-to-do folks who were coming to her home might see her modest place as beneath them.

With mutual reassurance, the ladies embraced before Jane alighted from the train and waited on the platform to wave goodbye. She thought fleetingly that it was a shame that Woolston was too far away from Netley; otherwise a perfect solution, for the positive benefit of both ladies, would have been for Jane to become Harriet's permanent lodger. It was not meant to be and so, just as the train was pulling away from the station and both ladies were smiling with a confidence that neither felt, they arranged to meet again in a fortnight.

Chapter 13

AT THE END of April, Sarah was saddened, but not surprised to receive a heartbroken letter from her mother:

25th April 1912

Dear Sarah,

I'm sure that you have heard the tragic news of the Titanic. Two families on St John's Road have lost their fathers, Patrick Cookson and Alex Porter, but so many of the crew also came from Woolston. Jennie from next door has been distraught since her brother George is missing too. We are taking it in turns to provide dinners for the Porters and the Cooksons because they've been given no support at all. It appears that spring is mocking us because, as the daffodils shine brightly, all around here is gloom.

I'm so sorry to be so despondent, but I hope that your lives are much happier now that you and Anthony are finding joy in little Timothy.

All my love to you
Mother

May 17th 1912

Dear Mother,

What can I say? Please send my condolences to all of the families, especially the Grooms. I cannot imagine George Groom gone, after all, he is the same age as me. Poor Jennie! The last news I had of her was that she was in service over in Marchwood, but I expect she's come home to support her parents.

Life here is fine, Mother. You will be surprised that I like being a mother and Timothy fills all my moments. He is sleeping through the night now and we are getting out for some fresh air every day. I enjoy that and so does he, waving his little arms if a seagull flies overhead. He can be so sweet and you would adore him too.

I'm thinking of you all,
Sarah

In fact family life suited Anthony and Sarah and both experienced an air of contentment as they found a routine around their little Timothy. Sarah continued to record the few exciting events at Gilkicker in her letters to her mother:

12th July 1912

Dear Mother,

Little Timothy is now beginning to climb over everything. He can walk a few paces without help but he likes to hold my hand. Oh Mother, you should see him. He likes to play with the shells and stones on the beach and he has a fixation for aeroplanes, just like his father.

We saw such a sight the other day as the Fleet left Portsmouth Harbour on exercises. Everyone watching was spellbound as several aircraft flew above the ships and then they gave us such a display. You can imagine the view from Gilkicker Point.

At one time they were flying low over the water like enormous seagulls searching for food. Anthony said that they were searching for submarines. Then suddenly they would swoop up into the air and hover, circling above the sea. What a sight.

At one point, as father and son stood watching together holding hands, both pointed simultaneously skyward and I felt quite emotional at the sight. Anthony draws pictures of aircraft for Timothy and he's really quite good. Timothy has them on his bedroom wall.

Nell and Irene are both well. Nell's son is just a little older than Timothy and looks after him like a big brother. You should hear them talk. It's so sweet.

I do hope that the folks of Woolston are beginning to recover from their great loss. I think of them often in my prayers. I also hope that you are well, Mother, not working too hard and enjoying looking after your guests. Don't worry about me and please give my love to the family.

All my love,
    Sarah

Christmas at the fort was quite a magical affair. The bleak setting was transformed on the inside with garlands of yew and holly and the ladies had worked hard to make beautiful Christmas cards. They bought candles in the nearby village of Alverstoke and planned a shared meal on Christmas Day with all of the families eating together. The Chaplain had held a small service on Christmas morning and the men had crafted figures to make a little tableau of the Christmas Story. When the children saw it on Christmas morning their faces lit up in delight. At lunch Nellie, Irene and Sarah beamed at each other as they ate; everyone was merry and cheerful. It was the happiest Christmas she remembered since she was a child and with the thought of her absent mother and her father she felt a moment of sadness, which soon passed as the men organised games for the children to play. She watched the children, usually encouraged to be quiet in the barracks, screech with laughter as they played tag in the yard and then the quieter games of hunt the thimble and pin the tail on the donkey as they were beginning to tire. Irene, Nell and she had been planning this day for months, squirrelling away treats for the children and deciding what they would need. It had given them so much pleasure, their secretive meetings adding to the excitement.

The months after Christmas were the hardest for Sarah but it was Nell who kept her from sinking back into depression as she fought with the sensation that she was imprisoned at the fort, despite her happiness at watching Timothy grow into a mischievous little boy.

Occasionally Nell would offer to look after Timothy while Sarah went for a walk along the empty shoreline, the piercing wind weaving through the long grass and the sea gulls arguing overhead. Unlike in the past, when Sarah would dream of escaping across the water, now the lure of her family and friends back at their barracks was greater, making her return both warm and cheerful.

'You've blown your blues away, then?' Nell enquired as she looked up to see Sarah's smiling face enter the room.

'Down, down,' demanded her cross son as she lifted him up off the rug where he had been happily playing with his favourite wooden soldier and horse which one of Anthony's men had carved for him.

Sarah laughed.

'Yes, I just needed some air. It feels so claustrophobic here in the winter but I'm fine now.'

'Make yourself useful and put the kettle on then,' ordered Nell, grinning as she looked up from her mending.

'Yes, maam!' teased Sarah. 'Thanks. I really do feel human again. We get out so little at this time of year.'

'Count your blessings,' reminded Nell. 'Life's not so bad here, really. You've just got to relax a little and enjoy it.'

Life at the fort continued in much the same routine for the months ahead and Sarah had little time to fret.

Chapter 14

BACK AT ST John's Road Harriet was too busy to worry, as there was hardly a night when she had a bed to spare in the coming months. Local people came to know her reputation for a warm welcome and wholesome home cooking. They often recommended Harriet's place as a place for their relations to stay, rather than the more expensive hotel; so much so that when a larger establishment called Bourton Villas, with five spare rooms, came up for rent on the Portsmouth Road, she was tempted to take the unexpected opportunity.

One night Ernest spent the evening with her, debating the merits and pitfalls of such a venture and Harriet was so grateful of his support, especially when considering the implications of the greatly increased rent and expenses. Nevertheless, Ernest could see by the enthusiasm in his mother's eyes that her mind was set. With the expanding industries in Woolston and rumours that a company was soon to be making aeroplanes close by, he agreed to support her initially, but also arranged an appointment with the local bank manager. Harriet explained her decision in a letter to Sarah the next weekend:

17th July 1913

Dear Sarah

I hope that you are well and that little Timothy is growing big and strong. It seems a long time since I saw you all at the Christening and I am sad that I am missing my grandson's growing years, and missing you of course.

I have been extremely busy with my guests, which is good because I never feel lonely. The majority of my guests are courteous and kind, usually writing positive comments in my guest book, which makes pleasurable reading.

I have some important news for you. A wonderful opportunity has presented itself to me and after a long discussion with Ernest, I have decided to move to Portsmouth Road, where I will rent Bourton Villas. It has five extra rooms which I can furnish as a guest house and the position could not be more central, being close to both the station and the Floating Bridge. I am so excited, Sarah, since this will give me a project to work towards which will be all-consuming. I have to admit that I still feel lonely at times, despite my guests, and so this will be ideal for me.

I am so thankful that you had the insight to clear out many things when you stayed with me before Anthony's return, and I am grateful that Ethel has kindly agreed to help me to clear the attic, if I mind Bethany and little Samuel. Going through your father's things was a task I did not relish.

I am looking forward to the fresh start with enthusiasm and hope that I will have your blessing, especially since this venture was your idea in the first place.

Just before I finish, please tell Anthony that Jane and I were lucky enough to witness a Sopwith Bat Boat. Yes, it's quite a good name for it! Jack and Ernest have told me that they saw it arrive in Woolston in the middle of May, the 17th I think. They tell me that a huge crowd gathered down by the

Floating Bridge to see it, but I was too busy at home. Mind you, they were quite jealous when I told them about our experience.

We were standing on the pier at Netley Hospital looking over the water. It was a beautifully sunny day with just a gentle breeze. We heard the now familiar buzzing, clattering sound that you once described in one of your letters and at first we looked up, excited to watch the air machine go over head. Soon it was clear that this craft was quite different. Before our eyes we watched a boat flying in the sky, but the boat had wings! Can you believe that! In fact its hull was quite pointed, and the double wings were each as wide as the boat was long. It flew over us no less than six times, gliding down to a marker buoy on Southampton Water and back again over the trees and out of view.

As you can imagine, quite a crowd had gathered by this time and we all waved as we witnessed each amazing circuit. A medical naval officer standing nearby explained the details to us, which Anthony might appreciate. Apparently the pilot, Harry Hawker, was taking part in the Mortimer Singer Prize competition where the plane must be a British amphibious aircraft (that's one that can alight on the water and move on dry land, using its own wheels, to you and me!) and must be flown by a British pilot. Can you imagine it, Sarah? A flying boat. Whatever next!

We've also seen several aeroplanes flying over Woolston of late. I know that Ernest and Jack were both so excited to tell me all about that newspaper's flying display which they saw last summer, the Daily Mail one, but even they were jealous when I described today's events. Ernest, more than your other brothers, was so enthusiastic when I told him, he being a skilled boat builder now. He hears so many rumours down at the The Yacht Inn. Who knows what we will see next.

Well, I must close now. Give Timothy an extra special hug

*from grandma and send my best wishes to Anthony. I was
hoping that I would be able to visit you this summer but life
has become so very busy.*

*All my love
Mother*

Only a few months later, early in October 1913, the news
reached Harriet that a famous person was living in a yacht
on the banks of the River Itchen, just up from White's
Boatyard where Ernest and Jack worked. It was the talk of
Woolston and Itchen Ferry village and while the lads were
gossiping in The Yacht Inn one evening, they were barely
surprised to see the two now familiar gentlemen coming
up to the bar and the whole room fell silent. One was
Hubert Scott Paine₅, who had taken over the running of
the yard, but rumours were rife that the other gentleman
was a man called Noel Pemberton-Billing and that he was
living up river on the yacht the *Princess Hannah*.

The normal banter was subdued, so they could only
eavesdrop upon snippets of information. After a while, the
prestigious gentlemen left to resume their talks back at the
Hannah, away from the prying eyes of the locals.

'What do you make of that, Ernest?' Jack asked as soon
as the door was closed.

'I heard the words "flying boat" mentioned and
something about a skilled workforce. Sounds pretty obvious
to me.'

'Would be a perfect location, here on the Itchen, so close
to Southampton Water. I think you might be right.'

'Would mean much more security for the workforce.
Couldn't be better for the village,' Ernest added.

'I'd be the first to volunteer if I had the choice to be
involved. What about you, brother?'

'Yes, I think it could be quite a challenge. Not much different to boat building, I don't think. We shall see.'

The men did not have to wait long because a few weeks later, several men at the boatyard were taken aside to begin the construction of a new flying boat, much like the one Harriet had seen at Netley. Ernest came to see Harriet that very evening with the news that both he and Jack had been chosen for this important work. She had never seen Ernest, usually so reserved and quiet, so animated as he described the visits from this extremely rich and famous gentleman.

By the end of the month it was obvious that it was going to be impossible to meet the present orders for boat building as well as work efficiently on the designs for this new flying boat and it was not long before men were employed to build vast new sheds nearer to the *Floating Bridge*. It was a good time for the people of Woolston and Itchen Ferry and, with plenty of work, all prospered.

For Harriet, this meant business was always busy and she had no reason to regret her decision to move to Portsmouth Road.

In the middle of November, on the 13th to be precise, Jack came to see her with more exciting news and persuaded Harriet to take a stroll down to the water's edge near the Floating Bridge, where a large crowd had gathered. Expecting to see another air machine or flying boat, she was surprised to see that the crowd was taking a trip on the ferry. It took a lot of persuasion for Harriet to go with Jack, but it was half way across the river that she realised what all the fuss was about.

'What does it say, Jack? "Super" what?

'It says Supermarine!' Jack exclaimed proudly. 'It's the name for the new company that Ernest and I now work for.'

There, emblazoned on the roof of the building in huge letters, only clearly visible by air or on the ferry, was the word 'S U P E R M A R I N E'.

'What does it mean, Jack?' Harriet shouted over the crowd.

'You've heard of a submarine which glides under the ocean? Well, this is an air machine which flies above the sea and one of its purposes is to seek out submarines. What do you think, Mother?'

The ferry had reached the Southampton side but, instead of walking off, Jack paid for the return journey and they remained where they were standing. This seemed a waste to Harriet, who had known enough hardship over the years not to throw money away if she could, but nevertheless she was pleased for her sons and their families and hoped that this would mean stability and prosperity for them all. She could not help but be a little fearful at the mention of submarines and a cold chill of foreboding seeped into her as she tried, but failed, to join in with the exuberance of the crowd. Fortunately Jack did not sense her fear because, when they reached the Woolston shore yet again, he picked her up and spun her around as if she were a child. Memories of Edward doing the same on the jetty on Riduna flooded back to her in that instance.

Harriet's laughing protests brought her back to her feet again as she tried to regain her breath. They walked past Bourton Villas and Jack gave his mother an affectionate hug as they parted. She had little time to dwell on her feelings because that night, for the very last time, her home in St John's Road was full of guests. She took no particular notice of a mysterious young man from London, whom she would see many more times in the years ahead.

With only two weeks to sort out and pack up all of her

belongings, Harriet was relieved that Ethel had offered to sort out Joe's things for her. His clothes were still hanging in the closet which they had once shared and she had never had the heart to remove them. Ethel was putting them all discreetly into sacks to give to people in need while Harriet was downstairs in the scullery, busying herself with a lifetime of belongings. There was the large pudding basin which she brought out to make birthday cakes and Christmas puddings over the years. All of her children had stirred the bowl and made wishes on numerous occasions on Stir Up Sunday. Joe had teased her that it was essential she made the pudding on that particular day. Harriet looked over to where Bethany and Samuel were playing on the rug, a pang of regret that Joe would not be with them to share future celebrations.

Whilst Ethel was in the bedroom she decided to pack away all of Harriet's clothes too and so she went up into the attic in order to fetch a trunk to put them in. She began to sort out Joe's old trunk, full of objects and toys from foreign lands.

'Harriet,' she called. 'What should I do with all of these strange things?'

Harriet climbed up into the attic and, seeing the wonderful gifts Edward had brought her children over the years she smiled as she thought of the countless days of pleasure they had brought.

'I think it would be a good idea for you, Jack and Sarah to share them between you. You never know when times might be hard and they'd make lovely gifts for your children as they grow up. What do you think?'

'Where did they come from?'

'The children's Uncle Edward brought them from his travels around the world. You should have seen their faces light up when he arrived. We never knew when he was going to turn up and they knew he would always bring them something special.'

'I'll leave them in the trunk then, and we can carry them downstairs and sort them out.'

Ethel climbed down and Harriet passed the trunk to her. Harriet paused before following her down. The attic was empty but for an old oak wardrobe which had been there when they had arrived all those years ago. There was something familiar about the wardrobe that she'd never noticed before. With a weird sensation of a living dream she opened the door to find a small scratched and dusty mirror hanging on the inside. She shivered. She should go on down but Harriet stopped briefly and glanced in the mirror. Momentarily, she saw Sarah's face and not her own in the reflection and just for a second it was as if she was transported back in time to Sarnia. She closed her eyes and it was if she was searching for something but what it was eluded her.

'Are you all right, Mrs Newton?' Ethel called out with concern.

Shaken back to reality Harriet shivered.

'Yes, I'm coming down. There's nothing else up here now and please call me Harriet, Ethel dear.'

When she went into the empty shell of her bedroom later that night, there was nothing but memories remaining. It was time to start afresh and with new beginnings in her mind she slipped off to sleep.

At first she dreamed that she was searching though all of her belongings. At one moment she was on Riduna and the next on Sarnia. All the time her eyes were looking around her, peering into the corners of cupboards and feeling at the back of drawers. Then she was aware that she was here at St John's Road and all the time her eyes wandered from place to place, looking, searching, seeking out something but she couldn't recall what it was. Her last vision was in the attic and as she opened to peer into the dim mirror there was a thud at the window.

Harriet came to with a start. It was nearly daybreak and she suddenly realised that it was the day of her move to Bourton Villas. She felt depressed, sadder than she had done for months, almost guilty that she was leaving the home she had shared so happily with her husband Joe all those years. What did he think? Would he be angry with her?

Once she had left the warmth of her bed she shivered with cold and quickly struggled to put on some clothes to keep out the chill. Once downstairs she threw on her coat and gingerly opened the back door. A small robin lay lifeless on the door mat but when she bent down Harriet realised that its heart was beating really fast. Gently she picked up the tiny bird. It lay on its back for a moment in the palm of her cupped hands, drawing from the warmth of them, eyes tight closed. Harriet held her breath. Suddenly the robin struggled to right itself, opened its eyes and hopped off on to the ground. Harriet stood spellbound as it shook itself and flew up into the branches of a hazel tree at the end of the yard. It looked back at Harriet for a moment before disappearing into the bushes.

Although Harriet could no longer see the little robin she suddenly felt as if Joe was watching over her. As it disappeared, for some inexplicable moment she could feel that he was at peace and gave her his blessing.

Chapter 15

HARRIET HAD SAVED well over the last two years and she was putting the finishing touches to the curtains for her newly furnished dining room, ready for opening just before Christmas. To her surprise and pleasure she noticed a little robin at the end of the now tidy but small back yard. Quietly she opened the back door and was just talking to the robin, welcoming it into her garden when there was a strangely familiar knock at the door. Instinctively Harriet knew who the visitor would be.

'Hello Edward,' she said as she opened the door. 'And how did you find out that I had moved house?'

'That's a fine greeting for an old friend!' exclaimed Edward, clasping Harriet's free hand in his and looking around him with a puzzled expression. 'I thought I could hear you talking to someone.'

Harriet's face reddened as she remembered the robin and so, evading his question, she replied. 'I often talk to myself, but where have you been to, Edward?'

'I know I should have called in before now, but it wasn't until I heard from one of my crew who lives in Woolston, that you had taken over the Bourton, that I realised it has been nearly two years,' he replied sheepishly.

In truth, although Edward had made a promise that he

would support Harriet if he could, each time the thought of visiting had entered his head, all manner of excuses caught the better of him and he had dismissed the notion.

Without waiting to be asked, Edward walked inside, looking around with mock wonder in his mischievous eyes.

'You *have* gone up in the world, Harriet. I'm proud of you,' he said as he walked from room to room, admiring the handy work of Harriet's sons, who had worked most of their free evenings to help Harriet whitewash the walls and arrange the modest furniture.

'I'll put the kettle on,' she replied, turning towards the kitchen. 'I'm bearing up well as you can see, and keeping myself very busy,' she added in a knowing way, 'and how are you?' she asked.

'I'm happy enough,' Edward replied.

He had returned to the kitchen, where he stood by the fireplace looking at the family photographs, picking up each one in turn. He paused, holding the one of the family taken at Sarah and Anthony's wedding, with Joe standing proudly next to his daughter.

Harriet glanced up and, seeing the happiness shine from the photo in Edward's hand, she felt her eyes glisten over as she remembered how happy she and Joe had been that day.

'You have a lovely family Harriet,' spoke Edward softly not adding how fortunate he thought Harriet had been, but she could hear it in his voice.

She handed him his cup of tea but continued to busy herself with making bread, which reminded him so very much of his mother. He took a sip of tea and grimaced.

'You always did have the ability to rise with remarkable haste from difficulties and get on with life.'

Harriet smarted at his sharp words and realising that he was alluding to her hasty marriage to Joe, once she thought that Edward had been lost at sea, she was dumbfounded.

You have no comprehension of what I went through, were the words Harriet silently fumed as she struggled to reply. She was so distraught that she was determined not to share with him the reasons for her hasty betrothal. She certainly had no regrets. Joe had been her rock and her best friend. They had struggled together over the years to give a stable and contented upbringing for their children and the smiling faces in the photos were proof that they had succeeded. No, she certainly did not have to justify her actions.

Edward was sitting beside the unlit fireplace staring uncomfortably into its depths while Harriet busied herself with kneading some dough. He broke the silence first with a peace offering to change the subject,

'When do you officially open?'

'I am hoping to have my first guests this month,' Harriet replied. 'We are nearly ready now. Jack and Tom helped me to decorate all of the rooms and Ernest has been so supportive, looking out for suitable furniture and guiding me with financial arrangements. I am so fortunate to have them.'

'I am so glad to hear it!' exclaimed Jack as he marched in through the back door without knocking. 'Have I interrupted anything?' he quipped, looking at Harriet's startled expression. 'How are you, Uncle Edward?' he continued, holding out his hand in greeting.

'Good to see you, my boy,' replied Edward taking Jack's hand in his enthusiastic grip and relieved that Jack had provided a diversion to their conversation, which had become as dangerous as sailing round the Cape. 'Still plenty of work at the boat yard?'

'Enough to keep me busy,' Jack replied, 'and I can always find a job or two if we're finding it hard to make ends meet.

What do you think of Mother's new enterprise, then?'

'I think you should all be proud of yourselves and looking at the fruits of your hard labour I'm now convinced it'll be a success.'

After a pause, when Edward gulped the last dregs of the tea, which he didn't have the heart to refuse, he added,

'I'm afraid my visit must be a short one, because I'm due back on the *Princess Ena* shortly.'

'I'll walk you down to the ferry,' offered Jack, thus curtailing any chance of further conversation between Harriet and Edward.

'Did you call for a particular reason, Jack, or was it just a social call?' asked Harriet as her son headed for the front door, this time followed by Edward.

It seemed to Harriet that her friendship with Edward had always been haunted by ill-timed interruptions such as this.

'Oh yes, I nearly forgot. My boss asked if you might have a couple of rooms for the night. He knows you don't officially open until the weekend but he is expecting some important visitors from the military and they are reluctant to stay at the Cliff. It would be impossible to keep the lid on their visit if they did.'

'I expect I could cope in an emergency,' smiled Harriet. 'You know that you can count on my discretion.'

With that she glanced towards Edward, who nodded his head in acknowledgement as he and Jack headed down the Portsmouth Road together. Harriet sighed.

Fortunately she had little time to dwell on Edward's visit because her two guests arrived just after dark, enjoying a hearty supper before heading for their evening meeting at the boat yard. They arrived back just before midnight, requesting an early breakfast, before they slipped discreetly upstairs.

The following morning little was said to lessen the mystery and soon they had left for the early morning train. It was only later in the week, when Jack came to say goodbye, that the mystery was solved. The gentlemen had called a meeting of the entire skilled workforce and had requested volunteers from the experienced engineers, to be taken to Calshot. They would be trained to work on the frequent repairs needed on the engines of the sea planes and flying boats at the newly formed RNAS station there. It was strategically placed, since Calshot Spit pointed into Southampton Water, looking over towards the Isle of Wight. Jack was one of the first to volunteer and his news only heightened Harriet's feelings of disquiet and, even at her busiest, she could not quite shake her fear.

On the other hand, Jack was excited. Although he was realistic enough to know that he'd never realise his dream to learn to fly, at least now he felt that he would be where he thrived, at the centre of the action.

For the next few months Jack enjoyed the excitement of working at Calshot, with a constant flow of sea planes and flying boats leaving the base on reconnaissance missions. It was also an important station for the training of new pilots in the unique skills required to successfully fly these unusual craft and thus the engineers were kept busy with repairs and engine maintenance. One of the trainee RNAS engineers, Patrick Jones, soon became his closest friend.

'When are you going to join up?' Patrick teased his tutor one day as Jack prepared to leave the base.

'When I'm good and ready, Patrick,' Jack replied, grinning as he headed for the Fawley Flyer, a horse drawn coach which sped along the track from Calshot village, through nearby Fawley village to Hythe, where he had caught the Hotspur ferry to Southampton. Within hours, Jack was home, amusing his family with tales of planes capsizing, somersaulting in the water or swooping so low over people's heads that they nearly took their caps off.

In February he came home for the birth of his adored daughter Phyllis and for a while she was the highlight of his visits until the end of June when he appeared uncharacteristically subdued. He spoke to no one of his haunting memories of the day Commander Rice and Lieutenant Cresswell, met their deaths. Jack had become quite close to the Lieutenant, the natural bond developing between mechanic and pilot of equal respect and trust as he was responsible for preparing Cresswell's plane for service. Jack was standing at Calshot Spit watching the Short 128 sea plane fly overhead and he was concerned and puzzled when it changed course as if to return to base. Jack watched in horror as he heard a loud explosion and the plane broke up in flight and crashed into the sea, narrowly missing a sailing yacht *The Guiding Star*. The pilot and observer had died instantly.

Patrick, who was standing by Jack's side whispered,

'When are you going to enlist Jack?'

'Soon, very soon, my friend,' Jack replied.

'I'm on my way north next week, did yer know?'

Jack gave Patrick a knowing look in a silent reply.

After retrieving what little there was of the wreckage for the incident enquiry there was no time for Jack to brood, as all hands were working flat out to prepare for the impending Naval Review. His uncharacteristic despondency was uplifted somewhat by mid-July as they watched no less than thirty eight aircraft flying overhead at Calshot to be positioned around the Solent ready for the King's Review of the Fleet.

Jack had a privileged position at Calshot Spit, which juts out like a finger into the mouth of Southampton Water, where all the action was to take place. Thus he watched in awe on one side of Southampton Water as Anthony, Sarah and Timothy viewed the spectacle from the other side of the water at Gilkicker. Unbeknown to them Jane also witnessed many planes heading towards the event as patients and staff mingled on the pier at The Royal Victoria. In fact the aeroplanes stole the show and although the atmosphere was dampened by the threat of war, none who watched could help but be excited by the event.

It was whilst watching the Review that Jack was resolute to join the RNAS as an engineer, making a decision that he knew would be unpopular at home. During his time at Calshot he had helped to train many mechanics. He had watched them, like Patrick, move on as they were stationed elsewhere in the country and Jack now longed to be away from the base and his haunting memories.

At first his life changed little, but only a month later, as sea planes were beginning to assemble in numbers once more between Calshot Spit and Netley for the Daily Mail Round Britain Seaplane Race, Calshot was gripped with the excitement of the preparations.

Jack stood spellbound. Planes were making trial take offs from the Solent and flying in every direction from the Spit, giving individual displays of daring as each made ready for the event.

Within twenty four hours everything changed and the atmosphere was charged with electricity. He'd heard rumours of the hostilities in Europe and the implications for Great Britain, but was filled with a mixture of disappointment and excitement since, before the actual race had even had a chance to begin, war was declared. Jack and his team waited with nervous anticipation while all the planes were pressed ready for military action by the RNAS and the race was cancelled.

Jack could have remained at Calshot throughout the war,

but the death of the lieutenant had affected him greatly. Also, he had an inbuilt enthusiasm to be at the centre of the action which overrode any responsibilities he might have had for his family or fears for his own safety.

As Jack was signing his name at Calshot, giving a commitment that he would be prepared to go wherever he was sent, Tom was also at the front of the queue in Southampton signing up for 9th (Cyclists') Battalion of The Hampshire Regiment. He had told no one of his motives for going across the water to Southampton that day, but he seemed compelled to do so. He had been encouraged to join by Old Mr Palmer at the Bicycle Shop. Mr Palmer felt that it might cure his restless spirit since his twin brother had departed for Calshot.

In Woolston it was Harriet's role to try to keep the family together. Now that Jack had enlisted he asked his mother whether his wife Hannah could move in to one of her guest rooms with their baby daughter, Phyllis. Harriet agreed since business was slow now and she was also pleased to have the company. She still had the occasional fee paying guest, but rarely for frivolous matters. Usually they were from the military or sometimes from London. She never asked questions and all the household knew that discretion was vital. There was one young man in particular who visited from time to time, the first time being just before she had left St John's Road. He was reticent to divulge the true purpose of his visits but as time went by he relaxed and began to entertain Harriet with brief accounts of his days. He seemed especially excited about sea planes and enjoyed talking to Ernest about the early days of Supermarine. On his last visit, just before the start of the war, he had started an animated debate about the work at Calshot with Jack at the time of the preparations for the Round Britain Sea Plane Race. He decided to return with

Jack on the Hotspur that evening, taking the Fawley Flyer with him to Calshot, but of course the race was called off.

In fact, he had been sitting at Harriet's breakfast table a couple of mornings later when the news of war was announced. She was just hovering at his table, replenishing his tea cup. The radio was on quietly in the background and as the news sank in Harriet looked at the gentleman with obvious alarm.

As she started to clear away his empty breakfast plate, she tried to make light of the announcement to calm her shaking hands.

'They say 'twill be over by Christmas.'

'That's very unlikely madam, I'm afraid,' he had replied in a tone imperceptible to her other guests.

The serious nature of his statement contrasted with his normally light-hearted air. Noting the folded newspaper by his side she wondered what article he had read to give him that assumption, but had no opportunity to ask, since he explained that he would now have to return to London early and curtail his visit.

As he had left he had handed her his newspaper with the name Harry Harper$_2$ ringed in red ink. He winked at her as he touched his cap and then put his finger to his lips as if to acknowledge that Harriet would keep his secret and nodded towards the range.

'I hope the war will be kind to you and yours,' he said. 'I may not return until it's over. Good day to you and thank you for your hospitality.'

With that said he had donned his cap and disappeared in the direction of the station.

As Harriet had cleared away, putting the newspaper into the glowing embers as she felt she had been instructed, she wondered if she had really guessed correctly that he was truly the The Daily Mail reporter, and if so, she wondered why he would have chosen to stay at her humble dwelling. Anonymity was the only solution she came up with but later that day, as she was faced with the more pressing news that her sons had decided to enlist, she had dismissed all thoughts of the stranger and concentrated on getting by from day to day.

When Jack and Tom, smartly wearing their respective uniforms, came to see Harriet for the last time before leaving for training, she could not help but notice the difference in the characters of her two precious boys, born only minutes apart. On the one hand Jack had regained his spirit and was full of life with a defiant enthusiasm for the adventure he was about to begin, whereas Tom looked nervous and withdrawn. She felt that, if he were given the chance to change his mind, he would leap at it with open arms. The moment when each twin enlisted had been simultaneous although their paths and roles in the war to come could not have been been more different.

Chapter 16

BACK AT FORT Monckton, so many air machines flew over the heads of the officers and NCOs that it was becoming almost commonplace. For some time now, an airfield had been established by the Portsmouth Aero Club based at Grange Fort, less than two miles away inland.

It was not until summer 1914, when Anthony heard the news that The Grange had been taken over by the War Department for the Royal Flying Corps, that he ever imagined his dream to fly might become a reality. The news of the hostilities in Europe filtered though to them and though it did not have immediate impact on their daily routine, it was the tense atmosphere of anticipation, and in some cases dread, which pervaded life at Gilkicker.

Since the commencement of the war on 4th August, the inactivity at Fort Monckton became a constant frustration for him. At times it was so unbearable that occasionally he even wished that he was joining the troops training in the grounds below them or travelling on their way out to the Western Front. Each time a ship passed, brimming with uniformed men, his regiment would stand to attention and salute as the sound of enthusiastic singing floated towards them. His men would be heard humming or whistling 'It's a long way to Tipperary' and 'Pack up you troubles', long after the ship had disappeared from view.

Aeroplane activity was also a regular distraction, with the sleek and more robust Avro 504s and BE2s, used for training in the months leading up to war, flying overhead. The inexperience of the pilots made it clear that they were often lucky to return to the aerodrome in one piece.

On the day the *Gamma* airship circled above, the whole community gathered with excitement. Timothy, now three years old, sat on his father's shoulders. At the moment it passed above them he ducked his head and closed his eyes, to the amusement of those around him.

'Come on, little man,' teased Anthony, tickling his son under the chin. 'You're missing the show.'

By early September Anthony knew that his time with his family was precious and so on the next free afternoon they took a stroll together along the pier, eerily empty of holidaymakers on this hot September day. A hopeful ice cream seller was forlornly peddling his wares and so Anthony bought them each a vanilla cornet as a treat, which also put a temporary smile on the face of the pedlar.

While Sarah and Anthony watched their son playing on the beach amongst the shingle and shells, oblivious to the changing mood around him, he spoke quietly to her.

'I wanted to tell you myself that you and Timmy will be evacuated shortly.'

'When do you think it will be?' Sarah replied in surprise, glancing towards Timothy.

'Very soon. I can't say when, but I wanted to give us time to plan. It's common sense really. If England were ever invaded, then these forts along the coastline would be the first line of defence and the initial target for attack. It's not safe for you to stay here.'

They sat in silence for a while as the implications of his words sank in. Rumours had already been very unsettling for the residents at Gilkicker and so it wasn't a total surprise.

'I think you should go to stay with my parents in Hamble. They have plenty of room and it would be a good environment for Timmy. I think it would be safer than in Woolston; quieter too.'

'No, Anthony. Your parents are very kind but I really think my place is with my mother. She may need my help, what with both Jack and Tom away and I would feel out of place in Hamble'.

'If that's what you wish,' replied Anthony, unable to conceal his frustration and yet trying so hard to avoid conflict.

He so wanted their parting to be an amicable one.

When she returned to their rooms to pack, Sarah was flooded by a sense of relief that she was to be released from the place which felt more like a prison than a home to her. This was followed by a wave of guilt as she thought of leaving Anthony behind. Nevertheless, she had little time to dwell on this because within hours the formal announcement was made and there was a frenzy of activity as everyone prepared for the evacuation. Everywhere in the barracks wives packed items needed for the trip, trying to decide what to leave behind for their husbands.

There was an air of nervous excitement, with the children inquisitive and mischievous. Just before Sarah closed her second case she felt at the far back of her underwear drawer and pulled out the small velvet pouch. As she had done so on several occasions before, she poured the contents into her hand and held the silver locket to her neck. She was daydreaming about its meaning when Anthony burst into the room unexpectedly.

'What have you got there?' he asked accusingly.

'Oh Anthony! I wasn't expecting you so soon.'

There was a moment's pause as they stared at each other, Sarah wishing she had confided in her husband at a more opportune moment.

'I can see that but where did you get that locket from? I've never seen it before.'

'There's not much to tell,' began Sarah, sitting on the corner of the bed, staring at the locket which she now held in her lap. 'When I was clearing out my father's trunk one day, in Mother's attic, I found it. I had never seen it before and it puzzled me, but I didn't want to upset Mother by mentioning it so soon after Father's death. I have asked a couple of people if they knew anything about it but have found out very little so far.'

The expression on Anthony's face relaxed and Sarah was relieved that he believed her.

'I just called in to let you know that I won't be off duty until late tonight and to see how you were getting on.'

'Have you time for a cup of tea? I'm nearly packed. There's no point in taking too much because they say the war'll be over soon and we'll be back.'

'No Sarah, I can't stop now.' He hesitated looking into her eyes. 'Come over here,' he said gruffly, 'I'm going to miss you.'

Dropping the locket on the bed Sarah went to him and Anthony held her in his arms. This rare show of affection took Sarah by surprise and she treasured the precious feelings of warmth and belonging.

After Anthony had gone she put the locket carefully back into its pouch and placed it at the bottom of her trunk before going to find Nell, who had been looking after Timothy and her son Ben this last hour.

'I'm finished, Nell,' she exclaimed.

'How about a well deserved cuppa, then?'

The children were playing with some wooden soldiers on the rag rug, quite oblivious to the turmoil around them. As Sarah watched them she tried to remember a phrase in the reading by Fort Monckton's chaplain at the service last Sunday. What was it, she pondered, as Nell busied herself in the small scullery. It was something about seeing life like little children, wasn't it? Oh, if only life were that simple. The war was tearing families apart and yet she was so mixed up inside. She went through to join Nell, out of earshot of the children.

'You know Nell, although I hate to leave Anthony behind like this, I have to admit that I'm really looking forward to moving away from here for a while. You know I've never truly settled here and it makes me so restless.'

'There's no need to scold y'self. Why shouldn't you look forward to seeing your mother and family again and spending some time in Woolston? After all, you grew up there.'

'You're so wise, Nell. You've been such a good friend, catching me when I've been heading towards rock bottom and lifting me up with your fun and laughter.'

'Come 'ere you silly girl. I'll miss you too, you daft thing.'

They hugged each other tightly, trying not to imagine what the war might bring. Tragic news of the loss of men over in France had already filtered through to them and although their men still spoke with bravado, it didn't help to try to look too far into the future.

The following morning Sarah had little time to say good bye to Nell, who was travelling by train to Fareham, but Irene and her little girl were able to travel with them as far as Bursledon.

Anthony and Irene's husband waited with them on the station platform at Stokes Pier, holding on to the small hands of Timothy and Annabel, and when the train arrived they helped their wives with the luggage and pretended to say goodbye as if the group were going on a family holiday to their grandparents. The children waved out of the window for as long as they could still see their fathers and then settled down to enjoy the unexpected journey on a steam train, which gave a conversational whistle as it sped past Grange Fort and the airfield. Timothy stared out of the window at the aeroplanes, which were lined up beside their hangers like a flock of enormous birds, waiting for their time to migrate south.

Irene and Sarah longed to talk about the implications of the war on all of their lives but their conversation was restricted in front of the children.

'Good luck to you both,' Irene said as she and Annabel prepared to alight.

'You never know, we may be back at Gilkicker to celebrate Christmas together,' Sarah replied cheerfully.

'Let's hope so. What a celebration that would be!'

Irene and Annabel waved from the platform and now Sarah was quite excited about seeing her mother again. It was a year since Bourton Villas had opened and her mother's last letter had been so enthusiastic. It was the first time Sarah had visited since she had left for Gilkicker nearly four years ago and she was amazed how much quicker and easier the journey was in the luxury of a train.

Chapter 17

ERNEST WAS WAITING for them at the station and seeing him on his own gave Sarah a few pangs of regret.

'You're looking well, Ernest,' she exclaimed as he bent to kiss her on the cheek. 'What news of Tom and Jack?'

As they walked the short distance from Woolston station, with Timmy holding on to Sarah's hand and Ernest striding by her side, he talked about their brothers, only pausing to cross the busy Portsmouth Road, dodging behind the buggies speeding down towards the ferry.

'Everyone was surprised when Tom volunteered as soon as war broke out; none more so than Mother.'

'I can imagine, and where is he now?'

'He signed up for the Hampshire Regiment in the 9th (Cyclists) Battalion and was sent to Louth in Lincolnshire.'

'Well, that suits him anyway, but I can't imagine Tom wanting anything to do with the war. He's too sensitive. Have you heard from him?'

'Mother received a couple of dutiful letters. They were very short and said little of his life on patrol. He sounded quite relieved to be on British soil though, doing coast patrol duties between Grimsby and Skegness. He hinted that he regretted his hasty decision and didn't really know why he was there.'

'Poor Tom! Sounds just like him. Gets himself into a situation and wonders how he got there. It's a relief he's still in England, though. Hopefully war will be over soon and he will come home unharmed. What about Jack?'

'You should have heard Jack's wife when she found out that he had volunteered too. I've never seen her so upset. She's such a quiet sort usually.'

'How has Mother taken the news, Ernest?'

'You'll see for yourself. She hides her real emotions and she rarely lets her guard down, not since father died, but you could see she was afraid on the day they left. We all walked to the station to see them off, apart from Mother. I don't think she could bear it. We waved goodbye on the crowded platform as they boarded the train bound for Southampton. From there they changed for Winchester, but Jack continued up to London.'

'Jack would relish an adventure like that, but what about you, Ernest? What's that badge on your lapel?'

Ernest reddened.

'It's to show that my occupation is vital to the war effort,' he explained briefly.

He did not mention that because of his work there was no pressure for him to join and that although it signified the importance of his work at Supermarine, many of his workmates had already volunteered for service and this had started to cause friction in the community left behind.

It was only a short walk from the station to the guesthouse, where Harriet was waiting impatiently for Sarah and Timothy to arrive. Fortunately for Sarah, business was now very quiet, when only essential travel was taking place, and so there were rooms to spare which Harriet had prepared for them.

They fell into each other's arms and soon both mother and daughter were shedding tears. Ernest, in his embarrassment at such an open show of emotion, turned to Timothy.

'Well, young man, while these ladies are blubbering, so pleased they are to see each other, let's walk down to show you the *Floating Bridge* and leave the women time to chatter. What do you think?'

And so, looking as grown up as possible and trying not to be concerned about his mother and grandmother's tears, Timothy took Uncle Ernest's hand and they strolled purposefully down to the River Itchen to watch the ferry come in from Southampton.

As they stood at the water's edge Ernest was pleased to see a flying boat pushed down the slipway. Little Timothy stood beside him in awe as the boat was guided into the water and a few moments later it took off into the air above their heads.

'I help to make flying boats like that, young Timothy, and that's where I work.'

Ernest looked down at his nephew, seeing a mixture of uncertainty and interest in the child's silent expression.

'We'd best get back and tell your mum all about it, don't you think?'

Timothy nodded in reply and gripped his uncle's hand. He had been excited by the train journey and now he'd seen a flat ferry and a boat take off into the sky. He didn't really know why they had left daddy behind at home but he was determined to be brave. When they reached Bourton Villas Sarah was unpacking in the room which would be their home for some time to come.

'I think your mother's busy upstairs, Timothy,' gestured Ernest.

Timothy paused a moment listening and then rushed upstairs and into his mother's arms.

'What did you see, little man?' asked Sarah but Timothy was too confused to answer.

'Let's go back downstairs to grandma then and see if she can find you a biscuit.'

'I can do better than that,' exclaimed Harriet as they entered the kitchen. Would you like a piece of my fruit cake and a glass of milk?'

Harriet was rewarded by a nod and a cheeky grin in response.

'Let's eat it up at the table so that we don't get crumbs everywhere, shall we?'

'Grandma makes lovely cakes, doesn't she? I'll have to have some lessons from her while we're staying here,' Sarah added as she settled in one of the chairs beside her son.

'And how's the business going, Mother? Are you glad you made the decision to move?'

'It hasn't been easy since war was declared, but before that I hardly had a night with a room to spare.'

'I can see by the comments in the guest book that you have been been very busy. Popular too!'

'Yes, with the help of the boys I opened quickly and it's been wonderful. I don't know what I'd have done without them.'

Harriet smiled at Ernest, who could not help but notice the worried frown which passed her features momentarily as she was obviously thinking of the twins.

'You said that Tom has gone to Lincolnshire, but where is Jack now and what's he doing?'

'He's at a training camp somewhere near London. We had a postcard from London but haven't heard from him since.'

'I'm sure we'll hear soon, Mother. No news is good news and I'm sure if he'd set sail by now he would have sent word to us.'

Harriet smiled at her remaining son.

'At least you're still here and now I've got you too,' she brightened as she smiled at Timothy, noticing Ernest winking at Sarah.

'Well, I must be off now. It's good to have you home, Sarah. Truly it is.'

'I'll walk along the road with you,' Sarah said, standing up and reaching for her coat.

Once out of earshot of the Villas, Sarah turned to Ernest. 'How's Mother really?'

'She's always been strong, Sarah, but she's worried sick about the boys. Every day she waits for news that they are to be posted and she dreads it.'

'It's just as well Mother has had you nearby, then.'

Ernest looked wistfully into the distance for a moment as if he wished to say something but couldn't find the words and his eyes fixed on a poster in the corner shop window. 'Your Country Needs You,' it read, pointing accusingly at him. He shivered.

'I feel so guilty at times, Sarah. The boys are off doing their bit for the country and I wonder if I should join too.'

'Don't be so silly, Ernest. If every skilled man said that, we'd have no one to build ships and aeroplanes to fight the war.'

'Don't you be so sure, Sarah. You'd be surprised, but there are already rumours that they will be taking on women workers at Vickers soon, and they've already taken children out into the fields in Sholing to help harvest the vegetables. Times are changing.'

A lady passed them by and glared accusingly at Ernest as she disappeared into Lipton's.

Sarah was thoughtful for a moment.

'I'd better go back now but please don't do anything hasty and sign up. I'm not sure Mother would be strong enough to see you go away too. She needs you, Ernest. Please try not to take any notice!'

Ernest lowered his voice to barely a whisper.

'That lady's just heard the news that her youngest was

lost in action so I'm not surprised at her bitterness towards me.'

Sarah took hold of Ernest's hands.

'I'm so glad you're here, Ernest. Don't forget you're doing an essential job for the war effort and I'm so proud of you.'

With that said she turned and walked quickly back up the street to the place she would now call home. As she entered, she had a pang of regret, remembering the little terrace she had grown up in on St John's Road.

Chapter 18

LIFE WAS EVEN more unbearable for Anthony at Fort Monckton after Sarah and Timothy had left. Watching, waiting and anticipating for any sign of unexpected vessels on the horizon, ever on the lookout for distinguishable movement on the surface of the water which could signify enemy submarines in action. Drill, equipment cleaning, watch, eating and resting, each in regular monotony. He was increasingly envious as planes flew over him from Grange Airfield, where pilots were being trained before leaving for France. Sometimes he could even hear the trainer yell out instructions from the cockpit behind the pilot, as they veered dangerously low, or the plane banked too steeply. On one occasion, Anthony and his men watched with concern as an engine stuttered so erratically that it cut out altogether and the pilot had to make an emergency landing on the uneven grassy slopes below them, its nose dipping into one of the moats as it blip, blip, blipped to an abrupt halt. Some of his men rushed to the pilot's aid. It was the first time this pilot had flown independently, but fortunately he was unharmed. Anthony ordered some of his men to load the damaged plane on to one of their carts, to be taken back to the airfield for repair.

His chance finally came when his Commanding Officer

came to inspect Fort Monckton with new instructions to inform him that the numbers of regular personnel they could spare for this operation, however important for the security of British shores, was going to be reduced. The Territorials would take up the slack. His men were to be posted as gunners. They were asked to prepare immediately for a short leave to visit their families before heading for Southampton Docks, ready to embark for France. Anthony hesitated at first and his Commanding Officer took him aside to speak in private.

'What's on your mind, Bombardier Parker?' he asked.

'Sir, I wonder if I may be so bold as to request permission to be transferred to The Grange to learn to fly?'

After a few moments' hesitation as his Commanding Officer considered a suitable reply, he answered,

'This is an unusual request from your rank, Parker. If I recommend you for this transfer on the basis of your exemplary record and it is refused, do I take it that you would volunteer to go with your men?'

'I certainly would, sir. I am most grateful, sir.'

'You will hear by the morning, Parker, but meanwhile I suggest that you prepare to travel home as ordered.'

They saluted one another, Anthony returning to his barracks to pack the few items that he would take with him, whatever decision was made. That night he hardly slept. He was tossing and turning, at one moment in a dark damp cold place and in the next he was high in the sky. In the early hours of the morning he gave up trying to sleep and dressed to join the night watch as the sun rose on the horizon.

At breakfast he found it difficult to eat and he noticed that it was the same for the small band of men preparing to leave on the early train. As they lined up to walk to the platform, their packs on their backs and their rifles by their sides, Anthony saw his Commanding Officer riding towards them.

'Bombardier Parker, see your men on to the train and report to Grange Fort at 0900 hours,' he ordered.

'Yes sir. Thank you, sir!' Anthony saluted, finding it very hard to stifle a grin, knowing that his CO must have pulled some strings to gain him the required promotion.

At the end of the day, as he settled in the single bunk in the accommodation for the trainees at the Grange, he wrote an excited letter to Sarah:

12th November, 1914

My dear Sarah and little Timothy,

I hope that you are comfortable in your mother's new guest house and that Timothy, you are being good for Mummy and Grandma. I have missed you these last few months and it's been so quiet without you.

I have some exciting news for you. I have been transferred to Fort Grange and I am going to learn to fly in an aeroplane. It is a dream come true for me and I know that you will be so proud of your daddy.

I start my training tomorrow, but it may be many weeks before I get into the air. I need to learn all about aeroplanes first and as soon as I have more news for you I will write again.

Yours as ever,
Anthony

The next morning, Anthony began his training in the makeshift classroom at Fort Grange. Initially he sat fighting off the irritation of irrational impatience, much like the other naive young men in the room. His experienced trainer had such a businesslike manner, but it was tinged with a down to earth sense of humour, which was in fact the best combination for a military instructor. Soon he had Anthony at his ease and had instilled in him a vitality and enthusiasm to excel.

The weeks passed quickly and Anthony passed his examinations, progressing on to the more practical part of his training: that of understanding and maintaining his aircraft. He found this more of a challenge but was surprised how quickly be began to understand the workings of the engine and to recognise irregular noises, suggesting a plausible diagnosis. The instruments inside the cockpit were still an irresistible mystery to him and he longed for the moment when he would one day take control.

The next part of his training was back in the classroom, poring over numerous maps and photographs, for initially Anthony was to be trained as an Observer, to sit behind the pilot on reconnaissance missions. So far Anthony had been at the Grange for several weeks and still he had not been up in an aeroplane but the day when he passed his last examinations was a cause for great celebration in the mess.

The following day he sat behind the pilot, nervously waiting for takeoff. The mechanic stood at the ready for the signal. As soon as contact was confirmed, the mechanic spun the propeller and the engine burst into song. It was certainly a tune familiar to Anthony's ears by now and it filled him with anticipation in the depths of his stomach. Almost as soon as the chocks were taken away from under her wheels by the attendees, the aircraft started to taxi over the bumpy ground. The vibration of the engine in front of him was as startling as its deafening noise. The throttle was opened and they sped off across the turf. There was no time to take a breath because within seconds they had lifted into the air. He felt exhilarated and was almost distracted from his mission by the amazing sights around him. As they flew over Portsmouth Harbour he tore his gaze from the coastline. As they banked to the left, he began to note key features such as ships off the coast and sea planes readying themselves for takeoff on Haslar Beach and he was proud of himself when he sighted a 'friendly' submarine, just submerged below the surface of the water.

After a few more weeks of training, when he suppressed his enthusiasm to be master of the controls rather than seated as an observer in the front cockpit, he was relieved to pass all the tests and achieve a reasonable level of accuracy in target practice. He was given three days' leave to visit family and caught the train to Woolston. It was an emotional reunion and he spent the precious few days with Sarah and Timothy, jealous of the times they shared with her family in the now overcrowded household. Keeping three rooms for Harriet's fee paying guests left one room for Sarah and Timothy to share, and another for her sister-in-law Hannah and her child Phyllis. On the following Sunday afternoon, Ernest kindly agreed to take them to Hythe by horse and trap, borrowed from the drayman in Itchen Ferry village, where Anthony felt less claustrophobic and there they were able to spend a civilised few hours taking tea in his parent's large garden. His mother was so proud of his single wing sign on his uniform with an 'O' which signified that he was now a trained Observer, although it was clear that she was unsure as to why her son was not yet a pilot.

All too soon it was time to leave for Southampton, where he would meet up with his new unit before crossing to France. Sarah was overcome as they had one last embrace before he caught the *Floating Bridge* and it was all she could do to hold Timothy to restrain him from running after his father. This time there was no hiding from this little man that his father was off to war and even in his young intelligent mind he had observed the tears from neighbours as men folk had not returned. Sarah held him firmly by the hand and encouraged him to wave as Anthony disappeared from view on the farthest shore of the River Itchen.

Anthony walked amongst strangers along the busy streets to the docks. He was drawn towards the Bargate where shoppers were lining the streets to cheer regiment after regiment of infantry, some who had walked all the way from Winchester and were marching proudly to the docks. He also watched some Avro 504s being loaded on to a waiting ship. He was struck by the greyness of the multitude of vessels which was a bleak contrast to the usual colourful sight of ferries and liners in the port.

It was a smooth crossing and they disembarked at Le Havre, where they faced a long journey by train to the airfield at Amiens. He settled in to his makeshift world of Nissen huts, taking time to sort out his few personal belongings with the utmost care, in order to dispel the unease he felt at being near the Western Front at last.

After a fitful night he had no time to dwell on the danger of his position as he was scheduled to make his first sortie over enemy lines that very evening. He and his pilot were encouraged to make several flights that morning in order to regain their confidence in flying, to get to know each other and also to get their bearings so that they would be more familiar with landmarks pointing back to base. It was a bitterly cold November day. The wind was blustery, making flying difficult and the rain was piercing. Despite the inhospitable weather, Anthony was relieved to be back in the air again and the two men soon became an inseparable team, treating each sortie as an adventure, though they cursed the rain as an inconvenience.

It was late one afternoon, when they were sent on their first mission to cross enemy lines and report back the up to date positions of the Hun, that it really struck Anthony psychologically, almost as hard as a real bullet might have hit him physically. At first hand he witnessed the British troops in the muddy trenches below and the close proximity of the enemy. When he realised that a strange heap of muddy rubbish littering the sodden ground beneath him was in truth the remains of bodies, left where they had fallen, he almost vomited out of the cockpit, his instructions forgotten.

It was only the short sharp orders from his pilot which brought Anthony to his senses and he resumed his important task of recording what he had seen. His training came into its own at that moment and he concentrated wholeheartedly on his task, so that when they eventually returned to base, his Commanding Officer was pleased with what he had to report.

It was only late that night, when he longed for the oblivion of sleep in order to erase the vivid pictures still flickering through his mind, that he realised how wise it had been to test his resilience as an observer initially, rather than to waste time training him as a pilot in the first instance. As the idea closed on him like the shutter on his camera, he hardened his resolve and sank into a deep dreamless sleep.

Chapter 19

IT WAS WITH her family around her, apart from Tom and Jack, that Harriet prepared for the frugal Christmas ahead. With no end to the hostilities in sight, and more young men volunteering from the village every day, she remembered Harry Harper's words and shivered. After Christmas, Hannah and Sarah offered to be trained at Supermarine to join the growing force of women workers who kept the industry afloat, since the demand for aircraft was ever increasing. Harriet's role was now to look after the children as well as to run the guest house.

Although money was no longer an issue with both young ladies at work, she found there was less and less in the shops on which to spend the housekeeping. They only had a back yard for guests to sit in when the weather was good and no room for growing many vegetables, though she had put some tomatoes in pots and some lettuce, parsnip and carrot seeds in the place where there had been a very small lawn.

One day she was tinkering in the garden to get some fresh air, to avoid spending this spring morning doing the large pile of darning and mending in the corner of the kitchen, when, to her surprise, the little robin came and sat on the handle of her trowel. His presence brought calm to her otherwise troubled world and she gained strength from the feeling that Joe was close at hand.

'What would you think of all of this, Joe?' Harriet asked the robin.

'I don't know what Joe thinks, but I think that if you were talking to me like that I'd recommend that you be sent away for your own safety,' remarked Edward, grinning.

When finding no one in the kitchen, unbeknown to Harriet, he had crept out in to the yard behind her.

'Don't do that to me, Edward!' Harriet replied crossly. 'To what do I owe the pleasure?' she added, unable to hide a hint of sarcasm, referring to the fact that she had not seen hide nor hair of him since before the outbreak of war.

'Well, that's a fine way to greet your oldest friend,' he added, his face continuing to show signs of his unrepentant amusement.

'I'm sorry, Edward. I was far away. It's just this horrible war. It gets to you sometimes. I'll make a cup of tea, shall I?'

Feeling a little braver this time, Edward replied,

'I'll have coffee if you've got some,' but he wished he hadn't made an issue of it as he watched Harriet reach far into the back of a cupboard and spoon out what was obviously the last of her coffee.

'How are you Edward and how has this war affected your life?'

Edward seated himself comfortably at Harriet's large kitchen table and began his tale, uninterrupted by Harriet, who sat opposite him, glad of an excuse to have a rest.

'Not long after war was declared I knew my easy days of being Captain for a ferry of travellers and businessmen would soon be at an end, but I wasn't sure how it would affect my life. It happened all too soon. My ship was commandeered to be a troop ship and repainted grey. At first it was quite exciting and the enthusiasm of the young soldiers I carried to France, not long out of nappies some of them, I can tell you, was contagious. I found myself singing their songs in my sleep. Since then it's been tough. I'm always watching out for enemy submarines and trying to close my eyes to the state of the poor sods we bring back.'

Edward noticed Harriet's face turn pale and thought at first that she was cross with him.

'Excuse the language Harriet, but you should see them!' he exclaimed in anger, but when Harriet didn't reply, he realised his thoughtlessness. 'And what news of your boys, Harriet?' he asked more gently.

She tried to regain her composure and forget the images Edward's words had conjured up for her.

'Oh, Edward. I really don't know. Jack's an engineer for the RNAS and he and his brother left a couple of months ago. The last we heard was that he was undergoing some military training in a place near London. Tom has signed up for the 9th (Cyclist's) Battalion and he's somewhere in Lincolnshire.'

'That's good. They're still safe on English soil, then. Maybe the war will end before they get into danger.'

Unfortunately, neither Harriet nor Edward believed that this might be the case, but it sometimes helped to pretend.

'What about Ernest and Sarah? Where are *they* now?'

'Fortunately, Ernest is still at home, working at Supermarine. Sarah and Jack's wife, Hannah, are working there too now, much to my disgust. Anthony and Jack aren't too pleased about it either, but needs must, I suppose, and I enjoy looking after their children when they're home from school.'

After a pause, Harriet was surprised to hear her own voice ask,

'How is Marie, Edward?'

Realising the significance of Harriet mentioning Marie's name, Edward was flustered momentarily.

'Marie. Well, she got religion just after the start of the war and volunteered to help out at the docks with the Salvation Army of workers. They wouldn't let her wear a fully fledged uniform, her and I not being.... well, you understand....... but they were certainly grateful for the extra pair of hands.'

'What does she do?' asked Harriet, ignoring Edward's hesitant embarrassment.

'She meets the injured soldiers coming off the ships from France. If they're seriously injured she writes a postcard from them to their families to let them know that they've safely arrived back in England. She gets them to dictate or write the address if they can, before the men are sent on to hospital. Marie and I usually travel over on the Hotspur together, but a neighbour was sick today and so she stayed at home.'

Harriet realised that this was the true reason for the length of time since Edward's last visit, but decided that she should be diplomatic and change the subject rather than to challenge him, but couldn't think of anything to say. They sat quietly for a little while, each with their own thoughts, the uneasy silence heavy between them. Reluctantly, Edward decided that he must make a move and return to his ship. He was saddened that they were unable to relax in each other's company the way they used to on Riduna. All that history between them.

As he stood up, their eyes met and for just a few seconds it was as if time stood still, but at that very moment two children burst through the door, coming to an immediate halt as they saw Edward standing there.

'Don't be shy, Timothy and Phyllis. Come here and meet

your Uncle Edward. He's a sailor and sails big ships to faraway places.'

Forgetting his shyness, Timothy came forward and took hold of Edward's outstretched hand.

'My dad flies in an aeroplane,' he exclaimed proudly as he shook Edward's hand.

'And what about you, little lady?' asked Edward as Phyllis went to hide behind Harriet's chair.

'Phyllis's dad mends seaplanes, doesn't he, Phyllis? Don't be shy and say hello to your uncle.'

Phyllis stayed behind Harriet for protection but as Edward moved to the door he winked at her and she beamed a beautiful cheeky smile.

'I'll call again as soon as I can,' said Edward as he reached the open doorway, smiling briefly at Harriet as he disappeared down the road towards the *Floating Bridge*.

Chapter 20

As for Harriet's son, Jack, he was now a competent and skilled mechanic, and having specialised in sea planes he was an asset to the RNAS. He travelled with his twin brother, Tom, to Winchester where Tom was to be transported north east with the rest of his regiment, following a short period of training. They said their short goodbyes and Jack continued on the train to London. His first visit to the capital was a little daunting, even for the brash Jack, but he had no time to dwell on the sights before finding his way to Liverpool Street Station where he caught a train to Harwich, reassured by the sight of many young men like him, nervously setting off into the unknown.

Once at the dock he was sent to a nearby training camp where he was put through drill and other preparations for the dangerous sea voyage that was to come, including basic strategies for defence and attack, to ensure he was prepared for any eventuality.

Jack's role on board the tender would be to maintain and assist in the launch of the sea planes: no mean feat, as he discovered when they attempted a mock launch of a Sopwith Schneider sea plane in the harbour a month later. The plane was launched successfully from the 'flying off' deck at the front of the ship and made a few graceful circles before alighting on the water, taxiing towards the side of the ship. The hardest and most dangerous part was attaching it to the winch to be brought safely back on deck and he put life and limb in danger at each attempt. Excitedly, he wrote home to Hannah:

15th April, 1915

My dear Hannah,

I have enjoyed the most exhilarating time here in the port. You cannot imagine my joy when we finally embarked on HMS Ben my Chree, what a funny name for a ship. I thought I would be on a grand ship called the Majestic or Princess Elizabeth. Nevertheless it has been good finally to set sail and to leave the claustrophobic training camp. I had thought my training days were never going to end.

Today I was so proud when we launched one of our planes directly from the ship. It was wonderful, just like watching our little Phyllis take her first steps. How is she by the way? In fact the only thing to mar my joy at being here is that I am so far away from you and I cannot see her sweet face.

I know you are angry at me for volunteering so soon, but you'll see. We'll be sending out our sea planes on such successful missions that we'll surprise the enemy, catch them on the hop and soon the war will be over. I'm sure you cannot begrudge me wanting to do my bit for my country.

Please give my love to Mother and Sarah and send news to Tom that I am well. I do believe that he has the hardest task in this war on the ground and my hope is that he too escapes the wet muddy fields of France and is given a chance to see a bit of the world. My part is just fun, mending and maintaining sea planes and sending them on their way. It's what I do best. I'll be fine, you'll see.

Yours,
Jack

Jack was standing on deck, full of excitement when on 3rd May 1915 the *Ben my Chree* left Harwich to take part in the raid on Norddeich but his heart sank when his unfortunate ship was forced to return to harbour due to fog. When back at Harwich, he was pleased to receive a letter from Hannah:

26th April, 1915

My dear Jack,

Phyllis and I are both well and settled in at your mother's. She is very kind and good company for us and it means that we have saved so much in rent we could ill afford with you away.

We had a very quiet Christmas but we made the occasion as cheerful as possible for the sake of the children. You should have seen Phyllis open the picture of your ship you sent for her and she has proudly put it up on her wall beside her bed. It is a very strange looking ship, I must say, but I expect it is because of the deck where you launch those sea planes you so love.

After Christmas, Sarah and I made an important decision which I must tell you about. We began training at Supermarine under Ernest's supervision. The benefits of this are many. Firstly, it means that we are able to make a greater contribution to the household expenses, since there are fewer fee-paying guests in these difficult times. Secondly, and more important, is that we feel we are contributing to the war effort.

I can't say that we enjoy the dirty dusty tasks, but the girls we work with are such fun that we make the most of it. Now

*it's spring time it's easier to keep our spirits up and believe
that war might end soon. I do hope so with all my heart.*

    *Phyllis and Mother send their love to you, as does Sarah.
Please keep safe, my dear Jack, and don't go and do anything
heroic.*

    Yours,
      Hannah

Jack's letter in return was less optimistic:

7th May, 1915

My dear Hannah,

    *Thank you for your letter. It was good to hear that you are
well but I am worried that you are working at the factory.
That's no work for a young lady such as yourself and you
should be at home looking after our daughter. I'm not happy
with the arrangement at all and cross with Mother for allowing
it to happen. I expect it is Ernest putting these ideas into your
young head or that headstrong sister of mine.*

    *I am afraid that here we are back in dock for minor repairs
to our ship, which was rammed by one of our own, would you
believe! We also had no end of trouble with the Schneider and
had to abort its launch. That's one of our best sea planes. You
cannot understand how frustrating it is to be back with so little
to show for it.*

    *The only fortunate circumstance to come out of this delay is
that I received your letter and though some of your news worries
me, I will still treasure it close to my heart in the voyage ahead.*

    *I cannot tell you where we are bound shortly, because it is
a secret but I do know that it will be a long way away. It is
sad that there is not enough time for me to visit you but rest
assured that I am thinking of you.*

Please send my love to Mother, Ernest, Sarah and Tom if you are able to and to Phyllis as ever.

I do love you, even though I do not tell you very often. By the way, I found out that 'Ben my Chree' means 'Lady of My Heart'! My fondness for this ship grew when I heard of its apt name and I'm sure that it will bring us good luck.

Yours,
   Jack

Jack felt relief as *HMS Ben my Chree* finally set off from Harwich towards the Mediterranean and it was a long time before the family at Bourton Villas heard from him again. Once the voyage was underway Jack was uncharacteristically nervous as to what might lay ahead, but as his ship arrived at its first destination, his role of preparing the new Short seaplanes for reconnaissance work became quite routine.

He was just beginning to think that this work was no more exciting than his time at Calshot when on 15th August one of their best pilots, Flight Commander Charles Humphrey Kingsman Edmonds[3], made the first ever successful aerial torpedo attack on a Turkish ship in the Dardenelles. When this was followed by more success, Jack felt in his element. So proud was he to be part of this mission that he wished he could share his joy with the folks back home.

His wish was to be granted because a few months later they headed to Port Said.

20th February, 1916

My darling Hannah,
   You would be so proud of your husband now! We have given

the Turks what for and our planes have been at the centre of the action. When we rehearsed in England I would never have believed how much good we could do with these beauties. They are truly like my children and as I see them fly into action I feel such a glow in my heart.

How is Phyllis, by the way? She must be quite a little girl now and chattering so much too, I expect. Does she remember her daddy, I wonder?

All our practice for launching sea planes from the deck at home was a complete waste of time because we found out the hard way that it was much too risky. Now we always use a winch, hoisting the aircraft carefully over the side and on to the water. They have fitted long poles at the sides of the ship to fend off the planes and stop them bumping into the ship, or worse still, into one of us. They are a godsend. My job is made all the more difficult by the heat here, which creates havoc with our engines. Having enough spare parts to keep these babies flying causes me a constant headache, but me and Patrick Jones, he's my right hand man here like he was in Calshot, usually manage it in the end.

After the excitement of our success with the Turks we did a good job in rescuing some Australians from their sunken ship, which I'm sure you will think was worthwhile, and then we headed towards Egypt. It was fortunate that we were near port when the SS Uganda came along side us. You wouldn't believe it, but we collided! In fact I was amazed when it happened too, and couldn't in my worst nightmares dream that we might be nearly sunk by our own side a second time. Fortunately, nothing of that nature happened, but nevertheless we are now here at Port Said waiting for repairs to be done.

Being in port has its compensations. With a bit of ingenuity we cleared the hangers and have been able to have quite a party, putting the piano we already had on board to even better use. What a time we've had! Who said there was a war on?

Another good thing to come out of this mess is being able to write to you and at least I can reassure you that I am well and safe. I hope that this confounded war ends soon and that I am able to return to you in one piece. Please give my love to Mother and a big hug to our little Phyllis.

Yours as ever,
  Jack

Chapter 21

FOR TWO MONTHS after he had said goodbye to his brother, Jack, Tom's battalion was in Lincolnshire. Dawn had broken and although tired from his night's activities, cycling along the coastal track between Skegness and Grimsby, he had enjoyed the bracing autumn air and the freedom of the ride. Once back at camp, instead of falling into his tent for a well earned rest, he was informed of orders to break camp and prepare for a journey south. It had not been confirmed, but rumours were that they were to return to the south coast. Morale was low among the men since they feared a possible posting to France. Once everything was packed, the men hung around listlessly waiting for orders. Tom's group grasped the opportunity to settle on the ground for a well earned nap, their packs under their heads. A couple of hours later, Tom was shaken by a mate as his Commanding Officer was preparing to give orders and all too soon they were back on their bikes, but this time cycling inland in a southerly direction. It was not until they had arrived at Portsmouth several days later that Tom took the opportunity to write to his mother:

12th October, 1914

Dear Mother,

I have some good news for you. I am writing from Portsmouth and we are having a well earned rest, having cycled all the way from Lincolnshire. We stopped at Kettering, Oxford and Basingstoke to break up the journey. You should see Oxford, Mother. It is such a lovely city with its sandstone colleges and many church spires, so much nicer than home, but then you'd expect that in such a place of learning.

I am to be posted on the coast near Chichester, which is so much closer to home now, and you'll be pleased to know that the plan is for us to remain there for some time. Our role will be to continue to patrol the coastline, much like our work in Lincolnshire. That suits me, of course, even though it's frustrating to be nearer home but to have no leave to visit you. Never mind, Mother, because I'm always thinking about you.

Your son,
    Tom

Tom was stationed near Chichester until April 1915 when he wrote home to say that his battalion had been moved on to St Leonard's on Sea. The tone of his letter was relaxed and cheerful, reassuring his mother that he appreciated his fortune to be stationed on the south coast of England. Beneath this light-hearted facade Tom started to feel restless. With the war showing no signs of abating, he was beginning to wish that he could do more for his country and wondered if he would be posted to France as a messenger cyclist after all.

For a while Harriet worried a little less about her two sons, realising her good fortune that both were still safe from harm. Each time she heard tragic news from another of her neighbours and friends she was aware that luck was running out for her twins and so she was not surprised to receive this short letter.

12th November, 1915

My dear Mother,

I'm afraid that my news this time is not so hopeful and I fear that soon I will be posted abroad. I had just returned from my patrol along the shore, cycling briskly to keep warm on this frosty morning, when I was informed that our battalion was to join forces with other units to be retrained for infantry service. I will miss my trusty bicycle, but even more than that, I wonder what the future might hold for me now.

I do so wish that I could travel to see you, Mother, but we are to move on to our training camp soon, (I'm afraid I can't say the exact location) where we are to undergo some serious training. I will write again as soon as I know more.

Your son,
Tom

It was in February 1916 that Harriet received the news that her dear, quiet son Tom was ready to be posted overseas. He was in Devonport awaiting the *SS Ceramic*, but it was not to France that this vessel would carry him, but to India. His own wish to be sent to France as a cyclist messenger for the troops had long since evaporated. Once his Battalion had been retrained for regular infantry work, he had expected to be sent to France at any moment. It was not to be, and so on February 4th the *SS Ceramic* left harbour, and as it sailed into the open waters of the Atlantic his only thoughts were that he longed to share with his brother his dread of travelling so far away from home.

Tom had gained news of his brother through spasmodic letters. Jack's light-hearted tales of danger and the chivalrous acts of the pilots whom he served so diligently only intensified his sense of loss at their distance. (The censored marks only added to his fear as he inserted thoughts of his own from his vivid imagination.) As the English shoreline disappeared on the horizon, he tried to immerse himself in the discipline of routine and leave thoughts of his family to his nights, when he often dreamed of St John's Road and his happy childhood experiences. These dreams were a continuous comfort to him as he faced the uncertainty of the months ahead.

Once they had reached India he was stationed at Bangalore until December and it took him a while to acclimatise to the unfamiliar surroundings; the contrast between the dusty poverty stricken streets with almost palatial buildings; the accosting of his senses by welcoming smells of spice filled markets and the less savoury odours of the slum dwellings and animals which disorientated his progress; the bright, almost fluorescent colours of clothes and furnishing with the grey of the unwashed.   These elements aside, his patrols were mostly as uneventful as his coastal patrols on the Sussex coast, and the men certainly made the most of any leisure time they had and so his long awaited letter home was received with relief:

10th November, 1916

My dear Mother,
    Though I am far away and I know you must worry, I would like you to be reassured that my stay here in India is more like an adventure than a battle. Our barracks are clean and certainly more comfortable than living in a tent and I write home to you from my bunk. I have put up the photo of the

family at Sarah's wedding to remind me of you all. Not that
I need a photograph to help me to think of home.

Thankfully, our duties at night are uneventful, but what is
more surprising is that we enjoy our spare time to the full. We
swim in the nearby lake, play polo on bicycles and last week,
you will find this hard to believe, but we took part in a
six-a-side football tournament at the stadium here in Bangalore
against a team from Calcutta. The stadium was packed and
even though we lost the match 1-0, I know that Jack would
be so jealous if he knew about the event.

Mind you, it's our games of bicycle polo that I am most
partial too, and I'm quite good at it, if you'll forgive the boast.

Unfortunately we are to move on from Bangalore next
month, heading north (so I've been told) and so I'm not sure
when I will be able to write to you again. Wherever I am
though, you are in my thoughts.

Your son,
Tom

In December, Tom's Battalion left Bangalore on the long
train journey north to a village near Peshawar called
Burham, during which he found himself absorbed in the
interesting sights of the countryside and villages which they
passed en route. Here they set up camp to commence their
mountain warfare training, but although their canvas homes
bore nothing of the relative comfort of the barracks he'd
just left behind, the men were blessed with warm days and
cool nights, perfect for their strenuous mountain warfare
training. It was during this time that Tom was promoted
to corporal, due to his diligent training and positive attitude
towards his unit.

It was one night in early January 1917, whilst sleeping
deeply after an exhausting day that Tom suffered from a

nightmare so real that it left him with pneumonia-like symptoms of fever and breathlessness.

He dreamt that he was on board a ship. There was a deafening explosion which woke him up and everywhere there was panic. As he struggled to put on some clothes, unable to grapple with his breeches, he hopped about helplessly and the ship began to list. He raced towards the cabin door, wrenched it open and joined the crew who were rushing towards the deck, falling into each other as the ship listed dangerously to one side. On deck he could see that it was no use heading for a life raft, since there was total chaos. With one dive he felt himself falling towards the sea, which he hit with such force that it winded him completely and he blacked out for several seconds. It was during those seconds that Tom saw his brother Jack sinking lifelessly before him, but when Tom tried to reach his brother the current lifted him to the surface and he spluttered, coughing up water as he regained his breath. He was just calling out to his brother, when one of the crew shook him awake.

As Tom woke up, he found a fellow Corporal crouched over him in his tent with his hand on Tom's shoulder. He was taken to the medical tent where he continued to sleep fitfully for two days, observed by the puzzled doctors, who initially thought he must have contracted malaria.

Tom was confined to the small medical tent while his symptoms persisted, but the doctors could find nothing physically wrong with Corporal Tom Newton. During the day he would doze off and the dream would repeat itself, but as the feelings of suffocation consumed him, he would have such a coughing, gasping fit that he would awaken drenched in sweat. One night he seemed to escape the dream loop at last:

He found himself back in the water, but by now he was swimming to the shore. Once sitting safely on the beach to recover from the ordeal, he sat in a trance as he watched his ship sink below the waves. Once the swell had subsided it seemed impossible to imagine that the ship had been there at all, but as he strained to identify the many men swimming to shore he was so relieved to recognise the face of his brother, Jack.

For the first time in forty eight hours he sank into a deep and undisturbed sleep, so much so that in the morning he was fully recovered and returned to his unit. Even though, to everyone around him Tom appeared to be well again, the fear he experienced for Jack was palpable. Unfortunately, two weeks later, Tom experienced an equally disturbing nightmare. When he awoke the following morning his whole body was seared with excruciating pain. His head throbbed and he had little feeling in his legs.

He was helped back to the medical tent and the doctors attempted to question him, but from that point on Tom hardly uttered a word, disappearing more and more into his own little world, any communication with his fellow men perfunctory. Though his physical symptoms waned, his mental ones were as acute as ever.

In March, as his battalion prepared to travel on to the Simla Hills, it was obvious that Tom was not fit enough to join them. Instead he remained at the makeshift medical tent and was cared for by the VAD nurses stationed there. It was not his symptoms which worried the doctors most about Tom and deemed him unfit to serve, even before he had reached any action, but a mysterious mental state, which the doctors had only witnessed in cases of shell shock. Tom hadn't spoken a word since his admission and though his body had recovered physically quite quickly, his deep eyes were vacant, as if life itself had drained away.

Rather than to continue as a burden to his platoon, the decision was made to send him by cart back to Karachi. He was kept company by a few injured men and those who were suffering from severe dysentery or malaria and it was this uncomfortable journey which sowed the seeds for Tom's poetry.

Once in Karachi he was not a priority for the ships in harbour waiting to take the injured back to Blighty. He remained in Karachi Military Hospital, under the watchful eyes of the nurses there, for over a month.

During that month, one nurse in particular had taken a special interest in this man with the faraway grey eyes, when others had dismissed him for more urgent cases in need of desperate medical attention. In her spare time, Nurse Gladys Rees sought out Corporal Newton and spent time reading and talking to him. His lack of response did little to deter her; neither did the disparaging remarks from the other staff, who had no patience for a malingerer.

She wrote a postcard for him to his mother, explaining that he was well and that he would soon be on his way home. Gladys was pleased when she persuaded the corporal to write the address of his mother on the card. This was the first positive response from this young man, at which point, as he concentrated intently on his painfully slow moving hand, she noticed a tear creep inadvertently into the corner of his eyes and wondered what haunted this corporal so severely.

The doctor felt that he should be given time to recover and possibly could be sent back to active service, but a month later, with no visible sign of improvement, Tom was dispatched for home. Gladys watched him as he boarded the ship and was rewarded by a slight lift of his hand, which could barely pass as a wave in her direction, as he turned and disappeared. Although feeling a little despondent at her failure to reach this corporal, with a shrug of her shoulders she returned to her all-consuming duties. Having carefully written down Tom's mother's address, she placed it safely inside her diary, alongside the unfinished poem she had found in his pocket, which she had not been able to bring herself to return. She hid this in the cramped quarters which she shared with three other nurses and tried to forget his haunted eyes staring straight through her.

Occasionally, as she wrote in her diary at night, she would reread the poem and wonder who Jack was, the man who seemed to have stolen her corporal's heart.

I miss you, Jack, with all my heart and soul;
If only I had followed you;
If only I could have kept you safe;
Who knows your pain?
Who was with you when you needed me most?
As we journey along God forsaken paths I think of you.
As the sun beats down relentlessly upon my back I am so alone.
Who are these men?
Why am I here?
Where are we going on this rough road?
What is this desolate, dusty place of rocks and mountains?
I cannot go on another day without you . . .

After this, there were a few words crossed out, *duty, home, Jack, illness, pain....* and then it was as if the writer had given up trying and she imagined him pushing the paper into his top pocket before slipping into the relief of sleep.

One day, Nurse Gladys Rees decided, she would follow the trail to Corporal Thomas Newton's mother as soon as she returned to England and see if he had recovered. She deceived herself that her motives were of curiosity and concern for his wellbeing and tried to forget that she had fallen in love with this silent soldier.

Chapter 22

IT WAS IN May 1917 that Anthony came home on leave. His request to learn to fly had finally been approved and he was allowed forty eight hours with his family before reporting back to Fort Grange. He was overjoyed to see Sarah and Timothy, who was a little shy of his father and hid behind his mother's skirts when they met at the station.

'Hasn't my little man grown up? Have you been looking after Mother for me?'

Anthony held out his hand and Timothy's curiosity overcame his shyness as he reached up to take his father's hand in his.

'What news of Tom and Jack, then?'

'Grandma heard from Tom last week. We can't quite work it out, but having travelled all that way to India, he is being sent home. He's not injured as far as we can tell but it's a bit of a mystery.'

'He's safe, anyway. That's the main thing. And Jack? Is he still at Calshot?'

'No, he isn't. Hannah and Grandma were cross with him when he volunteered and what with Tom being sent so far away, we were distraught when one of his letters to Hannah announced that his ship was going to Turkey.'

Sarah didn't add that she was very concerned about Jack, because Timothy was listening.

Taking her cue Anthony asked,

'And how is my little man? Are you too big to sit on your father's shoulders now?'

Without waiting for a reply he swung Timothy up so that he straddled his father's neck, one foot tapping on the half wing sewn on to his uniform.

'That'll be full wings soon. You'll see. You'll be proud of your father then.'

As if on cue three sea planes flew over head and circled the area before preparing to alight on the Itchen River near the Supermarine factory. Following their flight, Anthony suddenly frowned with a memory of one of Sarah's letters.

'I'm not happy with you working at the factory, Sarah. That's men's work. You should be at home looking after our son.'

Sarah sighed, not wanting to have an argument as soon as her husband had arrived.

'Timothy's fine with grandma and anyway he'll be starting school soon. I had no choice really, Anthony. I needed to pay my way since grandma rarely has fee-paying guests now and they are desperate for workers at the factory.'

'Are you saying that the money sent from me isn't enough, Sarah?'

'I'm not saying that at all, but Hannah and I wanted to do our bit for the country. With few young men left here, the work wouldn't get done if women like us didn't play our part.'

'And what are you doing there that's so important?'

'We're sewing linen bags for the wings. It takes a lot of patience since we have to fray the edges so that when they are stretched on the wings and sealed with layers of dope it is all neat and tight.'

Anthony wanted to mend their differences by saying how the airmen appreciated the painstaking work, and that there was no doubt in his mind that the skills of the seamstresses saved lives on the Western Front, but unfortunately for Sarah their conversation was brought to an abrupt halt as they reached Bourton Villas. They piled into the kitchen, joining Harriet and Hannah, who were preparing the supper.

Harriet gave Anthony a warm welcome, passing a questioning look towards her daughter, since she already sensed the tense atmosphere between them.

'It's so good to see you, Anthony. Come and sit down and tell us all of your news!'

She would have liked to have given her daughter a piece of her mind for being so selfish. After all, so many families had received such tragic news of loved ones lost forever that Sarah should be grateful to have Anthony home. His visit, albeit short, was proof that young men *did* come home and this gave Harriet renewed hope for Tom and Jack in the months ahead.

'Yes, Anthony. So good to see you back! What news of France?' asked Ernest, who had just come in the back door to join the now crowded kitchen.

With thoughts of their little tiff on the backburner for a while, Anthony gave a vivid description of how it felt to be in the air and of the many the antics of the pilots when they were relaxing after harrowing missions. He omitted to describe the desolation and devastation he had witnessed below, for the sake of the children.

Ernest bade them farewell and Hannah and Sarah served a meal of potatoes, broad beans and a little ham, which Anthony did not realise was the best meal the family had eaten for weeks. He noticed with dismay how little the women ate themselves, preferring to give part of their portions to the children and himself and his attitude towards his wayward wife softened.

As they were finishing their meagre meal Ernest rushed back inside brandishing a newspaper in his hand.

'Look at this, Mother!' he exclaimed, barely acknowledging Anthony and Sarah.

The family crowded round Ernest as he read the front page article aloud.

'*HMS Ben My Chree* was hit by shellfire off the coast of Turkey last week. The ship sank in Castelorizo Harbour but all the crew were rescued or swam safely to shore.'

Hannah went white with the news and gripped hold of her little girl's hand. Seeing the effect his words had on his sister-in-law, Ernest added with enthusiasm,

'Don't worry, Hannah. That means Jack might be home soon.'

Harriet sat down in her armchair taking the newspaper from Ernest, willing herself to be reassured by the words she reread. Once the significance of Ernest's words sank in, she smiled encouragingly at Hannah.

'That'll be something to truly celebrate, won't it, Hannah?

Just before she handed the paper back to Ernest she noticed the now familiar name of the reporter Harry Harper in print at the bottom of the page and wondered if he too was in Port Said or still in London, gleaning what news he could to encourage people not to lose heart.

Once normal conversation had been resumed, Ernest suggested that Anthony come out for a jar and leave the women to clear away, but however tempting it sounded, Anthony declined. Out of the corner of his eye he saw Sarah's shoulders relax a little and when he offered to put Timothy to bed he was rewarded by a genuine smile. That night, as if both were aware that their time together was precious, they put aside their stormy differences and united in love once more.

The following morning, Sarah, Anthony and Timothy caught the train to Hamble to spend a night at his parents before he continued on to Fort Grange for his training, with Sarah and Timothy returning to Woolston. Anthony thought of attempting to persuade Sarah to remain with his parents for the duration of the war. It was obvious that, although the meal they had shared was less lavish than before the troubles began, it was still more abundant than those at Bourton Villas. Nevertheless, he remained quiet and was aware that there was an unwritten code of silence between them, of forbidden subjects which might cause a further rift.

At the station he shook his son's hand and embraced Sarah, looking deep down into her eyes as they drew apart.

'Take care of our little man, Sarah. I hope that I will be able to call in once more before returning to France.'

'You know I will,' replied Sarah, gently.

After Sarah and Timothy had stood on the platform to wave Anthony goodbye they sat in the waiting room for half an hour before they journeyed in the other direction.

Chapter 23

HARRIET WAS ALONE when there was a firm knock at her front door. Her last guests had left an hour before and she was tidying up the bedrooms to prepare for any unexpected arrivals; a large pile of linen to be washed sat on the landing behind her. She climbed over it and rushed downstairs, but even before she opened the door she could make out the dark uniform of the telegram boy through the long narrow window.

In a dreamlike state she opened the door, leaving just enough of a gap for the envelope to be pushed towards her. It was as if she hoped that she could keep the bad news at bay. The young lad touched his cap out of respect before racing off on his bicycle. Harriet shut the door and sat down on the stairs. Her eyes filled with tears as she held the envelope between her shaking fingers. It didn't help that so far the family had been blessed with luck. She had watched so many people torn apart with grief as they struggled to come to terms with the loss of loved ones.

Suddenly, for the first time in what felt like a lifetime, her mind was transported back to Riduna. She closed her eyes, trying to hold back the tears and a vivid picture of her parents' graves appeared before her. In her mind she saw herself as a young girl kneeling by that grave, carefully placing wild flowers on the loose earth mound. She had experienced so much loss in younger life that she had hoped against hope that she'd left it far behind her on Riduna. Life wasn't like that and you couldn't run away from it.

Harriet struggled to her feet, the envelope slipping on to the floor in front of her. She ignored it, struggling to reach the back door and slipped outside for air. Falling to her knees she picked up some of the soil which slipped though her fingers. As she did this, in her dreamlike state, she was aware that she was being watched. Looking up she noticed the little robin a few feet away and it was at that moment that she let out an agonised cry and the tears began to flow freely.

It was Sarah who found her mother like this and, wishing to protect Timothy from witnessing her mother's grief, but guessing the worst, she ushered him upstairs to their room, noticing the unopened envelope at the bottom of the stairs. She left Timothy with his prized wooden soldiers which his father had given him, and some paper and a pencil, encouraging him to draw a picture for his father. Timothy looked quizzically up at his mother.

'What's the matter with grandma?' he asked.

'I don't know, Timothy, to tell you the truth. I'll just pop down to see her and make a cup of tea. Will you be a good boy for Mother and stay here?'

Timothy nodded solemnly and Sarah rushed back downstairs, picking up the envelope as she went. For a few moments she held it between her fingers, her mind racing with disjointed thoughts. It couldn't be about Anthony because the telegram would be addressed to herself and not to her mother. There again it was unlikely to be about Jack, since the recent news was that he was safe. Surely it couldn't be Tom. No, not dear Tom.

She prayed to God that it was not so. After all, until the telegram was read, they really didn't know the truth.

Gently Sarah encouraged Harriet to sit on the garden bench and she put her arms about her mother's shoulders. It was so distressing to see her like this so soon after she had recovered from her father's death. This horrible war, she thought.

'It may not be the news you fear, Mother. Why don't you open it? Then at least we'll know.'

When her mother didn't reply she asked,

'Shall I, then?'

Just at that point Hannah came in through the back door with Phyllis but seeing the distraught faces she froze. She looked down at the envelope in Sarah's hand and read *Mrs H Newton*.

'That's addressed to me,' she said in an angry tone as she grasped the envelope close to her.

Straight away she ripped it open and slumped down on to the garden bench, covering her mouth to stifle a gasp. Phyllis stood fearfully watching her mother's distraught face like a lost soul, her hand reaching out and resting on her mother's arm. The telegram fell down on to the path in front of Hannah.

Sarah glanced down and the less than comforting words of:

'*...regret to inform you that Jack Newton was killed in an unfortunate accident whilst performing his duties in Port Said...*' swam out of the page before her eyes. As she picked up the telegram Sarah couldn't hold back the tears, all her thoughts were of her lively, cheerful brother. She had no need to show it to Harriet because her mother's sixth sense already knew the truth.

After a few moments Sarah encouraged her mother to come into the kitchen and sit down beside the hearth. As she did so, she heard Hannah rush upstairs, followed close behind by Phyllis. After their bedroom door banged shut there was silence. Sarah followed them upstairs, not wanting to leave her son alone for long, and feeling in a daze she picked up the pile of washing, encouraging Timothy to follow her.

'How is Grandma?' he asked as they were on their way down.

'I think Grandma needs you to cheer her up,' Sarah replied.

In a daze she took the laundry out to the scullery, putting it in to soak in the large tin bath on the floor under the long wooden airier.

When Sarah returned to the large homely kitchen she had to smile when she found little Timothy snuggled on his grandmother's lap, with his arms tightly around her neck, her face nestled in his hair.

Chapter 24

TOM ARRIVED AT Southampton Docks in early June 1917 following a harrowing journey. Without the care and encouragement of the kind nurse in Karachi, Tom was a shadow of his former self. His mute, vacant, demeanour gave him the appearance of someone not quite sound in mind. Marie stood at the dockside, watching while the injured and sick walked or were carried off the ship. She went to the most serious cases first as she always did, offering them words of comfort and welcoming them home with good humour. It was while she was encouraging an armless young man to dictate his address to her that she noticed the quiet distant young man propped up on a bollard nearby. Marie walked over to him and gently asked him if he would like to fill in a postcard for home.

'How are you, ducks? Glad to be home I expect.'

There was a silent pause as Tom barely registered her presence. Not being one to give up too easily, Marie continued,

'Here's a postcard for your folks at home. Just to let them know you're safe, like. Can you fill in the address y'self or would you like me to do it for you?'

Marie waited another few seconds aware that she needed to see many more men before they were ushered or carried to the nearby transport. Just as she was about to give up, Tom held out his hand for her to stop, and his grey piercing eyes nearly broke her heart in two. Tom wrote the address slowly and deliberately and, when he had completed the task, he slumped back down on to the ground, head bowed low, as if it was just too much effort. Marie sighed and moved on. She had no time to spend with individuals but the encounter made her so despondent. She had wanted so much to do some good. The fleeting thought that these were the lucky ones did little to dispel her sadness; in fact it only made the situation acutely more painful.

On numerous occasions over the last year she had waited for Edward to come home then watched him arrive, low and dispirited after transporting a shipload of injured men back to Blighty, hardly saying a word to her, so unlike his normal hearty self.

One Sunday morning her sadness had been so uplifted by the sound of a Salvation Army band playing and singing hymns on the pier opposite their cottage that she went out to talk with them. She was so impressed by the calm positive nature of a lady called Alice that, there and then, she resolved to make her life count and offer her services in some way. Alice came back for a cup of tea and a bond of friendship was formed. Once Alice had heard Marie's story she realised that she would not be accepted in 'the fold' under her marital circumstances, but instead she suggested that she might help on the dockside. Here Alice was organising the volunteers somewhere nearby as Marie moved on to the next wounded soldier, the silent young man soon forgotten.

Tom was carried by cart to the train where he and the men with him were transported to The Royal Victoria Hospital at Netley. There he was met by the same derisory, mocking comments he had received in Karachi. No, he had no external injuries to justify his presence at the hospital, but it was as if his body was an empty shell and that the real Tom was lost somewhere in the world and that not even he could reach himself. He sat with his head bowed in a chair with a blanket draped over his lap half way along one of the endless corridors, no need to take up valuable bed space. He would rarely respond to the offer of food and, if anyone tried to feed him, with sheer exasperation he pushed them roughly away.

One nurse was just grumbling as she attempted to clear away the mess of food which had fallen on to the floor as Jane passed by.

'Why did you do that? It's such a waste! My family don't have half the food we have here and you go and push it on the floor. You're a disgrace to the country,' the trainee nurse muttered, not realising that Staff Nurse Jane Hanwell was right behind her.

The girl leapt to her feet.

'I'm sorry, Sister. I didn't know you were there,' she exclaimed.

'What is the meaning of this? How dare you speak to one of our patients like that, nurse! Go to my office at once, Nurse Bertha and wait for me there.'

Once the young nurse had gone, Jane bent down to look into this young man's eyes. She was shocked at seeing one of Harriet's sons staring vacantly through her as if she wasn't there.

'Hello, Tom,' she said in a gentle but cheerful voice, 'It's good to see you home safe. Your mother will be so relieved to have you back. We'd best get you to see the doctor and then hopefully we can discharge you.'

Tom barely registered her presence.

'Would you be kind enough to come with me?'

She offered Tom her arm, but when he didn't move she

knelt down beside him and looked into his downturned eyes.

'Do you remember me, Tom? I'm your mother's friend, Jane, down from London. She's always talking about you and she's going to be so happy to see you again.'

Jane realised to her dismay that she was speaking slowly as if he were a child. Upset by her own insensitivity she was about to fetch the doctor when Tom lifted his head slightly and stared through her, as if he was trying to remember who she was or, to be closer to the truth, those vacant grey eyes were pleading, 'Who am I?'

This response, albeit slight, was less than a second before his head dropped back to his chest and the thread between them was lost. Although, in some people's eyes, Jane had more pressing cases to attend to, her mature understanding of the sickness of the mind led her to different priorities. Jane knew that, without help, this young man might be lost to this world forever. In fact, if he continued to eat and drink as little as he was willing to at present, his days on this earth would be numbered.

Usually Jane was strict with her emotions, keeping them in check in order to cope with the sights of the desperately injured she saw at the hospital on a regular basis. With frustration she knew that if the soldiers had been given the correct medical support at the point of injury, their condition would have been far less critical today. It wasn't the first time that she longed to be back in the field and yet she knew in her heart that her role to train the young nurses here, keen to follow in her footsteps, (or the famous Florence Nightingale's, more likely) was as vital to the war effort as her presence could have been in one of the many makeshift hospital camps both in France and further afield. It was often equipment or supplies they lacked these days, rather than the enthusiasm of very knowledgeable young nurses. Youth was not on her side. She sighed as she paced along the corridor to talk to the doctor in charge of this wing of the hospital.

It was eight o'clock in the evening when she finally left his office, two hours after her long shift should have ended, and yet she couldn't help but to return to Tom once more. He was in a deep sleep, his head now back to one side and it was obvious that a more conscientious nurse had placed a pillow behind him. His head was resting on it, mouth open wide. Seeing his whole face for the first time, Jane was more concerned than ever. His regulation blue hospital uniform hid, to some extent, his thin limbs and torso, but nothing had prepared her for the sight of his gaunt grey face, and several days' stubble, giving the appearance of a man in his latter years of life, rather than the young lad he truly was.

With this image imprinted on her mind she returned to her office and, seeing a note on her desk from the trainee nurse she had long since forgotten, she realised quite how tired she was and sat down. The note apologized profusely for her thoughtless behaviour. Having waited half an hour for Jane to return, the nurse had decided to leave the note and return to her duties. It was obvious to Jane that this young girl had probably placed the pillow behind Tom's head and she smiled inadvertently at the thought.

Before leaving the hospital for the night Jane reached for her notepad and began to write a letter to Harriet. It was several weeks since she had visited the family in Woolston, lacking any free time, energy or inclination. Once more her world was so far removed from that of her friend's that she was concerned she would not know what to talk about. Jane preferred to spend any spare time she had talking with the VAD nurses in the huts behind the hospital, where unspoken experiences were acknowledged and where anger and frustration were understood. Now at last Jane had a point of contact with her best friend, unfortunately one that filled her with concern, but nevertheless a bridge between them.

10th June, 1917

My Dear Harriet,

I am so sorry that it is such a long time since I have been in touch with you but I'm sure you understand how demanding work is at present. At the end of my day, all I can do is sleep and sometimes even that bliss is illusive, leaving me tired and listless, not good company for anyone.

I have some important news for you and wanted to be the first to share it. A few days ago your Tom arrived on one of my wards. I'm sure that you would have heard by now that he is back in England but initially I know that the family are rarely informed as to which hospital their loved ones are sent.

I can understand your frustration, but this policy is for the wellbeing of all of the patients, who are encouraged to write home as soon as they can. It was quite a coincidence that Tom was brought to my attention, because my intervention is usually demanded for the more seriously injured cases and to support and advise the trainee nurses I work with. I was walking along one of the corridors today and I came across Tom quite by chance (if chance ever has anything to do with life and I sometimes doubt this). I need to warn you, Harriet, that he is seriously ill, but not in injuries which are easily recognised, diagnosed or healed, but in his mind.

After a long conversation with the doctor in charge of that ward, we believe that Tom is in some kind of living nightmare of his own and that the best place for him to recover is to come home to you. We hope that, when he is living amongst those who love him, he may return to us in mind, body and spirit. If anyone can reach young Tom, it is your good self.

With this in mind I hope to organise transport for us to come this Sunday morning. It means that I will miss the service here, which I am loath to do, and yet I do believe that I need time to talk with you and prepare you for what might lay ahead. I hope that my words have not shocked you too much.

I look forward to seeing you on Sunday.

Much love,
*   Jane*

With the letter completed and ready to post in the morning, Jane trudged slowly away from the hospital. She paused briefly, as she always did, to look out over Southampton Water, where the lights of ships, like glow worms in the dark, were following their relentless course both to and from the mouth of the river. They were almost certainly carrying more troops over to France but, worse still, they were returning with as many injured.

Chapter 25

IN THE FEW months after the news of Jack's death, the atmosphere at Bourton Villas had been subdued. Phyllis was understandably tearful, which seemed to irritate Hannah, whose despair had now turned to anger. Timothy, always the sensitive one, was forever offering gestures of affection to Phyllis, but this was more often than not rejected as Phyllis clamoured for her mother's attention. On the other hand, he warmed the hearts of his mother and grandmother, especially when he listened to one of Harriet's stories. Even when he presented them with gifts of little bugs and spiders in his father's empty matchboxes, it caused such amusement that it was a welcome distraction from the sufferings of war.

Harriet had received the mysterious postcard from Tom, reassuring her that he was safe on English shores but that he had been taken to hospital. She placed the postcard alongside her family photographs on the mantelpiece, a constant reminder of her ignorance as to his whereabouts. She was filled with frustration as she longed to be able to visit him, but had no way of finding out the location of the hospital. Harriet was unaware that the presence of the postcard was also a catalyst for Hannah's resentment that Tom's life had been spared but her beloved Jack had been taken from them.

The household was quiet, when Harriet had an unexpected visitor. Sarah and Hannah were at work and the children were at school when one of Jack's crew members, his best friend, Patrick Jones, kindly paid a visit. He arrived at Bourton Villas hobbling with a stick to support him and it was from Mr Jones that Harriet heard the truth about Jack's death. Once Harriet had settled him beside the hearth and made a cup of tea, he recounted the whole story.

He described Jack's bravery in launching the sea planes out in the Mediterranean and expressed his admiration for Jack, whose knowledge, experience and intuitive sixth sense when it came to maintaining their 'birds' had given them a reputation in the Navy for reliability and fortitude. The disaster at Castelorizo Harbour had been a sad end to a wonderful record of daring and success, as they prepared for mission after mission. Their pilots had come back with tales of bridges and roads destroyed to impede the progress of the enemy, trains and vehicles hit and useful intelligence and photos obtained. Mr Jones was so excited as he told his tale that it was sometimes difficult to believe that he had come to impart such bad tidings. Nevertheless he continued to describe how devastated they felt when the *Ben my Chree* was hit, but fortunately everyone was rescued.

'Jack and I, being strong swimmers were soon ashore, and watched with disbelief as she sank into the harbour. We were picked up by a French destroyer and taken back to Port Said where, as you can imagine, we went out to celebrate our safe return and fortune at being sent back to Blighty. We were just returning to the hotel which was our temporary quarters while we waited for news of our departure. The hotel was on the corner of a narrow junction, leading down to the harbour. We were feeling quite merry after our revelries. We weren't drunk, I can assure you, Mrs Newton, just very happy. Anyway, it was already dark and we were unprepared for the sight of the coal truck heading towards us. It was late arriving at port and in its hurry had taken the corner far too sharply, hitting both Jack and myself head-on, like. Jack had no chance, taking the full impact first and shielding me too. I was fortunate to come out of the accident with just a broken leg. All I can say, Mrs Newton, is that I'm truly sorry, but your Jack saved my life.'

There was a moment's pause as Harriet digested the news, her brain trying to register whether it eased the pain at all, or quite the opposite.

'I am really grateful to you for coming to tell me about my son. The telegram was so short. It didn't really tell us anything, but I'm glad that I know the truth now. Will you be able to stay to talk to Hannah, Jack's wife? There is a spare bed and you'd be more than welcome, after taking all this trouble to come to see us.'

Feeling slightly embarrassed now, and wishing to get away, Mr Jones made the excuse that he had a train to catch to return to London, but that he had come as soon as he had been able.

Just as he was about to leave, he hesitated.

'This was in Jack's pocket,' he said as he handed her an unsealed letter, which Jack had not had the chance to post. You might also like this picture. It was taken on our previous docking in Port Said. There's Jack, meself and some of the local crew members.'

Harriet thanked Mr Jones for coming, grasping the picture and letter tightly in her hand. Once he was out of sight along the road she looked down at the picture. A group of dishevelled men wearing tin hats, which she assumed was to keep off the sun, stood grinning from the deck of HMS *Ben my Chree*, standing proudly in front of a

Short sea plane. One of the men was holding the hoist hook in his hand, as if ready to begin their role of lowering the plane into the water for the next reconnaissance mission.

She sat down in her armchair looking at the cheerful face of her son, drawing comfort from the realisation that he was where he wanted to be, right in the centre of the action, yet feeling cheated that, but for a most unfortunate accident, her cheeky son would soon have been at home with her once more.

She placed the photo next to the postcard from Tom and thought of her two sons, so similar in looks but so different in nature. She could do nothing about her dear Jack but she fretted listlessly as to how she could find out about Tom's whereabouts and maybe visit him in hospital, yet there was no clue on the card as to where he was being sent. With frustration, she got to her feet and absentmindedly began to dust the over-dusted furniture. Harriet had little purpose in life but to keep her family alive and as nourished as they could be, with the little she was able to grow or purchase. There were few visitors staying with her now, but since both the girls were working at Supermarine they had no financial concerns. Compared to most she was fortunate. All but one of her sons had safely returned to England and yet with no challenge to occupy her days, there was something missing in her life. Everyone else seemed to be 'doing their bit' for the cause, whatever that may be.

A few moments later, as if answering her plea, the letter from Jane arrived on the mat. Eagerly she tore the seal and read the contents. Her mind raced and oscillated between hope and fear as she tried to imagine her quiet, gentle son, Tom. What had happened in his war to cause such an extreme reaction?

That evening she shared her news with Hannah and Sarah after the children had been put to bed. Hannah took the sealed letter which Mr Jones had left, but did not open it, fearful of the emotions it might unleash, giving her hope when she knew there was none. She would read it later when she was on her own or leave it until she was stronger. She too was drawn to gaze on the photograph, that same cheeky grin which had wooed and won her heart, much to the amazement of her parents. They had been a mismatch and yet she knew that Jack, in his own way, had been as devoted a husband and father as she could have ever have wished for.

Harriet noticed Hannah's damp eyes as she headed for bed that night and with a lump in her throat wondered how long her guests would remain in her household now that there was no hope of Jack's return. She was consoled by the fact that her daughter-in-law's parent's lived in a tiny cottage in Itchen Ferry village and had no spare room for Hannah and Phyllis whereas, at present, Harriet had rooms to spare.

Sarah, on the other hand, seemed content to remain with her and she was so grateful of her daughter's presence. Sarah's sometimes fraught relationship with her husband, Anthony, was a concern, but Harriet knew that those petty arguments were meaningless at a time like this and she noticed that even her stubborn daughter had softened in her attitude since the death of her favourite brother. Harriet was under no illusion that Anthony and Sarah's difficulties were one-sided and she had to admit that she felt more sympathy for Anthony on many occasions.

The next few days seemed endless to Harriet as she waited impatiently to see her son Tom back home once more. When the day finally arrived she was glad that she had had the foresight to send the rest of the family to church, so that, when she finally heard the sound of the horse and trap stop outside her front door, she was alone. As she headed for the front door she braced herself, fearful of what she might see and yet nothing prepared her for the first sight of her gaunt, lifeless son.

It was Jane, with her skills as a nurse, who was able to coax Tom down from the buggy and into Bourton Villas. Tom registered neither recognition nor emotion as he set eyes on Harriet for the first time, although he did lift his head for his grey eyes to pierce through hers, as he had done with Jane a few days ago.

It took all the courage Harriet could muster so that she did not break down at this encounter and Jane was proud of her friend as she pulled herself together and came to Jane's aid, taking Tom's other arm firmly in hers, talking to him enthusiastically as they made the painfully slow progress into the kitchen. Jane bade the porter goodbye, thanking him for his kind gesture of giving up his Sunday morning to bring her charge to Woolston. She would return to the hospital later by train, but didn't think she could have coped with Tom on the train without support.

Harriet busied herself with making tea, ever conscious of the presence of her lifeless son, who, now seated in his father Joe's armchair had allowed his head to slump on his chest yet again and had fallen into a fitful sleep. Harriet fetched a pillow and blanket from upstairs and gently placed the pillow behind Tom's head and blanket over his knees. The ladies held their breath as Tom made an audible sigh before sinking into a deep sleep and Harriet drew comfort in the fact that maybe he knew that he was finally at home.

Jane and Harriet sat up at the large kitchen table so as not to disturb Tom, and whispered greetings, sharing their news of the family and talking of the food shortages. When they got on to the difficult subject of Tom, Harriet indicated that they should move to the guest house dining room.

'How is he, Jane, and what can I do to help him?' Harriet asked when they were alone together.

'I will be frank with you and say that I cannot give you a true answer. We know so little about mental trauma that I can only make suggestions. In fact, watching your intuitive thoughtfulness and care, I believe that your wisdom will know how to help Tom come back to us. When I spoke to the doctor, we both felt that maybe Tom's mind might begin to recover once back in your loving environment.'

'You say "maybe", Jane?'

'Yes Harriet, we have never been anything but honest with each other. We don't know what's wrong with Tom or what triggered such a bad reaction. What we do know, from the notes of the doctor on board his ship returning to England, is that he wasn't involved directly in fighting over there. If he had been, then it may have shed some light on to his disturbing condition. "Shell shock" is a condition we are only just beginning to understand. By all accounts, Tom began to show signs of a disturbed mind long before that. Not long after he'd reached India, in fact, but I'm afraid I can't be more help to you.'

'Has he spoken at all since he's been at the hospital?'

'His notes say that he's not uttered a word since arriving at Karachi, maybe before that.'

Harriet's face showed the deep furrows of concern for her son and Jane was sad that she could offer no false hope or reassurance, though she added:

'I can only say that often, when patients have gone through some trauma, they can sink into themselves and Tom may well come out of it as suddenly as he was afflicted.'

With that glimmer of hope the ladies returned to the kitchen where Harriet prepared the light meal for her family and honoured guest. It was so good to have Tom home, regardless of his state of mind, and such a reassurance to see Jane again. Harriet had to cling on to the hope that her son would come back to her, in mind and spirit as well as in body.

Jane noticed the photograph of Jack over the hearth. Harriet told her about the visit of Jack's friend, Mr Jones, and recounted the story of the sinking of the *Ben my Chree* and the tragic accident in Port Said. Looking over towards Tom, a glimmer of a thought began to form in her mind. As if feeling her eyes upon him he stirred and, with his head resting back on his pillow, his eyes met Jane's and she thought that he showed a fleeting sign of recognition. Jane grasped the opportunity and took the photograph over to show Tom and was surprised to see his eyes water and a couple of tear drops fall down his cheek. Soon the moment was gone and, as if it was all too much effort, Tom's head slumped back down on his chest.

Harriet ran to his side and gently placed the pillow so that his vacant eyes could see her. She took the photograph from Jane and placed it back on the shelf, glancing momentarily at her son. They were quiet for a few moments.

'How is the business going?' Jane asked to change the subject, although she already knew the answer.

'It was going so well before the war and then there was a steady trickle of visitors, but once there seemed no end in sight to the war and food became in short supply, people stopped travelling altogether. Times are hard for everyone; so much bad news,' Harriet's answer trailed off between them.

'... but with Sarah and Hannah working full time at Supermarine we make ends meet and we're fine.'

Jane sat thoughtfully for a few moments wondering if it was the right time to make her suggestion. Finally she reasoned that you never really knew the right time.

'I have had an idea, Harriet, but you may not think it's a good one. Why don't you offer your spare rooms for convalescence for soldiers returning from the war? They may not need nursing care anymore but some just aren't ready to return home. It's natural for you to be kind but firm, like you are with Tom, and we are desperately short of places like that. It would free up beds at the hospital for more urgent cases. What do you think?'

She watched Harriet, who was obviously mulling over the idea before she replied.

'I know what you are saying, Jane. I have felt lost without a purpose great enough to distract me since losing Jack. You must feel so fulfilled in your kind of work. I'll certainly think about it seriously, but I must concentrate my attentions to settling Tom home for the time being and that might take some time.'

At that moment the rest of the family piled in from church and apart from signalling for the children to talk quietly, they ignored their uncle and Tom did not stir from his slumbers. Finally, when he did wake up, lunch was nearly over. Tom lifted his head up and Sarah beamed at him.

'Hello, Tom. Welcome home! Come and say hello to your Uncle Tom, Timothy.'

Shyly Timothy came forward and in his usual sensitive way he took Tom's hand and held it between his own and smiled up at Tom saying, 'Hello Uncle Tom. It's so good to have another man in the house!' to which everyone laughed, which eased the tension of the moment.

Phyllis was far too shy to come forward but hid behind her mother's skirt as Hannah came forward and gave Tom a peck on the forehead. Harriet and Sarah could not fail to notice Hannah's watery eyes and knew that she couldn't help but wish that it was her husband, Jack, who was before her.

'It's time I went back to the hospital, I'm afraid. You don't know how wonderful it's been to share a family meal again. Will you manage, Harriet?'

'We'll be just fine,' exclaimed Harriet who was

successfully encouraging Tom to eat some food.

At first Harriet had attempted to feed Tom, but another sign of hope was when he pushed her hand away gruffly and began slowly and painstakingly lifting the bread to his mouth himself. Harriet glanced up at Jane and they shared the first glimmer of a hopeful smile that day. Sarah came to sit by her brother as Harriet rose to follow Jane to the front door.

'I'll try and come over again in a couple of weeks, but you know how it is.'

Harriet didn't like to imagine Jane's everyday life at the hospital. The suffering she'd experienced between family and within their close community was more than enough for her to bear at present.

'Do you think he will ever truly come back to us?' she whispered, a touch of desperation colouring her voice.

Jane hugged her friend.

'I truly hope so. I've seen cases when the patient improves gradually like Tom, but occasionally it happens very suddenly.'

Jane didn't like to add that she also knew cases when nothing changed at all. 'It was a good sign that he shed a few tears when saw the picture of Jack.'

Harriet looked puzzled for a moment.

'How did he know that Jack was dead? How could he possibly have known? He's only just returned to England himself and from a totally different part of the world.'

Jane looked confused and then it was if a light went on in her memory.

'I don't want to give you false hope, but I know I've read something somewhere which might shed some light on Tom's situation. So far, Tom's condition has mystified the doctors, but I think I might know what's happened, but I need to do some research before I share it with you.'

Jane gave her friend one last hug as if she needed the reassurance herself.

'It's so good to be close to you again,' she said as she walked briskly away up the road so that she didn't miss the Sunday afternoon train.

Harriet stood watching her leave and waved as Jane turned the corner and was out of sight. She was wondering what on earth her friend was thinking about. Harriet smiled to herself. This was the Jane she remembered and loved from their early days on Riduna and she wouldn't even try to guess what was on her friend's mind. At least Tom was safely home. That was enough for now.

In fact, Tom improved gradually over the next couple of weeks. He didn't speak, but by the time Jane came over two weeks later he had taken over the work in the garden from Harriet and seemed to find some comfort from weeding, watering and tending the plants. When they glanced out of the back door towards him, Harriet audibly drew breath as they witnessed Tom holding a handful of crumbs out to a little robin and they gazed in awe as the tiny bird hopped on to Tom's outstretched hand.

The ladies crept back into the kitchen, their spirits enlightened by what they had just witnessed and Jane could barely wait to share her news.

'After I left you the other Sunday I went back to my lodgings and searched through my journals until the early hours of the following morning. Working a full shift the next day was a challenge after that, I can tell you, but I was so excited to share my findings with the doctor in charge of Tom at The Victoria.'

'What was it about?' asked Harriet eagerly.

Not wanting to shorten her story, Jane continued,

'I had a long discussion with Dr Stevenson and he agreed that I might have a plausible solution to Tom's case and congratulated me and asked if I would keep an account of Tom's progress and write an article myself.'

Harriet, finding it impossible to contain her impatience any longer, exclaimed, 'What on earth are you talking about Jane? You've completely lost me and you're talking in riddles.'

'I'm sorry, Harriet,' Jane replied, realising that, to her friend her research was meaningless and that Harriet only wanted to know what was the matter with her son.

'I believe that Tom is showing sympathetic symptoms with his twin brother, Jack. His notes are consistent with showing that he began to suffer nightmares when Jack's ship went down. After that, he recovered somewhat, but the impact of his brother's death hit him hard subconsciously. His nightmares returned and he fell into a world of his own.'

'But he didn't *know* that his brother had died. How could he know?' exclaimed Harriet, sitting down suddenly.

'That's what I am trying to explain, Harriet. We don't know how, and we can't be certain, but some articles have been written about twins being so close that they knew instinctively what was happening to each other.'

Harriet remembered the many occasions her quiet son was home and suddenly inexplicably, he would yell out in pain. Running to Tom's aid she would find that there was nothing amiss but a few minutes later would be surprised to see the boisterous Jack returning from some scrap with his friends with some part of him injured. It certainly had a ring of truth. If he really "felt" his brother's death, then it wasn't surprising that he'd retreated into his own shell.

'Would you mind keeping a diary for me, Harriet? Note down anything you notice, any changes good or bad, even if there is no change at all. It could be of great help to us.'

'Of course I will, Jane. It may help me to understand my son a little more.'

'Have you thought about my suggestion?'

'Yes, I have as a matter of fact, and I've already discussed how we can change the arrangements here on a temporary basis with Ernest. Although Tom can get upstairs, we thought of turning the dining room into a combined eating and rest area, freeing the front room to be turned into a bedroom for maybe two men. That would leave another room free upstairs next to Tom's. I feel that Tom needs his own space for now but the family spends most of the time in the kitchen, or in their rooms, so it will be no hardship for them. What do you think, Jane?'

'I'm impressed but I shouldn't be surprised,' laughed Jane. 'You are a wonderful lady and the best friend I could ever have.'

The following week two 'patients' arrived to take up residence at Bourton Villas. Their injuries were healing nicely, but in both cases it was their mental states which caused concern and the doctors felt that, though they couldn't continue to occupy beds on the wards, they needed recovery time before returning to their families. One had lost an arm and the other had incurred such chest injuries that he would never fight again. With encouragement from Harriet and a quiet secure environment with no pressure, they began to heal mentally from their traumas. Each man took a differing time to recover and at the end of their stay many were reluctant to leave the security of their life at Bourton Villas.

Harriet helped to prepare them for the time ahead, getting the men to help with chores as soon as they were able. Integrating back in civilian life would be far from easy, since they would rarely be able to resume the roles they held before the war. In fact, seeing Hannah and Sarah return from a full day's work helped in some ways to prepare them for the difficulties which lay ahead. The old order of women at home in their place was possibly over for good and this was often the hardest lesson for the men to learn.

Patients came and left, but Tom's progress had reached a plateau. Sometimes Harriet despaired that Tom would ever speak again, as she listened to the light banter between her residents, but she continued to keep her journal for Jane, nevertheless. In fact, this was encouraging because it made her more observant of the slightest differences in Tom's demeanour. Apart from her concerns for Tom, Harriet felt more at peace than she had since the start of the war. With two of her three sons safely nearby, she knew that she was fortunate and had at last found a purpose in life to replace those feelings of listlessness of a few months earlier.

Chapter 26

ANTHONY STARTED HIS training in earnest on the following morning after leaving Bourton Villas. Initially he was back in the classroom again, trying not to let his impatience show, but a month later his dream to take controls of an Avro 504 finally came true. As he sat in the cockpit of this sturdy wooden biplane, with his instructor a few feet behind him, he was full of nervous anticipation. His lifeline was a headpiece which had a pipe in contact with his trainer. This new invention was the talk of the whole fort. He was lucky enough to be using it since 'The Gosport Tube' as it became known, had only come into service in the last couple of months after the famous Major Robert Smith Barry[6] came to the training camp and saw the disastrous effects of the haphazard methods of communicating instructions in the past. Looking back, it was surprising that they had not lost most of their pilots, since instructions had either been flagged from the ground or bellowed out from the cockpit behind the new recruit, in a two seater that is.

The propeller was spun, the engine fired on the third attempt and then, with the chocks removed, the Avro 504 finally rolled forward. Anthony concentrated hard on his training and the endless stream of instructions he was hearing, so much so that he was hardly aware of the moment he was airborne. One moment the plane was bouncing along the ground, his hands gripping the stick before him. He took a deep breath, opened the throttle, faster and faster she sped across the grass and finally the tail lifted, and as he eased back on the control stick, gently lifting the nose up, she was away!

Once in the air, the instructions from behind were more spasmodic and Anthony began to relax, breath normally again and feel his control of the aircraft as if he and the plane had become one. He was a natural and the instructor soon realised that only an occasional prompt was required before they were preparing to land.

Anthony's training was a mere six weeks before he was deemed proficient enough to be sent back to France and his Commanding Officer proudly presented him with his full wings. With only fifteen independent flying hours on his record he wasn't chosen to fly in the 'ferry' squadron, who were taking the planes over the water. That following afternoon, before heading to the train station, he watched in awe as the squadron made ready for their departure across the channel. The pilots donned their leather coats, sheepskin boots, polished goggles and mufflers, finally climbing into their waiting aircraft. One by one the planes, wings shining in the sunshine, turned on their engines and eased forward, taking off at three minute intervals. Gradually the deafening roar was replaced by a gentle hum as the aircraft became small birds in the cloudless sky above. All that remained was the pungent smell of burnt engine oil wafting towards him.

Anthony was given three days leave before he had to report to Southampton Docks for his ship, bound for Le Havre. Once he had arrived at Bourton Villas he learnt the news of Jack's death and it was as if both he and Sarah were given a wakeup call, suddenly aware just how precious their moments together would be. The atmosphere at the guesthouse was quite subdued. With less and less to eat, Anthony was alarmed that all the women in the household had lost so much weight, especially Hannah, who understandably looked constantly listless as she tried to come to terms with her husband's death. Nevertheless, although he was sorely tempted to repeat his suggestion that Sarah move to Hamble, he resisted, knowing the friction it would cause. Instead, they went for walks together when they could. They visited his parents in Hamble for a day, where it seemed that the troubles of the war were far away for a brief few hours, and otherwise he just enjoyed the company of Sarah and his beloved son.

On the last morning, Anthony came down to find Sarah looking lovingly at the photograph of their wedding day on the mantelpiece. She looked up with watery eyes, and with the memories of their passionate moments during their last night together he folded her in his arms. As Timothy came into the room with Harriet they separated, Anthony lifting his son up on to his broad shoulders, his legs now brushing against Anthony's full wings, worn so proudly on his tunic above his heart.

All too soon it was time for Anthony to leave. Sarah wished to go with him to Southampton but he persuaded her against it, knowing that the sights she might see could distress her all the more. Just as they had done before, Sarah and Timothy walked Anthony to the *Floating Bridge*. They said little as they embraced and all the while the ferry journeyed slowly to the other side of the river Anthony kept his eyes on the lonely figures standing on the hard, the large chain, which pulled him further and further away from them, clunking noisily beside them.

After an uneventful crossing to Le Havre, Anthony was

transported by barge up the river towards Rouen. The small poverty stricken hamlets they passed by, with tin roofed cottages and muddy, rubbish strewn back yards, were such a contrast to his comfortable home in Hamble, with its floral garden and beautiful view of the river. It was a relief to see the church spires of Rouen on the skyline and pass the splendid shuttered buildings. From there he was transported by train to St Omer, the RFC Headquarters and the place where he would learn the real art of flying, before being let loose on his own missions at the Front. The depot was buzzing with activity but his Commanding Officer showed him to his 'home' for the duration, a tepee style of tent set in rows alongside the aircraft hangers in front of which a flock of single seater SE5As were waiting in eager anticipation to take off.

It was during the following month of July 1917, here at St Omer, that Anthony truly learnt to fly, swooping and turning his aircraft into a dive, judging the speed precisely and recognising the distinct differences in the sounds of his engine. He began to understand that a shudder, or unfamiliar vibration, was more likely to be due to his own mishandling rather than the fault of the plane itself. His respect for both his aircraft and those with obvious skill and experience around him grew and grew. He flew higher than he had known was possible, far up into the blue summer sky and he relished the freedom of flight and the glory of the successful pilots, for whom he had great admiration.

When he was finally sent for active service, to join a squadron at Estrée Blanche, a large base with several squadrons in the north near Treizennes, he was confident, enthusiastic and ready for action. His moment had come at last.

After his first few days at the base he wrote home excitedly to Sarah:

15th August, 1917

My dearest Sarah and son Timothy,

   How are you all at Bourton Villas? It seems like an age since we were together. After I left you I travelled to a base in France where I realised that, despite my training at The Grange, I really didn't know how to fly at all. I was like a toddler who had learnt to walk and thought I could go anywhere. It was here in France where I was given the training and practice to handle my SE5 with confidence.

   I have recently been posted to my active service squadron. I am not allowed to give you any details but I can first reassure you that I am in luxury compared to those poor chaps in the trenches I see below me, when I'm flying near the Front.

   Secondly, I want to reassure you that my safety is of great importance to my Commanding Officer here. It's not a bit like those damning reports of the Royal Flying Corps in the early years of the war, when each man was for himself and many lives were lost. We now fly in formation, a little like a dance in the skies, when several aircraft fly together, ever watchful and protective of the other pilots. In fact, as one of the new men here, I have been instructed to fly at the back of my patrol of five aircraft and, if I sense danger, I should fly under one of the experienced pilots who will protect me, much like a mother goose protects her young.

   I am so thrilled to be here and I will have such stories to share with you when I'm next home. My leaders fill me with so much confidence that I am both optimistic and enthusiastic that this war will be over soon.

   I hope that you are both well and feel happier now that you have read my letter. Give my love to Timothy, my not so little man and to all the family.

   Yours with affection,
      Anthony

Following the writing of this letter, even Anthony's positive enthusiasm was dampened rather by the change in weather, making flying conditions difficult and at times nigh on impossible. No pilot on patrol could help but be moved by the sight of the men wallowing in the mud-filled trenches below, but each had to focus, since a slight lapse of attention, succumbing to melancholy, put both his own life and that of those below him in jeopardy.

Chapter 27

HARRIET WAS SINGING one of her favourite advent hymns as she prepared breakfast and she could hear Sarah teasing one of their patients in the dining room. Sarah had received no more news from Anthony since his encouraging letter in the summer and his optimism had penetrated their lives at Bourton Villas, through into the autumn. Certainly life was never boring since Harriet had opened her home to convalescing patients of the war. Harriet was uplifted by a sense of purpose, which numbed the pain that she still felt deep within her. Jane had praised her last weekend for acting as a successful bridge between hospital and home. All but a few responded to her positive encouragement to be as active in the household chores as possible. Harriet didn't know how she would have coped without Sarah though. Her daughter's cheerful disposition did wonders for morale and she was aware that several lost their hearts to her before they departed for home. Harriet felt that no real harm was done, since Sarah was strong-willed and the men were soon put in their places if they strayed beyond a mild flirtation.

There was one young man, though, whom Jane had brought personally in early December, who was different. As soon as Jane realised that the young man was from

Riduna, she knew that Harriet's home was the best place to send him until he was fit enough to return to the island. The young man had injured his leg and was being sent back home to be part of the Home Guard there. He made no secret about looking forward to this. Harriet had noticed a subtle difference in the way Sarah spoke to him and had seen her uncharacteristic blushes as he flattered her incessantly. He was certainly a likeable person, although a bit loud at times, but she was puzzled that he seemed to recognize Sarah. She was determined to question her daughter next time they had a moment to themselves.

The family always ate breakfast together in the kitchen, before Sarah and Hannah went off to work and Phyllis and Timothy headed for school. Just as they were settling down to egg and bread, washed down by a cup of weak tea, Ernest came in. He had tried to be a dutiful son since his father's death, calling in on a daily basis at first, until Sarah returned. Even now he stopped by to see his mother when he could, balancing the needs of his own growing family with his loyalty to her.

At first he was concerned about his mother's new venture and liked to check out the new patients as soon as they arrived, just in case there might be trouble. He need not have worried because Jane ensured that no one unpredictable or unstable would be sent to Bourton Villas. He was frustrated that his brother was still mute and privately felt that it was time Tom did something more useful, but his mother would have none of it. Tom had taken on a couple of hens, as well as tending to the garden, hence the treat of eggs for breakfast.

'Good morning, son. Would you like me to cook you one of Tom's eggs?' smiled Harriet.

'No thank you, Mother. I've had breakfast with Ethel and the children but just called by to see how you're getting on.'

Harriet knew that her son was just checking on the new

arrivals and so walked with him through to the next room, leaving the family eating at the kitchen table.

'Ernest, this is Mr John Wilson from Winchester,' she said as she held her hand towards a young man with a nasty scar down the side of his face and splint on his arm. 'My son, Ernest Newton.'

Ernest carefully shook John's outstretched good hand.

'Pleased to meet you, sir.'

'And this is Mr Victor Le Page from Riduna!'

Harriet smiled at Ernest's obvious surprise, as the man hobbled to his feet and shook his hand firmly.

'What a strange coincidence,' Ernest exclaimed.

'Yes, I hear you have family connections with our island.'

'Yes, indeed. I expect you know by now that my mother was born there. I've never been to Riduna myself but my sister Sarah has.'

'I know,' Mr Le Page replied with a mischievous smile. 'We met.'

'That's not quite true,' explained an embarrassed Sarah, who had followed Ernest into the dining room. 'It's such a small place that we passed each other on several occasions.'

Harriet, knowing too well how easy it was to 'meet' someone on Riduna, especially if you had no wish to, smiled at her private memories of the island.

'You soon recognise everyone on Riduna, Ernest, friends and strangers alike. In fact, it's easiest to recognise the newcomers. It's hard for you to imagine an island as small as it is. It's not like Sarnia.'

'Well, I welcome you to Bourton Villas, Mr Le Page. I'm sure you will be more than comfortable here with my mother Mrs Newton and my sister Mrs Parker to look after you,' he added as if to emphasise the fact that Sarah was married. 'Mind you, isn't it time you were at work?'

'My brother's a slave driver,' Sarah laughed as she headed

for the front door, Hannah not far behind. 'Mind you, he manages to keep control of all of us women,' she teased, looking over her shoulder at Ernest, who followed them out of the house.

Once they had gone, Mr Le Page started to clear away their plates from the table.

'Leave it to me,' Harriet exclaimed. 'You don't have to do that.'

'You don't need to wait on us hand and foot,' laughed Victor with a cheeky grin, glancing between Mr Wilson's hand and *his* damaged foot. John Wilson didn't seem to take offence, even though he was obviously still in some pain and embarrassed at his clumsiness without his hand. They were all surprised when Tom, who had been sitting silently watching and listening to the exchange, got up from the table and started to clear away, taking the plates from Mr Le Page's hand.

'Tom is my son too, Mr Le Page,' said Harriet by way of explanation, as Tom headed for the kitchen.

'Oh, I understand. Please call me Victor,' he added with a sympathetic look as Tom disappeared out of the back door. 'Is there anything I can do to help you,

Mrs Newton? I hate being idle.'

'You could go down to the corner store and see if there is any meat today.'

'Will do,' said Victor cheerfully, hobbling to get his jacket.

Watching him limp out of the door, leaning on his stick, Harriet felt a touch guilty that she had not found him a task to do at home. She turned and jotted down the new development with Tom in her journal before she started to wash the dishes.

Over the next few weeks, Victor continued to tease Sarah and provoke her embarrassment whenever he could. Harriet was secretly pleased that Victor would be gone soon because she could see that her daughter was growing in fondness for this Ridunian and could see no good coming of their growing friendship. At times during the following week when Harriet was ready to go to bed, they would still be deep in conversation and she had to remain downstairs as a chaperone. It was beginning to irritate her that Sarah was being so thoughtless and a little more familiar with Victor than was proper. This was the only downside to the arrangement, but in all the weeks that Harriet had taken patients into her care, she could honestly say that it was the first time that any of the men had caused her concern. Harriet was glad that Jane would be visiting in a couple of days so that they could have a long talk about it.

On the other hand, Tom seemed to be making progress of late, getting himself involved in household chores. This may have been due to the fact that, as winter approached, he was unable to do more than check on the chickens outside in the garden. Tom always did like to be busy.

After Jane's visit, it was decided that Victor was ready to return home before Christmas. Two days later he had just gone into his bedroom to finish packing and Sarah and Hannah were getting their coats on ready for work when there was an unexpected knock on the door. As Sarah opened the front door, her face turned pale and her cheerful mood evaporated in the foggy air. The telegram boy thrust something into her hand and escaped, touching his cap with respect as he turned and fled. Sarah walked slowly back into the kitchen and sat down at the table holding the dreaded telegram in her trembling hands.

Lieutenant Anthony Parker was killed in action when his plane was shot down in France on November 20th 1917 while he was serving his country.

Harriet put a cup of hot steaming tea into her daughter's hand, slipping some brandy in the cup before she passed it over. She took Timothy by the hand and quietly asked Hannah if she would go and fetch Ernest, to let him know the bad news and that Sarah wouldn't be at work for the near future. Sarah bowed her head, her mind swimming with raw emotion, and Tom came in and stood quietly beside her, resting his hand on her shoulder. Then, in an act that surprised even Harriet, he came over and lifted Timothy up and gently sat him on his mother's lap. Timothy wrapped his arms around his mother and started to sob. Mother and son clung to each other as Sarah's tears finally started to flow.

It was into this scene that Victor strolled unawares, but he was quick-witted enough to guess the nature of the news, as he saw the opened telegram in front of Sarah on the table. He returned to his room to write a note:

Dear Mrs Newton,

Many thanks for your hospitality and making my stay so pleasurable, as I learnt to find my feet. I realise that this is a difficult time for you and would like to offer my condolences to Mrs Parker for her loss. I hope that you will forgive me for slipping away to catch my ferry. If ever you or your family are on Riduna then please drop by to say hello and I hope to goodness that this war will be over soon and happier times will come for you and yours.

Many thanks,
    Victor

With that Victor crept out and made his way slowly down to the Floating Bridge. He was so looking forward to returning to the safety of his island home, but he wished that he had left in happier circumstances and had been able to say goodbye to Sarah. He was afraid that he might never see her again and that made Victor uncharacteristically sad. This feeling just lasted long enough until he could feel the salty wind through his hair as the steamship left the dockside in Southampton Water and he was suddenly filled with anticipation. At last he was on his way back home to Riduna, the island of his birth.

Chapter 28

ON THE FEW days leading up to Christmas an air of melancholy hopelessness filled the atmosphere at Bourton Villas, so much so that Harriet could stand it no more. She decided to take the children for some fresh air and, wrapping them up in their warmest clothes against the cold, she took them all the way to Weston Shore. It was a crisp sunny day, when the rays of the sun penetrated through the strong northerly wind, a bitter sweet tonic to their lives. Harriet was pleased that the tide was low and that she could walk along Fisherman's Walk. Out of the corner of her eye she was reassured that the children were playing happily on the beach and she relished the feelings of freedom and danger by being surrounded by water. She thought of her husband Joe and gave a silent prayer for their life together, picking up a smooth, almost white stone, so solid in her hand, and threw it far out into the water.

Her thoughts turned to Jack. Dear young Jack. What a waste. He was the life and soul of the family, full of mischief from the moment he was born. Harriet bent down and picked up a brightly many coloured pebble, wet and glistening. She held it in her hands for a moment or two, wondering at its rugged beauty, as if she'd never noticed it before, and then, holding her arm aloft, tossed the pebble as far as she could.

At that point she felt a hand on her shoulder and turned in surprise as Edward guided her back to the shore. She knew that she had been a little foolish, especially with the children nearby, and yet suddenly she felt at peace, strangely elated by Edward's guiding presence. Her heart seemed to beat faster as the children ran to him and in turn he picked them up to swing them above his head. He tickled them with his beard as he gave each a kiss, even Timothy who wiped his face in mock disgust as Edward placed him back down on the pebbled shore. When was the last time she had heard their laughter, she thought.

Edward hinted at a surprise deep in the pockets of his large overcoat and so they headed for home, the children running in front of them, trying to hurry them up in their anticipation, reminding Harriet of Edward's visits when her own children were young. Bless him, she thought.

Edward and Harriet's conversation was warm and relaxed, sharing their news and anxieties, talking about her work with the patients whom he could see had fulfilled a great need in her. At one point, when she whispered her fears about the state of Sarah's mind and Tom's condition, Edward grasped hold of her hand and she did not remove it, feeling comforted by their closeness.

Back at Bourton Villas, after offering Edward some very weak tea, Harriet drinking only warm water, the children could contain their excitement no longer and the noise brought Sarah down to the kitchen. Edward made no sign of recognising the pained expression in her usually bright face, but as he winked at her he produced a roughly wrapped package and passed it to Phyllis, before his hand dived deep into his pocket once more, to retrieve another intriguing parcel. Phyllis was beside herself when she pulled off the paper to find a beautifully carved and painted wooden doll and she hugged it to herself on the hearth rug, looking far younger than her seven years.

When Timothy carefully uncovered a small model aeroplane Sarah gasped with a mixture of sadness and fear. All eyes were on the young lad. The little boy's eyes misted over at first, then there was a moment of pure magic as he lifted the plane high above his head, sweeping it about, making familiar air machine noises. Sarah held her breath as the lad gently landed the plane on the kitchen table and ran to Edward, giving him such a hug that her sigh was audible, and she was able, at last, to smile at Edward over Timothy's shoulders.

'Where did you get these lovely presents from, Uncle Edward?' she asked. Harriet, knowing that Edward was too modest to say that he had made them himself replied,

'Uncle Edward is clever like his father before him and like Ernest too for that matter. Give them a piece of driftwood and they can work their magic.'

Harriet smiled at him warmly and Edward's heart melted in her presence.

'Do you like your doll, Phyllis?' Harriet asked.

Realising that her grandmother was prompting her to be polite, Phyllis thanked Edward, too shy to offer a spontaneous sign of affection, yet the way she hugged her doll was thanks enough.

'How is Marie?' asked Hannah, with an unknowing knack of disturbing the pleasant atmosphere.

'She is looking after her sick neighbours, I'm afraid, but she herself is fine,' replied Edward getting to his feet, ready to depart. 'I must be on my way, but I just wanted to call before Christmas. It's been lovely to see you all again and I'm sorry I don't call that often.'

'You always did surprise us with your visits, Uncle

Edward. Thank you so much. You have made our Christmas, especially for the children.'

Sarah walked with Edward to the front door and he glanced over his shoulder at Harriet before he disappeared from view.

Christmas came and went with very little else to celebrate. It was very quiet because all of their patients had moved on and Harriet would not be receiving new guests until January. The winter was hard and Harriet longed for it to be over.

The following few months were the most difficult. The sense of 'the war will soon be over' was now replaced by relentless pain and grief. Sarah was listless and withdrawn. She ignored the guests, preferring to take Timothy up to their room and close the door, taking a pile of mending with her during the evenings, which she worked on by gaslight. Harriet longed for her company and was worried that Sarah was sitting alone in the cold, but aloofness in her daughter had created a barrier between them and Harriet didn't have the courage or energy to try to break it down.

Her son Tom slept most of the time and now that it was winter, he rarely ventured outside the back door and his presence, for Harriet, was a constant concern to her. It was as if the progress made earlier in the year was replaced by little will to live at all. Even the chickens produced so few eggs that Harriet more than once looked longingly at one of them, her mouth salivating in the wonder of what cooked chicken might be like. Next she was filled with remorse when she observed the only glimmer of emotion shown by her younger son as he tended the birds, the only task he truly engaged with during each short day.

It was Hannah who was the most difficult. Harriet could understand her grief and felt sympathy for the girl, but she had given her a roof over her head and had shared all she had to make sure that Phyllis was fed at least twice each day. It was Hannah's attitude towards Tom which hurt Harriet most, though she believed that her son barely noticed. It had certainly soured Hannah's friendship with Sarah and that added to Harriet's sadness. It was as if Hannah resented the fact that Tom had returned, although Harriet could understand that the likeness between Tom and Jack could be unsettling.

The children were also understandably sullen and though they had more than their fair share at meal times, Harriet was losing the ability to dream up interesting ways to prepare their meagre provisions. The harvest last year had also been poor and she was aware enough that the less fortunate in the country were starving to death, compounded by their grief. When there was a bright day at the weekend she would encourage Phyllis and Timothy to come out for a walk with her. It was only during those times, when they were able to run about and play, that Harriet felt a glimmer of cheerfulness. Fortunately, the children both enjoyed to walk and since most of the grassy areas near their home had been dug up for growing food, or even for infantry drills, there was little place to play near home. Since the success of their pre-Christmas walk they made a habit of taking the long walk to Weston Shore. This gave Harriet such a sense of freedom, to see the children chasing and playing along the beach. She often sat on a log and watched them, or gazed at the ships on their relentless path up and down Southampton Water. In the winter sunshine, even the grey mottled ships looked dull. Grey, grey, grey! Even on a sunny day they could not escape the greyness of the war.

Chapter 29

BY MARCH 1918, when the days were becoming longer and the mornings lighter, there was a slight shift in the mood at Bourton Villas. The first change Harriet perceived was in Hannah. The first noticeable difference was that she had started to wear a shorter skirt, much to Harriet's consternation. This fashion had gained in popularity by women, especially in the towns and cities, where many working women argued that their long skirts were an obstruction to efficiency. Harriet resisted commenting on her daughter-in-law's apparel, because Hannah appeared to be no more amenable at home. Harriet had also noticed, with concern, that Hannah seemed to come home from work later and later, leaving Phyllis to play by herself in the kitchen after school. The young women had stopped walking to and from work together long ago, Sarah preferring to reach home quickly, to spend as much time as possible with Timothy before he went to bed, whereas with Hannah it was quite the opposite.

'Why is Hannah always so late, Sarah?' Harriet asked as her daughter came home that night.

Sarah, feeling that it was not her place to betray Hannah's trust, replied,

'Don't fuss so, Mother. Hannah has worked some

overtime, that's all. You know that Hannah now works in a different department to me. I am content to continue to do the sewing for the wing assembly, whereas Hannah has been trained to do welding now. Rather her than me, I must say.'

Harriet let the matter drop but watched with increasing concern as Phyllis grew more and more introverted, barely saying a word to anyone, just cuddling her doll quietly on the rug. When Hannah finally arrived home, she was always in a fluster, rushing in and whisking Phyllis up to their room and closing the door.

Harriet's suspicions were heightened one weekend, when Hannah had gone out for the evening with friends after putting Phyllis to bed. As Harriet stoked the fire early the following morning before preparing breakfast for her two patients, she was horrified to hear Hannah creeping in and was not surprised that neither Hannah nor Phyllis joined them at church that Sunday. By the time the family had returned, Harriet was angry to find Phyllis playing in the kitchen, alone once more. She was not, strictly speaking, totally alone, because Tom was out in the back yard feeding the chickens and the patients were relaxed in the back room, but nevertheless that didn't excuse Hannah for her neglect of her daughter and as Harriet prepared lunch she fumed.

Just before lunch was dished out Hannah rushed in. Harriet was just about to rebuke her when it was obvious that her daughter-in-law had been crying;, her eyes were red and her thin cheeks blotchy. Suddenly Harriet was filled with compassion for the girl, remembering her own troubles when she was young. She bit her tongue, reasoning that it wasn't fair to speak in front of the children. Lunch was a strained, quiet affair, each adult with their own thoughts and the children too frightened to speak, praying that they had not committed some unknown misdemeanour which had made the grown-ups so cross.

Sarah, realising that it was time Hannah spoke to her mother, suggested that she take the children out for a walk and though Harriet regretted missing this opportunity to enjoy special moments with her grandchildren, she was grateful to Sarah for her wisdom.

As the children headed for the door, Hannah made to escape upstairs.

'I could really do with some help clearing away, Hannah, if you don't mind,' Harriet exclaimed, stopping the girl in her tracks.

Reluctantly her daughter-in-law turned and began to clear the table. Once Harriet knew that they were alone, she ventured to ask,

'Hannah, I know that you are suffering in some way. It would really be better for everyone if you talked about it.'

Hannah looked towards the closed door as if she was about to escape, but, having second thoughts, she slumped down on a kitchen chair and sobbed, her head bowed low.

Harriet sat next to her and put her arm gently over Hannah's shoulder.

'I'm pregnant,' she whispered, 'and I don't know what to do.'

The news was such a shock that it took Harriet's breath away, but the last thing Hannah needed right then was the condemnation she was rightly expecting from Harriet, less than a year after Jack's death.

'Tell me about it?' she asked quietly, gently persuading Hannah to move to the more comfortable armchairs by the hearth, leaving the dishes strewn over the kitchen table, unwashed.

'He is a foreman at work. He returned from the war with

injuries and he couldn't be sent back. Not that he'd want to go. Anyway, he persuaded me to work late and I enjoyed the flattery and attention. After all there's not much to be cheerful about in this dreary war.'

Harriet thought of Hannah's sad and neglected daughter, but held her tongue once more.

'Go on, Hannah. You'll feel better when you've told someone. What happened next?'

After a few moments, when Hannah's sobs had subsided, she continued.

'Somehow he managed to get hold of some rum. How, I didn't like to ask, but one night he got me drunk and I couldn't stop myself. You'll hate me now!' exclaimed Hannah, knowing her confession was likely to have both her and her daughter thrown out on to the streets.

Harriet thought for a few moments before asking the question which needed to be asked,

'And why can't this young man marry you, Hannah? You are free to marry now. It's not unheard of, to begin your life again after the suffering you've had. It might be good for Phyllis to have a father figure once more. No one can replace Jack, I know, but your life has to go on.'

At this Hannah began to wail, totally uncomforted by the words, so much so that a possible truth dawned on Harriet and she whispered,

'Is he already married, Hannah?'

'No, not married, but it's complicated because he's been engaged to his childhood sweetheart for three years now and they plan to wed when the war is over.'

As the implications of Hannah's words sank in, Harriet began to think in a rational way.

'You go and freshen yourself and have a rest and I'll see what I can do.'

Harriet encouraged Hannah to go upstairs and it was

while she washed up that Harriet decided the course of action that should be taken.

After making sure that her two patients had all they required, she put on her coat and bonnet and made her way along to Ernest's cottage in the neighbouring village of Itchen Ferry. Since it was unusual for his mother to visit, Ernest realised that it must be important and so, after pleasantries were exchanged with his wife and children, he made an excuse to walk his mother home. They took a detour down to the water's edge where they could talk undisturbed.

Ernest was not entirely surprised to hear his mother's news, since he had already heard rumours at Supermarine. Although the company now had a large number of employees, everyone knew everyone else and secrets were hard to keep. He had been concerned when he had witnessed Hannah's flirtatious behaviour with Mike the foreman on the assembly area for aircraft fuselages, but there had been little he could do about it. Even when he had tried to warn her, she had scowled at him, telling him to mind his own business, which is what he had done.

When he heard the extent of Hannah's predicament, at first he was stubborn that she had only got her just desserts but, once Harriet had pleaded her daughter-in-law's case and he was made aware of the suffering a scandal would cause all of the family, he agreed to go around and talk to Mike Burton. By the time Mr Burton was made to realise that he had little choice and that his reputation at Supermarine and in the community would be marred forever if he didn't 'do the right thing,' thankfully Mike Burton agreed to break off his engagement and to marry Hannah. The date for the quiet civil ceremony in Southampton was set for the following month and so by the beginning of May, Hannah and Phyllis had moved out of Bourton Villas for ever. The crisis had been averted to everyone's relief; apart from the aggrieved betrothed and her family, that is, who fortunately lived up at Pear Tree Green, so that the only awkward moments were when members of the families met in the street, when the atmosphere was more than a little frosty between them.

Times were tougher financially without Hannah's contribution to the household expenses but, with the money Harriet received regularly for the men in her care, she was just able to make ends meet. After all, it wasn't as if there was much to buy. With chronic shortages still in the shops, ladies like her had to use all the ingenuity they could muster to ensure that no one starved, though she was aware from her conversations with Ernest, who read a newspaper regularly, that she was one of the fortunate ones, as suffering and starvation was rife, especially in the cities. The motto of 'make do and mend' had always been a key to survival in her family, but as she observed the shabby garments her family wore now, which no amount of washing and darning could ever improve, she longed to be able to buy some fabric to make something new for them all, but it was out of the question.

It was on Sarah's birthday in May 1918 that Harriet also noticed a change in her daughter's demeanour. She had received a surprise birthday card from Riduna but was very secretive as to who it was from. It could have been from any of the family she had met on her visit a few years before, but Harriet reasoned that this was unlikely to be the case, because as far as she was aware, Sarah had not heard from any of them since her visit. No, the likely answer was that the card was from Victor Le Page and when, over the next couple of months, regular letters also arrived from Riduna addressed to her daughter, Harriet believed that she had guessed the truth.

Thanks to Edward, even Timothy seemed to have found

a purpose in his life. On his last visit Edward had been his usual mischievously, secretive self and had taken Timothy off for an afternoon together. When they arrived back home later that Sunday afternoon Timothy was beaming with pride as he produced his first ever catch of trout from the River Itchen. Timothy had been quick to learn the art of fly fishing and had soon caught two small fish, which he held up proudly to his grandma.

'Oh Timothy; how clever! Did you catch them all by yourself?' exclaimed Harriet, giving him a smile. 'We're going to have such a lovely supper tonight.'

'Uncle Edward showed me how to do it but I caught them by myself, Gran,' Timothy answered with pride.

Edward winked at Harriet over Timothy's head.

'He's a natural, Harriet. These chalk stream rivers are great for trout and bream. There'll be no stopping him now.'

'Go and fetch your mother, Timothy, but leave those fish on the kitchen table first. We don't want them upstairs!'

As Timothy raced to tell his mother, Harriet felt tears prick her eyes. She hadn't seen Timothy so happy since he had arrived at Bourton Villas and yet again she had Edward to thank for his joy.

'What's the matter, Harriet? Have I done something to offend you?' Edward asked, with obvious concern in his voice.

'Oh no,' smiled Harriet, unable to halt the flow of tears now, 'I can't remember seeing little Timothy looking so happy.'

Fortunately Sarah came down at that moment preventing further questioning and Harriet was grateful to turn her back on them to prepare the tea, whilst listening to their animated conversation. She pulled herself together, wiping her eyes on her sleeve, so that by the time she turned again she was both composed and smiling.

'Uncle Edward is going to leave me this rod and line, so that I can go out and catch us some supper sometimes. Isn't that wonderful, Gran? Aren't I lucky?'

Timothy rushed over and gave Harriet such a big hug that she was winded for a time.

'You certainly are, Timothy! I'm proud of you. Let's prepare them, shall we, and Uncle Edward can share some supper with us, since he's helped to catch it.'

'No, I'm afraid I'd best be off,' said Edward, reluctant to leave this happy family scene. 'Don't you forget all that I've taught you today, my young man, and I'll come back in a few weeks to see how you're getting on.'

Sarah walked Edward to the door, with Timothy by her side, while Harriet busied herself in the kitchen preparing the small fish for their supper. Their own private 'Santa Claus' had arrived yet again and Harriet smiled at the memories it gave her, trying to shake off the longing she was beginning to have for Edward to stay longer.

As Harriet tried to sleep that night she thought of her family. Each member, apart for Tom, seemed to be healing from the ravages of the terrible war and his continued disturbed state of mind dampened an otherwise lovely day. Even her daughter and her grandson were finding reasons to smile again and with that she drifted off into a dreamful sleep.

Her dream was a little like a fairy story her father used to tell her when she was young, only this one seemed the wrong way around. She dreamed that she visited Fort Clonque, a castle like fort on the coast of Riduna. Walking along the causeway, with water on both sides she reached the imposing wooden doors. Once inside, she was shown to a room with a large four poster bed and there was her son Tom in a deep sleep and no one could wake him up. Everyone tiptoed around the young man in order not to disturb him. Day after day she would sit by his bedside but there was no change in him and there was a hush all over the fort. One day while she was sitting holding his hand there was a knock at the window and, when Harriet opened the window, in flew a beautiful angel. She glided over the sleeping figure and then stopped by his pillow, giving him a gentle kiss. Harriet sat open mouthed, witnessing this strange happening and then, to her astonishment, Tom woke up and the angel vanished.

Chapter 30

SARAH WAS BEGINNING to walk with a spring in her step once more. She had received two letters now from Victor Le Page and although their tone was both cheerful and chattering, with no hint of any deep feelings or emotions, Sarah was still encouraged by them and found that she was watching out for the post each day.

Timothy too was less clingy and quiet since Uncle Edward had taken him fishing. He would never be a sociable lad, like his Uncle Jack had been, but was more thoughtful and studious like his father. Fishing suited him well and through this useful activity he had also formed a reliable friendship with another lad in the village and they liked nothing better than to spend their weekends and evenings at the river.

Sarah found herself day dreaming of Riduna once more. She closed her eyes, momentarily imagining her young son sitting on the rocks near Braye Beach, fishing rod in hand, Victor standing protectively by his side: silhouettes against the evening sky. She smiled.

That night, Sarah wrote her reply to Victor, keeping her tone light and of a friendly nature:

10th June, 1918

Dear Victor,

How good of you to write to me so soon. I so enjoy hearing about Riduna and how you are all coping in this endless war. Receiving your letters has certainly cheered an otherwise quite dreary life and for that I heartily thank you.

You asked me to call you Victor in your last letter and if that is appropriate I would like you to call me Sarah. After all, we did live under the same roof here in England for two months and so we must be closer than passing acquaintances.

I have one piece of really good news which concerns my son Timothy. A month ago our Uncle Edward came to visit us and took Timothy fishing. He has taken to it like a duck to water, as it were, and it has made him much more content. I am so grateful for Uncle Edward for being so considerate and thinking of just the right way in which he can lift all of our spirits. Not only do we see my son much happier now but Timothy also feels proud that he is providing a nutritious supper for the family. Everyone wins, don't you think?

I call him my Uncle Edward but that is not strictly speaking true. He used to be a neighbour of my mother's when she lived on Riduna until he went to sea, but he has always kept in touch.

I must go now and help my mother with our patients because there is always much to do. Thank you again for your kindness in remembering us.

Kind regards,
Sarah

After completing her letter she began to sort out her belongings. Her mother had suggested that, since Hannah and Phyllis had vacated the room next to hers, maybe Sarah would like to move into a room on her own, in order to give her growing son a little more space. When Harriet was able to have paying guests again in the future, apart from her patients from the hospital that is, then this arrangement may need to be reviewed, but meanwhile it seemed silly to leave the room empty.

It was while Sarah was clearing out one of her drawers that she came across the small but familiar pouch. She could not resist emptying its contents into her hands. The silver locket was a little tarnished now, but nevertheless it was still pretty and its mystery no nearer to being solved. Sarah sighed. Maybe she should do what Jane had suggested and talk to her mother about it, but something stopped her and so she slipped it back into its pouch and carried it into her new bedroom, hiding it once more.

It was a few weeks later that she received a reply from Victor and she could not wait to open the letter in private. Once alone in her room she eagerly broke the seal and sat on her bed, the pages in her lap.

14th July, 1918

My dear Sarah,

I was so pleased to receive your letter. I remember with fondness my time at Bourton Villas and I am glad that my letters have cheered you and helped you to forget your sorrows in this dreadful war.

What a lovely picture your letter painted of uncle and son fishing beside the River Itchen near to your home. I believe that there is no activity which can fill me with as much peace as fishing, especially with the satisfaction of catching our own supper. There is only one picture which I feel could be even better and that would be fishing in the sea off our coastal waters here on Riduna. Oh, how I would love to spend a few hours sharing these joys with Timothy! One day perhaps, when the war is spent.

I really hope you don't think that I've been prying into your family past but I was talking to some folks down at The Divers the other day and I mentioned your Uncle Edward. Straight away they mentioned your mother Harriet and how close Edward and Harriet were when they lived on the island. One said that he was even surprised when he heard of your mother and father's wedding. Do you think there was any truth in it?

I really hope that I have not upset you, or said anything which might cause you offence. I will await your reply with nervousness since I truly wish for us to remain friends.

Yours,
    Victor

Sarah allowed the letter to drop on to the floor. Surely it could not be. She would have noticed over the years if there were signs that her mother and Uncle Edward had been sweethearts. Her mother would have said something. Surely Sarah couldn't believe the gossip in the letter and at first it made her quite cross. She placed the letter back in its envelope and put it deep in one of her drawers. She wouldn't allow herself to dwell on the words and it was a long time before she re-read the letter or faced writing to Victor again.

Life at Bourton Villas continued to cling on to any glimmer of optimism as Harriet filled her life with the care of patient guests, supported by Sarah as best she could after a hard day at Supermarine.

Chapter 31

WHEN VICTOR FIRST returned to Riduna he could often be seen fishing on the rocky shoreline to the right of Fort Raz on Longy Bay, a lone silhouette of a figure standing statuesque off an outcrop not far from the sweeping sandy bay. In fact, at first glance he almost looked like a dark rock himself, protruding upright from the shore: a reflection of the Hanging Rock nearby.

Unfortunately, this familiar place where he had always loved to fish with his father and grandfather before him gave him no peace. The coast of France was clearly visible to him. Even with the sound of the sea, it was impossible to block out the echo of distant gunfire, fetching the true reality of the war right to the shoreline. There was no real way of escaping the horrors and the memories.

Instead he began to join the many young lads, fishing for mackerel and mullet off the Breakwater. He stood cheek by jowl, with just enough room to cast the twine into the sea from his long heavy pole. His younger brother William stood on the ledge behind him, attaching the bait and retrieving the captured mackerel, which Victor flicked expertly, as near to William as he could. Their catch was certainly adequate to fulfil the bodily needs of his family, although he still yearned to fish in solitude.

One afternoon he could bear it no more and so, instead of heading for the Breakwater, he began to clamber over the rocks by Fort Doyle. With his brother William holding the rod and bait, skipping lithely from rock to rock, Victor was embarrassed as he struggled and slid over the wet rocks, using both hands to steady himself as he coped with his painful shoulder and injured leg. Many times William looked back and wanted to give Victor support but in the end looked onwards, knowing full well that his older brother would be too proud to accept help. Finally they reached a ledge of rocks which jutted right out into the swirling waters and Victor settled there to gain his breath. William prepared the line for him, untangled the twine from the quill and cork float and attached some mackerel flesh to the hook as bait, carefully squeezing it between his thumb and forefinger. He handed the rod to his brother, knowing instinctively that Victor wanted to fish alone and then went to look for shrimps in the rock pools nearby.

Before Victor cast the line he sat and looked around him. His eyes spanned between Fort Groznez to his right, standing with pride to defend the harbour and breakwater, to the imposing sight of Fort Tourgis to his left, and the long barracks sweeping down from the horizon towards the stony shores of Clonque Bay. Just across the sea from Fort Tourgis lay the deserted island of Burhou, with dangerous waters swirling around outcrops of rocks as far as the eye could see. As Victor's eyes swept along the bay and out towards the open sea, he sighed with a rare moment of contentment. He cast his line and as he watched the float bob in the waters in front of him he began to relax. He breathed in the salty air, filling his lungs and clearing his mind. His thoughts drifted in and out of a pleasant emptiness until it rested, as it often did, on his feelings for Sarah.

Although he longed to share her company and enjoyed a glimmer of hope that one day she might agree to marry him and move to Riduna with Timothy, he was realistic enough to know that this was a distant dream. He had no idea of the impact that his letter was having on her, but he was all too aware that, although the effect of war was harsh over in Woolston, with painful loss and hardship, the actual suffering on Riduna was tenfold. It was hardly the time or place to encourage Sarah to join him, even if she could do so in relative safety.

Before the war, Victor's parents had encouraged him to settle down and marry a local island girl, but try as he might, he could only see the face of his sisters or cousins in their features, nothing to allure him in the way Sarah had done the first moment they had met. She had been unattainable then, but her marriage, rather than lessening his ardour, had added to her magnetism towards him. He had not been surprised to hear of Anthony's death. He felt his union with Sarah was written in the stars which he gazed at in his wakeful watchfulness.

The few remaining men on the island were injured, elderly or very young. It was if a whole generation was missing. Each family waited anxiously for news and as tragedy struck, everyone suffered alongside the bereaved, since each man that was lost was a son, father, brother, uncle, cousin or friend. Absentmindedly Victor pulled up his line and rethreaded some fresh bait. As he cast it once more, he was aware of the sea pounding through the gully of rocks nearby. This was Victor's solitude, a time when he tried to block out the worries of the war, but even here there was no escape. They invaded his mind, like the relentless crashing of the waves on the nearby shore. The sea was restless today, reflecting his mood.

Families on Riduna were struggling to survive, with few

supply boats safely reaching their shores. He threw a few lumps of precious stale bread into the water by the rocks beneath his feet, an investment, he hoped, for the mullet he might lure towards him. He thought of the many frustrated moments when his favourite fish had given him and his father the slip. Fishing had become a necessity for the survival of his family, making such frustrations unbearable. Nevertheless, all he could do was settle down and hope.

After a while, the sun, which shone through broken cloud, began to calm him. He sighed with a rare feeling of wellbeing, barely noticing the sweep of the bay or the island of Burhou ahead of him, or even the rocks beneath his feet. Each was reassuringly unchanged in their familiarity.

His time back on the island had taken on a routine of its own. He was part of a small band of men who had been given the task of keeping watch over the island. He had volunteered for regular night duty which took place near to the harbour or from dugouts along the shoreline at Fort Clonque. They kept watch for any sign of submarine or enemy shipping attempting to slip unnoticed towards their shores. Night Watch suited him. This group of mainly elderly men, some drafted from Guernsey to boost their numbers, welcomed him as a hero who'd come home to them. Since returning from the Front he had often suffered from insomnia and frequent nightmares. These seemed to leave him be as he napped during daylight hours. His body was now accustomed to night time vigils and he prided himself on his alert state of mind.

It was in the morning that he caught a few hours sleep, preferring to remain in his small room at the hotel, rather than to stay at his parents, where the noise of his family would disturb him.

In the afternoon he worked for his boss, as much for

board and lodgings than for any remuneration. There were few paying guests at the hotel now. Those that came were usually from the military or the occasional dignitary, there to discuss the implications of the war on this strategic outpost, once called the Gibraltar of the north, since the island was the closest to both the French and English shoreline. Meetings were held and then these people left. Nothing really changed. Promises were made to ensure that supply boats were safe, but promises made were often promises broken. The islanders knew that their plight was not a priority to those in England, when resources were stretched to the limit. Basically they were on their own. If English homes were straining from a lack of basic supplies then Riduna was suffering many times over.

Nevertheless, the islanders were forever resourceful. They continued the time honoured tradition of collecting seaweed at sunrise, Vraic as they called it, which they used as fertilizer for their farmland and they dried cowpats and gorse for fuel to put on their stoves. Like on the mainland the islanders had suffered from a poor harvest. Fish was the obvious staple diet and though the fishermen's boats rarely ventured out because it was far safer to remain and fish off the shoreline. Victor tried to find a few hours to go fishing late each afternoon. Out here on the craggy rocks of Crabby Bay it soothed his spirit and gave him time to think. At one with the elements he allowed his mind free range, like the feral chickens that roamed the land above Telegraph Bay.

An almost imperceptible initial tug on his line brought him to his senses. Acutely alert once more, he gave expert battle with the fish, respecting its struggle for survival. Slowly and skilfully he began to coax the fish in. A bit of slack, then tension again. A fine balance between strategy and strength, but he prayed that his determination to succeed was the strongest. His emotions were a mixture of anticipation, excitement and a fear of failure; a struggle reflecting the battles taking place only just a few miles over the water.

Victor gave one last pull, feeling the tension of the arching rod through his arms, shoulders, tight stomach and down to his feet, which held firm to the rocks in his worn out boots. Suddenly his whole body fell back as the fish broke free from the water. Regaining his composure he swung this beauty in towards William, who had clambered over the rocks to help him land his catch. William caught and held the weighty fish in his arms. A ten pound mullet, Victor guessed in proud amazement, as he relaxed at last. The irony of catching this 'whopping great fish,' after all those years of near misses, made him laugh out loud at their good fortune.

William held the mullet up to him and Victor carefully removed the hook, taking the life of the fish as humanely as only a true fisherman can. The tail gave one last flicker, as he looked down on the many colours of its glistening skin and the beautiful symmetry of gills and fin. For some moments he held the fish in reverence and thanks: a life taken to save others as he thought of his hungry parents who would eat well tonight, and maybe their neighbours too, judging by the size of it. As he laid the mullet, whose brightness had already faded, out on the rock behind him, the smell of fresh fish was already whetting his appetite, saliva running freely in his mouth. He too would share supper with his parents before reporting for night duty at the harbour. He couldn't miss this feast.

As he walked up the beach Victor noticed a sizeable piece of driftwood. He bent down to pick up a large stone and placed it prominently on the top of the wood. Victor smiled, touched for the first time in his life by the simplicity of the trust he had in the honesty of his fellow islanders. He knew instinctively that when he returned to 'claim' his piece of wood, it would still be waiting for him and that the stone would act as a time honoured signal of possession. After that, Victor limped home, slinging his kitbag holding the precious fish over his shoulder, his injured leg causing him more frustration than pain. All the while he pondered sadly on the way the wider world had truly lost that simple trust.

He shook off this feeling of melancholy as he reached St Anne and he walked into his parents' tiny cottage on High Street grinning from ear to ear, holding the mullet out in front of him as he entered the door.

'My word, that's a mighty fine fish, son,' his mother exclaimed with pride and thankfulness as she put aside the mittens she was knitting for the war effort. 'Isn't it, father?' she added with a slightly raised voice as she turned to Victor's grandfather, who had been snoozing in his chair by the window. 'Wake up and look at the sight of this fish your grandson has brought in.'

Victor handed the fish to his mother, a prize offering indeed.

'Your father'll be so proud of you when he gets in. Maybe we should invite the neighbours to share in our good fortune!'

Little Tommy, Victor's youngest brother, had come stumbling down the steep staircase, curious to find out what all the fuss was about.

'Crikey,' he exclaimed just as his father came in.

Monsieur Le Page slapped Victor on the back.

'Well done my lad. What a catch!'

As four generations settled down at the kitchen table, Victor told the tale of his battle with the fish, embellishing the story as only a good story teller can. While he was speaking the neighbours came in and stood listening by the door. His mother smiled as she busily prepared the fish, filling the small room with a pungent smell as she expertly gutted the large mullet and placed it in the stove. By the time Victor had finished speaking the air was full of delicious anticipation and his father opened his last bottle of precious brandy to toast the moment.

The celebration was certainly welcome, to lift their spirits to cope with the difficult months ahead. At the end of the evening, after the neighbours had left, Victor put on his coat ready to face the night air. Ever thoughtful of the needs of tomorrow, he turned to his grandfather.

'You'll come out with us to lay the trots tomorrow night, grandfather,' Victor asked. 'Some exercise 'n fresh air'll do you the world of good.'

'I dun know lad. I'm getting too old for all that now,' his grandfather replied, shifting in his chair.

'Rubbish, grandfather. You can trip up to the inn sprightly enough when the mood takes you.'

'Yes, father,' encouraged Victor's mother. 'You should go and give them a hand. Victor and my George work such long hours, they'd appreciate your support.'

'I'll come,' exclaimed Tommy.

'Oh no you won't, my lad,' replied his mother. 'It'll be far too late for you to be up.'

'Leave the lad be, Mother. You used to let me help when I was about Tommy's age and Rachel too. You mollycoddle the lad too much.'

Victor's mother looked indignant at being contradicted about her dealings with her youngest boy, always her favourite since he was so unexpected. He had been the fifth arrival in the family and several years after Victor's two sisters, both of whom were now away in service at a house in Dorset. She supposed she did baby him a little but she wasn't going to admit it in front of the boy or Victor for that matter.

'It's good for the lad to learn,' added Victor gently, thinking that he might not always be there to help his father and sensing that, despite protesting otherwise, it would not be long before his grandfather was truly too old to help.

'Anyway, both of you, put your boots on and come down to Crabby to give me a hand with that piece of wood.'

The brothers enjoyed the stroll together and finding Victor's claimed driftwood just as he had left it earlier, they removed the stone and carried it between them back up the hill towards St Anne to their grateful mother.

On the following evening the men in the family set off towards Fort Clonque, in perfect time to catch the lowest tide. Tommy ran excitedly in front of them as they strode towards the Zig-Zag, the path which took them down to the shore.

Carefully they set their trots, several lines trapped between rocks and buried deep in the sand. William helped his grandfather, who showed him how it was done, patiently passing on techniques and tips he had learnt from his father and grandfather before him. Once the task was done the men stood back for a while, allowing their boots to be washed by the incoming sea. They checked that each line was secure before heading back up to the town for supper. Later, Victor walked back down to the harbour to resume his nightly duties. A gun was fired from Fort Albert across the bay, reassuring him that he'd arrived just in time to start his 9pm shift.

The following morning William and young Tommy ran down to the harbour to meet Victor as his shift ended. They took Victor's favourite route via Crabby and Platte Saline, under the brow of Fort Tourgis, towards Clonque. This was a windy and exposed side of the island where the waters were the most choppy and the sea feared by any who sailed though her and yet it was beautiful in its ruggedness.

Victor's father and grandfather were already on the beach and, not waiting for their help, they were retrieving the trots, collecting the night's catch of rock salmon into a large basket on the beach. The tide had reached its lowest yet again, exposing the lines still secure, despite being submerged for the majority of the night. Tommy ran on in his excitement and helped his grandfather with the remaining trots on the beach, unable to contain yells of joy as a fish was discovered at the end of each line. William, on the other hand, scrambled over the rocks with his father to retrieve the ones set out on the craggy outcrops near the fort. They worked quickly and methodically, few words passing between them, William instinctively following his father's lead.

Victor watched the scene, full of childhood memories when his own enthusiasm had matched that of his youngest brother. It was a good night's work. They had caught eight fish, three of which they would keep for their own use and the others they would barter for goods from Rose Farm. It was an excellent arrangement and it was cooperation such as this which kept the islanders alive through these difficult times. They were survivors. With each cheerful thought Victor felt a darker side pulling at his mind, but during daylight hours he could usually keep painful visions of the suffering of his closest friends at arm's length.

Chapter 32

IT WAS NOVEMBER 11th and Harriet had walked down to the grocers. The foggy morning seeped through the community with a sense of subdued anxiety. She passed by neighbours who barely acknowledged recognition as they nodded and swiftly went their way. Harriet didn't know what was drawing her to the river's edge but once she was there she could see little through the swirling fog. There seemed to be none of the usual movement of water traffic and she sensed calmness as she stood and listened to the water lapping at the water's edge.

In the far distance a single deep noted siren sounded, almost certainly from the direction of Southampton Docks. Another higher noted echo gave its light-hearted reply and then it was as if all the dormant vessels wished to muscle in on the conversation, as a cacophony of sound drifted up and down the river, ever gaining in enthusiasm and intensity. Harriet smiled. There could be no doubt about their message to everyone. The war was finally over.

Behind her Harriet could hear the people flock out of shops, factories and houses on to the main streets of Woolston. For a moment she stood still soaking up the atmosphere in a sense of disbelief. Armistice had been declared and Harriet looked on as her neighbours drew untapped energy from deep down to dance and sing in celebration. Then she made her way through the crowds of people; the carts and trucks brought to a standstill, stopped by the powerful surge of the celebrations.

Harriet reached Bourton Villas just as her two patients hobbled out of the front door to see what was happening. At that moment Ernest appeared and unlike his usual reserved self he took his mother's hand and spun her until she began to laugh in protest for him to stop. Timothy and Sarah came rushing over to her next and she gave both of them a hug as Ernest claimed Sarah for a dance. Looking up, she saw Tom standing alone in the doorway. When he saw her looking at him he retreated back inside Bourton Villas and as she followed him she found him sitting quietly on their garden bench appearing oblivious to the celebrations. She sat down next to him, her hands falling into her lap as they sat there in their own silence.

In that moment she became aware of her shabby coat, over-mended dress and worn out shoes. Her eyes were also drawn to her thin spindly fingers and she smoothed the coat over her bony knees; all exuberance drained from her as she was struck by the legacy of the war both in tragedy and hardship. How could they heal from such life and memories? Tom too was thinking of the suffering, but his thoughts were of his brother and many friends who had lost their lives over in France. On cue, their little robin made a well timed appearance, hopping on to the hard ground to peck at some crumbs Tom had just thrown out.

At that point the whole family streamed into the yard, shattering their haven of peace and the robin disappeared into the bushes. Ernest called everyone back into the kitchen where he poured the last drop of brandy into glasses and as a family they toasted the end of the war. After that they each drifted back to work, leaving Harriet quietly mulling over the implications of the day's events as she prepared the still meagre evening meal. The declaration of peace was certainly a wonderful start, she reasoned, but it would take so much more to return to any form of normality in their lives. Her spirits had certainly lifted, although it was far too soon for her to try to imagine better times ahead. She would continue to take a day at a time.

Chapter 33

ONE MORNING IN late November, when Harriet's last patients from the hospital had left and she was preparing her rooms to open as a guest house once more, there was an unexpected knock at the door. Family and friends would always come in through the back unannounced and she was not prepared for guests as yet.

Standing on the doorstep was a young nurse, who looked both tired and a little dishevelled, with a case in her hand.

'I'm afraid I am not taking any more patients,' Harriet exclaimed, thinking that there might be a misunderstanding from The Royal Victoria.

'I am sorry to trouble you madam, but I'm looking for a young man called Thomas Newton.'

'Oh, I see,' answered Harriet, still a little puzzled. 'But he doesn't need any nursing care as far as I am aware. I would have been informed,' she added, sure that Jane would have sent word to her, even if she was too busy to come herself.

'I am sorry. I think you misunderstand me. I'm not from the hospital; I met Corporal Newton in Karachi and just wanted to make sure that he was fully recovered. My name is Nurse Gladys Rees."

As realisation dawned, reluctantly Harriet asked the

young nurse inside, concerned that Tom might be upset by memories of his time in Karachi.

'Come in and tell me all about it over a cup of tea,' she offered, unable to find the words to send this young nurse away.

As Nurse Rees settled down at the kitchen table she began her story. 'There's not much to tell, really. When I was working in Karachi, Corporal Newton, was brought into my ward for a while. There was little we could do for him there and we had so many injured men to look after that I'm afraid to say some of the other nurses weren't very kind to him. I felt concerned for him since he was so alone and seemed so vulnerable. While he was waiting for a ship to bring him home, I visited your son at his accommodation a few times, just to check that he was all right.'

Harriet relaxed a little, finding the genuine concern this young girl showed for her son quite touching.

'I apologize for my rudeness. It is unforgivable of me. I am Harriet Newton and Thomas, Tom, is my son. He is asleep at present but I am very protective of him. Many people are like your nurse friends and they just don't understand his condition. When he wakes up I would be very happy for you to talk to him, but please don't expect too much. He still hasn't uttered a single word since his return, although in other ways he has improved a great deal. I've been writing a journal for a dear friend of mine at the Royal Victoria. Would you like to look at it and tell me what you think?'

Harriet stretched up to a high shelf and pulled out a thin black leather book and handed it to Nurse Rees, relieved to find another person with genuine concern for her son. She realised that she had misjudged this young girl, since it was obvious that Nurse Rees was still wearing the garments she had travelled in and must have come directly from her ship when it had docked in Southampton.

Gladys read the short notes in silence feeling admiration for Tom's mother's care and patience, but a little nervous now as to how Tom might react when he set eyes on her again. Harriet could see the hesitation in Gladys' eyes and so, to put her at ease, she showed her the photos of Sarah on her wedding day with all of the family and of Jack on the *Ben my Chree*. She hid the journal carefully away but it was while she was pointing out Jack, Tom's twin brother, and quietly explaining Jane's theory that Tom had somehow experienced sympathetic trauma at the same time that his brother had been tragically hit by a truck, that Tom came into the kitchen.

'You have a special visitor, Tom,' exclaimed Harriet, as she rose to fill up the kettle once more. 'Do you remember Nurse Gladys Rees?'

Tom came in and sat down opposite Gladys at the kitchen table and as she stretched out to cup her hands over his, their eyes met. Harriet tried not to watch, but was aware of the glimmer of recognition, as if Gladys had reached into the place of his nightmare and given him comfort.

'You *will* stay the night, Nurse Rees?' Harriet asked, wanting to hang on to this thread of hope. 'I have a room already prepared and it would be lovely if you could stay for a couple of days.'

'I would like that very much, Mrs Newton. You are very kind to invite a stranger to stay.'

'It's my job to welcome strangers, Nurse Rees, but you are welcome to stay as our friend, rather than as our guest.'

'That's very kind. I'm quite tired after the journey and it would be wonderful to rest before continuing on to my parents' home, but please call me Gladys.'

Gladys found it hard to take her eyes away from Tom.

Each time their eyes met she felt a surge of happiness, which wiped away the shadows of the last few years. Was she imagining it or did Tom feel something too? Harriet certainly noticed that his eyes had softened and a glimmer of a light had returned.

Over the next few days Gladys and Tom were inseparable. At first she would sit on the bench while he tended the garden, or he would sit beside her, both huddled in their winter coats. What Gladys spoke of, Harriet was unable to guess, but after Gladys could stand the cold no more, having just returned from the tropics, they began to take walks further afield. Neighbours gossiped that they had been seen watching the ferry come in and even walked as far as Weston Shore. One day Sarah noticed that they had stopped outside the bicycle shop and she was keen to tell her mother.

On another afternoon Harriet came in from the frustrating task of shopping for what little she could find at the grocers when she found them both in the kitchen. Their heads were close together and he was sobbing deep silent tears of sadness on Gladys' shoulder, the photograph of Jack in Tom's hand. Harriet crept back out of the room and gently closed the door, praying that Gladys was the angel who had come to unlock Tom's disturbed mind. Despite this hope, she was also impatient with herself, because she was aware that a small part of her felt excluded by Gladys' presence.

The following Sunday afternoon, Jane visited for the first time in a few weeks. During Sunday lunch Gladys had announced that she must leave the following day to visit her parents and so the pair had gone out for a final stroll. Their absence gave Harriet the ideal opportunity to catch up with Jane's news and to tell her about Gladys and the positive changes she had noted in her son since the young nurse had arrived.

'It must be so frustrating for her, since Tom is still

unwilling to talk, but in all other ways Tom seems to have healed. He is going to be lost without Gladys after tomorrow.'

'And what does she intend to do next?' enquired Jane, who was remembering how disorientated she had felt returning home, with no particular direction planned.

'It was very good of her to call in to see Tom as soon as she arrived back in Southampton, but she is going home to her family for a few weeks before she decides what to do next.'

'Will she go abroad again soon, do you think, Harriet?'

'I'm not sure. I think, from what I can see, that it all depends on Tom.'

They were unable to continue the conversation, since Tom and Gladys walked in the back door, and after the introductions Gladys and Jane spent several minutes talking of their time abroad, and it was almost as if both were oblivious to anyone else around them. Harriet busied herself with preparing a small supper and Tom went out into the back yard to check on the chickens. Harriet could see by the look on his face that he felt neglected and her heart went out to her son, understanding a little more how frustrating Tom found his situation.

'Do you like your work at The Royal Victoria, Jane? Gladys asked. 'It must be such a privilege to work there and so different to your time in the field.'

'It took a while to become accustomed to the sheer size of the hospital, and the last few years have been extremely tough, but they've certainly been rewarding. We are so short staffed though, with many moving on as soon as they feel prepared to travel. Some see serving abroad as a glamorous option and for others it is sheer escapism, but most are eager to go as soon as they are able. Do you hope to travel again, Gladys?'

'Not for a while, I don't think. I'd like to be a bit closer to the family for the next couple of years at least.'

'And where is your home?'

'Not far, Jane. My parents live in Chichester, just along the coast.'

Jane paused for a moment, an idea forming in her mind.

'After a few weeks at home, why don't you come to visit me at the hospital? If you think you would like to work with us, then I will put in a good word for you. It isn't difficult to travel on to Chichester from Hamble as you know.'

The words 'and you'll be closer to Tom,' hung in the air between them and Harriet admired her best friend for her astute summing up of the situation.

'I'd like to do that very much. Thank you, Jane. You must excuse me now, because I should go upstairs to pack.'

Gladys headed for the stairs and Jane and Harriet saw her glance in the direction of the back yard as she went.

'What a wonderful idea, Jane. You couldn't have come at a better time. Oh, it's so good to have you close again, but while I listened to you I wondered if there was just a small yearning in you to go abroad again.'

'You know me too well, my dear Harriet, but don't worry; I have no plans to leave you yet.'

Jane didn't like to say that she dreamed nightly of travelling again and wondered if anything would satisfy that yearning, which made her so restless at times.

Later at supper Gladys exclaimed, 'I have really enjoyed my stay with you, Mrs Newton, but I hope that I haven't outstayed my welcome.'

'It's been our pleasure and you're welcome to visit at any time, my dear,' Harriet reassured her and knowing the positive change in her son Tom since Gladys' arrival she added, 'I do so hope that you *will* visit again soon.'

'Your hospitality's been so generous, Mrs Newton. Yes, I do hope to return one day, if Tom would like to see me again,' she added shyly, looking up at him from the other side of the table.

'There's one more thing before I go: Mr Palmer at the bike shop has agreed to have Tom working at the shop again. He's so busy now that some of the men have returned from the war that he had been thinking of recruiting a young lad, but he would much rather Tom returned to work for him. He's getting old now and hopes that sometimes he can rest a bit and leave the shop to someone responsible.'

'That's wonderful news Tom. I'm proud of you,' exclaimed Harriet, her eyes brimming with tears of happiness. 'Look at me. Your mother's a silly one, isn't she?'

'I don't think she's silly at all,' came a familiar voice at the door as Edward breezed in once more.

'You seem to have the knack of appearing quite unexpectedly, Edward. Coffee is it?' she asked as she rushed to her feet to warm the kettle.

'By the way, this is Nurse Gladys. She met our Tom in Karachi and has been staying for a few days. This is Edward, an old friend of the family.'

'Less of the "old", Harriet! Pleased to meet you, Nurse Gladys. You can look after me any day!' he added as Harriet glared at him across the kitchen.

'Charmed I must say by your welcome, Harriet. Yes, you could say we are very *old* friends,' he added with a wink at Gladys, which made her blush.

Sarah, who had just come in behind Edward and witnessed the altercation, looked quizzically at her mother, recognising the hidden implications in the tone of Edward's words, which she had never noticed before.

'I don't know about friends, but I heard a rumour once

that you were childhood sweethearts,' she ventured brashly.

Seeing that her mother was immediately flustered by her words, Sarah regretted her hasty comment. Nevertheless, it made her wonder if there was any truth in Victor's words after all, and that maybe she had finally unlocked the mystery of the silver locket, but how on earth had it found its way into her father's belongings?

'What a disrespectful way to talk to your mother,' Edward chided, for which he earned a grateful smile from Harriet. 'Young girls today! No respect.'

'I'm sorry Mother. That was uncalled for. You sit down and I'll make Uncle Edward's coffee. Don't take any notice of me. It was such a difficult atmosphere at work again today with some of the men back. They resent us being there and I'm not sure that I can take much more of their bullying.'

'Oh, Sarah. You're so young. You must remember that they've lost their self esteem, coming back to beg for their jobs and finding women in their place. It's only natural that they feel resentful.'

'But we've suffered too, Uncle Edward. It's easy for you to take their side but what would I do if I had to give up my work at Supermarine?'

'What do you do there, Sarah?'

'We sew the bleached linen bags for the wings. I'm quite good at it now. In fact I've been praised as one of the neatest workers there.'

'I'm sure there'd be plenty of sewing you could do here for your mother,' Edward responded without thinking.

Sarah put his coffee firmly in front of him and with a rush of apology, not trusting herself to remain polite, she disappeared upstairs to her room.

'I'm afraid that was the worst thing you could have said, Edward, though I know that you were only trying to help.'

'But couldn't Sarah help you with the business here, Harriet? Those men have suffered so much that it's unfair for them to be fighting the women for their jobs, now that they've been lucky enough to return in one piece.'

'If you don't mind me saying so, Mrs Newton,' Gladys added, 'I think Sarah would be an asset to you once you're fully opened. It would take the pressure off you and solve Sarah's frustrations at work too.'

Gladys was rewarded by a smile of approval from Tom and noticed that Edward was looking a little smug.

'I'll think about it,' Harriet replied, bringing the subject to a close, 'but what brought you here today, Edward, or is it just one of your usual surprise social calls?'

'I promised I would call to check you were coping from time to time and I'm just keeping my promise. In fact I must be gone because my ship won't wait for me. Nice to meet you, Nurse Gladys. Good to see you too, Tom.'

With that, Edward headed for the door and Harriet followed behind. With just one brief glance over his shoulder, when his face seemed to be asking Harriet a question, which he obviously decided not to ask, Edward disappeared down the road towards the ferry.

Harriet stood silently in the hall for some minutes, wondering whether to go up to talk to Sarah. With a sigh she decided that she had best leave it for now and she returned to the kitchen. Timothy came in at that point and was disappointed that his Great Uncle Edward had left, because he had landed such a big catch, a six pound trout no less and he held it out proudly in front of him.

'Well done, Timothy. That'll make a wonderful last supper to share with Gladys before she leaves in the morning.'

Harriet gave a silent prayer of thanks for Edward's thoughtfulness at teaching Timothy to fish. Not only was it excellent therapy for the lad, but it also relieved her headache of trying to provide nourishing meals every day since rationing had been introduced.

'Where's Mother?'

'She's gone upstairs for something. Why don't you go and tell her your exciting news!'

As Timothy raced enthusiastically towards the stairs, fish held triumphantly in front of him, he stopped in his tracks at his grandmother's voice.

'Come and bring that fish back here, young Timothy!'

Sheepishly Timothy returned and left the trout on the kitchen table and Harriet was relieved when Tom took it out to the scullery to clean it up. While he was out of earshot Harriet took the opportunity to thank Gladys.

'Tom has made so much improvement since you've been here, Gladys. It's obvious he thinks very highly of you.'

'Do you think so, Mrs Newton? I do so wish he would say something. I can't understand how he is still so locked up inside. Do you think he'll ever speak again?'

'I hope so, Gladys. In fact it's hope that keeps me going. I know I'm protective of him but it will do him so much good going out to work again, that I don't know how to thank you.'

'You don't have to thank me, Mrs Newton. To see his face brighten is all the thanks I need, but if he'd only say something before I leave, it would give me so much joy. You can't imagine!'

Neither Harriet nor Gladys realised that, with both the kitchen and scullery doors open, Tom could hear every word that they had said. He'd been so happy to see Gladys again and didn't want her to leave without realising how strong his feelings were for her and yet he had been quiet for so long now, he didn't know where to start. He just prayed that he would have the courage to speak to her before she left.

Sarah, meanwhile, had retreated to her room and to calm her temper she had reached deep into her drawer and pulled out the silver locket. She prised it open for the first time and inside she was surprised to find two colours of hair entwined, one was obviously her mother's auburn hair but the other was jet black. Her father's had been dark brown and so it couldn't be his. Was it possible that Uncle Edward's greying hair was once black, she pondered?

It was at that moment that Timothy came rushing in with his news. Sarah had no time to hide the locket and so Timothy stopped in his tracks, intrigued by what was in his mother's hand.

'What is it?' he asked.

'It's a special locket which is very old. I think it might have been Grandma's but she doesn't want to see it anymore. It might make her sad and so we must keep it a secret. Can we do that, Timothy? And what makes you look so excited today?' she asked, quickly changing the subject.

'I've just brought home the biggest trout ever, Mother, and you must come and have a look at it. Grandma says we'll have it for supper and Uncle Tom's about to clean it up.'

While Timothy was speaking, Sarah had slipped the locket back into the pouch and into its hiding place. For Timothy it was soon forgotten, because he was too excited to show his mother the fish. They went downstairs and into the scullery.

'What a fine catch. Your father would have been so proud of you,' Sarah exclaimed, always feeling that it was important for Timothy to think of his father at such a time.

Sarah knew that fishing with his son would have given Anthony so much pleasure and that made her think of Victor.

Tom handed it back to Timothy who took it through to his grandma to be cooked gently on the stove. After supper she was glad to see Tom and Gladys go out for a walk, since it gave her a little time to talk with her daughter.

'I can understand why Edward made you angry earlier, but in some ways he has a point. It was your idea to start up a guest house and now that the war is over and I can open up again, it will take more than one person to make it a successful business. I would really appreciate your ideas and I'd also enjoy letting go of some of the reins of responsibility to have a bit of time to relax myself. I'm not putting you under any pressure, Sarah, but I *would* like you to think about it.'

'You mean that we would share the business, rather than me working for you?'

'That's exactly what I mean. We could sit down and decide who would be best doing the different work. You might like to manage the finances, since you were always good at maths. Anyway, we don't have to decide today.'

'I really hate the atmosphere at Supermarine now, Mother. I never like resentment and although I don't like to admit defeat, this would certainly give me a positive future for Timothy and me, and I could spend more time with him, too.'

Later that night after supper Sarah bade her mother goodnight, following Timothy upstairs. He was still bursting with pride, so much so that it took a while to settle her little man to sleep. She smiled down at him, her eyes gleaming, sharing his pride.

Once all was quiet she decided that it was about time she replied to Victor's letter. It was while she was writing to him, sitting in the light of a small gas lamp, that she made her mind up to accept her mother's offer. It seemed a perfect solution to her future and she wondered what he thought.

20th January, 1919

Dear Victor,

I apologize for not writing for several months. I must admit at first to being a little upset by your comments about my mother and Uncle Edward. At first I dismissed it as evil gossip but a couple of things have made me doubt this judgement. I wonder if we will ever know the truth.

I have some exciting news from Timothy. He came home with a six pound trout today and we are so proud of him. You should have seen his face! I couldn't help but imagine how much he would enjoy fishing with you on Riduna. One day, perhaps.

For me, life has been quite hard since the end of the war. The men resent me working at Supermarine and Mother has offered me a share in her business. What do you think? This will be a good opportunity for me and give us the security we need right now.

Another interesting piece of news is that Tom has had a surprise visitor, a nurse from Karachi who met him when he became unwell. They are sweet on each other but unfortunately he's not uttered a single word since he's been home with us. I'm concerned, because I'm not sure if she'll wait for him to wake up from his nightmare and she is about to leave to go to her parents. I do hope she has patience and returns to us because I can see it in his eyes that he adores her. Love isn't easy, is it?

Well, that's all for now and I hope that you are well and that island life is returning to normality, if that can at all be possible. I have to admit that I have missed receiving letters from you and look forward to hearing from you soon.

Kind regards,
Sarah and Timothy

Downstairs Gladys and Tom came in after a short stroll and Gladys called goodnight to Harriet as she headed to her room. Tom paused as if to speak, but then smiled at his mother before heading upstairs himself.

Harriet sat heavily in her armchair, enjoying the quiet around her. It dawned on her that yet again she had Edward to thank for sewing the seed of thought in her mind about Sarah. She had no doubt that eventually the idea would have occurred to her too, but nevertheless albeit clumsily put, Edward had helped her family to heal yet again. If only Tom could heal too, and with that, she nodded off to sleep. It was a couple of hours later that she awoke again stiff necked and disorientated. Tom was gently tapping her on the shoulder. She smiled up at her handsome mute son and struggled to her feet, stiff and aching.

'Life can begin again now Tom, can't it? We'll never forget, but maybe at last we'll find happiness.'

She looked up at her son with love in her eyes. It was a pure moment between mother and son; agape, a love which was totally unconditional.

To Harriet's surprise and delight Tom whispered,

'Yes Mother, I hope so!'

At first Harriet stood in silence, overwhelmed by what she had just heard, half disbelieving her son had spoken for the first time since his return. When she looked up at him, his expression was as surprised as hers.

'Oh Tom!' she exclaimed, eyes streaming with tears as he hugged his mother tightly as if he didn't want to let the moment go.

Harriet looked up at her son and wondering if she'd dreamt it all she asked,

'How are you feeling, Tom?'

'I'm feeling much better, Mother, but it's still hard sometimes,' Tom began in a faltering, quiet voice. 'It's like

I expect Jack to come home any moment. When I smile I can see his smile and when I walk I can feel him walking by my side.'

'He'll always be with us, Tom, but you've got so much to live for now,' she said, thinking of Gladys.

'That I know,' Tom replied and with that Harriet felt more content.

She would remember this moment for the rest of her life.

The following morning, Gladys left quite early but the glint in her eyes as she said goodbye and expressed her thanks to Harriet spoke volumes. After her departure Tom headed to the bike shop, leaving Harriet feeling quite at a loss. With a sigh she went back upstairs to put the finishing touches to preparing the guest rooms. The curtains were washed and rehung, rugs shaken and walls scrubbed clean. Everything was looking fresh and ready to begin the new chapter in the life of Bourton Villas. If anything, she felt just a touch lonely and really hoped her daughter would make up her mind soon. After all, they had bookings for the weekend and the future looked just a little bit brighter, despite the limit of the ration books, now stored safely in the kitchen drawer.

Chapter 34

IT WAS NOT long before Sarah's decision was made for her. With falling orders for flying boats since the end of the war, in January 1919 Sarah and many of her fellow workers were laid off. This was no surprise to Harriet, who had hoped that her headstrong daughter would have made that sensible decision long ago. Nevertheless Harriet was quite proud that Sarah settled quickly into life at Bourton Villas.

Harriet was tired. Her own health had suffered since she had shouldered the burden of keeping the family afloat throughout the war and it was a great relief to shed some responsibility. The business proved to be a success despite local hardships, with a steady flow of guests during the spring and early summer, most stopping off on their way to catch steamers from Southampton. Harriet continued the role of shopping, cooking, washing and generally meeting the day to day needs of their guests, whilst Sarah dealt with the finances, kept the rooms clean and took on the role of meeting and greeting. Sarah also spent a couple of evenings a week mending and sewing, a task she knew her mother disliked.

By summer there were even rumours that there might be exciting times ahead for Supermarine and it was not a surprise to Harriet that her friendly London reporter returned. Early one evening she found Harry Harper in deep conversation with Ernest.

'What do you think of your new Chief Engineer, Mr Mitchell7, Ernest?' the mysterious gentleman asked.

'I admire him, to tell you the truth. At first, we wondered what this upstart was doing, joining us with so little experience, but his knowledge and understanding has won over even the most sceptical.'

'Supermarine is one of the few fortunate firms which seem to have survived the downturn. Why do you think that is?' asked the reporter.

'I have to admit that it's thanks to the management's vision of the future. They have an enthusiasm that carries the workforce and we're full of optimism.'

'Who, in your opinion, is the driving force of this vision, as you call it?'

'Well, certainly Mr Paine and Mr Mitchell seem to think along much the same lines, as far as I can see. I just supervise the implementation of their instructions. Of course I'm not privy to the management meetings. You'll have to ask them.'

'Yes, I certainly will if I can, but why do *you* think they've been so successful?'

'Well, I think the main reason is their forward thinking, to move on from the dependency on the military.'

'Do you think that civil aviation is the way forward, then?'

'Almost certainly, it's what's saved us. You'll see for yourself tomorrow no doubt, as we launch the first flying boat passenger service, certainly in Europe.'

'Do you think there's much call for trips to Bournemouth, then?'

'I think you're missing the point if you think that Mr Mitchell will be satisfied with that. Talk is that Bournemouth is a trial run for future flights to the Isle of

Wight but almost certainly to France and maybe to the Channel Islands!'

'But at seven pounds and nine shillings return, it's hardly competitive with the steamer or train, is it?'

'No, but there are those who'll pay for time and those who'll pay just because they can. You'll see,' argued Ernest.

Harriet moved quietly back to the kitchen, proud of the way her son was handling the interview. She was certain that Ernest was unaware of the true nature of Harry Harper's profession, though. That bothered her a little, but it was not until a couple of days later that realisation dawned.

On the morning after the exciting launch of the Supermarine Channel biplane on 14th August 1919, watched by the Mayor of Southampton, Ernest was reading the account in the Daily Mail. The bold headlines 'The First Flying Boat Passenger Service in the World' captured his full attention and then to his shock he recognised snippets of his conversation with his mother's guest. Although not displeased with the version in print, nevertheless he vowed that he should be more careful in future as to what he said to strangers.

Three weeks later, Ernest was not surprised to see the young gentleman stopping off at Bourton Villas once more. Woolston was still buzzing with speculation and hearsay about Supermarine's Sea Lion's failed attempt at the Schneider Trophy; an event which would draw Harry Harper like a gull to a trawler. This time he was on his way back to London after experiencing his first flight from Bournemouth to Southampton.

The men shook hands in greeting.

'Welcome back, sir. I must be careful what I say to you in future, now that I know the true nature of your work.'

Ernest saw the young man wink at Harriet.

'I can see that you already know who this man is, Mother. You didn't warn me. I might have said something controversial and could have lost my job.'

'But you didn't, Ernest, did you? You're far too proud of what Supermarine does to give away any secrets.'

'So, how did you find your flight in our flying boat, sir? May I call you

Mr Harper now that the truth is out?' Ernest asked the reporter, glad to be the one asking the questions.

'I'd be happier if you'd keep the knowledge between yourselves, if you don't mind.' Ernest and Harriet nodded in understanding. 'The flight was excellent. Though I must admit that it wasn't my first. It is a wonder to slice at speed through the water, spray everywhere. The noise: you can't imagine it. Then, just as you've become accustomed to the sensation, whoosh, you are airborne. Although you know it's going to happen, it doesn't lessen the surprise. Quite different to any other aeroplane I've had the privilege to fly in.'

'Privilege' is the word, thought Edward, although he was far too polite to comment, showing no signs of jealousy that his different status made such an experience for himself virtually impossible.

'You say that it wasn't your first flight in a flying boat?'

'Indeed no. What with the unfortunately timed rail strike last week, my boss was willing to fly us down to Bournemouth from London, rather than for us to miss the event.'

'Did you enjoy that experience as much?' asked Ernest, his eyes unable to hide his keen interest.

'Amazing! I'd been up in aircraft before, of course, but to fly over the coast and to land on the sea… well, it was like being a young lad again. I was so excited. If you're asking me to compare planes though, then I certainly felt more secure in your aircraft. The takeoff and landing was smoother and the pilot obviously had great experience. Biard was his name.'

Ernest beamed with pride.

'It still makes my heart race, seeing the aeroplanes glide over Southampton Water. Nothing will change that for me, either.' Ernest paused. 'Do I still need to convince you that there's a future in civil aviation for flying boats?' Ernest asked with interest.

'Oh, no indeed. I've heard it argued that it will be the main vehicle for flying from Great Britain in the future, us being an island: much safer that way, because you can land on the water and float if you get into any difficulty.'

'It should certainly give the traveller more peace of mind when flying over the English Channel,' agreed Ernest.

'Yes, I must say that I'm impressed. What do you think of Supermarine's effort in its first Schneider Trophy competition?' the reporter asked Ernest.

'I'm sure that our Sea Lion was capable enough, but I gather that it was the typical British weather that let us down.'

'Yes, the fog was pretty bad in Bournemouth. Your Sea Lion put up a good attempt despite hull damage early on. They even had to alight to find out where they were apparently, but then the Sea Lion hit something in the water.'

'Did you see anything from where you were standing?' Ernest asked.

'Not a thing. I was on the shore near the pier, but it was a real pea souper! The only information we got was by word of mouth from the organisers. Most unfortunate for the first of the competitions to be held on English shores. I'll give credit to your flying boat though, it took off again OK, so I'm told, but then flipped forward, pushing the nose down as the hull filled with water from the hole made by the earlier collision.'

'"Tossed the pilot into the sea" was the report that came

back to us here at Supermarine, but it was our first attempt and we're already excited about the next competition.'

'It's a shame there was no overall winner and hard luck on the Italian's for running out of fuel though. I've heard it might be in Venice next year and we shall see if your man Mitchell can prove himself and come up with the goods this time.'

'Let's hope so,' grinned Ernest, enjoying this conversation immensely.

'And what about you, Mrs Newton?' asked Harry Harper, turning to Harriet, who was busily clearing away the breakfast plates. 'You seem to be very busy at the moment.'

'It's been excellent business for us. We are fortunate that The Cliff Hotel still recommend us if they are full and we're so convenient for the *Floating Bridge* and the port.'

'I hope that your good fortune continues, Mrs Newton. Well, I must be off to catch my train back to London. Good day to your both and many thanks for your warm hospitality.'

Harry Harper bowed and tapped his hat as he paused at the front door before striding purposefully across the street.

Chapter 35

THIS PERIOD PROVED to be both busy and exciting at Bourton Villas. The recent events involving Supermarine had ensured that Harriet's guest house was quite popular and had gained a reputation for its welcome and convenient location. What with the cross channel flights planned for the end of the month, with departures from Southampton to Le Havre at twenty five pounds a head, Harriet found that most of her clientele were both well to do and fascinating.

Harriet's peace of mind was only dampened by two happenings in the coming weeks. Firstly Sarah started going out a couple of evenings every week and leaving Timothy in her care. Although Harriet enjoyed the precious time she spent with her grandson, she feared a repeat of the scandal the family only just avoided with her daughter-in-law, Hannah. When she discovered the nature of Sarah's evenings a couple of weeks later Harriet did not know whether to be relieved or equally concerned.

'I'm only getting involved in the meetings, Mother, because I feel so strongly that all women should have the chance we've enjoyed in running our own lives,' Sarah explained.

'But we've only been forced to think about opportunities

out of tragedy. Even if we had started a business such as this, I would never have taken on this responsibility if your father was still alive.'

'That's the whole point I'm trying to make, Mother. You've made such a successful business woman; why shouldn't others be allowed that opportunity?'

'Many have been forced into it, but not out of choice, Sarah. I know for a fact that they would much rather their menfolk had returned to them after the war.'

'Oh Mother, I know circumstances have been difficult for women, but they've also been empowering. So many of us tasted independence, working in jobs previously not open to us, that young women especially think differently to you. We feel that we should be given the same opportunities and that we should be able to vote. Tell me why we have so few rights? It's unfair and doesn't make sense!'

Harriet sighed. She would never truly understand her daughter but at least they had a good working relationship in their business. Once Sarah had gone out and Timothy had been put to bed she sat and thought for a while and had to acknowledge that Sarah had a point. She just wished that her daughter was just a little less headstrong and prayed that it did not lead her into any trouble.

Harriet was thinking of Sarah one evening. She was just about to take a well earned rest after clearing away supper when there was a knock at the door and she was surprised to find Edward standing there looking drawn and tired. She invited him into the kitchen where they would have some privacy. She offered Edward a brandy and sat next to him with a cup of tea, sharing the news of her family, the new developments at Supermarine, their success in the guest house and finishing with her concerns for Sarah. Edward just listened, uncharacteristically quiet, so much so that Harriet came to an abrupt silence and was suddenly embarrassed.

'Oh, I'm sorry, Edward. I must bore you with my ramblings!'

'Not at all, Harriet. I've known you long enough to be honest with you. It's just so good to listen to you talk, to sit with you just like in the olden days.'

Harriet looked at Edward with concern. She had never seen him look so unhappy.

'What's the matter, Edward? You really don't look too well to me.'

Edward sighed, while he tried to decide what to share with his childhood friend and his thoughts turned to the end of the war. Where should he begin? Should he describe the sights of ship loads of injured soldiers returning from the Front; hundreds of haunted soldiers passing though his care on the *Princess Ena*? Some of these men had been fine, just looking forward to reaching home at last, but most were dispirited lost souls, whose eyes glazed in empty resignation. At the news of the Armistice he had been full of hope, but how could he explain how he felt now, even to Harriet?

Getting no response and filled with concern, Harriet asked,

'And has your life returned to normality now that your ship is taking passengers across the channel again?'

'Normality? I'm not sure what that is.'

This time, as his eyes looked at Harriet, his mind drifted back to their life on Riduna and the everyday joy he used to feel as they shared their early years together.

'Where did our lives go to, Harriet? What happened to our dreams?'

This was not the Edward Harriet knew and loved and she was suddenly quite fearful. She shivered.

'How is Marie?' she heard herself ask.

'Umm, well, I feel a little like yourself regarding Sarah's activities. Marie is rarely home at night. She, too, has fervour of spirit, giving as much time as she can to the Salvation Army, both during and since the war. She goes out most nights. We have so much of this influenza around us that she spends all her time visiting and tending the sick.'

'That's to be commended, isn't it?' Harriet asked gently.

'It's all very fine but I never see her. She stays an hour to see me fed but then goes out, returning when I'm fast asleep. She often rises before I get up and leaves my breakfast on the hearth.'

'It must be rewarding for her,' Harriet commented, remembering her desperate need to have a role in life before Jane suggested that she took patients though the war. 'We all need to feel that we're doing something worthwhile.'

'But isn't looking after me worthwhile enough for her, Harriet? It always used to be.'

Suddenly Harriet understood her daughter Sarah's motives and felt a little impatient with Edward's lack of understanding. She was just about to express these thoughts when she saw such painful emptiness in his eyes that she softened.

'Oh, Edward. You mustn't feel so put out. I expect Marie just wants to feel needed.'

Edward looked straight at Harriet for the first time since his arrival and feeling his old emotions and desires stirring unbidden he paused, his eyes moist.

'All that time we threw away, Harriet. It could have turned out so differently,' he added with an expression of longing.

It took all of Harriet's will power to remain seated and not to fall into Edward's arms but at that moment they heard Timothy rush down the stairs, wanting a drink of milk.

Edward shook Timothy's hand and Harriet watched his

expression lighten as Timothy spoke proudly of his six pound trout. Of course he'd caught some fish since then but none quite as big as that.

When Harriet mentioned that it was about time for Timothy to go back to bed Edward decided that he should leave, thus breaking the spell between them. As she followed Timothy up the stairs she glanced over her shoulder at Edward. He smiled a warm smile, saying only, 'Thanks,' as he opened the front door and disappeared.

As Harriet settled Timothy for the night, she looked down on him as his eyelids closed and he drifted off to sleep. As she watched over him, Harriet suddenly realised that her life hadn't been thrown away at all. It had just turned out differently. She had her children and grandchildren who made her life so fulfilling. As she slipped off to sleep an hour later, she was moved to give thanks for each of them in turn. First there was Ernest who, of all her children, was fortunate to come out of the war most unscathed by tragedy. He supported his family well, now that he was a respected supervisor at Supermarine. Next there was dear Tom, who was now talking again, and although Harriet knew that in his heart he would never fully recover from the death of his twin brother, he was certainly living a normal life once more and she had high hopes that Gladys would soon return. Then there were Hannah and Phyllis who had settled into their new lives and had the imminent arrival of a sibling for Phyllis to look forward to. Last, but by no means least, were Sarah and Timothy whose presence at Bourton Villas helped to soften the emptiness she sometimes felt. She thanked God that their supportive relationship in both their private and business lives was mutually beneficial. Finally she remembered Joe, who would have adored all of his grandchildren and would have been her rock throughout the difficult times, but it was not to be.

As she always did, she also gave thanks for Edward, who still appeared unexpectedly and, like replacing a missing cog in a broken wheel, helped her world to continue to turn. Finally she prayed for herself and, hearing Sarah slip into the house, she drifted into a deep sleep.

Chapter 36

SARAH REVELLED IN her new life and responsibilities. Since she held the purse strings it was her role to deal with the bank and local businesses who supplied their needs. Her confidence grew, as did her respected standing within their community. She was answerable to no one, except her mother of course, and theirs was a partnership in the true sense of the word. No, she hated to admit it but Supermarine had done her a favour. Also Timothy was growing into an intelligent, caring lad and although she knew he still missed his dad, it was maybe now the memory of having a father which he longed for rather than the man himself. Unfortunately her son was not alone in that respect since nearly three quarters of his classmates were likewise bereft.

She was also enjoying her social life; the suffragette meetings she attended over in Southampton fed her self esteem as she was able to share her positive experiences and be inspired by others. Wearing her only decent outfit, which she had sewn during the recent light evenings of June, this morning she was striding along Victoria Street, nodding and smiling at people she passed by. After a successful meeting with their local bank manager she began to daydream, wondering if she should try to set up a local group of suffragettes here in Woolston. Once in sight of Bourton Villas she was concerned when she saw her mother frantically waving to her from the front door. Sarah rushed the couple of hundred yards up the Portsmouth Road, aware of the concerned look on her mother's face.

'It's Timothy, Sarah. He has been sent home from school with this influenza. I have just put him to bed, but I think we should call the doctor.'

Sarah rushed upstairs to find her son feverish and flushed, drifting in and out of a fitful sleep. As Sarah looked down on her son she berated herself for not paying heed to the signs she had tried to ignore that morning, of Timothy's lethargy and sweat drenched brow. How thoughtless and self-obsessed she had been that she'd put her meeting with the bank manager first and sent her precious son to school. She lifted some cold water to his lips and wiped his brow with a damp cloth, left beside his bed by Harriet a few moments before. Sarah looked over her shoulder and Harriet did not need words to read the guilt and grief in her daughter's eyes. Harriet rushed out of the house to call on the doctor but when he finally visited later that afternoon he could offer no words of comfort, but to demand that they close the guesthouse and send their remaining guests on their way.

For the next three days mother and grandmother sat beside Timothy in a constant vigil, each taking only a couple of hours to take a fitful rest. On the first day Harriet watched and listened as her daughter continued to blame herself for the neglect of her son, the phrase 'pride comes before a fall,' overshadowing her guilt-ridden face. On the second day Harriet found Sarah shedding silent tears of remorse and it was virtually impossible to persuade her daughter to take a break, but by the third day, with Timothy's condition deteriorating, an overriding calmness had filled the room. Harriet wanted to reach out to Sarah but felt an unseen barrier between them and in her own helpless despair, her prayer of thanks of just a few days before turned to a heartfelt supplication to the Almighty, expressing neither blame nor anger, just a silent entreaty for help to come.

On the following morning there was an unexpected knock at the front door and thinking that she would be turning away another hopeful guest Harriet reluctantly walked downstairs, only to find Gladys on the doorstep. Seeing Harriet's exhausted expression and greyness of pallor Gladys soon summed up the situation and, not hesitating to think of her personal safety, rushed inside and embraced Harriet, leading her into the kitchen where she noticed the range was cold and the room strewn with cloths and damp rags. The first thing she did was to light the range and sit Harriet down. This Harriet did under little protest as she watched Gladys tidy the room, placing all of the rags in a large pot to be boiled, talking constantly as she worked. Finally the water boiled and Gladys made the tea, slipping a drop of liquid into the steaming cup before passing it to Harriet. Few words had passed her lips since Gladys' arrival, apart from to protest that she should leave at once because Timothy was infectious with the Spanish flu.

A few moments after Harriet had drunk the tea, Gladys was pleased to see her relax and drift into a deep sleep. Leaving the rags to soak and taking another cup with her upstairs she found Sarah, limp, by Timothy's bedside. Her eyes showed just a glimmer of recognition, relief, and was it gratitude, as she too drank the proffered tea? Before Sarah had a chance to allow the soothing content of her drink to drift her into oblivion, Gladys took her by the arm and guided Sarah to her own bedroom across the landing. She then turned to her third patient, assessing his needs before returning to the kitchen for a bowl of warm water and a clean cloth. Back upstairs she lifted the covers from the shivering Timothy and gently smoothed the sweat from his face and body, finally lifting him to replace his drenched and stained sheets. Once Timothy was more comfortable she returned to the kitchen to prepare a warm liquid for him and although reluctant at first, she was pleased that he eventually began to take small sips which slipped down his burning throat. Soon he too relaxed and slept, his fever abating just a little and Gladys settled in the armchair, turning to the coffee she had prepared for herself in order to keep awake by Timothy's side.

It was not until late that evening when Tom came into the kitchen to find his mother still fast asleep and the room tidy that he guessed correctly that Gladys had returned. He smiled. Taking two stairs at a time he reached Timothy's bedroom and caught Gladys' eye through the open doorway; without hesitation she rushed into his arms. They stood thus on the landing for several moments, drinking in the security and warmth of their embrace. Sarah, disturbed by Tom's appearance, gratefully took over Gladys' vigil and Tom led Gladys downstairs and out into the yard.

At first they sat in silence, enjoying the moment of togetherness. It was Tom who broke this quietness with his concern.

'You shouldn't be here, Gladys. I don't want you to put your life in danger.'

Surprised at first by Tom's ignorance of the nature of her profession she replied tactfully,

'I think I'm meant to be here, Tom. It's what I do best, to care for people in need and hopefully I can do some good too. Would you rather your mother and sister suffer from exhaustion and despair? If I can only share their burden then I will gladly do it.'

Tom looked down into her eyes.

'I'm so pleased you're here,' he said with genuine warmth which melted her. 'Last time you were with us you made me well again and I can only hope you can do the same for young Timothy.'

'I think it was your mother who made you better and not me. I was only the final catalyst to make you believe that living was worthwhile after all.'

'Will you marry me?' Tom asked, taking Gladys by surprise.

'Yes, I will!' she replied and they embraced once more, for the first time allowing their lips to meet in a gentle, sensuous kiss.

Harriet, who had awoken by this time and heard voices in the back yard, witnessed the encounter and although her fear for her grandson was undiminished she felt hope return.

The next few days were critical for Timothy but with Gladys' guidance the routine of joint care continued like a smooth seamless garment, woven into the fabric of their lives.

It was on the fifth day that Timothy gave up the fight and passed away, like so many children in their neighbourhood. Sarah was overwhelmed by grief and even Harriet lost any drive to keep believing. After a quiet funeral the hardest task of looking after Harriet and Sarah began for Gladys. Tom, who had moved back into the room above the bike shop by this time, looked on with grateful concern as Gladys tried to support his family. Her presence reassured him and he had no doubt that his mother, and certainly his sister Sarah, would have lost the will to live without her support. After a month had passed by, when he watched his mother and sister wander about listlessly, he felt that the sooner his family opened Bourton Villas for business again the sooner they would start to heal of their overwhelming sense of loss, but he also knew that neither had any inclination to do so. He discussed this with Gladys on one of their evening walks.

It was September before the decision was fortunately taken out of their hands. Ernest called in one day with some news. Harriet thought it must be important because he took the cup of tea Gladys offered and sat down, making sure he had gained his mother's attention.

'Supermarine is to begin flights to France, Mother.'

'That's good for you, isn't it?' replied Harriet, trying to sound interested.

Tom had come in behind Ernest and heard the news.

'Why this sudden decision, Ernest?' he asked.

Glad to have a more appreciative audience Ernest continued,

'What with the national unrest we've read about in the papers, LSWR have gone on strike. This has also affected the steamers of course and many travellers have been stranded, unable to journey to France. Well, Supermarine, like Avro, took this unfortunate happening and turned it into an opportunity. Avro dropped leaflets from the sky offering a private service to stranded travellers but Supermarine grasped the outstretched hand of fortune and have started a regular service.'

'That's excellent news, brother. It's what we've been hoping for, though, isn't it?'

'I know, but look at the paper today.'

Ernest handed the paper to his brother's eager outstretched hands.

The words in the Mail read that Supermarine was a pioneer in offering 'The First International Flying Service' to Le Havre for twenty five pounds per person.

'Well, Mother. You know what this means?'

Harriet, who had not quite caught up with the

conversation, tried to focus on her son's words. Unusually exasperated by her lack of response, he continued,

'There will be urgent need for overnight guest accommodation. I have been asked to try to persuade you to open for guests again, Mother. What do you say?' Ernest waited for a reply and since there was none it was Gladys who responded first.

'I'll be here to help you, Harriet. We can manage together and it would be such a good opportunity to get the business going again.'

Reluctantly Harriet agreed but at first Sarah would have little to do with the business. Soon though, she was coaxed back into the practical matter of the running of Bourton Villas, since Gladys claimed to be useless at financial matters. Thus Gladys took over the front line tasks of meeting and greeting guests and serving their meals, enabling Harriet to remain in the background, cooking and running the household. Although Sarah kept charge of the purse strings, she spent most of her spare time in her room, carrying out any mending required. She had no interest in meeting people now and rarely ventured out of the house, sending Gladys as a go-between, to attend any meetings at the bank or to liaise with suppliers.

It was during this lonely time that she began to write more regularly to Victor and his replies became more frequent.

9th September, 1919

My dear Sarah,

I am so sorry to hear your news of Timothy. I was devastated when I received your last letter. I wish I could be there with you, although I know I could not ease your suffering. I only wished you had been able to bring young Timothy over here to

see our island. I would have enjoyed getting to know him so much. Allow yourself time to grieve, Sarah, but try not to hide away.

Nothing can take away the sadness you feel, but I am glad that your guest house has now opened up again. Nurse Gladys sounds like an angel and I'm so glad that she's there to help you. Work certainly keeps the mind active and eases the pain just a little. I find this so when trying not to dwell on my many friends who have not returned from the war. There are so many gaps in our lives over here. The older generation are having to work harder and continue to work into old age because their sons are not here to take over.

Women too have taken over roles previously not open to them and in their case they have no choice, since few of my generation have returned in one piece. I am one of the fortunate ones. I have a limp but I do not allow it to hinder my activities. I still enjoy to go fishing both for pleasure and to make a little extra money for my parents. Oh, I do so wish I had been able to teach Timothy the skills of fishing in the sea.

Please write again soon, Sarah. I still remember with fondness my time staying with you at Bourton Villas and I want to reassure you that you are constantly in my thoughts.

Yours truly,
    Victor Le Page

Sarah penned a reply by return of post:

30th September, 1919

Dear Victor,
    It was so good to receive your prompt reply. I try not to hide away but find it easier to keep away from people and their meaningless platitudes. I know that I am not the only one

suffering, but that does nothing to lessen the pain. To lose a husband or, in your case friends, is hard enough, but you cannot imagine what it is like to lose your only son. I cannot even begin to describe my emotions and yet to write to you and receive your letter was a balm in an otherwise cruel world.

It is good to keep my mind occupied with figures and sewing, but it is still hard to have the will to keep on living. I wish I had the desire to continue in the works of the women's movement here, but I have no enthusiasm for even such a good cause as that.

I sometimes think of Riduna. I wonder whether Timothy might still be alive if I had brought him over there sooner, as you had so often suggested. That particular train of thought is futile, though. It only adds to my burden of guilt, which is already far too heavy for me to bear.

I thank you for your continued kindness towards me and am grateful to you for giving me meaning to my otherwise barren life.

With affection,
Sarah

Life continued in much the same manner for the next few weeks in Bourton Villas. Although there were only regular flights to Le Havre for a few days while the strike lasted, Supermarine's flights to the Isle of Wight, Bournmouth and the Channel Islands continued, which, combined with the nearness of the Port of Southampton, ensured that Bourton Villas thrived.

The guesthouse was busy with travellers eager for their journey ahead. Some only stayed one night, preceding or following their first trip in a flying boat and were enthusiastic to talk of their experiences from the excitement of the flight along Southampton Water, to the surprise as the aircraft lifted free. Some found the turbulence unbearable but others, who'd been blessed by calm weather, enthused about the sights they'd witnessed from above, describing in detail the birds' eye view of The Royal Victoria, The Isle of Wight and the Needles.

Only a few weeks later, Sarah received a reply from Victor. She had fretted that he might have been discouraged by her melancholy, but was relieved that this was not the case:

October 10th, 1919

My dear Sarah,

How my heart was heavy when I received your letter and I felt so powerless to help you. I will not fall into the temptation of writing meaningless comments in order to try to ease your grief because I know that they would only irritate you. All I can say is that I'm thinking of you. I know that it is little consolation but it is all I have to offer.

Nevertheless, I felt that I was brought closer to you last week when a pilot called Evans was flying a flying boat from Supermarine and it came down in fog at the end of the breakwater. Do you know him, by any chance? It caused such an excitement here but unfortunately the plane was wrecked and brought on to Braye Beach.

Apparently it was one of two planes flying to The Channel Islands, the other successfully reaching Jersey; I was told by a local fisherman.

The thought of regular services to Riduna gives me little hope for seeing you sooner, since the cost, I know, will be way beyond either of our purses, but it does make the distance between us seem more accessible, somehow. I honestly think that a regular service to Riduna is only a pipedream, since the waters around us are much too dangerous for flying boats to land safely, even with the Breakwater. We shall see.

I hope that business continues to thrive, Sarah, and that you will begin to feel more at peace. If only you could come to Riduna for a rest. I'm sure that the sea air and scenery would help to heal you, but I know that this is as unlikely as the hope of regular flights to our island. I am thinking of you, nevertheless.

If only I could be at your side to give you comfort.

Yours truly,
Victor

When Sarah read Victor's letter she closed her eyes and thought of Riduna. She imagined the ride down to the harbour and the vivid picture of Braye Beach gave her strength to carry on. She knew that a visit was out of the question although, if her father was still alive, there might have been a slim chance that she could have taken a trip to Sarnia with him, but not now.

Chapter 37

DOWNSTAIRS, HARRIET TOO was in her armchair dreaming of Riduna. Thoughts of the island seemed to come unbidden more frequently now. It was as if the grief had dislodged suppressed emotions in her heart and whenever she closed her eyes she seemed to be transported across the waters to the island of her birth. Sometimes her dreams took on an existence more real than reality itself.

That afternoon Jane had called and so it was easy for Harriet to remember their girlish talks as they grew up. That afternoon her friend had been firm in a kindly sort of way.

'It's time you picked up the pieces of your life and took control again, Harriet. It's doing you no good relying on Gladys all the time.'

Gladys, who had been making the tea at the time, blushed and protested that she was happy to help, but it did not deter Jane from continuing.

'We desperately need your skills at the hospital Gladys, even if it is only for six months. Your talents are wasted here. Harriet is quite capable of coping now.'

'That's kind of you to say so, Jane, but I'm quite happy helping out here,' Gladys replied.

'I know you are, Gladys, but you are an experienced nurse and I feel that it is such a waste.'

It was Tom who spoke up next, with a response which surprised everyone. He had seen the deterioration in his mother's will and his sister's lethargy and he realised that Gladys' support, although highly appreciated and beneficial initially, was now hindering their progress to normality.

'I think Jane's right. You've done so much to support my family but I feel you should not waste your skills now, even if it is only for a while.'

Tom and Gladys had previously agreed that they would wait for six months before they got married and he saw no reason for Gladys to waste this opportunity.

After lunch, when Gladys and Tom had gone out for a stroll together, the atmosphere between them was tense. Gladys felt that Tom was pushing her away and that he was saying that she wasn't needed anymore. Once Tom had explained his reasons she felt more reassured, but as she looked down at the sleeping Harriet that evening, creeping about the kitchen, working, she suddenly realised the truth of his wisdom. For the last couple of months she had felt pleased to be needed, but Tom was right. She had been on her feet working from sunrise til dusk and she was nearly as exhausted as she had been at the hospital in Karachi. It was time that Harriet and Sarah began to take responsibility again and if that meant she spent some time apart from Tom, then so be it. Not waiting for another conversation with Tom, she went to her room and penned a letter to Jane.

2nd November, 1919

Dear Staff Nurse Jane Hanwell

   Thank you for the offer of a nursing post at The Royal Victoria Hospital which you put to me informally this afternoon. It would be a wonderful opportunity for me to continue to serve my country and practise my profession. Like yourself I would be happy to pass on any knowledge gained through experience working abroad on to the younger trainees at the hospital.

I would like to inform you at this point that Tom and I have plans to marry next July, but nevertheless it would be an honour for me to accept the position if under these circumstances it is still offered.

Yours sincerely,
Nurse Gladys

A week later, as Gladys was clearing away the breakfast plates, the postman arrived and she was pleased that she intercepted the letter in Jane's familiar handwriting, before Harriet was able to see it. She tore open the envelope and read it while standing in the hallway:

12th November, 1919

Dear Nurse Gladys

Congratulations on your engagement. I have discussed your situation with my superiors and we would be pleased to have you join our staff on 20th November. There will be accommodation provided in the vast complex behind the hospital, now less crowded since the end of the war, and I suggest that you travel by train, from which you can catch the branch line directly into the hospital grounds.

Looking forward to greeting you on the 20th and I will personally take on the task of your induction to the hospital.

Kind regards,
Staff Nurse Jane Hanwell

Once she had read the short reply, Gladys looked up to see Harriet's quizzical face. Without saying anything, she handed Harriet the note. Harriet's face went white in an expression of denial and dismay.

'What will Sarah and I do without you, Gladys? I'm not sure we'll cope.'

'You will be fine, Mrs Newton. It's for the best, really.'

There was a long pause, when it was as if Harriet was being dragged out of a dream.

'What's wrong with me, Gladys? I must wish you well, of course. My son Tom is such a lucky man and I'm so grateful for all you've done for him and for us.'

It was as if Gladys' decision to leave had reawakened her inner strength, as her son had hoped it would. She reached out and embraced her future daughter-in-law.

'I am so pleased for you,' she said with tears in her eyes.

Only a week later, Gladys left Bourton Villas with only the small valise she arrived with three months before. She was nervously excited about her life ahead but painfully bereft of the life she was leaving behind. As Jane showed Gladys around the hospital, Jane could not help but reflect on the changes there in the past year. During the war the wards had been packed to overflowing with patients in varying degrees of agony and more casualties lined the station platform as they had waited helplessly to be carried or wheeled to some makeshift shack or tent in the grounds awaiting further attention. Now everything was calm, orderly, clean and efficient. Maybe it was the less sterile chaos she yearned for which made her restless to be on the move again. She shivered. She certainly did not long for the trainloads of seriously injured men who had arrived on a daily basis for nearly four years.

As for Gladys, whose experience in a large hospital such as this was limited to her early years of training, she relished the opportunity to practise her skills without the pressure of conditions abroad. She also looked forward to her role of supervising the new recruits. In fact the next few months passed by very quickly for Gladys. Her life at the hospital took on a regular pattern. During the weeks she worked extremely hard and then on each alternate Sunday afternoon she would visit Bourton Villas to see Tom and on the remaining Sundays he would return the visit, sometimes travelling with his mother in order to see Jane.

Life at Bourton Villas also took on a more positive routine. Harriet and Sarah, though reluctantly at first, returned to their original roles, leading to the smooth running of their enterprise. Christmas came and went in a subdued fashion. Gladys had returned to her home in Chichester, inviting Tom to join her for the first time, and with no guests staying over the festive season, life was very quiet. Harriet visited her other grandchildren at Ernest's cottage to protect Sarah from further pain and was glad when a new influx of guests arrived for the New Year. On New Year's Eve Harriet sat and reflected on the past year and wondered with a small amount of indignation why Edward had not made the effort to pay them a visit, but fortunately she had little time to dwell on the past as she prepared supper for their guests.

Chapter 38

BACK ON RIDUNA, Victor was standing amongst a large crowd of supporters for the Muratti Cup Final. All of the islanders were in a state of nervous excitement, tinged with a sense of relief. The Ridunian team, having successfully reached the final of the Channel Islands football tournament that year, had been about to lose some of its key players when lady luck shone on them. Two of the team had planned to emigrate to America, but their ship, the *Imperator,* outbound from Liverpool, was delayed, allowing the much anticipated event to go ahead with the original team. The islanders knew the stark truth that without these two men there would be no team to play, with so few young men returning after the war. Victor had also been persuaded to leave for America with his two friends and so he stood alongside neighbours and family with mixed emotions. Before the war he would have put on his kit and played for his island but now it was out of the question.

It was an excellent match, supported by an exuberant crowd and it was soon obvious that the home team was going to win. The celebrations lasted throughout the night and so the small crowd which gathered on the quayside to wave goodbye to the three departing islanders were still in good spirits, albeit a little jaded. Victor and his friends, Sam and James, were sailing alongside the defeated team and so the banter and lighthearted insults between the men continued throughout the journey to

St Peter Port on Sarnia. There was no direct ferry from Riduna to the mainland and so their route was via Sarnia and then on by steamer to Southampton. From there the travellers would rest before taking a train on to Liverpool in time for the new date set for the *Imperator* to set sail.

Secretly Victor wondered how his two best friends had persuaded him to come on this venture, since he was already missing Riduna, but he reasoned that he could always change his mind and take the next available ferry back from Southampton. This also gave the added bonus that he could call in on Sarah, whose correspondence was getting increasingly encouraging. After all, none of the island girls had caught his eye in quite the same way, although a number had tried, and there was a certain quality in Sarah which attracted him magnetically. What was it, he pondered. There were certainly signs of fearlessness and a stubbornness of spirit, but surely it was more than that. Whatever it was, his heart fluttered at the thought of seeing her again. Not only that but she also gave him an escape route, a reason to hesitate and maybe to change his mind completely. With options clear in his mind he settled to catch up on some much needed sleep, keeping his doubts about the proposed journey to America from his two friends.

Once in Southampton, late the following day, he left his friends at a small lodging house near the docks and made his way to the *Floating Bridge,* explaining that he had to check up on some friends of his and would return to the lodgings the following morning to catch the train to Liverpool. He left them before they had a chance to argue with him or ask for further explanation.

It was Sarah who opened the door to Victor and she was so surprised to see him that she dropped the pile of washing.

'Why didn't you warn me that you were coming to see us?' she exclaimed, bending down to pick up the pile of laundry.

Victor bent down to help her, but as they stood up again their heads nearly collided and for a moment their eyes met and both were still. Victor knew in that instant that he had made the right decision and it took all his self-restraint to refrain from taking Sarah into his arms and kissing her.

Sarah was caught off-balance by his gaze and nearly succumbed to his magnetism, but at that moment Harriet bustled into the hallway. She summed up the situation in an instant and took control, thus protecting her daughter from the embarrassment and shame of gossip from passers-by.

'Welcome back to Bourton Villas, Mr Le Page. What a lovely surprise. Are you hoping to stay with us for a couple of days, or is this a flying visit?'

Rather hoping that it was the latter, she was relieved to watch the young people straighten and separate, regaining their composure.

'I would appreciate a bed for the night, Mrs Newton, if that's possible. I am just passing through on my way to America with two friends from Riduna. We are planning to emigrate, but I just thought that I would call by, since I really didn't have the opportunity to thank you for my last visit.'

With that, he passed over to Harriet a small bunch of flowers which he had purchased on the docks at St Peter Port. He glanced over towards Sarah and was pleased to note a glimmer of incredulity in her composure.

'These are all the way from Guernsey,' he added, aware of the altered expression of disappointment, which Sarah tried so hard to disguise, as the flowers were handed to her mother.

'That's so kind of you. Come in and tell me all about your exciting plans while Sarah prepares your room for you.'

Fuming, Sarah felt that she'd been dismissed and so it was with some amusement that Victor watched her retreating up the stairs. He was surprised that he was invited into the kitchen, usually reserved for close friends and family, and encouraged to settle in one of the armchairs beside the range.

'Well, there's not much to tell, Mrs Newton. I'm sure life on Riduna has been no tougher there than here since the Armistice. At first I settled back into my life at the hotel since the manager relies on me when he is away, which is quite frequently. It was difficult because we lost so many of our friends in the Royal Guernsey Light Infantry but life had to go on. A couple of my closest pals, who also returned from the war, got restless and decided to emigrate. I'm not sure how they persuaded me to join them, but here I am.'

'So you're not too sure of your decision to go to America, then?' asked Harriet.

'I must admit that it wouldn't take much to change my mind,' Victor explained with honesty, just as Sarah came back downstairs, catching the tail end of this conversation.

She had been wrong-footed by his remark at the front door and was angry that Victor had come back into their lives so suddenly, only to be leaving so soon. She didn't like to acknowledge, even to herself, the seeds of feelings which led to her disquiet. She smiled shyly at him as she entered the room and the smile he returned was enough to disarm her once more.

Harriet felt the tangible thread strengthen between them and knew that her daughter had taken Victor's last remark as a challenge. With sadness and fear for her own sanity, she was suddenly aware that Mr le Page held a weapon which might destroy her partnership with her daughter in an instant. The vulnerability of life's pathways was suddenly exposed and what had seemed, until that moment, a comfortable and mutually beneficial arrangement, was now filled with uncertainty. Of course, Harriet only wanted the best for her daughter, including her future happiness, but she could not help but fear for her own future.

After a light lunch, when Victor talked more openly about island life after the war, Ernest called. Encouraged by Ernest's enthusiasm, Victor then recounted a moment by moment account of what would become the most famous football match in the island's history. There was a pause when he finished his tale with a flourish and Harriet was not at all surprised to hear Victor asking if Sarah would like to go out for a stroll, leaving Harriet to mull over the implications of his visit as she cleared away.

'How are you, Sarah?' Victor asked as they walked up the Portsmouth Road. 'I was so sorry to hear about you loss.'

'I can't say that any day is easy, Victor. I can call you Victor, can't I?'

'Of course; that goes without saying,' Victor replied.

'Working with my mother has helped, though,' Sarah continued more brightly. 'I was angry to give up working at Supermarine too, but now I'm really pleased it happened because I have much more independence and standing within the community since Mother left me to organise the finances.'

'You have become quite a business woman, Sarah. You should be proud of yourself.'

'Oh I am,' exclaimed Sarah. 'It certainly fills my brain with other concerns so that I have little time to dwell......
well, you can understand, I expect.'

'I can't say that I have a right to believe that I know how

you feel, but I have lost some dear friends and life is never quite the same again.'

There was a pause.

'Are you really planning to go to America?' Sarah asked.

'Now, that depends,' replied Victor teasingly, hoping to lift the solemn expression from Sarah's lovely face.

'Depends on what, may I ask?' replied Sarah inquisitively.

'That would be telling,' continued Victor, glad that Sarah's frown had been replaced by a lighter, more puzzled expression.

'What do your parents think of you leaving Riduna?'

'They're devastated, to be honest with you. They nearly lost me once before and they can't see why I am going this time. It's not as if I had no prospects.'

'Were you still working at the hotel, then?'

'Yes I was. My boss is furious with me, because he's come to rely on me so much. It would take a long time to train someone to take my place and, to be honest with you, he has little inclination to do so.'

'Why is that, then?'

'He knows that he can trust me to stand in for him when he is away, and is confident the hotel won't fall apart in his absence.'

'So, if your parents didn't want you to go, your boss was more than reluctant to lose you and I also detect that your own attitude was less than enthusiastic, may I ask you why you are planning to emigrate?'

Victor put his head to one side with a boyish smile.

'I don't know, really,' he replied.

There was another silence between them as each digested the implications of their conversation. Sarah, although glad that Victor was with her, wondered how he had been so gullible as to be persuaded to join his two friends. Realising that this might be in Sarah's thoughts, Victor wondered how he might give Sarah a more favourable impression of himself without sounding too eager. With this puzzling dilemma he remained silent longer than he would otherwise have done. Sarah was aware of the slight limp in Victor's walk as he strode beside her.

They had reached Miller's Pond: an area of wasteland which had been unsuitable for vegetable growing or target practice during the war and so had remained remarkably unspoilt. Without discussing the matter, they ambled through the well trodden paths, thus turning away from the busy road. There were few people about and so Victor paused.

'I might have had an ulterior motive to come to England, Sarah,' he said, giving Sarah a knowing look.

'And what might that be?' Sarah responded, pausing to look up into Victor's eyes.

'Would you really like to know?' Victor smiled questioningly down at Sarah and was pleased to see her return his smile.

'And when might you sail for America?' asked Sarah, wanting to break the spell between them and probe deeper into Victor's intentions, 'If you decide to go, that is.'

'If I sail, then we leave next Thursday, but my friends are planning to catch the train to Liverpool tomorrow.'

Victor's use of the word "if" was not lost on Sarah, as she realised that they had less than a day. She returned his gaze once more and they drew closer, his hand gently brushing a lock of Sarah's hair from her cheek. Within seconds their lips met, brushing each other's gently at first but soon both were swallowed in a passion neither had experienced before.

Several seconds later, as they drew apart, Sarah whispered,

'And when do you sail for America?'

'I don't think under the present circumstances that I *will* be sailing for America this Thursday after all,' Victor replied as he swept Sarah into his arms and kissed her once more.

They walked back to Bourton Villas in a pleasant silence, each with their own private thoughts. Sarah was suddenly aware, much like her mother, that a few unexpected moments had altered her destiny. She had no idea where her life was about to take her, but of one thing she was certain, it would not remain the same.

Victor, on the other hand, was elated. He was thinking through the various options. It wasn't quite true that going to America was ruled out in his mind, but he did not wish to frighten Sarah at this stage. He reasoned that, if he went to America Sarah would be going with him. This would take time for her to adjust to and also to organise. Alternatively he could remain in Southampton. Although jobs were scarce, he was sure he could find himself a position in one of the Southampton hotels with a good reference from his boss on Riduna. He wasn't one hundred percent convinced about this option, because he was realistic enough to know that he would be like a small minnow in a large sea rather than a large fish in a tiny pond, as he was at home. Home? Would Sarah ever consider leaving her mother and family and moving with him to Riduna? Once the seed of that thought had planted in his mind Victor was sure that this was the option to take and was quite excited about discussing the prospect with her. Meanwhile, he must return over the water to talk to his friends and enable Sarah to have time to consider the options herself. Already, he realised that she would not take too kindly to finding out that Victor had made the decision for her and so he would have to tread very carefully. With cunning planning, he hoped that Sarah would make the decision for herself, thus thinking that it was her idea in the first place.

On returning to Bourton Villas, Sarah had work to do and so they parted company, but it was not difficult for Harriet to observe a lift in her daughter's spirits and that her eyes were shining brightly.

Feeling pleased with himself, he went up to his room and wrote a letter to his boss saying that he had experienced a change of heart. He asked if he could have his job back and warned him that he might be returning with a lady, who also had experience in the hotel business and might need a position herself. He took the letter to post before returning to the dining room to join the guests for supper.

The following morning was Sunday and as the family were getting ready to go to church he took the ferry over to Southampton. He picked up a message left thoughtfully by Sam Allen at Atlantic House, a place where many passengers stayed the night before embarkation, and met them in the Royal Albert Hotel, a nearby hostelry.

'There you are, boy,' exclaimed Sam on catching sight of his friend. 'We were just wondering if you'd show up today after all. How are you?'

'Couldn't be better, Sam, thanks. I'll just get a jar. Are either of you ready for one?'

'I never refuse an offer like that,' Sam replied, 'not unless there's a better one going, that is,' he grinned, looking over towards a young woman, leaning provocatively over the bar towards him.

'Come on, Sam. It's Sunday morning. Have you no decency? There's a time and place for everything,' exclaimed James, always the quietest one of the three. 'I'll not have another, thanks Victor.'

Victor went to the bar to order two pints of the local brew, giving the lady in question a wide berth, to make it quite clear that he wasn't the least bit interested.

Victor settled happily next to Sam to have his drink and

they grinned at each other. Sam, Victor knew, was more talk than action. His friend would run a mile if the lady had really approached him. Victor paused, not quite sure how he would explain his change in circumstances.

'I've decided not to go to America after all. Well, not on Thursday at any rate,' he said abruptly.

'Why's that, then?' James asked, but not giving Victor a chance to answer, Sam interrupted.

'You can't change your mind now, Victor. We're all agreed. We're a team here and I'll hear none of your weak excuses.'

There was silence for a moment.

'I've made up my mind that I won't be going next week, but that doesn't mean that I will never follow you.'

Victor didn't want an argument and hoped to see his friends off on the train in good spirits before he admitted that he had decided to return to Riduna so soon.

'What's your excuse, then? What's so important to you to keep you here?' Sam asked.

'I've no excuses. I'm just not ready to go to America yet and I have unfinished business here in England to sort out before I leave.'

'It must be a lady. Only a lady would come between you and your friends after what we've been through,' Sam replied sarcastically.

'It is, as a matter of fact,' replied Victor, not wanting to deceive his pals completely. 'I met her when I was staying here in Woolston, before I returned to Riduna. We've remained in contact ever since and I need to know how things stand between us before I make such a journey.'

'Bring her with you, then. That's no problem, is it James?'

James, who had kept quiet through this exchange, paused to think before he responded.

'Well, you shouldn't rush these things and there's her

family to consider so I can see you'll not change Victor's mind, Sam. You can see that determined look on his face, so I wouldn't waste your breath in trying. Each to his own, I say.'

Not wanting to admit defeat that easily Sam started to argue,

'But...

'There'll be no buts, Sam. I've made up my mind. I'll give you the address and you can write to let me know where you've settled.' Victor interrupted his friend, thus bringing the altercation to a halt.

'Good luck to you, Victor,' exclaimed James, who was slightly envious of his friend's certainty. 'Of course we'll let you know what's happening. I never thought you to be the romantic one to be swayed so quickly by a lady, though.'

'When it happens it hits you like a ton of rock, James. You'll see.'

James slapped him on the back and congratulated his friend, whereas Sam's response was more reticent. Victor remained with his friends for the next few hours until it was time for them to catch the evening train to London. He hoped that it would also give Sarah some time to think on her own. There was so much to take in.

At the station Sam and James bought their tickets and they waited on the platform for the arrival of the train, three friends standing close together. Sam showed obvious excitement as he bid his friend farewell but James was unable to hide his nervousness. Victor, on the other hand, was surprised that the only emotion he could identify was a great sense of relief. At that point he knew, with a certainty which surprised him, that, whatever happened between Sarah and himself, he would not be following his friends to America at any time in the future.

Chapter 39

VICTOR MADE HIS way back to Bourton Villas early that evening. This time he held a bunch of roses in his hand which he knew would please Sarah. Harriet took him into the front room and called for Sarah to come down. For the last half an hour Sarah had been fretting over her appearance. She had little choice in garments and so decided to wear the suit she usually kept for business visits to the bank. It had a fairly tight fitting skirt which skimmed her hips and finished just below her knees. The jacket too followed the outline of her curvy figure. She knew her mother still disapproved of its length and that thought made her smile as she looked at her reflection in their only full length mirror on the landing.

She had no worries about weight since the discipline of rationing had continued until recently and it had become second nature to be frugal. No, she had to admit that she saw a fine figure of a woman staring back. Why was she so nervous? She knew that his friends had left for Liverpool that morning and so time was marginally on her side, but she did not know what he was thinking. 'If I went to America,' he'd said. How would she feel if Victor persuaded her to go to America with him? The idea excited her somewhat but in her heart she knew that she did not wish to be so far away from her family. It was a momentous decision and though she was adventurous she was not sure she had that amount of courage.

Sarah wondered whether he would consider staying here in England, but would that be fair for her to persuade him to do so, if his heart was still set on sailing to America? If only he would consider returning to Riduna. Now that was a big 'if'. She closed her eyes and felt the familiar pull towards the island she had fallen in love with during her short visit only a few years ago. She remembered the desperate yearning she had experienced when she was on Gilkicker and sometimes just thinking about Riduna had kept her sane. It was the obvious solution if you thought about it. Victor had a good job to return to and she had family roots on the island. Sarah was sure she could settle into life there but she could see only two difficulties to that perfect solution.

The first was persuading Victor to admit that he'd made the wrong decision and she knew in her heart that it might be a stumbling block for a man to admit that he was wrong. The second was her mother. She and Harriet had such a good arrangement here at the guesthouse, which had suited them both, so how could she consider leaving her mother now? Her eyes strayed to a photo of Timothy sat on a table on the landing. The cheeky boy seemed to be grinning at her and Sarah's eyes welled up.

'You'd have wanted to live on Riduna Timmy, wouldn't you?' she whispered.

'Yes, Mother, very much,' his eyes seemed to whisper in reply.

At that moment Sarah was brought back from her thoughts as she heard her mother's impatient voice repeating her request that she come downstairs. Putting all these conflicting thoughts aside she went into the front room to greet Victor.

'How lovely you look, Sarah,' Victor exclaimed, holding out the flowers towards her.

Sarah blushed as she lifted the roses to smell their deep scent.

'What a surprise, Victor. Thank you. Did your friends leave on time today?'

They sat down in armchairs facing each other and to Sarah's frustration Harriet sat on the chair between them, determined to be a chaperone. Sarah sighed, unable to hide her annoyance.

Ignoring the tense atmosphere Victor described the events of the morning in Southampton, as his friends continued their journey towards their new life.

'I can't imagine why people are so keen to uproot like that. It's so far away,' said Harriet.

'It's the lure of promising opportunities in the land of the free, Mrs Newton. Life is so tough here. They see it as a way of starting afresh.'

'But, to leave your family behind like that, it's not natural.'

Harriet remembered with warmth that Joe had chosen to bring all of his family with him when he came to England. Life was hard enough then, but the wrench of leaving Sarnia was painful at the time. Harriet wanted to add that there had been too much heartache already losing loved ones in the war, without families separating by choice.

Seeing where this conversation was leading, Victor tried to change the subject.

'While I was in Southampton I had a look for opportunities of work. It wouldn't be easy since there are many men chasing each job, but I'd have a fair chance of success with my good reference.'

'Are you seriously thinking about staying here in Southampton, Victor?' Sarah asked.

'I am looking at my options, Sarah. That's the best thing I can do, isn't it?' Victor's question seemed to imply that there was so much more he wanted to say, but felt restricted to do so.

'What opportunities did you find?'

'I'm afraid that I would have to start again at a lower level in a small hotel and try to work my way up. Trust is something which isn't built in a day, is it?'

Sarah was even more frustrated now because their conversation seemed so stilted with her mother present and so she was relieved when there was a knock at the door. It was her brother Tom who, having been introduced to Victor once more, seemed keen to talk to his mother in private. Reluctantly, Harriet followed him into the kitchen and was irritated when he closed the door behind him, thus giving the couple some privacy.

At last Sarah could say what was really on her mind.

'That would be a shame, Victor, when you have such a good job on Riduna. Would you consider returning, do you think?'

Victor couldn't suppress a smile emerging as Sarah had expressed just the words he longed for her to say. Not wanting to sound too eager and to try to give Sarah sole credit for the idea he replied slowly and thoughtfully,

'Well, I hadn't really considered it as an option, but now you come to mention it, the idea of returning to Riduna does seem quite attractive doesn't it?'

Straight away he could see the relief flood into Sarah's expression and he knew for certain that, not only was he winning the argument far more easily than he had imagined, but also it appeared that Sarah was just as enthusiastic about living on Riduna as he was. Sarah was one of those people who you could read like a book. She had never been able to hide her feelings and Victor decided to seize the moment.

He went down on bended knee in front of Sarah's startled figure and he asked the words she had dreamt of hearing,

'Will you marry me Sarah, and come back with me to Riduna?'

So unexpected was this, so soon in their courtship, that Sarah fell down on her knees too and they embraced, both overcome with emotion.

As they parted and struggled back to their feet, giggling, Victor asked,

'Do I take that as a yes?'

There was no hesitation in her reply.

'Yes,' she said. 'With all my heart. I've never felt so happy.'

Looking down at her, Victor realised with certainty that she was telling the truth. They had no time to continue their conversation though, because her mother and Tom burst back out into the hall, both beaming.

'Gladys and I have decided that we can wait no longer and we plan to get married next month,' exclaimed an excited Tom, and Victor found it hard to believe that was the same young man who had been so traumatised only a year before.

Seizing the second important moment of the evening he exclaimed,

'That's a coincidence because Sarah has also just agreed to be my wife and I can see no reason to delay. Maybe we could have a joint wedding.'

Congratulations were exchanged all round and, although she was stunned by the sudden news, Harriet hid her feelings well. She retrieved a recently purchased bottle of sherry, hidden in the kitchen for such an occasion, and they toasted everyone's good health, leaving the implications of their words to wait for another day.

As she looked at the young couples Harriet was suddenly transported in her mind to a time long ago when her parents were toasting Edward's departure to go to sea. She felt a sudden pain as she remembered the agony of seeing him leave Riduna. She closed her eyes. It seemed like yesterday. The reality of her love for Edward suddenly filled her with an intensity that surprised her. So many dreams which came to nought. So much love sacrificed for freedom. It was at that moment that her heart happily set her daughter free. How could she stand in the way of love? She knew that she should embrace it and wish her daughter well. After all, she had watched Sarah bravely bear so much tragedy, losing her husband and then her precious son. What right did she, as a mother, have to stand in Sarah's path to a second chance of happiness?

Suddenly Sarah was concerned.

'Are you ill, Mother? It must be the shock. Sit down over here and I'll fetch a glass of water.'

As Sarah rushed off to the kitchen Harriet returned to the present and the feelings of agony disappeared as if they had never existed. She shook herself, taking hold of the cup with gratitude and reassured her frightened children.

'I'm fine. Really I am. I'm so pleased for you all. It's time our family had some good news to celebrate, don't you think?'

Relieved that his mother's colour had returned to her face once more, Tom replied,

'Gladys is coming over on Sunday and I believe that Jane is visiting too. Why don't we invite Ernest and his family and then we can discuss the plans together?'

At that moment Harriet, Sarah and Tom each thought of Jack and Joe, the members of their family who were still deeply missed and Harriet's eyes started to mist over once more.

Chapter 40

JANE STOOD ON the wooden pier watching the vessels navigating their safe channels up and down Southampton Water. It calmed her after a fraught morning on the wards, caring for those who were still undergoing operations and treatment for the more serious medical and mental conditions. The empty wards should please her but instead they seemed to hang on to the ghosts of the war.

She should feel pleased and more relaxed, glad to have more freedom to pass the time of day with her colleagues and friends. On the contrary, Jane was dismayed to experience the familiar restlessness of spirit and as she watched a large vessel reach the Solent and disappear from view, that she finally made her decision. Her family in London wouldn't be the least bit surprised and her half-sister Edith had recently written her a letter:

10th May, 1920

My dear sister Jane,

I hope this letter finds you well and in good spirits now that the world can truly celebrate peace. How many years is it since we have been in touch? I find it hard to count, what with the war years in between. So much has happened since you last wrote to us that I don't know where to begin.

After I finished my schooling, my mother was quite disappointed that I showed no desire either to follow in her footsteps and become a teacher or to take your good example and train as a nurse. Although my memories of father are quite scanty, since I was only eight years old when he died, I know that both he and you would have been so proud of me if I had been clever enough to take a career in medicine. It was not meant to be. My mother was frustrated by my lack of enthusiasm and was determined that I should make my way in life and so found me a job in service at Saumarez Manor.

I can assure you that I did not relish the dusting and polishing, not to mention the bowing and scraping. You can imagine! When I saw adverts for girls to volunteer for duties in France I was more than eager to go. I may not have inherited yours or father's brain, or Mother's for that matter, but I must have gained some of your adventurous spirit.

Anyway, Mother wasn't at all surprised but decided to travel on with me to England, feeling that she would be far safer with her family in Sussex. I will write her address on a separate page. She sends her love to you and to Harriet, if you happen to see her. Her eyesight has failed her I'm afraid, otherwise she would write to you herself.

I digress. We set off for England and I travelled on with her to Sussex to see her settled with her brother and his family. I could only stay for a few days before reporting for duty at Dover. There I was taught to drive a truck, a brief and amusing experience, but I think they must have been so desperate for my services that I passed the test and soon I was on my way to France. You know only too well from your service abroad, that the cheerful camaraderie between us girls on our trip over the channel formed a bond which helped us to survive the months ahead. I will not describe the days in France, because I know that you can empathise with the conditions in which we worked.

Towards the end of the war I was stationed near Cambrai to transport the injured back to the field hospital. It was a sobering experience and at times service in Saumarez Manor seemed a much better option. More than once I thought I was mad to be there. Suffice it to say that there was a silver lining to my cloudlike life in France and that was mainly due to the luck, if luck is an apt word, that I met my own personal hero, a Canadian Officer called James. I was transporting him back to the field hospital for injuries on his hand, but the feelings we had for each other were instant; corny, I know, but that's the truth. Whether it was the constant fear, living one moment at a time, grateful for every second in each other's company and gnawing fear when we were apart, I don't know. Anyway, we met several times in the remaining few weeks of the war and so on Armistice Day he asked me to marry him.

We are getting married on 5th June and it would be wonderful if you could come to the wedding. Mother would be so happy if you could join us and we would like you to invite your friend Harriet too. I know they were mutual friends on Riduna.

If you cannot travel at that time, then I hope we will be able to meet up before we leave for Canada in the summer. We will not be leaving for Nova Scotia until August when the RMS Scythia sails from Liverpool. Unfortunately, Mother will not be able to travel but I assure you that I go with her blessing.

Kind regards,
  Edith

Having reread the letter Jane made some decisions. She would certainly try to make her way over to Sussex to be with Edith on her wedding day. She felt guilty enough that she had seen so little of Edith while she was growing up, especially since their father had passed away. She would also try to persuade Harriet to join her. She was sure that her friend would be pleased at the opportunity of seeing Mary again, even though she'd worry about her business. Mind you, she knew that Sarah was quite capable of looking after Bourton Villas for a few days. It was her last momentous decision which filled her with the most delicious anticipation and yet she knew would be the hardest for her dear friend Harriet to bear. She must go and see Professor Blackney for some advice.

Jane was walking back over the grass towards the chapel when she was surprised to see Nurse Gladys walking towards her.

'I am so pleased to find you here, Jane. May I call you Jane?' Gladys asked nervously, looking around her to see whether she had been overheard and not wanting to sound disrespectful towards her superiors in front of the other nurses.

'How are you, Gladys?' Jane replied, ignoring the question. 'I hear you have settled in well and have been a godsend on your ward.'

Gladys blushed.

'I've enjoyed every minute of my life here but......'

Her words trailed off as she struggled to say what was on her mind.

Jane summed the situation in an instant.

'Are you thinking of leaving us so soon?' she completed Gladys's unfinished sentence with her own question.

'Tom and I are planning to get married next month. We have no real reason to delay now but I must apologize that my service here will have been shorter than expected.'

'Congratulations are in order then, but the hospital will be sorry to lose such an excellent nurse.'

Gladys blushed again.

'We're not sure where we are going to live as yet but I

am going over to see Tom's mother on Sunday. He asked me to invite you to join us.'

'I was thinking of coming to see Harriet myself soon and so it's kind of you to ask.'

'Sunday it is, then. Tom will be borrowing a trap to pick us up following the service.'

'That's perfect, Gladys. I'll look forward to Sunday, then.'

Jane was wondering whether to confide in this young nurse and tell her of the dilemma she was facing but decided against it, making her way over towards the professor's office in the hopes of finding him alone.

That night, as she searched in vain for elusive sleep, her conversation with the professor echoed in her head:

'Don't you think you are a bit too old for travelling to India, Staff Nurse Hanwell?'

'But sir, I am still fit and have as much energy as a nurse half my age, not forgetting the experience,' she had replied with passion.

The professor had looked intently at Jane before answering,

'It is obvious from your expression that you've made your decision and even though I believe you are carrying out a vital role here, I cannot stand in your way.'

It was hardly an enthusiastic response to her request to be posted to India, but nevertheless permission had been granted, albeit grudgingly. Jane smiled. The professor's bark was worse than his bite, as they say, and she fell asleep knowing that he had been slightly envious of the ease with which she could uproot and go where she pleased.

Was it just a whim or a rational decision, she asked herself as sleep finally overcame her.

Chapter 41

ON THE FOLLOWING Sunday, the whole family converged on Bourton Villas after church. It was a joyful affair. Even Hannah, heavy with child, and her new husband, Mike Burton, joined them in the celebration. Harriet's cup was overflowing with love and gratitude as she heard the light banter between her grown up children, noticing with relief that Gladys and Victor seemed relaxed and already part of the family. She was also pleased to see her friend Jane again and hoped that they would have some time to themselves after the celebratory lunch.

'Where are you going to live when you are married?' Jane asked Tom.

It was hard for her to believe that the confident cheerful young man seated opposite her was in fact the same person as the young man whose spirit had been so severely broken when she had recognised him at the hospital.

'We haven't discussed it with Mother yet,' exclaimed Tom glancing sheepishly at Harriet. 'There's so little room in my flat above the shop that we were hoping to move back into Bourton Villas once Sarah and Victor have left for Riduna. Mother will need some support and

Gladys would be only too pleased to help out.'

'That's a wonderful idea. Don't you think, Harriet?' Jane asked.

Harriet and Sarah's eyes met over the table as the sudden realisation that the perfect solution to their main worry had been presented as a gift before them. It was Sarah who replied, unable to hide her relief and enthusiasm.

'That'll be perfect, Mother. I was so worried about how you'd cope.' She beamed at Gladys. 'You will be wonderful with the guests, Gladys. I'm so pleased it has worked out for the best.'

'You'd both be more than welcome,' replied Harriet and it was obvious from her smile that she shared Sarah's enthusiasm. 'I will be more than pleased to have your company, as well as your help.'

'I think that deserves a toast, don't you?' added Ernest.

'Here's to Tom and Gladys, Sarah and Victor and to Mother's new partnership in her business!'

There was an echo around the table as everyone clinked their glasses.

'I only hope Victor knows what he's let himself in for,' teased Ernest and everyone laughed, except for Sarah of course, who glared at her brother at the head of the table.

'We'll clear away, Mrs Newton. It was a lovely meal,' said Gladys, catching Sarah's eye, diplomatically trying to diffuse any bad feeling. 'The men can go out for a while, don't you think?'

Ernest, Tom and Victor didn't need any further persuasion and were soon heading for the door.

'That leaves you and me, Harriet,' said Jane as the girls started picking up the dishes and taking them through to the scullery. 'Do you have anything urgent to do or can we take a walk together?'

'That's just what I was thinking. It's a while since we had time to ourselves.'

They fetched their shawls and headed for the front door. Harriet was feeling quite light-headed by now, not only by the wine but also by the reassurance that she wasn't to be left to cope alone. It would still be painful to see her only daughter leave her but she was much more at peace now to see her go.

'How are you, Jane?' she asked when they were on their own.

'I'm restless, to be honest with you, Harriet. I feel that my main task at The Royal Victoria is now complete.'

'Surely you are not thinking of moving on again so soon, Jane?'

Harriet didn't realise how uncharacteristically selfish this sounded and was surprised by her friend's silence.

As they strolled down towards the *Floating Bridge* and stood looking out over the River Itchen she pulled herself together, aware that Jane was struggling to find her words.

'Are you trying to tell me that you are going away again, Jane? I can see from your expression that I am right but all I ask is that you keep in touch with me this time.'

Relief flooded into Jane and she hugged her best friend.

'You know me too well, Harriet. Yes, I'm planning to go to India. I'm travelling with some young nurses in three weeks' time. It will be my last opportunity to serve abroad but if I leave it much longer I will be too old.'

She didn't add that some people thought her too long in the tooth already.

'Of course I'll write to you this time.'

'Promise?'

'I promise!' she exclaimed as she saw tears creep down Harriet's cheeks.

'I'm sorry to be so emotional, Jane. There've been so many changes for me to take in of late.'

'I know, Harriet. It's me who should be apologising. I seem to have the habit of leaving you just when you need me most.'

The ladies both remembered standing on the dockside in St Peter Port when Jane left to train as a nurse all those years ago. It was so long ago but the emotions of their parting could be conjured up in an instant.

'I have a happier suggestion for us to share before I leave, though I'm sorry that I will not be able to attend your family wedding. I received a letter from Edith the other day and she is getting married in ten days' time. In her letter she mentioned that her mother Mary is now partially blind. I was wondering if you would like to come to the wedding. It would be wonderful for you to see Mary again, don't you think?'

'I'm so sorry to hear of Mary's affliction,' replied Harriet in a non-committal manner.

'I believe the condition is cataracts, not affecting her general health but certainly an inconvenience and probably makes Mary less sure of herself when travelling,' Jane explained.

Mary had been their teacher on Riduna, but after Harriet had left school she had worked with Mary, helping out with the younger children. It was because of this that their relationship had changed to more of a friendship, their ages not so many years apart.

At first Harriet was going to decline but then it occurred to her that it might be a good idea for Gladys to spend a few days working alongside Sarah before her daughter's departure.

'I would love to, Jane. What a treat it will be to spend a few days with you, and I haven't seen Mary since I left

Riduna all those years ago. To think her daughter is old enough to get married. That makes me feel quite ancient.'

'That's settled, then. I will get word to you as soon as I can make the arrangements.'

Once back at Bourton Villas Jane bade Harriet farewell and she and Gladys set off for the hospital for the last time.

Chapter 42

THE NEXT FEW weeks were hectic at Bourton Villas, with arrangements to be made and rooms to reorganise for Gladys' large family. Victor knew that his parents would not be able to make the journey but he was sure that he and Sarah would have quite a celebration when they reached Riduna, not only to welcome his unexpected bride but also in the joy of the return of their prodigal son. Nevertheless, he was pleased that his two sisters had agreed to travel from Dorset to be with them for the day.

Since it was not appropriate for Victor and Sarah to live under the same roof, to avoid gossip and unnecessary temptation, Victor accepted Tom's offer to stay at his flat. The makeshift bed of straw-filled sacking and a blanket was a far cry from the relative luxury of Bourton Villas but Victor enjoyed having time to relish his last few weeks of bachelorhood. He wasn't mechanically minded in the least and couldn't give assistance in the bike shop, but to pay his way he offered to help Tom organise his bookkeeping, a much neglected task since old Mr Palmer had recently given up the shop completely. Victor also made order out of the chaotic stockroom and suggested a system which would help Tom to keep account of his stock and the parts he needed to order. He would have liked to make some suggestions about the running of Bourton Villas, since hospitality was his trade, but his diplomatic alter ego ensured that he remained silent on that matter.

One week after the family celebration, Gladys left her position at the hospital and moved into Bourton Villas, leaving them only three weeks before the wedding. From the moment Gladys moved in, it was as if she had always been part of the household and Sarah began to feel that she was more like a sister to her. Sarah watched as Gladys took over tasks in such a subtle way that Harriet did not realise it was happening.

On the morning that Harriet was to leave with Jane to travel to Sussex to see Edith and Mary, Harriet was flustered, worried that the two young ladies would not be able to cope without her. In the end Sarah had to be quite firm with her mother:

'You are fussing, Mother. Gladys is a competent cook and is quite able to take over your role for a few days.'

Seeing her mother's crestfallen face, she added,

'Of course we'll miss you, but it'll be good for you to have break and we will need you to be rested to support us in the wedding preparations.'

'If you're sure that you can manage without me,' Harriet replied.

'It won't be easy, Mrs Newton, but I am sure we'll manage,' Gladys added diplomatically.

Sarah gave Gladys a smile. As she embraced her mother it brought a lump to her throat to think they would soon be parted and she could see tears welling in her mother's eyes too.

'Have a wonderful time, Mother. You deserve a break and some time with Jane before she leaves for India.'

This was just the comment that spurred Harriet to

collect her things together and make her way to the buggy, which was waiting outside.

'I'll carry those, Mrs Newton,' offered Victor who was standing behind Gladys.

He lifted her valise into the back of the buggy and held out his hand to support Harriet while she stepped up to join Jane.

'Isn't this exciting, the two of us having a few days together?' Jane exclaimed as they embraced.

And so, like two schoolgirls on a Sunday school outing they set off along the Portsmouth Road. Luck had it that one of the men who regularly delivered to the hospital had parents over in Brighton. He was travelling to see them for a few days and was more than happy to take the detour to Woolston, especially since Jane had paid him handsomely for his services.

Two days later as Harriet and Jane stood side by side at St Botolph's Church, Heene, near Worthing, watching Edith glide down the aisle towards her handsome Canadian officer, two familiar faces on the other side of the church caught their eyes. Both ladies blushed as two English officers, obviously quite high ranking, smiled back at them. Whether it was their dashing uniforms, or that age had been extremely kind to these men, Harriet didn't know, but as she puzzled as to what an odd coincidence it was, memories flooded back to her of when their paths had crossed years ago, when they had been corporals stationed on Riduna. She remembered the time when young Corporal Thomas had been sweet on her friend Jane and that Corporal Frederick had showed an interest in her too. The fact that she had rebuffed him had surprised many of the local girls, whilst she had continued to harbour her secret love for Edward.

Next to her Jane was experiencing quite different emotions. To see Thomas again after all these years, almost more attractive in maturity than he had been in his youth, her heart missed a beat and she found it difficult to concentrate on the service. She glanced at her friend, whose smile was full of warmth and understanding. On the one hand she longed for the service to be over when it was likely that he would come over to talk with her, but on the other hand she dreaded the mixed emotions such an encounter might give. What if he was married and she had to meet his wife? But, if he was married why was he standing side by side with Frederick? As questions filled her head, both ladies were transported in their minds back to the church of St Anne's on Riduna when on many occasions the soldiers, in their bright red uniforms, had sat at the back of the church, trying to catch the eye of any pretty girl they could.

When the service was over and while the family was gathering for photographs, Harriet stood alone whilst Jane was ushered to be part of the group photos. Jane watched with a certain amount of irritation as Thomas and Frederick joined Harriet and she was frustrated that she could not hear their conversation.

Ever the gallant one, Thomas held out his left hand to take Harriet's, brushing it with his lips,

'Good day, madam. How good it is to see you again.'

'What a strange coincidence to see you after all these years... May I call you Thomas?' Harriet replied looking at the shoulder pips which denoted an officer of high rank. 'You have certainly done well for yourselves. Good day to you, Frederick.'

'Good day, madam,' replied Frederick, bowing, holding his cap and standing a little aloof from them.

Harriet noticed the deep scar on Frederick's left cheek,

which she could see continued below his neck line, and she reddened at the thought. Pulling herself together, she turned again to Thomas and asked,

'And what has brought you to this wedding today?'

'It is a long story, madam, but it was when I was climbing into a truck to be transported to a field hospital near Cambrai that I stumbled and the young Canadian getting married today leapt to support me and helped me into the truck. As it happens it was young Edith who was driving the truck at the time and I became friends with them both and watched their romance blossom, as it were.'

By this time Harriet saw out of the corner of her eye that Frederick had wandered off to talk to one on the pretty bridesmaids. She also noticed for the first time that Thomas' right arm looked a little strange and realisation dawned that it must be wooden, the hand barely showing below his cuffs.

At that moment Jane came to join them and her eyes met Thomas' as he greeted her with a similar flourish, accompanied by a brilliant smile.

'How lovely to see you again, Jane! You look as beautiful as ever.'

'You were always a flatterer, Thomas,' Jane blushed, obviously pleased nevertheless by the comment.

'How is life treating you, Jane?' Thomas enquired.

'After I had trained in England I worked in Natal for several years before returning exhausted to London. After a much needed rest I worked at St Thomas' for a couple of years, in tropical disease research. Then I transferred down to The Royal Victoria at Netley where I now train VAD nurses for their work overseas. It was here my friendship with Harriet was able to resume. And you?'

'I served in India for a while before my unit was called back at the start of the war. I served in several skirmishes until lady luck ran out and I lost my arm in Cambrai.'

'You could say that you were one of the fortunate ones. After all, you returned to England still alive,' Jane remarked.

There were a few moments silence as each thought of their nearest and dearest who were less fortunate until Thomas relieved the tension.

'That's certainly true, but I can't say that I was too sad to be back in Blighty, although it was a wrench leaving my men behind.'

'I expect your wife thought differently,' Jane replied.

'You have me wrong there, Jane. Like you and your service as a nurse I have been married to the army. I have certainly met no young lady since you who might have made me think otherwise.'

Jane blushed and Harriet, who felt a little as she was eavesdropping by now, went over to speak with Mary, leaving the couple in peace. Later that night as she and Jane were having supper in a small but comfortable lodging house she quizzed her friend.

'Well, Jane. How did you feel meeting Thomas again after all these years?'

'To be honest with you, Harriet, I am now totally confused. Whereas I was so sure that it was my destiny to travel to work in India, I really don't know now.'

'What has made you doubt your decision, Jane?'

'As you know we talked quite a bit today and he has asked me to go to stay with him at his family's home near Cambridge. I really don't know what to do.'

'What harm will it do to go with him for a few days? At least you will give your heart a chance to tell you which path you should take.'

'You are very wise, Harriet, but this will mean that you will be travelling back to Woolston on your own. Would you mind that so very much?'

Harriet got up to hug her friend.

'I am a capable businesswoman now. Of course I can manage. I'll miss you, that goes without saying, but I will be fine.'

The following morning, after Harriet and Jane said their farewells to Mary and Edith, they set off in different directions, wondering when or if their paths would cross again.

'You'll come to see me at the docks when I leave for India, Harriet?' Jane asked.

'If you go to India,' Harriet replied, with a stress on the '*if*'.

Chapter 43

ON THE EVENING after her return to Woolston, Harriet sat by the range watching Gladys busy at work. Since she had returned from Worthing she noticed that Gladys already looked quite at home in her kitchen and the two young ladies worked well together, their complementing qualities working seamlessly: so much so that Harriet wished that her daughter would stay in England. How she dreaded that moment when she would be saying goodbye to her. As she sat staring at the photos above the mantelpiece, daydreaming of her daughter growing up, she remembered the time Edward had arrived unexpectedly. He had not realised Sarah's existence until he heard her whimper from the wooden cot. She could see him now, picking Sarah up in his arms and gently talking to her. In fact, it was from that moment that Sarah was Edward's favourite. Absentmindedly she wondered how he was and why he had not called in of late.

There was a sudden knock at the door. Harriet's memories had been so vivid that she half expected Edward to breeze through the door but it was the postman with a letter to Sarah. Harriet took it and handed it to her daughter. It was written in Edward's unmistakable handwriting and Harriet found it hard to contain her impatience as she watched her daughter read the letter.

5th June, 1920

My dear Sarah,

Thank you so much for thinking of me and inviting us to your wedding. There is nothing I would like more than to see you on your wedding day but I'm afraid there is still sickness over here so it would be wrong of me to come. Marie is exhausted with the care of her neighbours and she has no energy for the trip.

If at all possible I will try to call before you leave for Riduna, but if I am unable to make the journey then I wish you and Victor every good fortune. I must admit to being a touch envious. I try not to think of Riduna very often but recently I have found myself daydreaming of the island of my birth: so much so that sometimes I think it is calling me home. I know this is irrational, since I have a comfortable home here, but there you are.

I wish you a wonderful day and a successful and happy life together.

Kind regards,
    Uncle Edward

Sarah stood in the hallway rereading her letter, filled with disappointment that she might not see her favourite uncle before leaving England. She looked up, only to see her mother's quizzical expression.

'Uncle Edward's not able to come to the wedding, Mother. That's sad, isn't it?'

Harriet was lost for words. She couldn't understand it. She knew that Edward would come if he was able to and also knew that she had been looking forward to seeing him again, even though, out of politeness, the invitation had been directed to Marie also.

'I'm surprised he is not making every effort to be here for you. After all, you were always extra special in Edward's eyes.'

'I know, Mother. Yes I'm disappointed too but he's only thinking of us, after all.'

'It doesn't make sense. There's as much sickness over here too that I'm still surprised he won't make the effort to see you before you leave for Riduna.'

'He doesn't say that, Mother. He says that he will try to come over if he can and that's more than I can ask.'

Sarah was even more suspicious by the unusual irritation in her mother's voice but let the matter drop. She had just finished cleaning the range and was preparing to relight it.

'Why don't you make that cake now that you're rested? I need to go upstairs to continue to pack my things and then we need to sit down and plan the food for the wedding.'

Harriet smiled as her daughter left the room. Sarah was the organiser, always making lists and plans. Mind you, it was good to be busy because she didn't want to wallow in self-pity and so she found herself singing as she worked.

Upstairs Sarah was clearing out her drawers. They would sail to Sarnia only a week following the wedding and with only three days to the wedding there was a lot to do. At the back of her underwear drawer she found the locket. Her eyes watered as she thought of the last time she had lifted it to her neck and her little Timothy had noticed it. She so longed for him to be there, to share her happiness and to see Riduna and she daydreamed of him fishing off the rocks with Victor. Yes Mother, she thought. Sickness had come to them too. Could she ever truly recover from losing her only son? Even her present excitement was tinged with a deep sadness.

There were moments too when Sarah noticed that Victor also allowed his guard to drop on his usually cheerful demeanour, when a haunted look flooded over him and there was no way in which Sarah could reach him. She never asked what he was thinking at that time, knowing that his mind must be filled with such indescribable agony that he could never share the pain with her and in all honesty probably never would. Sarah loved him all the more at those times. Their love, built on mutual attraction and a scattering of good humour, also shared a firm foundation of empathy, unshared memories and grief that neither tried to express.

Sarah sat down and, as she had done so on many occasions in the past, she slipped the locket out of its pouch and into the palm of her hand and the chain slipped like a stream of water through her fingers. It was while she was staring at the locket, willing it to open to reveal its mysteries that a thought came to her. If Edward was not to come to the wedding then she resolved that she must find time after the wedding to travel over the water to see him.

The hive of activity at Bourton Villas continued to the morning of the weddings on 19th June, 1920. Victor's sisters had arrived, both vivacious and full of infectious laughter, and Sarah warmed to them instantly. Gladys' family had travelled from Chichester the night before and, once Sarah's friends Irene and Nell had arrived, Bourton Villas was overflowing with happiness. Once the guests had left to walk to the church Harriet was able to spend a few precious moments with her daughter as she put the finishing touches to her hair.

The sun shone and Gladys and Sarah looked beautiful as they alighted from the trap, which was decorated with pink ribbons and roses for the happy occasion. Gladys was wearing a traditional floor length white wedding dress with lace trim on the skirt and sleeves. In fact it was her mother's dress which had been carefully mothballed over the years. Although its colour had lost a touch of its original brilliance, it was feminine and flowing, fitting Gladys with hardly an alteration. She was so proud to be the first daughter to wear it.

Sarah, on the other hand, was wearing a modern dress of pale pink. It was plain with Romanesque shoulders brought in tightly above her waist and bound by a wide pink ribbon. The skirt fell to just below Sarah's knee, as high as modesty could permit, even in these modern times. She had a hairpin of pink carnations holding her flowing shoulder length auburn hair away from her face. Harriet had to admit that her daughter looked stunning. Nevertheless, she wished that the neckline was a little higher and the skirt a touch longer.

The church was overflowing with family and neighbours. There were also several of the survivors of Tom's Hampshire Regiment, proudly wearing their uniforms and the families of two members of Victor's regiment who had settled in the Southampton area after the war.

The two men stood side by side at the altar rail, nervously waiting for their brides to appear. Victor had bought a second-hand suit with some of his savings and Tom wore the only suit he possessed.

Gladys was the first bride to enter on the arm of her father, followed by her younger sister as her only bridesmaid. Tom beamed with pride as she walked slowly towards him and took her place by his side. Gladys turned to hand her flowers into her sister Anne's safe keeping for the duration of the ceremony.

Next it was Victor's turn to gasp as Sarah entered the nave. Her dress flatteringly flowing in pink over her curves, cheeks reflecting its rosy hue and her face glowing with happiness, just took his breath away. Ernest walked Sarah down the aisle towards him, taking on the role of their father, and

Hannah's daughter Phyllis walked behind them in a smock dress, cleverly trimmed with the same matching ribbon.

The ceremony was unusual, with each group of phrases said first by Tom and Gladys and then echoed by Victor and Sarah. All went smoothly, thanks mainly to the reverend, who took control and quickly put both couples at their ease. The congregation sang Blake's "Jerusalem" as the registers were signed and soon the couples emerged to walk down the aisle. Tom and Gladys were first to emerge into the sunlight, bowing under a guard of honour. This was formed by men from the Royal Guernsey Light Infantry and various Hampshire regiments, with the two men from the RGLI at the head.

A local photographer caught these auspicious moments on camera, along with a dozen more family photos, after which they all retired to the church hall for light refreshments, which had been prepared by Harriet, Ethel and Gladys. Under the circumstances it was a fairly frugal affair, but nevertheless it was enjoyed by all. Before they settled down for the speeches, Sarah spent a few moments with her old friends Irene and Nell.

'I can't believe you're both back at Gilkicker. It seems like a lifetime away for me now.'

'We're the lucky ones' Irene replied, knowingly. 'Once my George returned from the war it seemed the most natural thing to go back. I just didn't want to let him out of my sight.'

'And not because your George is one for the ladies, either,' teased Nell, always the one to have a joke.

'Oh, how I've missed our fun together,' Sarah exclaimed.

'Now, Sarah! Don't kid yourself. You hated the place, really. We only helped you along the way but your life is so much more exciting now,' replied Nell truthfully.

'I know, Nell, but even so it's good to see you both again,

but it's for such a short time.' Sarah groaned. 'Promise me you'll both write.'

'We will,' reassured Irene, who knew that she would probably be writing for both of them since Nell was certainly no scholar.

At that point Victor came over to claim his wife to be together for the speeches. As they sat together in the church hall they were suddenly overwhelmed by a keenness to escape. Victor squeezed Sarah's hand under the table as they listened to Gladys' dad finish his speech. The smile Sarah returned was both flirtatious and sensuous and so, wishing for the remainder of the day to be for Gladys and Tom alone, they made their excuses and crept away as soon as the wedding breakfast was over and people were mingling. They said their goodbyes as quietly as they could, Sarah finding her mother at the very last moment.

No words were shared between them as they embraced. Both were aware that tears could flow at any time and so they drew back, keen to be as light-hearted as possible.

'Now look after that man of yours, Sarah and treat him kindly. You are so fortunate to find someone who adores you.'

'Don't worry, Mrs Newton. I have Sarah under control,' returned Victor as he winked at his mother-in-law.

'What do you mean?' laughed Sarah, pretending to be indignant at the remarks.

'Just be happy, my girl; that's all I ask,' returned Harriet as the pair left the hall, waving back towards her.

'We are, don't you worry, Mrs Newton,' said Victor as he took his wife's hand in his and they made their way down the road and to the ferry.

Gladys and Tom, on the other hand, were staying at Bourton Villas, Tom moving back there from his flat for the first time since the end of the war. Ernest, sensing an awkward situation, had suggested that Harriet stay with them overnight in order to give the couple some privacy and so she happily shared a bed, top to tail with her two grandchildren, who giggled with excitement and the novelty of having their Gran to stay, thus soothing away any loneliness Harriet might have felt.

With the family and friends returning home directly after the wedding, Gladys and Tom were nervously in awe of the unusual quiet at Bourton Villas as they entered the house. As they stepped over the front door mat they were both overwhelmed by shyness and were at a loss as to what to say or do.

To ease the tension between them, Tom smiled and a cheeky uncharacteristic thought struck him. He swept his new bride off her feet and, ignoring her protests, he carried her into the house and up the stairs to the room Gladys had prepared for them to share. As their laughter subsided Tom was overwhelmed yet again by shyness, uncertain what he should do next. Finally it was Gladys who took control. She began to undress Tom gently and sensuously and so taking her lead he slid his arm behind her back and unzipped her flowing gown.

'You're so beautiful,' he whispered as they lay down together and he claimed her as his own.

Chapter 44

WITH SARAH'S CANNY whiles, she had persuaded Victor that it would be a good idea to spend their wedding night over the river at Hythe. They took the *Floating Bridge* and Victor and Sarah embraced the warm evening air as they strolled along to catch the *Hotspur*. As the small ferry, familiar to Sarah, chugged its way across Southampton Water, Sarah savoured the sights of places she knew so well.

Victor pretended to enjoy the view as he made several sidelong glances at his pretty wife, whose face was alive with happiness. He felt blessed with good fortune. Once in Hythe they walked along the wooden pier and booked into a small but respectable guesthouse near to the water's edge. Victor asked for supper and a bottle of wine to be brought up to their cosy room. First the landlady carried the wine and two glasses, saying that the food would follow shortly and as Sarah sipped her wine she began to relax. Unable to wait any longer, Victor swept Sarah into his arms and began to kiss her with an ardour that she had never experienced before, but at that moment there was another knock at the door.

Sarah fought hard to suppress her mirth as Victor talked politely to the landlady, answering her many questions about the wedding, as she brought in the dishes of food. When the couple were finally left alone they burst into uncontrollable giggles. They fell on to the bed laughing, but within moments their mirth was turned into passion and as naturally as if the world turned just for themselves, Victor and Sarah were made whole by the healing balm of their love, their food soon forgotten.

The following morning after breakfast they strolled along the water's edge. With the morning stretching ahead of them, Sarah explained what she had planned. She wanted to visit Uncle Edward before she left England for Riduna and hoped to introduce Victor to him. She did not explain her other secret motive, but as they walked along Victor noticed an unfamiliar silver locket around Sarah's neck. He was slightly irritated by it, because he wondered if it was from Sarah's first husband, Anthony, and could not understand how Sarah could be so thoughtless as to wear it on the first day of their lives together. Since it was a sensitive subject and he wished to avoid any conflict with his wife he didn't mention it, but he did express his uncertainty about the intended visit.

'If your uncle explained his absence from the wedding because of illness then maybe we should have respected his wishes and kept away. After all, he did say that he would get over to see you if he was able.'

Immediately after Victor had spoken, he realised that he had made an error of judgement, since he could see the glimmer of Sarah's stubbornness behind her shining eyes.

'It would mean so much to see Uncle Edward before we leave. Can you understand how important it is to me? I've known him all my life and since my father passed away Uncle Edward has been there for me.'

In the end Victor agreed, but only to please his pretty

wife. They stopped at a little cafe, where Sarah explained that initially she wanted to visit her uncle on her own but, if all was well, she would bring him to see Victor.

Irritated but resigned by this time, Victor reluctantly agreed to remain at the cafe, buying a newspaper to while away the moments and distract him from his irritated thoughts.

Sarah left the cafe with a quick backward glance over her shoulder at Victor, whose returned smile was less than reassuring, but resolutely she walked along to Edward's cottage. Nervously she knocked on the door, quelling her confused thoughts.

The cottage, which once seemed so small and quaint, was familiar and yet strangely challenging to her memory. The air of a cosy dwelling was replaced by one which looked both cold and neglected. At first there was no reply, and aware that curtains were tweaking in the cottage next door, she knocked again.

Finally the door slowly opened and a familiar but dishevelled man stepped back into the room, making space for Sarah to follow him.

'What's the matter, Uncle Edward? Are you unwell?'

'No Sarah. I'm not the one who's ill, but why did you come? I wrote a letter telling you why I couldn't see you. Didn't you receive it?' Edward spoke in an irritated tone, unfamiliar to Sarah.

He slumped down in an armchair.

As Sarah took her eyes off her uncle's face, she began to notice the disarray in the cottage. In the past it had always been kept spotlessly clean by Marie, reverberating with her laughter.

'I wanted to say goodbye, Uncle Edward, because I'm leaving for Riduna next week,' Sarah explained as she glanced around the room, showing obvious distress.

'What's happened?' she whispered.

Edward was silent for a while but then he replied in a tired, empty voice,

'She had to die didn't she? Worked so hard making everyone else better that she had to die herself. There's justice for you.'

'Oh, Uncle Edward,' exclaimed Sarah, falling to her knees at his side. 'I'm so sorry. When did it happen?'

'I didn't want to tell you in a letter - spoil your happy day, did I? I would have let you know in time, but not yet.'

'Oh, Uncle! I'm so glad I came to see you. Would you like me to make you a cup of tea?'

In the silence between them, Sarah noticed that the range was stone cold and she realised instantly that her offer would be impossible to fulfil because she knew that it would be unfair to leave Victor for so long.

'No, girl; I don't want you fussing. That's why I didn't let you know,' Edward snapped, staring at the flag stones beneath his feet.

As far back as Sarah could remember, she had always seen Edward in a cheerful, fun-loving state of mind. It was a bit of a shock to find her uncle like this. She was at a loss as to know how to respond and was aware that she must go and find Victor, otherwise he would worry about her. She stood up and was about to leave, muttering a comment about her regret for his loss. At that moment Edward looked up at her for the first time since she had arrived. But it was not into Sarah's face that he stared but at the locket around her neck.

'Where in the world did you get that from?' he croaked.

Sarah, flustered a little, moved her hand to her throat, suddenly realising that this probably hadn't been one of her better ideas.

'I found it in my father's belongings,' she replied, with a

barely audible voice. She backed to the door, now longing to escape.

Edward's eyes followed her, but it was as if the locket had finally bridged the void between them. She stopped, her fingers on the door handle, the silence fused with energy of years passed.

'I gave that locket to your mother on Riduna, long long ago,' Edward whispered.

Sarah sighed with relief.

'So that *is* the truth. You gave the locket to my mother because you were sweethearts.'

Edward sighed. It was as if the weight of the secret of all those years had been lifted.

'Yes, Sarah. Your mother and I were sweethearts long before she met your father. In fact she became close to your father when she thought I was dead. Oh, Sarah. It's such a long story, but many years before you were born, I can assure you. We were just children then.'

Edward's voice had softened sounding more like the uncle the Sarah knew and loved. She relaxed a little and stepped back into the room.

Reaching to unclasp the locket, she dropped it into Edward's large work-worn hands.

'Here it is, Uncle Edward. It belongs to you.'

She looked down at him with kindly but challenging eyes, both fully understanding her unspoken intent.

'I must go to find Victor now, because he's waiting for me and will be concerned but here's the pouch I found the locket in.'

Sarah handed Edward the leather pouch and their eyes met.

'Goodbye, Uncle and I hope that I've not upset you too much, but it was important to me to see you before I left.'

'Oh Sarah, I didn't mean to be unkind and I'm sorry that

you found me in such a state. I know it's been tough for you too, but when my Marie died, I started to wonder if all the pain and suffering I'd witnessed on my ship in the war had been truly worthwhile. I fell apart. You must understand. I heard about young Timothy. Such a fine lad, a tragic loss for you,' and Edward sobbed once more.

Sarah, fell to her knees beside him on the dusty floor and held his hands in his. For a while there was nothing to say in their shared moment of grief.

'I still miss him every moment of the day, Uncle Edward,' replied Sarah, tears falling gently on their joined hands. 'I will never forget him and every day I long for him to share my happiness, but I will not allow myself to feel guilty, Uncle. Timmy will always be with me but I am so fortunate to find someone who loves me so, and being with Victor will never take away the memories but it helps to ease the pain.' Sarah looked up, uncertain for a moment as to what to do.

'Of course you must go and find Victor now, Sarah. He's a very lucky man. I'll get m'self together and meet you on the pier before you leave. Go on, off with you.'

With that dismissal Sarah rushed out of the door, not really knowing whether to feel an overwhelming sadness at Edward's loss or relief that he had started to mellow again. She ran to the cafe but Victor wasn't there. Then she rushed to the pier and saw him ambling slowly along the wooden platform.

'Victor!' she called out and he turned to see her racing towards him. He held out his arms and she ran into them, sobbing with emotion. Fearing the worst, he lifted her face up to his and kissed her on the forehead.

'Don't worry, Sarah my love. I'm here for you. Let's get away from here. I knew we shouldn't have come.'

After a few moments Sarah pulled herself together.

'We can't leave yet Victor. Edward is going to come out to meet you but he just needs a little time. Then I'll tell you the whole story on the way home, or at least everything that I know.'

'Where did your locket go, Sarah? Have you lost it?'

'The locket wasn't mine, Victor. It belonged to my mother, but Edward has it now.'

'You're talking in riddles, girl,' Victor laughed affectionately, full of relief that Sarah was fine and that the locket had not belonged to his wife after all.

They sat on a wooden bench half way along the pier. The sound of the water lapping on the wood below them seemed to calm Sarah and Victor knew instinctively that it was better not to press his wife for more details at present. Instead, Sarah rambled on about the times when she and her father had visited Edward when she was a child. It was twenty minutes before Edward came striding along the platform to meet them. He had obviously washed and changed his clothes, a far cry from the ragged, broken man she had found in his cottage an hour before. As he reached them, Edward could not help but notice Sarah's striking resemblance to Harriet in her youth and he hesitated for a moment as Victor stood up. The feeling of uncertainty passed.

'You must be Victor from Riduna,' Edward exclaimed, vigorously shaking the young man's hand. 'I've heard so much about you since your stay at Harriet's place... Mrs Newton's,' he corrected himself.

'Pleased to meet you and you must be the famous Uncle Edward.'

Remembering in time that he shouldn't mention Timothy he added,

'I hear that we have one thing in common at least: that you're an expert fisherman.'

'Oh I wouldn't say "expert", but there's certainly nothing better for the soul than a quiet spell of fishing,' Edward replied.

'I agree with you there. Although recently it became a life saving necessity on Riduna, I can tell you.'

'I'm sure it did,' answered Edward knowingly.

He, too, remembered the time he'd taught Timothy to fish, not only to help the lad, with his father gone, but also to add to the family's diet.

'I used to fish with my dad on Riduna, but that was long before you were born,' he mused on far safer memories.

'Where was your favourite spot? Mine used to be at the Black Rock on Saye Bay though I don't go there much now.'

'Yes, I fished there for certain, but we didn't go to that end of the island very often. We used to fish off the rocks near our home in Crabby Bay most of the time.'

Sarah was amused by this exchange between Victor and Edward but she was also aware that they should be getting back.

'I'm sorry to interrupt,' she exclaimed and the men smiled, 'but I can see that our ferry's on its way.' Sarah paused. 'I was wondering if you'd come over when we set sail to Sarnia on Tuesday. I know that Mother would be pleased to see you too and she would certainly appreciate your support after we're gone.'

Edward could see the glint in Sarah's eyes, but was reluctant to make a promise he was unable to keep. He had some serious thinking to do first and needed to sort out his life.

'Will you give this back to your mother then, Sarah?' Edward asked, pulling the locket out of his pocket and fingering it lovingly. With reluctance he offered it back to Sarah.

'It's not mine to give, Uncle Edward and Mother doesn't

even know I've found it, so I think it's best that you keep it. After all, it was a gift from you in the first place.'

She smiled up at him and he gave her a peck on the cheek. He shook Victor's hand and they walked along the second half of the pier to the platform where the *Hotspur* was just arriving. They waved to Edward as their ferry began its journey back across the river to Southampton.

'Do I need to explain?' Sarah asked, once they had settled.

'I think I get the gist of the matter. Let me see if I'm right. Edward and your mother were sweethearts on Riduna.'

Victor gave Sarah a knowing side glance as if to say, 'I told you so'. Sarah gave Victor an affectionate nudge in the ribs.

'Anyway, as I was saying. Somehow the locket got lost and so did Edward, so to speak.'

'Yes, Mother thought that Uncle Edward was lost at sea. I've heard that story many a time since I was little.'

'Your mother then married your father, but what I don't understand is how your father ended up with the locket in his trunk.'

'Yes, that's still a mystery, and one I guess we'll never know the answers to now, I'm afraid.'

'Then Edward appeared alive and well, too late to claim your mother as his bride,'

Sarah laughed.

'You make it sound like a fairy story.'

'And my little scheming wife is hoping that it has a fairy tale ending and the prince sails in to claim his bride once more!' Victor grinned and turning his face towards her, he caught Sarah unawares and planted a kiss on her lips in full view of the other passengers.

'Just like our story,' Sarah replied in a whisper, oblivious to the disapproving looks around her.

Chapter 45

IT WAS EARLY in the morning just a week later when the whole family turned out to walk Victor and Sarah down to the *Floating Bridge* and Sarah was full of mixed emotions. With Victor by her side she longed to see Riduna again but her only real agony was in leaving her mother behind. Ernest and Ethel stood together with their two children and Tom looked happier than he'd done for years, with the loving support of Gladys by his side.

It was only Harriet and her friend Jane who were to accompany Sarah and Victor across to Southampton. Ernest and Tom were due at work in half an hour and Gladys was returning to cook breakfast at Bourton Villas, happy to have the offer of Ethel's help for the morning.

They travelled in silence, each with their own thoughts. Victor was full of enthusiasm to return home and he was so full of love for the lady by his side. Finally, when the moment came to say goodbye, he knew that all he could offer was reassurance.

'I promise that I'll take care of your daughter, Mrs Newton and don't forget that you will be more than welcome to visit us and thank you for everything you've done for us.'

Harriet's eyes welled up as she took his hand in hers.

'I'm so glad that my Sarah has found you and that she's happy. I wish I could say that I might come to see you one day but I'm afraid that's unlikely. Look after her for me, but keep an eye on that strong will of hers.'

Victor put his arm around Sarah's shoulder with affection.

'I think that I can handle it,' he laughed, as Sarah struggled to be free in feigned indignation.

'Oh Mother, how I wish you were coming with us. I had hoped that you'd change your mind.'

As they embraced, Sarah knew that she should be relishing her last moments with her mother but she was distracted, scanning the crowd over her mother's shoulder for a familiar but welcome face. Trying hard not to show the irritation she felt by Edward's absence yet again, she stood back and tried to concentrate on her mother.

'I'll write as soon as we arrive, Mother, and I'll so look forward to your letters too. I'll miss you but we'll come back and visit sometimes. I promise.'

With their goodbyes over, Victor took Sarah's hand as they walked together on to the waiting ship. Sarah glanced over her shoulder to see her mother and Jane standing patiently below and she lifted her hand as they disappeared from view and found their way along the corridors and up the steep staircase and on to the deck. In view again they waved down to the two ladies, familiar faces in a sea of well-wishers, all jostling for the best view. Yet again Sarah scanned the crowd and even as the water swept in between the ship and the quayside she still hoped to spot her uncle.

Guessing her distress Victor commented,

'From your account, your Uncle Edward wasn't the most reliable of types, Sarah. Don't worry about him. Your mother will be fine with Gladys, Ernest and Tom to keep an eye on her.'

Sarah sighed.

'Oh, I know, but I was just hoping...'

'We shouldn't interfere with other people's lives, my love, even if they are our parents. You would be the first to moan if your mother meddled in our lives and tried to persuade us to stay here in England, when she knows full well that our hearts wish to return to Riduna.'

Realising the truth in Victor's words she lifter her head towards his. Ignoring the fellow passengers yet again, they kissed.

'I'm so lucky to have found you,' she sighed.

'And don't you forget it,' he smiled, turning his lips to meet hers once more.

For a while they stood enjoying the breeze on their faces and the salty smell of the sea. Once they had reached the Solent and were heading for the open sea Sarah's thoughts turned to Riduna.

'It was strange the way we kept meeting each other on Riduna, wasn't it?'

'It was fate, Sarah. It was meant to be. I must admit that I was really disappointed when I saw your wedding ring, the time we met in the baker's.'

He didn't add that it was really no surprise that they kept meeting. Riduna was such a small island that after a while you were bound to meet the same people over and over again. Still, he did not like to dispel her beliefs and it was certainly fate which had brought him to Jane's attention at the hospital and on to Bourton Villas during the war.

'Will we live with your parents when we arrive on Riduna, Victor?'

'No, Sarah. We will have a room at the back of the hotel. It won't be much at first, but it'll be comfortable.'

Thinking of his parent's small cottage just off the High Street where they had managed to bring up five children, he was relieved that he had received a letter from his former manager to say that his job was still open to him. In fact, he'd written an amusing account of the lad who had tried to take his place. Young Jacob had mixed up the guest lists on more than one occasion, forgetting to follow the procedures in carefully recording all the new arrivals and departures. In the end, Mr White had needed to pacify several irate customers, so much so that the lad had been returned to his previous role in the kitchen, whilst Mr White was working all hours to man the reception himself. Knowing how his manager preferred to be messing about on his yacht, Victor had smiled when he had read the account, but was also relieved that he and Sarah would be able to use his old room. What with the war and the slow return of tourism to the island, money had been tight, so he had just saved enough money for this voyage. He still possessed the money for the fare to America, but that would not have gone far if they had needed to pay for lodgings.

At the same time as Victor was suggesting that they retreat from the fierce breeze to the lower deck, Jane was encouraging Harriet that it was time to go home. They had stood on the quayside long after the ship had disappeared from view. It wasn't the first time in her life that she was engulfed by a sense of loss. Jane placed a gentle hand on her shoulder, but as she did so, Harriet began to faint as her emotions overwhelmed her. Jane leapt to her friend's rescue but, as she struggled to catch the falling figure, some strong arms came from behind them, catching Harriet's shoulders and head, preventing them from hitting the ground. Jane reached into her bag for some smelling salts but instead of kneeling by her friend as she might have done by instinct, she passed them to Edward, who held them gently under Harriet's nose, encouraging her to come to her senses.

It was Edward's face and not Jane's that Harriet focussed on as she regained her composure and Jane diplomatically took a few paces away to give them some space.

'Oh Edward,' Harriet sighed. 'I'm so glad you're here.'

For a few moments Harriet remained still, resting on Edward's knees and looking up into his familiar, albeit rugged features.

'You've aged so,' she muttered with concern.

'That's a fine comment to fill a man with confidence, Harriet. You're not so young yourself.'

Harriet laughed and as she did so, she struggled to her feet, taking Edward's arm for support. 'But you're a few minutes too late. Sarah has just left for Riduna with her new husband, Victor. You've just missed them.'

'I know, Harriet. I saw them go, but I didn't wish to spoil your private moment with your daughter.'

'How did you know that Sarah was leaving today, Edward?' Harriet sighed, not giving Edward a chance to respond. 'Never mind,' she said. 'I don't want you to explain now. Just more secrets between you,' Harriet exclaimed in frustration.

'We didn't mean to keep secrets from you, Harriet but we didn't want to hurt your feelings.'

'You find a strange way of caring, Edward. You breeze in and out of our lives at will. We never know when you will appear and just when we get used to you being there you disappear again, until the next time it suits you to grace us with your presence.'

'Shall I walk you both to the *Floating Bridge*?' asked Edward, attempting to change the subject.

'We'll be fine, Edward, but thank you for coming. I expect you'll want to catch the *Hotspur* home from here and it would only be out of your way. Come over and visit us one day, when you can find the time.'

With that she turned from him and, taking Jane's arm in her own, she strode purposefully away.

Helplessly, Edward stood and watched Harriet and Jane as they disappeared from view and he walked dejectedly away to catch his ferry home. Once on the Hotspur he took the locket out of his breast pocket and held it thoughtfully, in the way he'd sometimes watched Irish sailors finger worry beads when they thought they were unobserved. He nearly threw the chain out into Southampton Waters but in the end he dropped it back into his pocket. It was then he resolved to go back to work as soon as possible. It was either that or turning to drink and he knew how that could damage a man. He shuddered.

When they were out of earshot Jane exclaimed, 'Don't you think you were being a little too severe towards Edward? After all, he came to your rescue and rushed forward to prevent you from hurting yourself.'

'But they always kept secrets from me, Jane. It's so frustrating. First I find out that, unbeknown to me, my husband visited Edward regularly, taking Sarah with him when she was only a child and now I find that Sarah is yet again in touch with Edward behind my back. It is so underhand.'

'I'm sure Sarah was only thinking of your feelings, Harriet. She has always been close to Edward. Even you admitted that and she was very disappointed when he did not turn up at the wedding. She had every right to let him know that she was leaving for Riduna.'

'I suppose you're right, as always Jane. I did behave rather badly. After all, he had made the effort to come to see her off.'

'Never mind, I'm sure Edward is of stronger stuff than to take offence so easily.'

'I do hope so,' exclaimed Harriet showing obvious concern. 'I hope he will still come and visit from time to time, even though Sarah has left home now.'

'I'm sure he will,' Jane reassured her.

Later that evening, as they were sitting companionably beside the hearth in Harriet's kitchen, Jane finally confided in Harriet about her trip to Cambridge.

'There's little to tell, really. Thomas' parents were very welcoming but surprised when I explained my plans to leave for India. They are elderly now, of course, and are all too pleased that Thomas has returned to them, almost in one piece, and is able to take over the running of their large arable farm.'

'Did Thomas hint that he might like you to stay there?' Harriet asked.

Jane blushed.

'He was very gentlemanly in putting no pressure on me and understood that I must follow my conscience, but nevertheless he gave me a clear reassurance that I would always be welcome in Cambridge, if I chose to return.'

'It's just like the saying of the caged bird isn't it? If you set her free and she flies back to you, then she's yours forever.'

'I don't know about that but I am certainly in turmoil as to what to do. Should I go or should I stay? All I am certain of is that Thomas and I will always remain good friends because there is such a bond between us.'

'What about that spark, Jane? I remember you saying a long time ago that, since you returned from Riduna, your friendship had lost a certain spark.'

'Yes, I remember explaining that in my letter to you, but it seems quite different now. We've both experienced so much of the horrors of life: me married to life as a nurse and he to his military career. Maybe, just maybe, it could be time to settle and find some peace and happiness at last. What do you think?'

Harriet paused before she spoke.

'You could follow your dreams and still return to settle when you are ready to do so. You might feel trapped if you changed your mind now, but anyway you have the few days at your brother's to make up your mind.'

Jane blushed again, almost as if she was embarrassed about withholding information from her friend.

'Thomas is travelling down to London to meet me while I'm there and I must admit that I'm looking forward to seeing him again.'

Harriet could see that Jane had been changed emotionally by this recent encounter and yet she had also lost confidence in her ability to choose her own destiny.

'All I can say is that you must follow your heart. If you no longer have that yearning to travel, then you should feel no obligation to go to India. You have given so much of your life for the benefit of others that maybe now is the time to think of your own wellbeing.'

'Maybe,' replied Jane firmly, making it obvious to Harriet that the matter was now closed for the time being.

The following morning the friends parted, with Jane taking the train to Southampton and then on to London and Harriet settling back into life at Bourton Villas. In the next few days her thoughts were never far from Sarah and Victor and their new life on Riduna or what Jane was thinking during her stay in London. She tried hard not to dwell on her recent encounter with Edward, since each time she did so she was filled with embarrassment by her bluntness and would be mortified if he'd taken offence and felt he was unwelcome to her home. In reality, she was at a loss as to what she could do to rectify the matter. It was at night when she found it hard not to relive the encounter, often imagining different versions of the scenario in her dreams, each with quite different endings. Much as she tried to dismiss the invading thoughts, each night they returned to her as she tossed and turned in her loneliness.

Chapter 46

DURING DAYLIGHT HOURS, Harriet and Gladys soon found an efficient rhythm of working side by side and Harriet was also glad to have her son living back home again. At Victor's suggestion Tom had hired a lad, not dissimilar to himself, to help in the shop and the boy was also more than willing to move into the flat above the shop.

Jane's visit to London was over all too quickly and despite her confusion she had arranged to meet Harriet at the dockside to say goodbye on the day of her departure to India. Each day Harriet had expected word from Jane to say that she had changed her mind but the telegram never came.

Harriet made her way over the water yet again and they met with a warm embrace. Harriet said no more about the matter of Thomas because she could see from Jane's expression that she was resolute.

'Promise that you will write to me this time, Jane. I don't want to lose touch with you again.'

'Of course I will, dear Harriet. I don't think that I'll be away for very long this time. After all, we're not as young as we were, are we? It's just that I have this desire to go one last time. I can't explain the feelings of completeness and satisfaction my work gives me, especially since I will be working with young girls much like I was all those years ago.'

'You *are* a wonderful person, Jane. I do so admire you, but I'm going to miss you so much.'

'I'll miss you too, but you've achieved a great deal in your lifetime, too. You should be proud of yourself. Think of your lovely family and the business you've built up. Times haven't been easy but you've come out shining.'

The ladies embraced once more and it was with reluctance that Harriet let her friend go.

'No fainting now, Harriet. Be strong for me, otherwise I will not have the courage to leave you.'

Harriet smiled.

'Look after yourself and come home safely.'

As Jane moved away, their fingertips were the last to part as she slipped on to the waiting ship. Harriet stood and watched the ship depart. She lifted her hand for as long as she could make out the familiar shape of her friend standing on deck, but just as the ship disappeared from view she turned, and there was Edward standing behind her. He held out his hand to take hers but instead she fell into his arms.

The couple stood there for some moments before Harriet lifted her face to his.

'How did you know?' she asked.

'Let's just say that a little bird told me,' he grinned through his scruffy beard, hoping that Harriet would not take offence yet again.

Harriet opened her mouth as if to say something, but Edward put his finger to her lips. After a few moments, Edward stood back, still holding one of her hands in his and looked down into her face.

Their eyes met and Harriet sank into his embrace once more. As he held her tightly, he gave a prayer of thanks that at long last they had found each other. After a few moments they wandered along towards the *Floating Bridge*, hand in hand. There was so much to talk about, but for now they were both silently content just to be in each other's company.

Chapter 47

'WILT THOU HAVE this man to be thy wedded husband, to live together after God's ordinance in the holy estate of matrimony? Wilt thou obey him and serve him, love honour and keep him in sickness and in health: and forsaking all others, keep only unto him, so long as ye both shall live?'

'I will,' answered Harriet, her eyes meeting Edward's, who beamed down at her lovingly.

She looked as beautiful as ever in her deep blue dress, wisps of her auburn hair escaping around her face as they always did.

The minister brought their hands together, wrapping them with his stole, and then he read the familiar words which Edward repeated in a resonance which echoed around the church.

'I Edward do take thee Harriet to be my wedded wife, to have and to hold from this day forward, for better or for worse, for richer, for poorer in sickness and in health, to love and to cherish till death do us part, according to God's holy ordinance: and thereto I plight thee my troth.'

There was hardly a dry eye in the small congregation as Harriet's words echoed Edward's and Harriet's heart was so full that she barely heard the minister's prayers. She was transported in her mind back to Riduna and she and Edward were standing side by side in the small church of St Anne's, as she always dreamt they would be. Suddenly the minister's final words boomed out across the pews.

'Those whom God hath joined together let no man put asunder.'

Harriet's attention was brought back to Woolston once more as Edward led her through the smiling congregation and out into the sunshine. On the steps of the church, Harriet was filled with a sudden nervousness as Edward leaned towards her. They had not kissed since he had left her on Riduna all those years before. She blushed but as their lips met it was if they had never been parted.

Family and friends mingled outside the church for a while, but since there was no wedding breakfast, people began to disperse, wishing Harriet and Edward much happiness as they left. Lastly Ernest and Ethel with their two children, and Tom and Gladys walked with them to the Portsmouth Road where they said their goodbyes. Harriet hugged her grandchildren, whilst Edward shook hands with Harriet's two sons. She was proud of them both and as they gave her an affectionate kiss on the cheek she could not help but notice how like Joe Tom had grown, standing there with Gladys by his side. Ernest, on the other hand, had a temperament and mannerisms similar to her. They had all turned out fine, she silently remarked to Joe, whose strong presence she felt, giving the union his blessing. She looked back on the tableaux of her family on the hard at Woolston, a photograph in her memory.

Edward had persuaded a reluctant Harriet to travel to Riduna for their honeymoon. Harriet's resolve had been weakened by the added incentive that she would see her daughter again, but she was full of anxiety as they set off from the quayside.

She had forbidden any of her family to watch their departure and so, with quiet anonymity, they stepped along the gangway and on to the quarterdeck of the steamer which would carry them to Sarnia.

It was a damp misty morning and they stood silently on deck, Harriet's hand resting on Edward's. Harriet watched the familiar sights of Weston Shore, the Royal Victoria Hospital and the Isle of Wight fill their view, dreamlike in the mist. Each held so many memories of family and friends. It seemed like only yesterday that she and Joe had arrived on England's shores, with little hands clutching hers with nervous excitement. That morning before the wedding she had stood with Gladys and Tom in their little courtyard. She was relieved to know that Gladys, with Ethel's support in the mornings, would be quite capable of running the business successfully in her absence and it seemed no coincidence that their little robin appeared almost as if it came to wish her well. Harriet smiled at the thought as two seagulls flew overhead, keeping up with the ship. Once in open waters the wind licked the upper decks and Edward led Harriet below. It was a long and stormy crossing and more than once Harriet wondered how Edward had persuaded her come.

They arrived on Sarnia, tired and subdued. Edward had sent word to his cousin, Pamela, that they would be arriving and Harriet was more nervous than ever that her sister-in-law would be reproachful of her actions. She need not have worried: Pamela and Walter could not have been more welcoming.

'Just relax and enjoy a couple of days with us before you sail for Riduna,' she reassured Harriet, as she offered them tea and coffee in their guest lounge.

'That's very kind of you, Pamela,' Harriet replied, the colour starting to reappear on her pale cheeks.

'Not a good crossing then,' Pamela added unnecessarily.

'You'd have thought the elements were doing their best to keep us away,' joked Edward, trying to ease the tension.

'A storm like that's nothing to you, Edward. That I'm sure of,' continued Pamela amiably. 'When are you returning to sea, then?'

'I'm having a couple of months' break but I haven't decided what to do next. After the war finished and our crew returned to taking normal trips to Caen, my heart wasn't in it. Then, what with everything else....'

He paused, not wanting to speak of Marie's death or to embarrass Harriet by talking about their coming together.

Pamela sensed his hesitation.

'We were so glad that you've found happiness in each other's company.'

She smiled encouragingly to Harriet, who had remained silent throughout this exchange.

'After all we went through in the war, catch some happiness while you can is my motto and I am very pleased for you both.'

'Thank you, Pamela. You're very kind.'

'Not at all, Harriet, I'm just realistic. It's good that you've found each other for company. Anyway, I must get on to prepare supper. Please make yourselves at home but would you like me to show you to your room now?'

'That would be lovely,' replied Edward.

As they followed Pamela upstairs they passed what appeared to be an old man on his way down. He glared grumpily at Harriet, staring through her with piercing eyes in such a disturbing manner. It was as if he recognised her instantly but she had no such recollection.

As they reached their room, Pamela held the door open for them to enter. She followed them in and gently closed the door, whispering apologetically,

'I'm so sorry about your cousin Luke. He's been living

with us since he returned injured from the war and he's a bit disturbed. Harmless, though, I can assure you. Well, I must be off now.'

Harriet couldn't believe that the man they'd passed on the stairs was her cousin, Luke. He was only five years her senior and yet he appeared to be so old. He had been a nuisance all those years ago when she'd lived with her aunt and uncle in Les Canishers on Sarnia. He had deliberately made her life difficult, telling tales and spreading rumours, but nothing to worry about and so she forgot the incident and turned to Edward.

'Well, Mr Johnson,' she said with a mischievous glint in her eyes, 'What would you like to do now?'

'Well, Mrs Johnson. I think we should lie down and have a rest, don't you?' Edward replied with an equally wicked smile.

Slowly and gently they came together and it was as if the years fell away from them. Afterwards they lay side by side, Harriet's head nestled gently on Edward's chest, her auburn hair falling around her glowing face and on to his skin.

'It's more comfortable than a bed of hay, isn't it Harriet?' he murmured, reminding her of their first time all those years ago in the farmer's barn on Riduna.

'Just as good, though,' Harriet smiled at Edward's rugged face.

'Well, Mrs Johnson, would you like a stroll by the harbour before supper?'

'That would be lovely Mr Johnson,' Harriet grinned.

They freshened themselves with the water from the bowl on the wash stand before Edward turned to the window, being respectful of Harriet's modesty.

They walked hand in hand down the steep hill and out into the evening sun, unaware that they were being watched. The weather had changed and it was now a beautiful evening, with the autumn light making pools of colour in the shimmering waters of the harbour. They looked out towards Castle Cornet and strolled along the Promenade. Neither Harriet nor Edward could remember the last time they had felt so content.

Once the light began to fade they retraced their steps and headed back to his cousin's guesthouse. It was as they turned the corner and into the dark, narrow passageway leading to Well Road that Edward saw a glint in the darkness. Suddenly he was taken back in his mind to the night crossings bringing back the injured from France, when occasionally he had to be wary of a soldier sleepwalking, experiencing skirmishes during their frequent nightmares. Edward sprang forward, instinctively coming between the flashing light and Harriet.

There was a yell of anger from the shadows as a shining knife struck a blow through his shoulder and, leaving the weapon, his assailant fled up one of the nearby passageways.

Edward slumped to the ground, with Harriet screaming for help as she fell on her knees by his side. Several people rushed to their aid from the nearby cottages, whilst Harriet cradled Edward's head in her arms.

She was barely aware of the commotion a few hundred yards away, as a man was pinned to the ground by two burly harbour men. She was more intent on watching Edward's face as he drifted out of consciousness.

'No,' she cried to him. 'Don't leave me now, Edward. It took so long to find you again. I couldn't bear to lose you.'

Tears rolled down her face as the doctor, who had been called to the scene, encouraged her to let Edward go, whilst he carried out a brief examination.

'Tell me he's still alive,' she pleaded.

'I can still feel a faint pulse. That's all I can say for now, but please give me some space.'

Harriet stood helplessly by, while Edward was lifted on to a stretcher and carried gently up to Les Cotils.

By this time Pamela had been called and she raced to Harriet's side, slipping her arm through Harriet's. They followed the stretcher bearers up the cobbled road to the hospital.

Hours later, Harriet remained seated outside the ward waiting for news. It was midnight, but nothing could persuade her to leave her vigil. Pamela found her in the same spot the following morning, just as the nurse came to say that Harriet could sit with Edward for a short while before he was taken for another operation.

Harriet sat at his side, holding his rough hand in hers, gently talking to him; willing him to wake up. She felt him slipping away from her and she cried out.

The nurse led her back to Pamela and they watched helplessly as Edward was wheeled away.

'They're doing all they can, Harriet. We are lucky to have such a skilled surgeon here and if anyone can save Edward then Mr Harper can.'

Harriet did not reply because at that moment she was distracted by a policeman, who was striding towards her.

'Would you mind coming down to the station with us, Mrs Johnson, to identify your husband's assailant?'

'But I can't leave Edward,' protested Harriet.

'You can't do anything here, Harriet and I'll come with you,' reassured Pamela.

'It will be several hours before your husband is returned from his operation, Mrs Johnson. You should go and get some rest,' encouraged the nurse, glancing sternly at the policeman, her eyes warning the young man that he should leave Harriet alone for the present.

'I will only keep you for a few moments, Mrs Johnson and then I will return you safely to your lodging house.'

Glancing apologetically over her shoulder at the nurse, Harriet was led out to the waiting carriage which took them both down to the police station, the wheels and hooves clattering noisily along the cobbled streets, piercing Harriet's gloomy thoughts. The bright sunny morning seemed to mock her.

Pamela held on to her arm tightly as they were led through the station lobby and out to a back corridor containing several guarded cells. The guard opened one of the hatches and the policeman beckoned to Harriet to look inside. Through the bars Harriet was shocked to see her Cousin Luke sat in a crumpled heap on the floor, his face lost and dejected.

She nodded her affirmation at the policeman who led her silently back into the lobby.

'Would you be prepared to make a statement now, Mrs Johnson?' the officer asked kindly.

She nodded again and was led into a nearby room, where she relived the incident by his painful questioning.

After she had finished her brief account the officer asked,

'Can you think of any reason why the accused would want to harm your husband, Mrs Johnson?'

'I think you've got it wrong, officer. I think my cousin wanted to kill *me* and not my husband. Edward rushed between us, but it was so sudden and dark that I didn't really know what was happening.'

'Can you think of any reason why he would want to harm *you*, then?'

'Cousin Luke never liked me. He always caused trouble when he could, while I was living with my aunt in Les Canishers years ago, but I still don't understand why he would try to kill me. I think my husband's cousin might know more. He's been living at her guest house since he returned from the war.'

'We will certainly ask her, Mrs Johnson, but can you think of any reason why the assailant would want to seriously harm either you or your husband?'

'No, I cannot officer. I am sorry, but there's nothing I can tell you to explain this.'

'That's all for now, then,' the police officer replied, bringing this unhelpful interview to an abrupt close.

With the interview over, Pamela was asked in for brief questioning and then Harriet was determined that she wanted to return to the hospital. Harriet and Pamela decided they need some fresh air and declined the offer of a carriage. They climbed the narrow cobbled streets, passing the end of Les Canishers, evoking strange memories for Harriet. They stopped at the corner of Beauregard Lane, pausing for breath and looking out over the harbour. It was such a beautiful view but neither had it in their hearts to admire it for long. There was not much they could say and nothing Pamela could do to comfort Harriet and so they turned and finished the climb to the hospital.

Edward had been taken back to the ward following the operation but he was still unconscious and the nurse came out to see them.

'How is he?' Pamela asked.

'We believe Mr Johnson is out of danger now but he remains unconscious. You will be relieved to know that he suffered no serious internal injuries. The knife wound, although deep, went through his shoulder, missing his lungs, for which we can all be thankful. It was the severe concussion he suffered, when his head hit the ground, which has caused him to remain unconscious for so long. We can only watch and wait, now that the swelling on his head has receded. You may go and sit with him now, if you would like to, Mrs Johnson.'

Harriet sat with Edward throughout the remainder of the

day but Pamela persuaded her to go back to the guesthouse for a rest that night. For several days she sat talking to Edward, willing him to open his eyes and speak to her. At night she relived the incident in her restless dreams and a week later, during cousin Luke's trial, she suffered further agonies of standing in the witness box. When she listened to Pamela describe how Luke had come home from the war and taken an instant dislike to members of his own family, she shuddered.

'No, your honour. The defendant has never been physically violent up until now, and since he has moved into the guesthouse he had been no trouble at all, just a bit bad-tempered and sullen. We had no way of anticipating this. Otherwise I would never have agreed to rent him a room.'

Harriet was so relieved that there was no question of cousin Luke's guilt and in the end the jury took only ten minutes to reach the verdict she expected.

Back at the hospital there was still no change in Edward.

'Maybe we were never meant to be together, Edward,' she whispered to him one day, when she thought that no one could hear her speak. 'Maybe this is a punishment for being so wicked when we were little more than children.'

She sighed, closing her eyes trying to block out memories of her and Edward when they had been so much in love on Riduna.

'Oh, I don't know about that. I like a bit of wickedness,' a mischievous voice replied.

'Oh, Edward!' Harriet laughed, sudden tears of joy streaming down her face.

'Come on, Harriet. Dry those tears now; we're on our honeymoon.'

With that Edward attempted to sit up. He winced with pain and lay back down again.

'What have we here?' asked the nurse, coming up behind Harriet. 'You're back in the land of the living again I see, Mr Johnson. You have given your wife quite a fright.'

'No more than the pain I have been inflicted trying to protect her. Can't you give me something to relieve the agony?'

'Just lay back and rest and you'll soon heal,' the nurse soothed. 'You'll just have to be patient and I'll get the doctor to come and see you as soon as I can.' She looked up at Harriet sympathetically. 'Now all your troubles begin. There's nothing like the moaning of a man in a bit of pain.' She smiled at Harriet as she left.

'Thank you, Sister,' Harriet called after her.

'Don't thank her. She hasn't done anything to take away my pain,' exclaimed Edward indignantly.

'Just be grateful that you're alive,' answered Harriet.

She laughed, sensing Edward's frustration at being so immobile.

'Be patient,' she soothed.

'How can I be patient when we're supposed to be on our honeymoon?'

'You'll just have to wait,' grinned Harriet.

'I quite agree. No over-exertion for quite a long while, Mr Johnson,' said the doctor who, unbeknown to either Edward or Harriet, had walked up behind them.

He winked at Harriet.

'Now, let's look at the patient shall we.'

It was another two days before Edward was allowed to leave the hospital, just to make sure there were no lasting effects from the concussion.

Chapter 48

TWO WEEKS LATER, Edward and Harriet finally set sail for Riduna on the *Courier*. Some fishing boats, returning to the harbour after a hard night's work, passed them by as they sailed through the harbour's narrow entrance, under the imposing gaze of Castle Cornet. The air was filled with such familiar smells and, as they peered into one of the vessels, they could see sizeable crabs and lobsters clawing for an escape route, as if they understood their fate.

Harriet savoured each second, aware of the sounds of the seagulls following in their wake and the sights of the smaller islands covered in sunlight. It was as if Edward too was aware of the magic of the moment, as he focussed on the sandy shell beach of Herm, not unlike those he had experienced in his adventures on the Caribbean Sea in his younger days of seafaring. A gull screeched overhead, awakening them out of their revelry and Edward smiled down at Harriet.

'Well, Mrs Johnson. What does it feel like to be going home at last?'

Harriet paused before answering. The last two weeks had been full of soul searching as she had waited for Edward to return to her. Now that he was by her side again she was overwhelmed by a sense of peace.

'To be honest with you, Edward, I'm just so grateful that I'm no longer afraid to go home. In fact, I'm quite excited to see Riduna again.'

Edward smiled at Harriet and placed his hand gently over hers as they gazed intently across the water. Both were sure by now that they could see the faint outline of Riduna on the misty horizon. Neither had wished to go below deck, both preferring to enjoy the anticipation of each moment, each deep in their own thoughts.

The crossing was kind to them and soon Riduna was close. As they passed Fort Les Hommeaux Florains, a fisherman stood out on one of the farthest rocks. Edward was reminded of his younger days with his father, when they had fished on that very spot and Harriet wondered if it might be Victor catching supper for his family.

Next they caught sight of Corblet's Bay, reminding Harriet of summer picnics with friends and family. Edward, who had usually been on Sarnia for the summer and had missed the village outings, instead remembered racing to that end of the island with his friends John and Michael, their goal to be the first in the sea.

As they passed Fort Albert and caught sight of Braye Beach, Harriet caught her breath and gripped tightly to the railings. It had hardly changed in the twenty five years since her banishment. Her hand moved to her throat as she remembered the evening before Edward's departure, as they had embraced in the dying sunlight on the grass above the shore. Fleetingly she thought of her lost locket, a symbol of their young love before, to her dismay, it had gone missing. She coloured at the memory.

Standing beside Harriet, Edward was thinking of all those times he had said goodbye to her and he had watched her lonely figure standing on Douglas Quay until she had disappeared from view. Instinctively he put his good arm around Harriet's shoulders and pulled her close. Harriet was reassured by his solid warmth and strength, as she fought with a familiar fear: so many memories she'd tried so hard to forget.

As the steamer drew close to the quay and was secured by ropes, both forward and aft, by young men who reminded Edward so much of his early days at sea, a young lad came on to the ship to take their luggage. Edward ushered Harriet in front of him and in a dreamlike state Harriet took her first steps on the island that had once been her precious home. It was hard to resist the desire to bend down and touch the sandy path.

As they followed the lad, walking along the familiar street, The Diver's Inn beckoning Edward as they passed by, they paused frequently for Harriet to look around her. She glanced towards Crabby Bay where she had lived with her parents and along the bay towards Fort Albert.

A short way up Braye Road, to Harriet's amazement, they turned through the impressive gates of Scott's Hotel. Harriet looked up at Edward questioningly.

'It's a surprise,' he answered to her puzzled glance, putting his finger to his lips. He had contacted Victor with the strict instructions to book a room for their first two nights on the island but had asked that Sarah should not know.

'Surely this is much too expensive' was the question Harriet was forbidden to ask as the doorman stood back for them. Harriet looked around her, her heart racing as they entered the hotel foyer, a place she had seen many times in her youth but never dreamed that one day she would have the pleasure of staying in as a guest. The word 'guest' summed up her emotions as she felt strangely detached from the reality of her island home.

As they entered the lobby, Harriet caught sight of Sarah, who was sat at the reception desk with Victor by her side, looking confident and happy in her role of meeting and greeting new arrivals and to put them at their ease.

Sarah looked up from the guest list. The names of the expected arrivals, Mr and Mrs Johnson, sounded strangely familiar to her, but she could not quite place them in her memory. She gazed in total amazement at the sight of her mother and Uncle Edward standing at the entrance to the hotel. After a moment of total disbelief, Victor was amused as he watched his wife give out an undignified yell and rush towards them, sobbing into her mother's arms, all composure lost in the moment.

Edward and Victor laughed as they came forward to shake hands.

'Welcome to Scott's Hotel, Mr Johnson. I hope that you and your wife will have an enjoyable stay.'

Carefully, Edward shook the proffered hand.

'Call me Edward, Victor my lad, and don't stand on ceremony. I lived here all those years without too much fuss and I'm too long in the tooth to begin now.'

'Thank you, sir, I mean Edward,' Victor replied. 'Shall I show you around the hotel while the women compose themselves?'

He smiled at Edward, who whispered his reply,

'A drop of the hard stuff wouldn't go amiss.'

'What a good idea,' Victor replied and he led Edward though to the bar where they waited for the ladies to join them.

Sarah was the first to regain control of her emotions. She glanced at Harriet's left hand and the bright new wedding ring on her mother's third finger.

'Are congratulations in order, Mrs Johnson?' Sarah smiled.

They both laughed and embraced once more, this time without tears, all raw emotion replaced by the joy of the moment.

That night as Sarah and Victor settled down to sleep, she remonstrated with her husband,

'Why didn't you tell me they were coming?'

'It was worth it just to see the look of amazement on your pretty face,' Victor joked.

'No, seriously Victor; we shouldn't have secrets between us.'

'Think of it this way, Sarah. How would you have felt if they hadn't arrived after all and by all accounts that nearly happened? You would have been so disappointed. You have settled so well here on Riduna that I wanted it to be my surprise. You're not angry with me, are you?'

Sensing Victor's irresistible boyish charm, Sarah laughed and fell into his arms, the tension between them evaporating with their passion.

'Are you still cross with me?' asked Victor, as he absentmindedly stroked Sarah's face, running his fingers over her flushed cheeks and down to her rosy lips.

'No Victor, I'm just exquisitely overflowing with happiness,' she grinned as she turned to him for another passionate embrace.

'You're insatiable,' Victor whispered as they enjoyed their pleasures once more, squeezed into their tiny bed.

Meanwhile the older lovers settled into a deep contented sleep in their luxurious room upstairs. Unbeknown to Edward, Victor had twisted his boss' arm and had arranged for the honeymooners to spend two nights in their most expensive suite at a lower rate. Their lovemaking before sleep had been gentle and sensitive, as Harriet had taken the lead, ever mindful of Edward's healing injury.

During the next two days Harriet sensed that her whole being was emerging from a chrysalis. On their first morning as they strolled up to St Anne and along Victoria

Street they were as strangers on vacation in a distant but oddly familiar land. They walked to the far ends of the island, at times wrapped together in shared memories and at other times deeply absorbed in their own private thoughts. Gradually the news of their return was spread among the islanders, who frequently stopped them in their tracks to greet them, some with enthusiasm and others with a certain reticence, shy to rekindle old acquaintances.

During their time on Riduna they met up with many of their dear old friends. On the first evening they were warmly welcomed at The Rose and Crown by Charlotte and John, who proudly introduced them to their extended family. On the following morning they called in on Michael and Rachel at the bakery and Harriet recalled their wedding on Sarnia all those years ago, when she had seen them last.

Together Edward and Harriet visited the graves of both of their parents, Harriet laying some flowers at the base of each grave in quiet thoughtfulness, as both remembered their happy childhoods and the times they'd shared.

Later that afternoon Victor took Edward to The Divers for a jar, to give Sarah a chance to spend some quality time with her mother, albeit for only an hour or so. They sat drinking tea in the hotel gardens.

'I can see that you're happy here, Sarah. You don't feel at all homesick, then?' Harriet asked.

'I love it here, Mother and that's the truth. I feel as if I belong to the island and Victor's family have made me so welcome.'

Harriet frowned momentarily as she felt a touch of jealousy at Sarah's remarks.

'Don't look so upset, Mother. Of course I miss you, but I do enjoy my work here and we are both fortunate to have good jobs and a roof over our heads.'

Knowing the truth in this remark, and realising how silly she was being, Harriet relaxed.

'It's just wonderful to see you so settled and happy again, Sarah. Please don't worry about your old mother.'

'But I *do* worry about you, Mother; it's so good to have you here with us, even if it's only for a little while. How does it feel to be home again?'

Harriet ignored the emphasis on the word 'home' as she replied,

'It was strange at first, like living in my own dream, but I feel more at ease today, now that we've enjoyed the company of some old friends and been recognised by some not so familiar faces. I had forgotten how wonderful it is to see children running about in the surf. It takes me back to my childhood, Sarah. I was so happy here too when I was young.'

Sensing her daughter's face cloud over momentarily, Harriet berated herself for her own thoughtlessness.

'You will always miss Timothy, Sarah. There's nothing wrong in that. Being here brings thoughts of my parents back to me, too.'

'Timmy would have loved it here, mother. I know he would,' Sarah choked, wondering when it would be that she could stop the tears creeping into her eyes when she spoke of her lost son.

There was silence between them for a moment.

'But I think I may have some news for you,' Sarah whispered, patting her stomach, the true meaning of the gesture unmistakable. 'I have not told Victor yet.'

At that point, Victor arrived back, a cue for Sarah to return to her duties; she passed a shared look of understanding with her mother as she headed back towards the reception.

'Edward is waiting for you down by the quay,' Victor

explained. 'It's such a nice evening that he thought you might enjoy a stroll before evening dinner.'

'Thank you, Victor. Yes I will go and join him.'

Sarah kissed her mother on the cheek at the door of the hotel.

'We'll join you for supper later. Have a good walk.'

'Thanks, love.'

Harriet squeezed her daughter's hand then waved back, as she strolled out of the hotel and down towards the harbour.

Harriet and Edward greeted each other as if it had been weeks rather than hours since they had parted and they walked hand in hand along Braye Beach. At the far end of the sandy bay, almost under the shadow of Fort Albert, they turned to retrace their steps before taking a path through the grassy sand dunes and up on to Braye Common. There they paused to admire the view, two figures standing side by side bathed in the orangey yellow light of the early evening sunshine.

A familiar sound overhead made them turn simultaneously skyward in the direction of the breakwater. A flying boat, with the distinctive word 'SUPERMARINE' on its hull, flew noisily over the bay and they guessed that it was on its way to Jersey or to the French coast. For Harriet it was as if an invisible thread had joined her to her family back in Woolston.

'You see; you aren't so very far away from Ernest and Tom over here, are you?' Edward remarked.

Harriet smiled at him and, squeezing his good hand in reply, turned back to watch the plane disappear from view.

Edward sensed that the moment was right and let go of her hand to rummage deep into his pocket, from which he pulled out a strangely familiar velvet pouch.

Harriet's eyes were full of wonder as he poured out the precious silver locket into the palm of her hands.

After a few moments Edward took it from her and gently lifted it to her neck. Then he looked down on her and smiled.

'But how did you find it?' asked Harriet, her eyes misting over with memories as she thought that it must have remained here on Riduna all these years.

'Let's just say that another little bird brought it to me and be pleased that we've found it,' he said, reaching to do up the clasp and then placing his finger gently on her lips.

'Oh Edward, I am. Truly I am,' Harriet exclaimed as she reached up to kiss him.

As history repeated itself and Edward folded Harriet in his arms once more a lonely figure, now of ample proportions, was watching them from Les Butes. Charlotte had come to watch her boys take their fishing vessel out for the night, as she often did. This time though she smiled indulgently when she noticed her two good friends who had found each other at last. She walked back to The Rose and Crown.

'My, my, how lovely it is,' she chuckled.

As Harriet and Sarah met that evening Sarah noticed the locket.

'That's lovely, Mother. Is it a present from Uncle Edward?' she asked.

'You might say that, Sarah; Edward gave it to me many, many years ago, but that's a long story.'

'We've got all night and I'd love to hear it,' encouraged Sarah, noticing Edward winking at her over her mother's head, as they were seated at the table.

Once they had made themselves comfortable and each had given the waiter their order, Sarah smiled expectantly at her mother.

'Well,' Harriet paused. 'When I was just a girl and Edward lived next door we were inseparable.'

She smiled at Edward, who raised his eyebrows at Victor who returned his grin.

'Mother?' exclaimed Sarah impatiently, 'What happened next?'

'For years we were best friends. We shared everything, even our secrets, and Edward, being that bit older, always looked out for me.'

'Oh, how sweet; that's much like Ernest and Ethel in St John's Road, isn't it? Don't stop, Mother.'

'As I said, we were very close but slowly, as I grew up, I began to realise that Edward meant much more to me than the boy next door and...' looking over to Edward for reassurance here, Harriet continued, 'I think it was when he went to sea for the first time that we fell in love.'

'What about the locket, Mother?' Sarah asked, unable to hide her impatience to know the truth.

'I was just coming to that, Sarah. It was on the night that Edward left to travel to England and on to far more exciting places...'

The words 'leaving me far behind' were on the tip of her tongue but instead she continued,

'We stood on Les Butes over twenty five years ago, virtually on the spot we stood tonight and Edward gave the locket to me. How I lost it I shall never know, but when I arrived on Sarnia it was missing.'

With a glance from Victor, Sarah took the hint and was uncharacteristically tactful as she joined him in a toast.

'To you both and may your happiness be long and joyful,' Victor exclaimed and they all laughed as they enjoyed their delicious lobster supper.

The following characters were real people, important in the history of the day:

Lieutenant Cresswell and Commander Rice [1]
Died in first seaplane accident in Britain off Calshot

Harry Harper [2]
Air Correspondent for The Daily Mail

Flight Commander Charles Humphrey
Kingsman Edmonds [3]
A decorated British Naval aviator in WW1

Colonel Grimstone [4]
of Peartree Lodge

Hubert Scott Paine [5]
Aircraft and Boat Designer

Major Robert Smith Barry [6]
Inventor of the Gosport Tube

Mr RJ Mitchell [7]
Designer of the Supermarine
Schneider Trophy winner and later the Spitfire

RIDUNA

by Diana Jackson

First published in May 2009

IF YOU ENJOYED reading Ancasta, you might like to read Diana Jackson's first novel Riduna. This is the prequel to Ancasta and tells the story of Harriet as a young lady, with flashbacks to when she was a child and teenager. Harriet and Edward, neighbours on the beautiful island of Alderney, (Riduna was the Roman name for Alderney in the Channel Islands UK) were brought up almost as brother and sister, and so it was a surprise to both of them when a romantic love was kindled.

Riduna explores not only the lives of Harriet and Edward, but also many of their close knit community on this small, unique island, and many of these characters will now be familiar to you. As you read Riduna, you will soon learn why this island remains close to Harriet's heart throughout her life.

Here is a tweet from a twitter follower, who was born on Alderney and now lives in Canada:

'You can take the girl out of the island but you can't take the island out of the girl'

In August 2012 The Historical Novel Society wrote of Riduna:Life was picturesque growing up on Riduna on the Channel island of Alderney. It was a place where the old ways remained steadfast even though "outsiders" were slowly creeping in. Lifelong friendships develop and, in the case of Harriet and Edward, these friendships blossom into love. As the two grow into adulthood, they find that their love will be tested, when each desires a different path for their futures. Edward's dream of becoming a sailor finally pays off, and he finds that life onboard a ship is very different from the strict morals of Riduna. Harriet has decided to wait on the island for her sailor boy to return, and during his Christmas visit, their actions lead to a possible pregnancy. After discovering that it's a false alarm, both are relieved. After an unfortunate accident that shakes Harriet's world, Edward becomes more distant as his taste for the sea takes over his life. Throughout their journeys, both Harriet and Edward must make sacrifices and decisions that will forever change their lives.

Riduna speaks volumes about the power of love and loss and is beautifully written with a fluidity that speaks to your soul. Author Diana Jackson's ability to portray the everyday ordinary yet life-changing events of those in a community is amazing; you get a true feel of what it must have been like living in Riduna during that era. Fans of *The Guernsey Literary and Potato Peel Pie Society* will fall in love with *Riduna*. --Angela Simmons